THE
DINNER
PARTY

ALSO BY REBECCA HEATH

The Summer Party

THE DINNER PARTY

REBECCA HEATH

HEAD
ℓ ZEUS

An Aries Book

First published in the UK in 2024 by Head of Zeus,
part of Bloomsbury Publishing Plc

9 7 5 3 1 2 4 6 8

A catalogue record for this book is available from the British Library.

ISBN (PB): 9781804546109
ISBN (E): 9781804546079

Cover design: Emma Rogers

Typeset by Siliconchips Services Ltd UK

Printed and bound in Great Britain by
CPI Group (UK) Ltd, Croydon CR0 4YY

Head of Zeus
First Floor East
5–8 Hardwick Street
London EC1R 4RG

WWW.HEADOFZEUS.COM

To Dave, Amelie, James and Claire.
For everything. Always.

TRAILER: THE CALLAGHAN BABY

Music playing: 'Something's Missing In My Life' – Marcia Hines

The music fades to the familiar sounds of a summer night. A faint breeze. Crickets.

Woman speaks:
If you head out of the city and drive, the bustle of cars and scurrying workers will eventually give way to pockets of quiet. There, the houses are more sprawl than stacked. Streets are wide, and footpaths free for bikes and evening strolls.

It's a safe haven, a place made for families.

Or it should be.

But behind the lit-up picture windows and closed curtains secrets can hide. Lies. And it's in one such community that we start our investigation.

I'm Ruby Costa and this is 'The Callaghan Baby Podcast'. Along with my team, I've been investigating a forty-year-old cold case. In these episodes you'll hear the results of our work. We thank 'The Megan Callaghan Foundation' and the 'National Radio Grant' for the funding to create this podcast.

Let us begin.

Male reporter's voice. The scratchy sound of the audio shows the age of the broadcast.
Tonight, police are searching for missing baby, Megan Callaghan. Only four months old, she is reported to have vanished from her home in Ridgefield. She was last seen around ten p.m. on the evening of Sunday the 9th of December. If anyone has any information on the whereabouts of baby Megan, we urge you to come forward.

There is no obvious link between Megan's family and notorious child snatcher Dominic Snave, who was released from prison yesterday morning. Police say they are following a number of lines of inquiry; however, there's increasing public pressure to investigate whether Mr Snave is involved.

Ruby:
It's summer 1979. The Knack, KISS and Blondie are big on the charts and Ridgefield, half an hour from Adelaide in South Australia, is experiencing its first real heatwave of the season. Throughout the day, windows are thrown open seeking a breeze, and fans are dragged from cupboards and plugged in, immediately whining at the effort of stirring air heavy with heat. Children swarm to the sprinkler in a neighbour's front yard, while parents – grateful for the respite – hide inside in the shade before luring their sun-dazed offspring home with the promise of an ice-block after dinner.

Late at night in this nice suburban community, full of young families on their way up in life with promising futures, a four-month-old baby is reported missing.

According to police reports, the call came in at eleven minutes past eleven p.m. on Sunday the 9th of December.

Due to the late hour, Megan's disappearance shifted to the front of the public consciousness on Monday December 10th, on the evening news, then making headlines in the papers the following day. That's nearly two days after Megan went missing.

I have in front of me copies of the newspapers, their message stark despite the grainy, faded print.

'MISSING BABY,' one cries in two-inch font. Then slightly smaller: 'Have you seen Megan Callaghan?' Beneath is a photo of Megan. Back then, it was popular to have a professional photo session for a baby and this was from only days before she went missing. It's good quality for the time. There were no smartphones enabling a new mother to share pictures one hundred times a day to social media, but there isn't much detail. Wearing a white, smocked dress with a ruffled collar, Megan lies on a pink-edged rug. Her blue eyes are wide and a few dark wisps of hair curl on her head.

To be honest, it could be anyone. This picture wasn't ever going to allow the public to find the missing baby. If Megan was going to be reunited with her family, they'd need a witness to come forward or for police to find a lead.

Evening news intro.

Male anchor:

It's been three days and there are still no breaks in the case of missing baby Megan Callaghan. We'll speak to the police about their progress at five.

Carol:

Please, if you have her, whoever you are, please bring her home. We'll pay you whatever you want, do whatever you want. Leave her somewhere anonymously if you must. She needs her mother. Please, please, please bring my baby home.

Ruby:

That agonising plea you've just heard comes from Carol Callaghan, Megan's distraught mother, who fronted the media several times alongside her husband Frank. The tragic events would prove to take an enormous toll on Carol and the rest of her family over the following years.

Carol:

I just pray that whoever has her is looking after her. She deserves to grow up, to have birthdays and friends. It's been so long now since she went missing. This year she'd be starting school.

Reporter:

Do you think your daughter is still alive?

Carol:

I have to believe she is, and that one day she'll come home.

Ruby:

For this podcast, we've collected police reports, information from the 2005 inquest into the investigation and interviewed a number of persons of interest.

Let me set the scene.

December 9th 1979 was one of those long, hot, early summer Sundays. Perfect for a gathering of friends.

Ridgefield was a suburb for those on the rise. Young couples and families building their dream homes alongside others with similar aspirations in a good school district with neighbours who fast became friends.

Trish and Ken Williams at number five Wattlebury Court, the largest house in the neighbourhood, invited their neighbours – a group who'd all built or bought in the street at the same time – over for an impromptu dinner party.

Often, the dinner parties were an opportunity for the host to show off a curated version of their home and marriage, like one Carol put on three weeks earlier. She'd served an entrée of garlic prawns, chosen veal parmigiana for the main and whipped up a Black Forest torte for dessert. The latter a recipe from that week's *Women's Weekly* magazine, selected to outdo her friend's tiramisu from the party before.

This event was more of a potluck affair due to its hasty arrangement.

In total, four couples attended that evening, including the hosts.

From number three there were the Marshes and they brought a huge pot of stroganoff and rice. Gloria aged forty and Ray at forty-five, parents of an only child, were the oldest of the group and were the first to arrive. They brought chips and dips for the table, and drinks of course. Gloria was famous for loving a port after dinner.

Barb and Larry Jones who had three children made their way from next door at number six with a decadent trifle for dessert, big enough to feed twice the expected number of guests. Larry had enough beer for all the men after having been ribbed mercilessly for forgetting to bring drinks last time.

And of course, from number eight on the corner, there was Carol and Frank Callaghan, parents of two, with Carol's trademark apricot chicken and a new fancy fondue pot. She couldn't wait to try it out.

So, we have it: four couples ready for a good time.

Something you might notice about the guest list is that I've only mentioned adults attending. The reason for this seems impossible to understand through the lens of today's thinking but didn't raise any questions at the time.

The children were not invited.

This was a common practice happening for as long as anyone could remember in the safe and friendly neighbourhood, where doors were left unlocked and every person knew their neighbour and would always stop to chat in the street. Parents dashed to the shops while their baby slept, and being young and happy made them invincible. This is Trish Williams, host of the dinner party, speaking at the 2005 inquest.

Trish Williams:
I know it seems strange now, but it was a different time. We lived in a safe neighbourhood on the edge of the world

and nothing and no one could touch us. At least that's how it felt.

It's not as though Ken and I forced them to keep their kids at home. You can't blame me for their decisions. Besides, it was common for us to get together at one of the neighbourhood houses once the kids were all in bed, and the dads would take turns going to check on them. That way they all got to sleep in their own beds.

Anyway, Ken and I didn't have children.

I think about it now, of course I do. I wish we'd done things differently, but we couldn't have known what would happen that night. No one could have. If you're asking whether I would have left my baby home alone to cross the road and have a party then the answer is no, but I never had that choice to make.

Ruby:

Over the years, all those who attended that night, at what came to be known as the 'dinner party from hell', have tried to explain leaving their children. They've described the sense of community, how they were all one big happy family. It's difficult to ascertain whether any of the parents had qualms about such a set-up and ultimately it doesn't matter. History shows the children were left behind.

At the Callaghans' home were baby Megan and ten-year-old Amanda. Next door to where they gathered at number six, Barb and Larry left nine-year-old Darren, three-year-old Vicki and their youngest, Rachael, who'd turned one a few weeks before. And sixteen-year-old Jennifer was home alone at number three. Larry Jones also spoke at the 2005 inquest.

Larry Jones:
I think the thing that affects Barb and I the most is knowing that there, but for the grace of God, go us. I can't judge Frank or Carol for their mistake. We, too, left our children alone that night. Our three precious children. And, honestly, part of me can't understand how we could have done it, raised as we both were in rougher parts of the city; but we couldn't imagine anything bad happening in this middle-class neighbourhood. Every day I live with the knowledge that it could have been our house broken into, our lives destroyed. If something had happened to Darren, Vicki or Rachael...

Ruby:
Larry sniffs and wipes at the end of his nose with a handkerchief.

Larry:
They were our world. It was for them I got up and went to work each day. Trust me, I didn't want to choke on a tie and banking wasn't my boyhood dream. It was for a better future for our children.

And I know that Frank and Carol felt the same for their kids.

Ruby:
It's been nearly four decades. Memories blur. Some of the most important players in the investigation have passed on, but we still don't know what happened that night.

When there is no official explanation, rumour and innuendo, whispers and accusations will linger. These haunt the subjects. Shadowing their lives and those of their children.

The public might demand an answer but those who have been wrongly implicated *deserve* one.

The foundation were initially reluctant to support the podcast; however, recent cases where such investigations have broken open cold cases and put the perpetrators on trial convinced them. Using my contacts and resources as a journalist, I've made it my goal to bring together everything known about the events of that night.

This podcast will investigate and interrogate like no one has dared to before – with unprecedented access to all the major players and new revelations that promise to shock and change everything you think you know about this case.

We have a four-month-old missing and a panicked call to the police. In its wake, a desperate search kicks off involving members of the police, emergency services and volunteers. So begins a case that would mystify all those involved for decades with its web of secrets, lies and murder. There has been a reward offered, a large sum of money, but no one has come forward.

And still we're here asking the question: *What happened to Megan Callaghan?*

1

Monday December 9th, 40 years later

Bleariness from the battle of trying to get her baby, Lola, to settle meant Billie Callaghan-Jones was already several steps into her kitchen before she registered the sharp, sweet odour of burning apricot chicken. Closer inspection revealed tendrils of smoke seeping from her oven door.

No, not today.

As she hurried to grab a potholder from the hook, a piece of paper dropped from inside it to the floor. On the bright yellow Post-it, in Nathan's familiar block scrawl, it said, '*You got this.*'

She blinked back the prickle in her eyes so she could see to remove the smoking dish from the oven. The pregnancy books all said her hormones should be getting back to normal now Lola was five months old but then the books were failing her on everything else, why not this too? Her husband had surprised her with a note on the bathroom mirror on the first day he'd had to return to work after their daughter's birth. In the months since, he'd left a message to brighten her day a couple of times a week. Each time she found one, she felt a little less alone.

Cradling the casserole dish full of charred remains, she went to step around Plank, her sleeping staffy boxer cross mutt, who'd helpfully positioned himself right in the middle of the kitchen. Smelling the food, he jumped up in front of her to investigate, his blunt black and white nose in the air.

Somehow, she didn't hit him or fall, but the potholder slipped. An explosion of heat lanced into her left palm.

'Holy fu-fire truck!'

Eyes streaming, she slammed the dish down and flicked the tap to cold. Grizzles echoed from the baby monitor and for a moment she didn't dare to breathe. They quieted, and she shoved her already reddening palm beneath the flow as Plank apologetically leaned his square head against her leg, assuredly getting white hairs over her black culottes.

The cool running water had begun to work its soothing magic when Plank trotted to the door to the garage, his stumpy tail wagging. Nathan entered a moment later, his tie adorably askew, reaching down to pat the dog as he took in the scene. He abandoned his bag and phone on the bench and approached her, concern in his eyes, eyes the green of a lucky clover.

'Let me see.' He took her hand in his. 'That looks sore.'

The skin had already begun to blister. 'It's agony,' she admitted. 'But at least I managed not to disturb Lola.'

As though she'd heard her name, the whimpers from the nursery became a wail, amplified to a screech by the baby monitor.

Billie's chest constricted. 'I was sure she'd sleep until we had to leave for Mum's. Is half an hour of peace to make the stupid chicken too much to ask?'

'Wait,' Nathan whispered. 'Maybe she'll settle.'

The cry continued. 'Not settling,' Billie moaned.

His mouth quirked up at the corner. 'Did you use fire truck again?' he teased. 'If you'd sworn properly, she'd have slept through the whole thing.'

REBECCA HEATH

She managed to muster a smile.

'Long day, huh? I'll get her,' he said pressing a quick kiss to her forehead before striding from the kitchen.

He'd made it clear he thought it silly not to swear in front of a five-month-old, but she'd read that babies could already understand some things by this age, and she wanted to get in good practice for the future.

Her younger sister, Eve, never swore. A fact Billie added to the long list of ways she was failing as a mum already. But Eve hadn't been the one entrusted to make the apricot chicken for the memorial for Mum's sister, Billie's aunt Megan, who'd disappeared on this day forty years ago. Her shoulders slumped. The chicken that had been charred black when she'd dragged it out the oven.

With Plank waiting hopefully at her feet for crumbs to fall, she'd managed to pick off the worst of the burned bits by the time Nathan returned, a freshly changed and happy Lola in his arms.

Billie had to ignore the stab of envy that even Nathan handled this parenting thing better than she did. It was all she could do not to flee. Run from the homely cottage, all the way back to her office at family business Callaghan Constructions, where she knew what she was doing. Although, given everything that had happened there since the podcast, maybe it was a good thing she was on maternity leave right now.

Instead, she exhaled hard and kissed the top of her beloved baby's head.

'Hey, Lola-love,' she cooed before turning to Nathan. 'I think your phone buzzed while I was trying to salvage the chicken.'

Something she couldn't decipher flashed across his face but

12

then it was gone and he was over by the counter, still holding Lola, checking the screen.

'Something important?' she asked.

'Nah, it's just Tim.'

She frowned at the mention of Eve's hubby. The once-famous footballer got along well enough with Nathan but didn't do casual chit-chat. 'What does he want?'

Nathan shrugged. 'Just wanting to know when we'd be there.'

'Are they there already? Mum said she wouldn't be home until six.' Then again, her sister had always operated on her own time and might have headed there early just to try to work out what appointment Mum had had that afternoon that she'd been so secretive about.

'Don't ask me.' Nathan bounced Lola up and down, getting a gummy smile that even distracted as she was, made Billie's heart go all gooey.

Billie sighed. 'We'd better go.'

After loading Nathan up with all they'd need for Lola, and checking Plank had water, Billie covered the now-cooler casserole dish and carried it out to the car. She replied to his raised eyebrows with a *'do not say one word about the chicken'* look.

He blew a raspberry on Lola's cheek and remained silent, but his eyes crinkled in that way she knew meant he was laughing on the inside.

And, suddenly, Billie was laughing too. The apricot chicken was just a symbol of that night long ago. Her mum wouldn't mind about a few brown patches as long as she had her family around her to remember Megan.

2

Billie's mother opened the back door to her house before Billie could knock. With her hand on her chest as though catching her breath, Mum glanced down at the dish in Billie's hands. She cupped Billie's cheek and managed a tremulous smile. 'Thanks, love. I knew I could count on you.'

Billie fought past a lump in her own throat. 'It's a little overcooked, but it should be fine.'

Mum accepted a kiss on the cheek from Nathan and took Lola from his arms, immediately snuggling in close. 'Put the dish on the stovetop, if you don't mind?'

With a parting wink, Nathan headed through to the lounge, where Tim had the TV on so sport could help him avoid too much missing-baby talk. Billie couldn't blame him when all this had happened before they were even born. The two men slapped backs in greeting and debated firing up the barbecue or leaving it until the next game break.

As she moved to follow the others, a hot breeze off the conservation park across the street teased at Billie's skin like tiny fingers trying to pull her this way and that. She shivered and stepped inside past her mother, immediately entering an open-plan modern kitchen/dining area where her sister Eve sat at the round wooden table, glass of white wine in hand.

Although she was two years younger than Billie's twenty-seven years, Eve's twins – Max and Matilda – were nearly four. They sat at the plastic table in the corner, colouring in. They were dressed in matching white and navy and somehow, despite what Billie knew about kids, both were perfectly clean, their blonde heads close together as they worked.

'Do not disturb the terrors,' Eve whispered. 'They've been a nightmare today.'

Billie nodded weakly.

Eve was her usual fresh and stylish self in white shorts and a floral shirt worn loosely over a tight white singlet. Blonde, like her children and with a little help from the hairdresser, her short hair was cut in a style that was somehow classy and perky all at once and made Billie wish she'd made the time to go to the salon since Lola was born. Lately her own style was more about comfort and breastfeeding accessibility than anything else. Some days she counted showering as a victory.

The dish in Billie's hands kept her from smoothing back stray strands of her long, mouse-brown ponytail as she rounded the bench to place the food where her mother had directed. There, fresh and golden, was a dish full of her mum's famous potato bake.

She caught Mum's eye across the kitchen. 'Too weary to make the chicken?' she teased.

Mum shrugged. 'You sounded like you could use the distraction.'

Billie thought back to that phone call last week where she'd been trying so desperately to pretend she wasn't struggling with Lola and missing work and feeling useless. Mum had known just how to make her feel useful again.

Other than the weariness she'd played up for Billie's sake,

Mum had been in as good a place as Billie could remember. Seeing a therapist one of the other parents involved in the foundation had recommended, and even talking about dating again.

Considering how much harder maternity leave was than Billie had anticipated, not having to worry so much about her mother was a blessing.

Eve raised her glass as Billie turned towards her. 'Wine's in the fridge.'

'Maybe after Lola's next feed.'

Although, Billie thought as she poured herself a sparkling water instead, there would be no 'maybe' about it. Gathering for the memorial for Mum's missing baby sister had always been emotional but now she had Lola, Billie hurt for her mum and her beloved Pop more than ever.

'Do you want to eat before or after you've fed this little cherub?' Mum asked. She didn't look at Billie as she spoke, too busy making faces at Lola who she'd placed in the baby swing close to where the twins were colouring.

'After.'

Billie couldn't help but smile at the scene. All the most important people in her life together in one place.

Except Pop.

She pushed the thought away knowing he was too unwell to come out of the care facility and probably unaware of what day it was. Given everything that had been revealed in the podcast, she needed to be here with her mum on the anniversary of Megan's disappearance. Needed to not eat the apricot chicken, nibble on the strawberries rather than use the fondue set that would come out after dinner, and listen to the stories of her sister that Mum wanted to share.

Conversation flowed easily around the table as Eve recounted funny stories of the twins and they all fawned over every sound and expression Lola made, while Billie tried not to yawn. Hopefully, Lola would sleep better tonight.

Give Billie a building site with too much rock, a client changing their mind every two days and a council notoriously slow on granting building approvals and in her role at Callaghan Constructions she'd have a dream home completed within timeframe and on budget, but convincing a five-month-old to sleep through the night seemed to be beyond her.

Just after the men had headed out the back to start the barbecue – the meal they'd actually be eating – Lola started fussing and Billie picked her up.

Mum clucked approvingly. 'My clever little granddaughter knows it's time for her dinner. You should mash up some chicken and rice – give her a taste.'

'Maybe afterwards,' Billie replied. 'I'll breastfeed her now.'

As Billie passed her to find a spot on the couch, Mum's hand pressed against her chest.

'Maybe you should sit down too.'

'I will,' Mum said in a surprising concession.

By the time Mum joined Billie in the lounge area, Lola was almost done with her feed and Billie had successfully managed to convince Max and Matilda that they didn't need to try some breastmilk. Billie didn't mention their charming request to Eve, knowing if she did it would end up being shared for likes on 'Waffles and Co', the Insta account Eve ran starring the kids and their cavoodle named Waffles. Billie tried to imagine her Plank with his own Instagram page and smothered a giggle. His mongrel combination of genes meant he had the look of a boxer dressed up in a staffy costume, not exactly aesthetic, but she doubted there was a kinder dog in all the world.

Mum plonked into the seat opposite. 'That's better.'

'Have you thought about going to the doctor?' Billie asked.

'Not sure they can do much for old age.' But Mum's hand went to her chest again, switching to checking the buttons on her top when she noticed the direction of Billie's gaze. 'Leave it alone.' A gentle smile tempered the order. 'Give me today.'

'Just today,' Billie warned smiling back. They'd always been close and she knew her mum's generation thought going to the doctor was admitting some kind of weakness. 'Now, what was this mysterious appointment you had this afternoon?'

Her mum's eyes twinkled and she jerked her head to where Eve had disappeared. 'Wait for your sister.'

Billie mock-glared but Mum mimed zipping her lips.

As Lola fed, Billie used her free hand to check her phone for any new emails. Despite being on maternity leave, it was automatic to look for any updates from Callaghan Constructions, where she – usually – acted as operations manager. The house they were in had been one of the company's early projects when her grandfather was starting out on his own and it was the quality and class of the design that they'd kept as a core value. Not always building the biggest houses but those of a calibre and style that meant they'd grown into a premier builder.

Her stomach clenched at the sight of an email from Trish, Billie's godmother and part-owner of the business, who had an honorary title of customer liaison officer but spent more days on the golf course lately as she approached retirement.

'Staff meeting re: Quarterly Figures.'

Maybe she could get her mum to babysit and go in for the meeting. Everyone would have to understand that she needed to be there; these were highly unusual circumstances.

'That's not work is it?' Mum asked before Billie could open the email to confirm the time and date of the meeting. 'Why are they bothering you? You're on leave.'

In the kitchen to get some tongs, beer in hand, Nathan's eyebrows lifted, echoing the question.

Billie closed the email app and dropped her phone onto the cushion next to her. 'Just keeping up with the water-cooler gossip.'

She knew they were coming from a good place, but neither of them understood how work needed her, and how at least there she might be useful. A gurgle from Lola had guilt stabbing through her. There was no more important job than looking after her baby. It was just a pity Billie wasn't very good at it.

When Eve returned a minute later and took the seat next to Billie, Mum cleared her throat. 'While I have you both here, there's something I need to tell you.'

EPISODE 01: INTRODUCING THE CALLAGHAN BABY

Music playing: 'My Sharona' – The Knack

The music fades into the familiar intro of a news bulletin.

Male anchor:
As the investigation enters its fourth day, police are no
closer to finding missing baby Megan Callaghan. Although
they refuse to speak publicly, we understand they have a
number of lines of inquiry underway.

Ruby:
I'm Ruby Costa. Welcome to the first episode of 'The
Callaghan Baby Podcast'. Along with my team, I've been
investigating the forty-year-old cold case of baby Megan
Callaghan who went missing at age four months on the
night of Sunday December 9th 1979. In these episodes
you'll hear the results of our work. We thank 'The Megan
Callaghan Foundation' and the 'National Radio Grant'
for the funding to create this podcast.

The first place to look for answers is those closest to
Megan.

Understandably, Megan's mother, Carol, was devastated

by what happened that night. It haunted her right up until she passed away ten years after Megan went missing. Although we can't interview her directly, we have recordings of her from over the years and we'll hear more from her and about her in later episodes.

Megan's father, Frank Callaghan, is eighty now and is in care as he suffers from dementia. We'll share statements from Frank that were collected by the police and the media in the past, including at the 2005 inquest.

For so long he's been painted as the grieving father; however, it is time to examine his testimony and actions with the kind of scrutiny that until now has been reserved for others. Frank's grief is undeniable, but grief and innocence are not the same thing. Already, interest from the trailer of this podcast is creating new leads and further lines of inquiry. We will endeavour to follow these without the bias that has prejudiced such investigations in the past.

Fortunately, we do have a direct link to the family.

Megan's older sister, Amanda, has kindly made herself available. She's shared everything she's pieced together over most of a lifetime spent searching for her little sister.

Amanda is the driving force behind, and creator of, 'The Megan Callaghan Foundation'. A non-profit organisation she set up in memory of her sister, to continue the hunt for Megan, and to aid other families who are searching for missing children. They do amazing work.

Although named for the missing Callaghan baby, the foundation has a broad scope for the assistance of those who have missing family members and who have exhausted police help. Money donated to the foundation is used to make information available to those left behind, to help raise media attention for families who can't do this on their own, to provide reward money where police agree it might help in the search and also to provide support services for those grieving. As well as taking generous donations from supporters they raise money by managing charity events including their annual ball and a fun run.

Notably, support from the foundation helped in the case of missing university student, Jasmine Bahri, with a tip-off encouraged by the reward offered by the foundation, leading to closure for their family.

Without the support of the foundation, and access to records Amanda has personally collected over the years, we wouldn't have been able to attempt this investigation. We'll share parts of our extensive interview with Amanda as it becomes appropriate in telling Megan's story.

We begin, now, as the police did, trying to determine a timeline of the evening that became known as 'the dinner party from hell'.

There was no official start time, rather a 'get there when the children had settled and bring a dish'. But by eight p.m. all the couples were at number five, the home of newlyweds Trish and Ken Williams.

The testimony of the parents agrees that apart from Jennifer, the only teenager, all the children were tucked up in their beds. This includes the Callaghan children.

In Carol's statement to police, she described the hours immediately before they left the house as a typical evening. She'd made a smaller version of the apricot chicken dish she took to the party for Amanda as it was her favourite. Then they tucked the girls into bed and kissed them goodnight.

Carol admits to having a little hesitation leaving Megan. She'd been a colicky baby but had begun to settle better and it seemed likely she'd sleep through until morning as she had the night before. Amanda promised to listen out for her sister, but Carol assured her it wasn't necessary.

With both girls asleep Carol and Frank headed out of the house, arriving around the same time as the others.

The police timeline tells us that dinner was put out straight away and guests served themselves food and wine while catching up on the neighbourhood gossip. Someone put on a record loud enough it was reported being heard a block away. The neighbour who always complained if the gatherings got too loud – a regular occurrence – was away, so there was no one telling them to keep the noise down.

None of the four couples were tested for drugs or alcohol that night but considering the number of empty bottles afterwards in the Williams couple's kitchen, it is safe to assume that none of them were entirely sober. Police notes include mentions of slurred speech, flushed cheeks and wild eyes but these could all be shock-related.

The children were checked on by principal Ray Marsh around eight-thirty p.m. and then Frank Callaghan around ten. When interviewed later, Jennifer didn't remember seeing him. When pressed as to whether he'd even come into her house, she admitted that she was focused on her study. However, Amanda recalls her father coming by.

Amanda Callaghan:
I remember that part of the night clearly. I'd just woken from a nightmare and I wanted to go to Mum but that would mean leaving Megan alone. As I lay there trying

to decide what to do, my bedroom door opened, and Dad appeared. He was red-cheeked and dishevelled, the top three buttons of his shirt undone and when I ran into his arms he was all sticky with sweat. He held me close until I calmed down, then he waited while I went to the bathroom. The whole time he hummed softly and when I asked him what the music was, he said he'd been dancing with Mum and twirled me in the hallway.

Then we checked on Megan together, tiptoeing into her room, seeing our way by the hall light. I could just make out the pretty twigs of lavender on the wallpaper of the nursery and then, as we got closer, I could see Megan's little face. Her lashes were dark little spikes and she had some of her hair stuck to her head, made damp from the hot night.

I reached out to touch her, but Dad whispered not to disturb her, so I didn't.

It... it was the last time I ever saw my baby sister.

Ruby:
According to reports, after tucking Amanda back into bed, Frank returned to the dinner party.

Later, Frank and Larry went out together in what would be the last check of the children. The three at number six were sleeping and Jennifer Marsh was reading in bed after finishing her homework. They promised not to tell her parents she was still up.

Frank's own home was the last that they visited.

That's when they discovered Megan missing.

To find out more, please join us next time on 'The Callaghan Baby Podcast'. If anyone listening knows anything further that could assist in making this podcast, if anything we say here jogs a memory about something you saw or heard about from that night, please contact me, Ruby Costa, on investigation@thecallaghanfoundation.com. If you know something that could help the police, please contact them.

Thank you for listening.

3

'Good news, I hope,' Eve said.

Billie loved that about her sister, that she always seemed to see the bright side of life. She studied her mum's face where a hint of pink bloomed in her cheeks as she drew out the moment, lips curved.

Although the annual memorial was usually a time of warm reflection on what Mum could remember about her missing sister, it always had its tinge of sadness too. This was something different.

'It is good,' Billie guessed, for a moment back to being a kid knowing there was a treat for her in the groceries as long as she helped pack them away. 'Tell us.'

Mum smiled fully, cheeks properly red now. 'I've been notified that I've been recommended for an award with the Australian honours system for my work with the foundation. For Megan.'

Her lips curved around the two syllables of her sister's name gently, like she wanted to hold each just a second longer before letting them go. Love and grief entwined.

Billie swallowed back the emotion that threatened to burst forth in more tears, happy ones this time. 'Congratulations.'

'Mum, that's brilliant,' Eve added. 'So deserved.'

Mum squirmed a little. 'Finding Megan and all those other lost souls is the most important thing.'

'No one doubts that,' Billie assured her. 'And recognition for you and the work you do getting sponsors and for the ball and maintaining media interest in all those cases will only help give the foundation more attention.'

'There's a ceremony and everything,' Mum said. 'But it's a plus-one only.'

'That's Billie,' Eve said immediately. 'She helped in the early days when the foundation was just an idea at the kitchen table.'

Thankful they wouldn't fight over the ticket like they had Nutcracker Barbie back in the day, Billie grinned. 'Thanks, and I'd love to.'

Mum smiled at them both. 'I'm just grateful that I've been able to do good in Megan's name, give her a lasting legacy beyond the story of that night.'

While Mum had shared her news, the warm milk feed had worked a minor miracle. Lola's deeply relaxed body, drunken parted lips and closed eyes suggested this time she was finally asleep.

Mentally, Billie kicked herself. She should've set up the port-a-cot before she started feeding. Mum would help in a heartbeat but the last thing she needed was to be lugging baby paraphernalia because Billie hadn't planned ahead. Picking up her phone again, she messaged Nathan who'd gone back outside.

'SOS. Bring me the pram, please.'

She waited, only relaxing when she heard the thud of the car's boot closing and then there was Nathan, wheeling in the pram.

'Thank you, you're a lifesaver,' she whispered as she manoeuvred Lola onto it.

With Lola settled, Billie caught Nathan's hand and tugged him towards her, then pressed a quick kiss to his smooth cheek.

His face split into that dimple-revealing grin that she'd first noticed about him. The one that still made her insides all melty. 'I'll forget to get the pram out more often if that's how I get rewarded,' he murmured.

She chuckled. 'That was for coming to my rescue no questions asked.'

'I'll do that too, then,' he said pulling her against him.

She let herself be held. As much as she was happy to be there for her mum, given Lola's age it would be harder than ever to hear the stories about Megan over dinner. As the oldest, Billie had always been Mum's biggest support with her dad moving interstate years ago.

When Mum and Dad finally divorced, he'd argued that: 'No one could live in a marriage where an invisible baby shared their bed day and night.'

Her mum and her dad – Darren Jones – both being part of that night after he was left at home when Barb and Larry went to the dinner party had brought them together. The shared history and not needing to explain so much of what shaped them had given them an understanding and connection that Billie had wanted in her own marriage one day.

Until her dad ran off with his secretary.

It could have broken Mum but instead she'd put renewed energies into her efforts to find Megan, thus creating the foundation that gave hope for so many families searching for missing loved ones.

Sometimes, Billie wondered why a normal guy like Nathan had married into a family so steeped in tragedy.

'You,' he'd reply if she ever said it aloud. 'I didn't marry *them*, I married you.'

A snort of amusement from a few feet away shook Billie from her thoughts.

'Get a room you two,' Tim said. Then he smirked. 'Actually, don't get a room. They lead to babies and if you want any advice from me, stick to one.'

Eve, her wine in hand, swatted Tim as she passed him. 'They are right there, you know; they can hear you.' She pointed to where Max and Matilda were set up at the small table, although only Matilda was there to smile back angelically.

Billie drew away from her husband, smiling at the banter, but unable to shake the heaviness in her heart. She'd always known her aunt went missing as a baby but since having Lola, the knowledge had sharpened.

When she moved towards the place left empty at the table for her, everyone else was already seated, passing around bowls, no one touching the apricot chicken like always. The twins had begun eating before everyone else, and their places showed only a smear of tomato sauce left on Max's plate and Matilda pushing salad around hers.

A faint musical sound came from beneath the edge of the tablecloth. No one else seemed to notice it. Billie paused, one hand on the back of the chair. She knew that tune. Was it someone's ringtone?

She pulled out the chair.

Bam!

Something exploded from under the edge of the white

material and Billie bit back a cry. It was faded red, blue and yellow with washed-out, grinning lips. And was it bouncing?

A familiar blonde head bobbed up after it.

'Max,' Eve scolded, but she was laughing. 'Where did you get that?'

He promptly burst into tears, his usual defence whenever he thought he might be in trouble.

The men, acting more like boys themselves, were almost in tears of laughter. 'Your face,' Tim said to Billie between gasps for air. 'You should have seen it.'

Mum pushed back her chair and held out her arms to the crying little boy. Max climbed onto her lap, nestling against her. 'You've all upset him,' she admonished, her tone gentle so as not to agitate Max further.

Eve leaned over and brushed his hair back, before dropping a kiss on his forehead. 'He's okay, aren't you? That was a funny trick on Aunty Billie but maybe not such a good idea at the dinner table.' She picked up the toy. 'Where did he even find this?'

Mum looked a little embarrassed. 'Put the toy up on the cupboard out of the way,' she suggested, still snuggling with Max. Matilda had joined him there, her little arms embracing both brother and grandmother, not wanting to miss a chance for cuddles.

Suddenly, it clicked for Billie. This wasn't some treat Mum had bought and put away for one of her grandchildren; it was a memento from her childhood, probably kept because it reminded her of her sister.

'It's not damaged,' Billie reassured her. She picked up the antique gingerly and placed it where Mum had indicated. Her heart was still hammering from the surprise.

'The toy was one of mine but I'd kept it to give to Megan,' Mum admitted quietly. 'Of course, she was too little to have played with it before that night, but I had ideas about us one day playing with it together.' Her lips curved. 'Maybe surprising our parents like Max did you. I was going through some old things and thought maybe it was time to pass it on to a family in need.' The way she swallowed gave away the lump in her throat, but she was smiling. 'Megan would have wanted that, I think.'

'Aww, Mum,' Billie and Eve chimed in unison.

Billie reached over and squeezed her mum's hand. 'Maybe it's time.' They shared a long look.

Lola woke, stirring with a sleepy whimper.

'I'll go,' said Nathan, already on his feet.

'Thank you,' Billie said, loving him a bit more.

Uninterested in the latest drama, Tim inhaled food like he was in some kind of competition.

Shaking her head and blinking away the shine of memory in her eyes, Mum held both twins extra close. 'Do either of you pumpkins need an ice-cream?'

The last traces of tears vanished at the suggestion. 'Yes, please,' they chorused.

'As long as you've eaten enough dinner and it's okay with your mother,' Mum added with an apologetic look at Eve.

Eve pursed her lips in consideration while Max and Matilda held their breath, little cheeks puffed and eyes hopeful. 'Okay.'

The cheers sounded out as Mum retrieved the treats from the freezer, then she and Eve helped to open them.

And then, over the ruckus, the doorbell rang.

Billie grabbed the opportunity to do something useful. 'I'll get it.'

She jumped to her feet, giving the little toy on the counter a bemused look as she passed it. Giving something like this away was such a big step for Mum. It showed all the therapy was giving her the kind of closure they'd hardly dared dream she might reach.

As Billie approached the door, the breeze from the park caught her again, sending a shiver skittering across her skin. The shape on the other side resolved to be an unfamiliar silhouette.

A woman.

Billie clicked the lock over, pressed down on the handle, and then opened it enough to confirm it was a stranger. The woman had dark hair loose on her shoulders and she wore a black, sleeveless top and khaki three-quarter-length pants. Older than Billie but younger than Mum, she clutched at the shopping bag in her left hand. But it was her eyes that had Billie's gut churning. There was something almost evangelical in their hazel depths. Like a devoted cult member keen to convert Billie to her beliefs.

'Can I help you?' Billie asked, but what she was really thinking was: *whatever it is you're selling, I'm not buying.*

The woman smiled and then cleared her throat. 'This is number 8 Wattlebury Court?'

Billie hesitated. Her mum had bought back the Callaghan family home not long after Billie and Eve moved out of the house they'd grown up in. The airing of the podcast and the renewed media attention had at first brought out a few less than sane individuals looking for attention along with fans who would turn up and talk to Mum for hours about their theories. There hadn't been anything like that in the last few months.

Her hand tightened on the doorframe as she measured the woman: fan or attention seeker? 'Why?'

'I'm looking for Amanda.'

'Why?'

The woman straightened her shoulders, lifted her chin, and took a deep breath. 'Because I am Megan Callaghan.'

4

Billie only just resisted the urge to slam the door on the woman who claimed to be a person missing for forty years. Instead, she narrowed the gap and lowered her voice. 'I'm sorry but this really isn't a good time. My mother doesn't need to be put through this today.'

The woman's face fell. 'But—'

'Please leave.'

Billie moved to close the door, but the woman's foot came out, keeping it open.

'Look, I've come a long way and I really think if I could come in and talk—' She caught herself as her voice broke. She gripped the shopping bag with both hands. 'I'm not here to make trouble.'

Billie hesitated. There was something familiar about her and she seemed genuine, but so had the others. And this day, of all days, none of them needed to deal with a fake.

While she dithered, the woman stepped closer.

'Let me speak to Amanda. Please.' Her voice had risen, become insistent.

'Who's at the door, Billie?' Mum asked. 'What are you doing?'

Billie felt Mum approach with the inevitability of a train

crashing when it had long since veered off the rails. If she'd had a chance to stop this thing, it was gone. It was like Billie had brought this to life by daring to think her mum was finally happy.

She turned, still shielding the view in or out, but Mum was closer than she'd realised, and reached to pull the door wider.

'Mum,' Billie said. 'I don't want you to get your hopes up.'

Mum rested her hand on Billie's shoulder. 'I'm sorry, this isn't really the time.'

The woman hesitated before lifting the shopping bag so she hugged it against her chest, the material inside lifting out the top. 'I'm not here to make trouble.' She bit her lip. 'I think I'm Megan Callaghan. I think I'm your sister.'

There was movement from near the table, followed by the crack of a glass breaking. 'Crap,' Eve said.

As well as one of her mother's wineglasses, Eve's knocking the glass managed to break the tension of Mum's wide-eyed stare at the woman. She shook her head as though to clear it, and then waved at Eve. 'Get a dustpan,' she said. And then, to the woman who was returning Mum's stare: 'You'd better come in.'

Billie didn't move from blocking the way although the fine hairs on her neck stood up at what she was seeing between the two women. A connection? Recognition? 'She's a stranger; you were going to send her away.'

'I was,' Mum agreed. 'But if the boys will take the children for a play under the sprinkler—' Max and Matilda immediately scurried in that direction '—then I think I'd like to hear what she has to say.'

Billie couldn't argue; after all the woman seemed perfectly normal, if a little nervous. The men had disappeared before

Mum and the stranger even got to the lounge area, and a moment later there was the hum of some sport commentary from a radio in the backyard. They'd be happy out there for however long this took, unless one of the children needed something.

The four women sat. Mum choosing the armchair and the stranger the adjacent couch. The woman's gaze kept slipping to the large black and white photo hung pride of place on the wall, the one of Mum, Megan and the grandmother who'd died before Billie was born.

Billie and Eve took the remaining seats. Evening light slanted through the huge windows overlooking the yard sloping down to Wattlebury Court. Across the road the towering face of the conservation park rose up, the brown grass all gold and shadows.

'Go ahead,' Mum said. 'Tell me why you've come into my home on the anniversary of my sister disappearing. And make it good.'

Billie shared a look with Eve.

Mum always started like this, firm and sceptical, but it wouldn't take long before her desperation to believe overrode everything else.

'My name is—' began the stranger, before pausing and clearing her throat. 'I always believed I was Donna Novak, daughter of Janette and Stefan. I grew up believing they were my biological parents and I had no reason to think otherwise. We lived first in the Blue Mountains and then in Sydney before settling on the outskirts of London in England. Dad was in IT and travelled a lot for work. Mum picked up casual shifts wherever we went. There were other cities and other homes, but they were the places we stayed longer than a year.'

Billie studied Donna as she recited her brief life summary, catching the hint of an accent that must be from her time in the UK, looking for signs of family resemblance, trying to remain objective. There was a sense of familiarity about her but that could just be the hope brought about by it being the anniversary. Could that be a hint of Pop in the shape of her eyes? Was her jaw like Mum's?

A glance in that direction showed Mum already getting caught up, hanging off every word, probably matching the story with all the different possible lives she'd imagined for Megan.

'What made you question what you'd been told?' Mum asked, her gaze darting towards Donna's shopping bag.

Had she seen something?

Donna swallowed. 'Maybe you want to hear that I always thought there was something wrong, but I didn't. I was happy. Dad died when I was ten. He was much older than Mum and he'd always been a distant but kindly figure so not much changed. It was Mum and I against the world and we were close.' Her voice caught. 'Close enough that I wouldn't have believed that she could have kept such a secret. It wasn't until my mother passed away that I began to have questions. Organising her affairs gave me purpose. Some of the dates and documents didn't add up with the stories I'd been told.

'There was no record of me being born in Springwood Hospital, and my research suggested it didn't even have maternity services back then. Also, there were no pictures of me earlier than about five months old. Together, these made me start looking for the truth.'

'That must have been confronting,' Mum said. 'All while dealing with the loss of your mother.'

'Yes and no. At first, I thought of it as a mystery, like it was happening to someone else. I followed the trail of the captions written on the back of the few photos I had and tried to contact people who Mum knew back then. That's how I learned she'd met Stefan Novak in early 1981, well after I was born. It was like I'd loosened a thread and the whole thing unravelled.' Donna's head lowered for a moment and when she raised it her eyes shone with tears.

Mum made a sympathetic noise.

'Then I found the medical records.' Donna waited a beat. 'Janette Novak couldn't have children.'

Despite the sympathy on Mum's face, Billie could sense the excitement building. For all she'd told Ruby in the podcast that she kept her distance from those claiming to be Megan and sensibly waited for the DNA results without getting sucked in, *this* was the truth. This was the cycle Billie had seen play out before.

Mum's hope couldn't be contained. And each time it wasn't, Mum lost her sister again.

EPISODE 02: MISSING

Music playing: 'Heart of Glass' – Blondie

The music fades to the sound of an old-style rotary phone ringing.

Ruby Costa:
Police received the call at 11.11 p.m. on the night of the 9th of December 1979, from Frank Callaghan. And the transcript is as follows:

Emergency caller (identified as Frank Callaghan): Help, please help. My baby is missing.

Operator: Sir, you need to calm down. I can't understand you. Are you sure she's missing? Maybe she's wandered off.

Frank: No, no that's impossible, she's only four months old. Please come, please!

Police were sent to the address immediately. Once the gravity of the situation became apparent, they sent for backup. A search was organised, and statements recorded. But there was no trace of Megan Callaghan and the only evidence at the scene was a broken window and a few stray cigarette butts outside on the path.

Amanda was found in her own bedroom by her father, and her condition was described as 'catatonic' in the police notes. One officer noted they'd never seen a child in such distress writing: *what unimaginable horror must she have seen?* However, apart from suffering from shock, she was physically unharmed. That night, Amanda was unable to answer questions to help police, nor has she been able to since.

I'm Ruby Costa and this is 'The Callaghan Baby Podcast'. Along with my team, I've been investigating a forty-year-old cold case. In these episodes you'll hear the results of our work. We thank 'The Megan Callaghan Foundation' and the 'National Radio Grant' for the funding to create this podcast.

Amanda Callaghan:
Believe me, I have tried everything to take myself back to that night, but the last thing I recall is Dad tucking me into bed.

The rest of that night is a blank until the police spoke to me, which I think must have been past midnight. It's a blur of strangers asking questions I couldn't answer, and light shining off broken glass, and Mum crying as though she'd never stop.

Ruby:
We can come back to this; I understand it must be difficult. Do you need a moment?

Amanda:
I've had forty years. Close to a lifetime of moments spent

not knowing what happened to my baby sister. That's why this podcast is so important. I didn't know much about podcasts when you approached me, but with your contacts and getting funding approval through the foundation we could reach a new audience. If it stirs someone's memory or leads to something that gives even the tiniest breakthrough...

Anyway, where was I?

Trying to remember that night has taken me to doctors, legitimate and less reputable, to try to get those missing hours back. In my head I can see Megan's cot, the sheet rumpled, and I can hear a sound I'm sure is her crying.

The heart-tugging cries of an upset baby grow from a faint background noise to a crescendo as Amanda's voice catches. She sighs.

But these memories could be from before she went missing.

Even if I remembered it all tomorrow, I'd be afraid it was a scenario created in the recesses of my brain. It kills me that I might have the answer inside me, but I can't access it. That someone is going about their lives unpunished because of me.

I lie awake in the dark hours and sometimes I believe I can almost hear Megan crying for me. I'm afraid she's out there somewhere and she needs me.

That's part of the reason the board of the foundation agreed to contribute funding to this podcast: we need new information desperately. I want listeners to be aware that there is a significant reward offered for any concrete information that leads to finding Megan.

Ruby:
We spoke to memory expert Professor Anne Jantzen about Amanda's inability to recall the night of Megan's disappearance.

Anne Jantzen:
The most important thing you need to understand in this is we're discussing first the observational ability, and then the recall and memory, of a ten-year-old. Children can be observant, but whatever happened in that house that night included significant trauma to Amanda. This reaction indicates that Amanda Callaghan personally experienced something that night. When you add in the fact Megan has never been found, it is not at all surprising these protective mechanisms have remained.

Ruby:
This helps us understand how Amanda could fail to remember, but the trauma has not been limited to the past. When I interviewed Amanda, we talked about the false Megans she's had to deal with over the years. Several years ago, Amanda formed a close bond with one before she learned the truth.

Amanda:
Obviously, it's been disappointing so far, but I haven't given up hope.

It's well known from early news reports that Megan had a birthmark on her torso and there's DNA testing; also some details about Megan have never been revealed to the public.

Ruby:

Although much has been said about police procedure around Megan's disappearance, it is noted that all of the couples who were at the dinner party were questioned separately to formulate the timeline of events and their explanations all matched up to the minute. Effectively, these eight people form each other's alibis.

Hindsight, of course, gives us an advantage that couldn't be had at the time and it's that perfect synchronicity of their stories that doesn't quite add up for me.

A photo taken that night that became synonymous with reporting of the 'dinner party from hell'. It shows the eight of them together. They're posed at the end of a table filled with food and drinks with the four men standing behind the four seated women. All their faces have that wide, happy smile of the completely carefree.

Certainly, none of them appear to have a clue about what's to come.

The sandy-haired and boyish Frank Callaghan dressed in a fitted white shirt with a wide collar stands behind Carol and her fingers are wrapped in his, where his hand rests on her shoulder. Her long dark hair is caught mid-swing like she's about to turn to say something to her husband. Her brown eyes are full of laughter. He's looking at the camera but somehow, he's focused on her and it's not hard to understand why. She glows, stunning in a simple light blue shift dress, not looking at all like someone who had a baby only months earlier.

The hosts are next to them. Trish, the immaculate former air hostess, looking exceptionally bored behind her smile, is striking in a tight, red, halter-neck jumpsuit.

Ken, already balding and pudgy, with the stunned grin of a man who can't believe his good fortune, has his brown and yellow striped shirt so far open it threatens to show his belly button.

I think if I didn't already know Gloria and Ray were teachers then I'd guess it from the photo. Ray's impressive sideburns not able to hide his faint disapproval at the world and his crisp shirt and brown jacket look like they could come straight from a classroom. Gloria's brown bob makes her rounded face even rounder and she's wearing a prim yellow dress.

Barb and Larry are on the other end. There's a distance between them despite their proximity. Her wild reddish curls tied back by a scarf and colourful, patterned blouse buttoned high, contrasting with his neat banker's cut and boring beige.

Although there's nearly two decades between Ray, the oldest, and Ken's new wife, Trish, they have a similarity between them that suggests they were all at home in this promising community with good schools; basically, couples on the rise.

We'll move in this investigation in the same direction as the police. Because what else is there to do when there is such an obvious suspect and public demanding he be investigated?

Therefore, we turn our attention to Dominic Snave.

Female reporter:
Twenty-four-year-old Dominic Snave today received a suspended sentence for the attempted extortion of his boss. Mr Snave was expected to receive a custodial sentence;

however, when delivering his verdict, Judge Pascal ruled Mr Snave was unlikely to be a further threat to his victims or the community.

Ruby:
You've just heard an excerpt from a news report relating to the first of Dominic Snave's convictions. Convictions that began with attempted blackmail and grew from there.

The most recent of his known crimes before Megan disappeared was kidnapping the child of a businessman acquaintance, not unlike Frank Callaghan. At the scene, Dominic Snave broke a window of the child's bedroom to enter late at night and left copious cigarette butts outside in the yard where he'd waited, observing the premises.

Dominic Snave's release that day, the cigarette butts at the scene and a recent industry article citing Callaghan Constructions, Frank's fledgling business, as being on the rise was enough to make him a suspect.

The police's suspicions were heightened when Mr Snave couldn't be located at his mother's house, a mere twenty-minute drive from Wattlebury Court.

However, it was a witness coming forward having seen Mr Snave near Wattlebury Court that night that solidified him as the main suspect in the investigation.

You'll see in the next episode how that impacted the rest of the investigation. Join us next time on 'The Callaghan Baby Podcast'. If anyone listening knows anything that could assist in making this podcast, please contact me on investigation@thecallaghanfoundation.com. If you know something that could help the police, please contact them.

Thank you for listening.

5

'What made you think you were Megan?' Mum asked, urging Donna to get to the part of the tale that mattered most to her.

'A search of the national missing persons database threw up her name as a possibility given the timing. There was no record of adoption papers for me and my mother had talked about an older man she knew from Ridgefield. The coincidence rang alarm bells.'

Again, Billie could see the cogs in her mother's brain turning, trying to align this with what they knew.

Donna sighed. 'She'd mentioned Ridgefield over and over in the delirium of her last few days. And she spoke to this man as though he were there at her bedside, telling him she owed him everything. At the time it didn't make sense but then I thought... maybe... She always said I was her everything. Like most of the country, I'd heard about the case and these things always strike a chord when you're the same age as the child. I'd listened to the podcast on her disappearance, too.'

'Hmm.' Billie didn't mean to say anything but she must have murmured her disappointment. Both Mum and Eve frowned at her obvious scepticism, but she couldn't help it.

Someone had to keep a level head, and – as always – that someone was Billie. So far, the story could be the concoction of some podcast fan of about the right age with half-decent acting skills hoping to get their hands on the reward from the foundation mentioned in an early episode.

'Go on, Donna,' Mum said. 'Don't mind her.'

Rather than appearing annoyed, Donna laughed nervously. 'Trust me, I didn't believe it either at first. It was a nagging idea until my mother... Janette's estate cleared and I was given a key to a security box. In it was this.'

She pulled a large envelope from the plastic bag she'd brought with her. Tipping it up, she shook it, so the contents fluttered onto the surface of the small coffee table.

'Newspaper cuttings,' Eve breathed.

Mum reached forward and picked up the closest, her fingers trembling, a faint wheeze in her breathing. 'Missing Baby,' she whispered, reading it. Then the next one: 'Have you seen Megan Callaghan?' Excitement lit her expression.

'When I saw these,' said Donna, 'I knew I had to find out for sure. It all fits. I believe Janette took that longed-for baby, me, from the older man who must have been involved with her kidnap. My mother wanted a baby so badly she didn't ask questions. Later, she married Stefan Novak, probably never telling him the truth about me. But guilt over where I'd come from got the better of her as the years passed, thus she collected these, suspicious that I could be the missing girl. I recently moved here with my son, but I've been waiting for the right time to approach you.'

'Why come forward today?' Mum asked.

'I've been here for a couple of months, settling into the city and trying to get the courage to approach you knowing this could change all our lives,' Donna admitted. 'I believe I'm Megan Callaghan and I was taken from this house forty years ago. Being the anniversary, I couldn't stop thinking about it, and I guess I just couldn't wait any longer.'

'I want to believe you,' Billie said carefully. But she could tell Mum was caught, reeled in by her own desperate need to believe. 'But you understand a few newspaper cuttings aren't proof.'

'I have a birthmark like the one mentioned in the podcast. I'll show you,' Donna said, placing the bag on the floor and getting to her feet.

Mum, Billie and Eve watched as Donna lifted her top. Beneath was the soft, white belly of a forty-year-old woman and just below her right ribcage, a light brown stain on her skin.

Heart, thought Billie immediately having to blink back tears. How many times had she heard the story of her grandparents jokingly arguing whether Megan's birthmark looked more like a music note – her Pop's suggestion, or a heart – this from Carol?

The memory of another birthmark, this on a tattooed fake pretending to be Megan, was the metaphorical cold water on the hope sparking in Billie's chest. 'Lots of people have birthmarks and there aren't any photos.'

'It *was* there,' Mum said, wonder threading her voice. 'I don't need photographs. I remember.'

A glance at Eve showed similar marvel in her face.

Billie forced herself to look out the window at the trees swaying in the conservation park and away from Donna's stomach. It was a good story. Too good? Someone needed to be sensible. They'd all been hurt before.

'May I?' Mum asked, reaching out to Donna, drawing Billie's gaze back inside.

Donna nodded her permission and Mum touched the mark lightly with a shaking fingertip. 'It's exactly as I remember,' Mum said.

'That little mark has been through a bit,' Donna said with a chuckle. 'Got well and truly stretched out when I was pregnant with my son, who's a teenager now. But I've had it for as long as I can remember.' She lowered her top and sat on the couch.

'We've had people come to us with birthmarks before, but they've been proved to be frauds,' Billie explained. 'A tattoo artist we know has explained how simple it would be to fake such a mark.' Even as she said it she couldn't help thinking her mother hadn't been this convinced last time. 'Do you have anything else?'

Mum chewed on her lip, her hope a tangible presence in the room.

'You're right to be sceptical,' Donna said reaching for the shopping bag on the floor. 'But there's more. This was in the security box, too. An article with a photo of Megan wrapped in a baby blanket was pinned to it. The woman I thought was my birth mother must have kept it.'

'The blanket,' Mum said on a sob, her eyes glued to that shopping bag, her hands covering her mouth.

Billie's heart jumped. So, this was the reason Mum had relented and let her in; she must have glimpsed the edge. This was new. This meant something.

She held her breath, understanding what had her mum leaning forward to the very edge of her chair. When she was seven her parents had a huge fight – one of many – about Megan, it was always about Megan. It was after some crackpot had shown up claiming she knew where Megan's body was buried. This much Billie found out later when her dad had had a few too many beers and swore that Megan Callaghan ruined his marriage before it began. He explained that there had been a search at an address two hours from the city. It had everything: all the media, TV cameras, helicopters, the works. But when they dug up a small box and unwrapped the remains, forensics showed it to be a deceased pet.

As her mum tucked seven-year-old Billie into bed, she'd said, 'Between us, I knew from the moment I saw the blanket that it wasn't her.'

Bleary and confused, Billie asked, 'What blanket?'

'The only thing that went missing with her.'

Billie didn't need to ask who 'her' was; Megan's disappearance was already a part of the fabric of her life, buried so deeply she'd never find the beginning of the thread. 'Why was it special?'

'We've never released to the media, but it had our name – "Callaghan" – embroidered on the edge.'

'And that blanket they found didn't?' Billie asked as her eyes closed.

'No,' whispered Mum. 'It didn't.'

Mum had explained the details properly when Billie got older. She'd told her how she'd know that someone claiming to be Megan was real if she had the embroidered blanket. It was Mum's secret insurance. And that knowledge had been passed down to Billie as the oldest, along with a legacy to never stop searching.

And now, this woman had a blanket as proof? Could this woman finally *be* Megan?

THAT NIGHT

He clicks his fingers.

It's not an order so much as an expectation that I will come to do his bidding. Immediately, I'm on my feet and crossing to Ken like he's yanked a string. The need to please my new husband enhanced by the second glass of wine that I somehow finished without noticing, while one of the wives told us the story of her youngest taking her first steps two days ago.

The warm, orange light spilling from the lamp in the corner, diffused by the rich, sweet scent of what the men are smoking, has softened Barb's usually disapproving gaze. Or maybe that's just how she gets when talking about her babies, when she forgets to let me know I'm the newcomer here.

I reach his side and wait while he finishes telling the men how the tan, leather couches they're sitting on were made to his specifications and imported from Italy. Of course not one of them is bright enough to ask how he affords it all on a dentist's income. Getting into his role as host and entertainer, he finishes by letting them know it's soft and warm enough to lie on naked, his voice suggestive, his smirk letting them know we've tried it.

Then he links his hand in mine. I let him pull me down towards him, so my other hand has to find balance resting on the open neck of his shirt, in the coarse hair curling there. He's damp with sweat, heat lingering in the night air despite our efforts to cool the space. I feel his tongue wet on my lips as his other hand finds the curve of my hip, possessive, cupping my arse for the benefit of the other men with their perfect view. Staking his claim.

One of the men says something I don't catch over the swirling, pulsing beat of the music, throbbing from the speakers in the corner, but I know the kind of sentiment from the throaty laughter that follows and I feel the wave of animosity radiating from the gaggle of women I left behind.

Like I'm the one in charge of this little show.

My husband lifts his head to come up for air, eyes red and shining. 'He's finished his beer, honey.'

There's nothing else needing to be said, just that expectation because I'm his wife now.

Obedient, I sway across to the fridge, letting the music move me, past the dining table filled with the congealing remains of casseroles and the chocolate fondue beginning to set. The food a mere prelude to the real purpose of the night, all of us knowing what's going to unfold later in shadowed corners under the lamp's glow.

I open the fridge door, and have to bend over again to pull a couple of bottles from the bottom shelf. I feel their eyes on me – all of them now, men and women both. Feel their heat of want and hate and just one filled with kindness – that's the hard one – but I have drunk enough that I can turn with my head high, knowing my bright red lipstick remains curved in that perfect hostess smile.

6

'What's so special about the blanket?' Eve asked.

Billie clasped her hands together so she didn't reach for it. It wasn't her place; instead she left it for Mum to explain.

'I'll show you, if I may?' Mum said to Eve. At Eve's nod, she held out shaking hands.

Donna handed over the yellowed material. Mum took it with such care it could still have held that newborn she remembered so dearly. She turned it over and there, on the corner, was 'Callaghan', embroidered in flowing script.

Silent tears flowed down Mum's cheeks as her finger traced each letter. 'You're really her. This is really happening.'

Then the two women were laughing and crying and hugging.

Billie wiped away her own tears and shared a happy smile with Eve. Could this really be true? After she'd taken her turn hugging Donna – her aunt? – and joining in the happy jig around the coffee table, she brought them back to practicalities. 'Shall we call the detective in charge of the case?'

Mum and Donna broke apart from another delirious hug.

Donna squeezed Mum's hand and smiled. 'I hadn't really thought about all the details of what would come next. I mean, I was just getting up my nerve to come here, and I didn't know what you would think or how you'd react. But Billie's right: better to make sure for all our sakes.'

Billie was relieved the prospect of a DNA test hadn't scared Donna off, another point in her favour. As well as what she was beginning to think was a definite resemblance to her mother.

But Mum took a shaky breath. 'I don't know.'

'What do you mean?' Billie asked. 'I'm sure I can find out the number. Or that detective from the podcast can help. I know his number is on the fridge.'

'Paul Lennard's number is there. As is the number for Detective Okely, who's currently responsible for the case,' Mum said. 'I'm perfectly capable of getting it and calling, but I'm not so sure I want to.'

'What?' Billie and Eve said in unison.

'Don't worry,' Mum said. 'I'm not an idiot.' She smiled at Donna. 'No offence.'

Donna shook her head. 'None taken.'

Mum's smile slipped when she looked back to Billie. 'You know better than anyone, this isn't our first time going through this. And each time there's been media intruding into our lives. All our lives.' Her gaze lifted to include Donna and Eve. 'Last time we had them camped on the doorstep and following us. There's nothing like a party gone wrong and the opportunity to judge other parents to inflame opinion pieces. Yes, the podcast brought the case some media attention but this would bring out the gossip magazines, all trying to get the next clickbait headline. There are young children to consider, as well as Donna's teenage son who might also be affected. None of us want to go through that again. Agreed?'

Billie couldn't argue with that. 'Then what do we do?'

'Darling, I'm already ahead of you, if you'll give me a moment.' Mum laboured to her feet and disappeared down the hallway, returning before anyone could speak.

She waved a package at them. 'In here is the answer to that particular conundrum.' She tossed it through the air and Donna caught it.

Donna read the label and looked up. 'A paternity kit.' She leaned forward like she wanted to rip it open right away.

Mum sank back into the chair with a sigh. 'We'll do it ourselves, remove the possibility for media speculation, unless anyone has an objection.'

'But it could take longer,' Billie argued. 'This time of year, postage is crazy.'

Ignoring Billie, Mum took both Donna's hands in hers. 'It's up to you but I'm not sure I can go through all that again. The way I look at it: we'll have the rest of our lives, what's a few more days?'

Donna nodded slowly. 'If that's what you want.'

Eve picked up the kit and peered at the instructions. 'It says paternity. That means...'

Billie didn't blame her sister for not finishing her sentence. Since the last few episodes of the podcast had aired, mentioning Pop at all tended to set Mum off. Discovering drugs were involved and the timeline of the night being brought into question had left her shocked and hurt and, thanks to Pop's condition, unable to ask him about any of it.

Billie wanted to believe in the grandfather who'd been such an important part of her life but she couldn't blame her mum for being upset. 'Okay, we'll do it your way,' she said into the beginnings of an awkward silence.

But rather than being satisfied by Billie's agreement, a frown creased Mum's forehead. Her eyes squeezed closed and she gripped the armrests so hard the veins stood out on the back of her hands. Hands that, to Billie, suddenly looked like those of an old woman rather than her indefatigable mum.

'I feel,' Mum began, 'a little...' she paused again, her chest rising and falling '... short of breath.' The last came out on a wheeze.

Billie scooted over to kneel by her mum, searching her face for signs of just how serious this was. Her brain raced. Heart attack? Stroke? Mum was young, only fifty, but it happened. Could Donna's news have caused such a thing? 'What is it?'

Mum's eyes opened. 'My heart is racing. Maybe it's the shock. I'm sure I'll be fine if I just have a moment...' More ragged breaths. 'A bit of rest.'

'Or maybe it's serious,' Billie said.

'Do you mind?' Donna had moved closer to bend over Mum. 'I'm a nurse,' she added.

Billie moved aside as Donna checked Mum over. The protective oldest child who'd always cared for her mum wanted to argue but she recognised expertise when she saw it in Donna's brisk, assured movements. She found herself praying that it was nothing serious, not when they finally had real hope Megan was home.

'How long have you been feeling like this?' Donna asked. At the same time, she picked up Mum's hand, turned it over to expose her wrist and felt for her pulse.

Mum shrugged. 'I haven't been the best for a while but... It's been getting worse.'

'Any other pain?'

'No.'

Donna tilted her head, concentrating. 'That pulse rate is high.'

'What's wrong with her?' Billie asked. She saw her worry reflected in Donna's gaze and felt the connection over their shared concern.

'Is it a heart attack?' Eve added. 'Does she have pain in her shoulder? I read online that shoulder pain is bad.'

Mum shook her head at Eve. 'Don't get so worked up.'

A small frown pinched Donna's features. 'We need an ambulance.'

7

'No lights and sirens, thanks,' Mum said at Donna's suggestion for an ambulance. 'I don't want any fuss. And what would the neighbours think? Today of all days.'

'I'll drive her to the hospital,' Billie volunteered, needing to do something to help.

'That's for the best,' Mum agreed. And then to Billie: 'Thanks, love.'

Upon arrival in the hospital's emergency department twenty minutes later, Billie described Mum's symptoms as best she could and filled in the required paperwork. The whole time she swung between studying Mum for signs she was getting worse and trying to imagine what was happening back at the house with the woman who'd claimed she was Megan.

It didn't take long for Mum to be preliminarily assessed, hooked up to machines that beeped and whirred in time with Billie's worries, and told a doctor would see them soon.

Two hours later, after Billie had fielded several messages from Eve, and one from Nathan letting her know Lola was fine, a man walked in with the stride of someone who'd have answers.

'Dr Wan Li,' he said. He shook Billie's outstretched hand

and greeted Mum while studying the monitors. Dr Li didn't look much older than Billie, but they'd been told he was the senior cardiologist at the hospital.

'Hmmm...' He pushed his silver glasses up on his nose. 'That is rather high.'

'What does that mean?' Billie asked, trying not to let her concern show in her voice in case it upset Mum.

For the first time since they'd reached the hospital, Mum's brow creased and she seemed to shrink into the bed. Her hand found Billie's and they held on tight to each other, sharing strength like they had so many times before.

Dr Li tapped his chin. 'Simply put, we believe Amanda has an abnormal heart rhythm, called an arrhythmia. We'll run a few more tests to confirm but I don't think it's anything more complicated. We'll keep her in, monitor her overnight, and see if it settles.'

'And if it doesn't?' Billie asked the question Mum couldn't.

'Then we'll have her back for a day procedure that lets us shock her heart back into rhythm.'

'Heart surgery?' Billie repeated, her own pounding.

'A procedure,' Dr Li corrected, kindly. 'For a common heart condition.'

While her mother was admitted to a room, Billie updated the others, explaining the diagnosis sounded scary but wasn't uncommon. Even as she reassured Eve, she mentally replayed the interaction with the doctor and how her usually forthright Mum hadn't uttered a word.

It wasn't until they were alone again and Billie had done her best to reassure Mum there was nothing to stress about regarding her condition, that conversation returned to their unexpected visitor.

'She's my sister,' Mum said softly. 'I know it.'

Billie hoped so too but she worried about the consequences for Mum's mental health if this was just a better-prepared fake. If they weren't already hopeful, the way she'd helped with Mum's scare had made her seem part of the family.

Mum chuckled. 'I must be sick.'

'Why?'

'Billie Callaghan-Jones biting her tongue. Wonders will never cease.'

Billie allowed herself a small smile. 'I want this to be true, I do, but I don't want you getting your hopes up.'

'I love that you're protective, but I have a really good feeling about this.'

By the time Billie quietly let herself in her house hours later, she had to fumble for the key in the dark. Inside, the silence confirmed Nathan's earlier message that he'd managed to transfer Lola to sleep in her cot.

She flipped the light switch.

'Shit.' Nathan who'd been stretched out on the couch, startled upright, dropping his phone to the floor with a crack. 'Shit,' he repeated, this time at the phone's screen.

'Sorry, I didn't realise you were in here. Is it bad?'

He rubbed at his eyes, his hair and clothes adorably sleep rumpled, and placed it on the coffee table. 'It's fine.'

'What were you doing in the dark?'

He yawned. 'Must have drifted off watching the races.'

'At this hour?'

'It's the doggies, under lights. Forget that. Will your mum be okay?'

'The doc seems to think so,' Billie said, sinking into the couch, suddenly exhausted. 'She'll be in for a couple of days.

I'm not really surprised. Massive day for her, and she's not getting any younger.'

'Fifty is spring-chicken territory these days, barely even old enough to be a cougar.'

'Yuck, thanks for that mental image. I do not need to think of her on the prowl.'

'Might be good for her,' Nathan said as he rounded the kitchen bench and got two glasses from the cupboard. He poured them each a glass of red.

She accepted hers with a heartfelt, 'Thank you,' and a check of the time. With a little luck, Lola would sleep, and Billie could enjoy her wine and catch a few hours' rest herself. She lifted the glass to her lips, breathing in the earthy and fruity aroma. After the day she'd had, she'd *really* enjoy this one.

Then she heard the whimpers from Lola that would soon escalate to a hungry cry. Billie sighed and stood, placing the glass on the bench.

'I'll get her,' Nathan said.

'That's okay. I'll feed her again and maybe she'll sleep right through.'

But Billie doubted it. Someone had helpfully warned her about the six-month growth spurt and Lola was almost there. Lately she wanted to feed all the time.

Nathan crossed the room to push a loose strand of Billie's hair back from her face. He kissed her gently. 'I could give her a bottle, give you a break.'

Her heart ached in that moment and she could have melted against his chest. He knew her so well. This was what kept her going in the long days and nights when she thought Lola would never stop crying: having this man as her partner.

'I'm tempted, but—'

'I want to preserve my expressed breastmilk,' Nathan finished her sentence in unison with a rueful grin that made her heart skip a beat.

'I'm up now,' she said. 'And the wine will wait.' Or more likely end up tipped down the sink.

The ding of the doorbell before she'd reached the nursery had her cursing under her breath. 'Who could it be this late?'

EPISODE 03: A SUSPECT

Music playing: 'We Don't Talk Anymore' – Cliff Richard

The music fades.

Ruby:
Welcome to Episode Three. I'm Ruby Costa and this is 'The Callaghan Baby Podcast'. Along with my team, I've been investigating the forty-year-old cold case of missing Megan Callaghan. In these episodes you'll hear the results of our work.

If you recall, we left off last episode with a witness coming forward who had the police looking for Dominic Snave. They might have looked in other directions if not for Danny Pratt's visit to the police station on the 10th of December.

Danny claimed to have seen Dominic Snave at his workplace, a service station two blocks from Wattlebury Court. If you remember, the news stations had already suggested the link in the media and shown Dominic Snave's face.

The police did all they could in the following days to find their man.

And discovered very little.

His mother insisted he was innocent; however, he was a known kidnapper, placed in the area by a witness and he couldn't be located. Add to that a crime scene like his others and, in Callaghan Constructions, a target flush with success. Thus, Dominic Snave became the police's number one, and I would argue from their efforts on the case that he was also the number two, three and four suspect. It was raised during the 2005 inquest that it may have been the very overtness of Dominic Snave as a suspect that prevented police properly considering other persons of interest.

The witness who placed Mr Snave near the scene, Danny Pratt, was called to appear before the coroner in the 2005 inquest into Megan Callaghan's disappearance.

Kate Emmett is a criminal lawyer who was the counsel assisting the coroner throughout the inquest. Blonde, intense and with a reputation for breaking witnesses with a look. You will hear a lot from her throughout this podcast via excerpts taken from the inquest recording.

It didn't take long for her to have Danny Pratt squirming on the stand.

Kate Emmett:
You stated, in an interview, that the man you saw that night was wearing a baseball cap and he had it pulled low on his head. If that was the case, how could you give police a description? Also, the time you reported to police was ten p.m., which is too early for him to have taken Megan. And, before you say anything else, you've described seeing a baby sitting in the back of Mr Snave's vehicle – something that would have been physically impossible for you to see.

Danny:
I don't know. It was dark and there were lights reflecting on the windows and they were across the far side of the station. And maybe my watch battery had stopped. It could have been eleven not ten.

Kate:
What you're saying is that you maybe had the time wrong and you forgot details in your preliminary police statement, and you may or may not have seen a baby. Is that correct?

Danny:
Yes, but you're making me sound all idiot-like.

Ruby:
Police soon hit a brick wall in their investigation, unable to question someone they couldn't find. Then, an associate of Dominic Snave, Axel Finch, came forward and admitted to having seen his friend for dinner that evening at a location four hours' drive from Ridgefield. The presence of Mr Snave's red panel van at the property seemed to back up his claims although Mr Snave couldn't be found.

Mr Finch was a known criminal, but under close interrogation he stuck to his story. Then again when he was questioned by Kate Emmett during the 2005 inquest.

Axel Finch:
Listen, lady, you can stand there in ya fancy clothes, looking at me over the top of yer glasses and shit but it

ain't gonna make me change me story. Cos it's the truth, the whole truth and nuttin' but the truth, so help me God.

Nic was at my place for dinner that night and couldn't have been taking some little'un in the suburbs. He wouldn't have done shit like that anyway.

I cooked chops and mash, me mam's favourite. We had a smoke and a beer after, and we sat out on the step to enjoy it cos it was so bloody hot inside.

Kate:

If your memory is so clear, you'll be able to tell us what time Dominic Snave arrived at your home and also when he left.

Axel:

It's not like I spent me days staring at the flaming clock, did I?

Look, Nic arrived before the evening news. I remember that much because we laughed about how they showed his mugshot on the screen.

Kate:

So, you're saying Dominic Snave arrived at your property before six-thirty p.m. What time did he leave?

Ruby:

If you watch the recording of the inquest, it's clear that Axel Finch takes an absurdly long time to answer this question, tugging at the collar of his shirt like it's choking him.

Police records suggest that Dominic and the older Axel met through a mutual associate when Dominic was looking to buy a weapon. As well as being criminal colleagues, the two men shared a love of Aussie Rules football and went to games together.

Finally, Axel shrugs.

Axel:
We'd had a few drinks and it wasn't safe to drive so Nic crashed at my place. I think he left the next day, taking one of my old dirt bikes.

Ruby:
This is the last time anyone is on record as having seen Dominic Snave. His mother insisted he never came home.

His disappearance fit well with police theories at the time. They believed he'd taken Megan intending to use her to make ransom demands, then got cold feet. He'd aborted the plan and gotten rid of her.

To me, it seems quite the stretch that a man with a non-violent record could cold-bloodedly dispose of a child. In all my career as an investigative journalist I've learned that killing, deliberate killing, is not as simple a task as it's often made out to be in books or movies. Something human must be severed inside.

More likely for there to have been a terrible accident, causing him to flee. This is Dominic's mother, Mary, speaking to a reporter.

Mary Snave:
You're all searching for my boy as a suspect, but has anyone stopped to consider that he might be a victim?

That Callaghan woman isn't the only one who lost a child that night.

Ruby:

In 2008 there was a development regarding Axel Finch. Thanks to information from a small-time arms dealer, police conducted a search on the Finch property and found human remains that dental records identified as Dominic Snave.

Police located Axel at the local pub where he drunkenly confessed to accidentally shooting Dominic Snave in the early hours of the 10th of December 1979 in a quarrel. Axel was charged, convicted and died behind bars.

Where to from there?

Technology has changed in the last forty years. At the time of Megan's disappearance, the scene was searched for evidence. DNA can be quite stable and the cigarette butts from the scene were stored. They were well preserved, and when DNA testing became viable police hoped they'd be able to find samples for analysis. They found nothing, confirming they were planted at the scene.

Dominic Snave was thus eliminated as a suspect in Megan Callaghan's disappearance.

The continuing lack of closure for the Callaghan family, culminating in the passing of Carol Callaghan, was brought to a head by Amanda's campaign for answers. Her dedicated work brought about the inquest into the handling of Megan's disappearance.

It is rare to have access as we do to both video and audio from the inquest and we thank Amanda Callaghan and 'The Megan Callaghan Foundation' for sharing their recordings.

The chances of a complete stranger happening upon that house that night are so slim as to be basically negligible. Therefore, it's likely the person who took Megan was close to, or part of the family. The Callaghans didn't have extended family close by and they socialised most often with their neighbours.

This is where police should have been paying attention.

All the surviving attendees of the dinner party were interviewed as part of the inquest. We'll share their testimony when it makes sense to do so.

First up was Frank Callaghan, a man who was mostly seen in the media as the stalwart husband, standing behind his distraught wife Carol as she pleaded with the public. Despite combing through all of the historic TV footage, we could not find one quote from Megan's father. Perhaps Frank was the strong and silent type.

Or perhaps he didn't speak because he had something to hide.

Don't they say in cases like these that the first place to look is closest to home?

Please join us next time on 'The Callaghan Baby Podcast'. If anyone listening knows anything that could assist in making this podcast, please contact me on investigation@thecallaghanfoundation.com. If you know something that could help the police, please contact them.

Thank you for listening.

8

'I'll get the door; you go to Lola,' Nathan said. 'Divide and conquer.'

Happy to leave him to handle the door, Billie went in to Lola. Her precious daughter lay on her back, sucking on her little fist in between low-pitched hungry cries that had Billie's milk threatening to leak.

'Oh, are you hungry, little Lola-bug?' She sniffed. 'Hungry and stinky. No wonder you're crying.'

At least the nappy change should give Nathan time to deal with their visitor.

But when Billie carried a freshly changed Lola out to feed in their favourite chair, Eve was sitting on the couch. 'Seriously?' Billie said, shaking her head. 'It's late.'

Eve smiled. 'I messaged you; it's not my fault you ignored it. I said to let me know if I shouldn't come by.'

'I've been busy,' she said wearily.

'I went past the hospital, but they wouldn't wake Mum.'

'Because it's late.' Billie said it slowly, carefully enunciating each word.

'Anyway, Tim has kid duty, so I figured I'd come by.' She must have noticed Billie's incredulous expression at last because she added, 'We need to debrief about Donna.' Then she spotted the glass Billie had left on the bench. 'Oh, is that a pinot noir? Be a love, Nathan.'

Billie settled Lola into feeding and Nathan brought over a glass of wine for Eve.

'Thanks, you are my favourite brother-in-law.'

Nathan snickered. 'I'm your only brother-in-law.'

'Don't forget you're driving,' said Billie, thinking of the white wine earlier.

Eve took a long sip. 'Who made you the alcohol police?'

Billie didn't flinch. 'You can be annoyed all you want; I'm not going to stop being the big sister. I care about you.'

'The *bossy* big sister,' Eve corrected, but her annoyance was gone. 'No more for me,' she said to Nathan who hadn't moved. 'Billie's orders. Anyway, what do we think about this Donna chick?'

'I don't know.'

'What about the blanket?' Eve countered. 'You can't explain that. I'd be annoyed no one ever told me but that's what happens when you're the youngest and the cutest. That never made the media.'

It was that detail that had Billie daring to hope. 'Maybe it's not that big a secret. Someone else might have known.'

Eve considered. 'Dad? She'd have had to tell him.'

'Precisely,' Billie said. 'And you know what Dad's like once he's had a few beers.' She adopted a gloomy expression, imitating him. '"Megan-bloody-Callaghan ruined my life." You know it's one of his favourite soliloquies.' Billie shrugged. 'Hell, half the country might know. It wouldn't be hard to get a blanket made.'

'Maybe,' Eve said. 'You have to say Mum looked pretty convinced and the script for the font would be hard to guess. No one is that lucky.'

'Or maybe Mum wants this to be true so badly she's forgetting the original.'

'But what does Donna get out of all of this?' Eve asked.

Billie couldn't help playing devil's advocate. 'What do any of them get? The thrill of being involved with the case? Some people like the attention. And this one is better than most; maybe she thinks she'll get her hands on the reward Mum set up through the foundation.'

Nathan looked up with a frown at the mention of the foundation. The finances were his area of expertise. 'But she'd have to know we won't clear anything without DNA proof. The rules are strict. And I'd question whether her being Megan would qualify as information leading to her whereabouts anyway – it would be unethical.'

'People don't always think straight with money involved,' Billie countered. 'She might not know all of that. And then there's Mum personally. There's not a thing Mum wouldn't give her if she believes Megan really has come home.'

'But we need to give her a chance.'

'You weren't here last time.'

Eve's face softened. 'I know, but Mum's different now. You heard her – she's not rushing into anything.'

'She said that then. Right before she let that woman into her life and lost most of her savings. Not to mention the rest of it.'

As usual Billie couldn't bring herself to go into detail. A lifetime of protecting her little sister hard to shake. It wasn't Eve's fault she was living overseas back then. It was the life of a football wife, travelling at her husband's side during his short but spectacular professional career before Tim's injury brought them home to a job for life at the club where he'd started. His lingering fame and local influence boosted Eve's social media profile enough that it seemed to be a job in itself. Not that Billie understood how all that worked.

'She won't have another breakdown,' Eve said with the blithe confidence of someone who didn't witness the last one.

In contrast, Billie just had to close her eyes and she was back there walking the hospital floors after the attempted overdose. She saw the grave face of the doctor informing Billie that Mum couldn't be left alone. As if Billie would have been anywhere but by her side.

And then, when she was released, the long nights Billie kept watch before struggling through a long day at work.

All of it she'd made sound lighter for Eve, stuck as she had been on the other side of the world.

'It won't happen again,' Eve repeated in one of those rare moments of understanding.

'You don't know that.'

'Yes, I do. I'm here now.'

Billie allowed Eve's confidence to quieten the turmoil inside.

'Besides,' Eve continued, her voice brighter. 'If she is Megan, we never have to have apricot chicken again. That reminds me, I brought your dish back.'

As Billie swapped Lola to feed from the other side, she saw the dish, clean and sparkling. 'Oh, you didn't have to wash it.'

'I didn't.' Eve played with her empty glass and didn't meet Billie's gaze. 'There was all that mess and it wasn't like the men were much help – no offence.' The latter said to Nathan.

'None taken,' he said.

That left one possibility as far as Billie could see. 'You didn't.'

'What could I say?' Eve argued. 'Donna offered and I was all worried about Mum. She might be family and that's what family does in times of crisis.'

'They let strangers go through their stuff?' This was Eve all over. Hopelessly optimistic and rarely thinking things through, yet somehow always ending up okay.

'She's not really a stranger,' Eve said. 'She seems genuine. Nice. She had the blanket, don't forget.'

'You're just saying that because she cleaned for you.'

Eve was biting her lip in that way that Billie knew only too well from their childhood.

'Spit it out,' Billie said. 'Your guilt's all over your face.'

'She might have locked up for me, too,' Eve said. Really fast, like somehow Billie wouldn't notice.

Billie noticed. She jerked, yelping when Lola remained stubbornly attached to the milk supply. 'You did what? Let her lock up Mum's house? Please tell me you didn't.'

'You weren't there. Tim and the kids were bored, and Nathan had done the bolt.'

'Don't blame me,' Nathan said. 'You said I could go.'

'Well, I didn't mean it.' Eve pouted. 'She said she'd do the last bit and lock the door behind her.'

Billie's jaw tightened. 'You left a stranger in Mum's house.'

'I knew you'd get mad. I'm sure she didn't stay long.'

'Eve...'

'Fine.' She held up her hands in defeat. 'I'll go past there on my way home, even though it isn't on the way at all, and make sure she's not throwing a party.'

'Or looting the place.'

'You'll be sorry you were so distrusting when we confirm she's telling the truth. Oh, and I told her it was you who burned the chicken.'

Billie didn't say anything.

'I'll go now and message you when it's all clear.'

'Be safe.'

Eve rolled her eyes and saluted. 'Yes, boss.' But she blew Billie a kiss goodbye on her way out.

As Lola finished her feed, Billie tried to get her head around her sister's thought process or rather lack of it. If Donna was an imposter, then her little sister had handed the woman the opportunity to go through Mum's house. If she wasn't, it was simply part of the family helping out.

Later in bed, Billie couldn't sleep.

Nathan's breathing suggested he, too, was still awake. 'Either she's telling the truth, or not. Why are you letting yourself get all worked up?'

'Who says I'm worked up?'

'Ah, the fact that you're lying there, tense as fuck.' She flinched as he brushed her shoulder. 'See? You're like that jack-in-a-box about to pop. By the way, that was pretty funny, you have to admit.'

'Maybe,' she conceded. 'It's just that Mum's not well. If she gets her hopes up again and it turns out this woman's lying, it could break her.' *And I don't have the strength to put the pieces back together this time.*

'Hey.' When he reached out again, she let him pull her back against the solid strength of his chest. 'We'll get through it.'

Billie should have realised the podcast would stir up the case. She'd been too focused on Lola.

She'd not expected Donna.

And she'd not expected the dread that warred with hope at how convincing she was and how strongly her mother already believed. Billie would do anything to protect her mum.

They needed proof before anyone got too close to Donna or the media discovered there'd been a break in the case.

Her eyes flew open. The test!

Billie would make sure they had it all in the post tomorrow.

9

Tuesday December 10th

When Billie pushed Lola's pram into her mother's hospital room the next morning, Donna was already present, ensconced in the chair next to the bed.

'Billie, hi,' Donna said with a smile.

Billie smiled back, but felt a stab of something like jealousy. For so long she'd been her mum's biggest support. 'Good morning. You made it in early.'

'Isn't it thoughtful of her?' Mum said.

Billie nodded. It really was. But it was also like the behaviour of those who'd tried to fool her mum into thinking they were Megan before.

As usual, it had taken forever for Billie to get out the front door. Sometimes she longed for her work days, longed for them with a desperation she didn't dare say aloud in case she seemed ungrateful for her healthy baby. Pushing her motherhood doubts to the back of her mind, Billie crossed to her mother and kissed her cheek. 'How are you?'

'Not too bad,' Mum said. 'Although the sooner they let me out of here, the better.'

'Any news?' Billie scanned the various monitors but didn't have a clue what any of the read-outs meant.

As though she'd summoned him, Dr Li entered. 'Lovely for

you to have your family around you,' he said. 'You should be okay to go home tomorrow but you'll need someone to stay with you.'

He looked to Donna who seemed in the process of nodding, but Billie cleared her throat, drawing everyone's attention.

'I can do it.' All the Lola-shaped reasons that would be impossible arrived in her head too late. Dr Li was nodding, the matter settled. He went on to confirm Mum would need to return for the procedure.

And all the while Billie was thinking how Nathan and Eve would be thinking she'd lost her mind taking on caring for Mum with a baby in tow.

After he left, Donna stood and gathered her handbag. 'You sit; I was just leaving.'

'Don't go on my account,' Billie said quickly, finding she meant it. Mum and hospital rooms brought back bad memories and some company might help. She didn't know if it was the familiarity of Donna or just the way her mum was so happy to have her there.

'I have to get to work,' Donna said. 'But I wanted to bring this since we forgot about completing it yesterday in the drama.' She held out the paternity test.

Billie took it, turning the package over in her hands. All the seals appeared intact.

'You could do your part before you go,' Mum suggested to Donna. 'I'm sure the kids won't mind if I keep you a minute.' To Billie she explained, 'Donna works at the children's hospital.'

Donna nodded. 'I was lucky enough to get the position ahead of the move here. It's shift work but it makes me feel like I'm making a difference.'

'That's wonderful,' Billie said, trying to keep in mind Donna still might be a fake.

Mum and Billie both watched closely as Donna scraped the swab on the inside of her cheek and sealed the sample as per the instructions.

As Billie placed it back in the packaging, Donna lingered near the foot of the bed.

'Pity in all the rush you didn't have time to have a tour of the house,' Billie said. She still couldn't believe Eve had left her alone at Mum's house.

Disappointment shadowed Donna's expression. 'It's unfortunate, but there's plenty of time for all that. Hard to believe I was in the house where it happened.'

'We'll correct that as soon as I'm home again,' Mum said.

'And sort out seeing Dad?'

They shared a look that suggested they'd already talked about it. Maybe Donna could be the trigger to get her mum talking to Pop again.

'Soon,' Mum agreed.

'I'll look forward to it. I want to know everything I can about my past, every detail.' Donna leaned over and squeezed Mum's hand. 'I'll come by after work. I know hospitals can be boring.'

'Please do,' Mum said.

And with a wave at Billie, Donna left.

Mum gazed wistfully after her before turning to Billie and the pram. 'Is my precious Lola awake?'

'Awake seems to be her default state,' Billie said, trying not to yawn after the long night of feeding and crying. Crying and feeding.

As though none of it had happened, Lola sat happily in her pram gnawing on the edge of a cloth book.

Billie carried her over but Lola immediately reached out for the wires attaching Mum to the monitors.

'Maybe not,' Mum said, blowing Lola a kiss instead.

Billie returned Lola to the pram. 'We'll need to get Pop's sample, too, before we can send it off.'

Her mother made a grunting sound. 'Post it to the care facility and ask a nurse to complete the procedure.'

Billie swallowed the lump in her throat that appeared every time she thought of what the podcast had revealed about her beloved grandfather, the man who'd mentored her at the company he'd created from scratch. 'It was a different time. You can't stay mad at him forever.'

'Watch me.'

'He made mistakes, but that doesn't make him responsible for someone taking Megan.'

Mum stared down at her hands twisting the edge of the sheet. 'He was high, Billie. I've carried all this guilt for being the one at home that night and not being able to remember what happened and he kept that a secret. It raises questions.'

'Like?'

She took a shuddery breath. 'Was he worried about the police finding out? Did he delay the call for help? Did he touch something else or move something? I believed in him.'

'The Seventies were a time of experimentation and living it up.' Billie didn't really blame her mum for feeling betrayed, but she hated what it was doing to everyone.

'I just need some time,' Mum said quietly.

Billie squeezed her hand. 'I'll go there,' she said. 'And once

I have his sample, I'll send both off to be analysed. Christmas will probably mean delays, even with express post. Are you sure you don't want me to contact the detective in charge of Megan's case? Was it Detective Okely? They can probably get an answer quicker.'

'I'm sure,' Mum said. 'You know what will happen if this gets out, especially since the podcast is so popular. I don't need the media camped outside the hospital.'

'I guess you're right.'

Lola threw the book on the ground and started grizzling. When Billie handed it back, she threw it again.

Mum followed the interplay. 'Look, you have enough on your plate with Lola and coming to stay, without running all over town for my benefit. All of this can wait until I'm out of here.' Mum picked at a loose thread on the sheet as she spoke. 'I mean, it's not like Donna is going anywhere.'

Billie knew her well enough to read between the lines. Part of Mum didn't want to know the truth in case it proved Donna wasn't Megan. But they needed to know.

'I'll go there today.'

THAT NIGHT

8.53 p.m. – Carol

I step into the kitchen, air pushed from warm to steamy by the hot water running in the sink. Tonight's hostess, Trish, a vibrant pop of youth and colour in the red of her ultra-chic jumpsuit stands there, head bowed, her hand pressed against her flat stomach.

A giggle carries from the living area where I left the men rolling their smokes with the excitement of a gang of private schoolboys going against the rules, and the other women whispering their delight at a gossiped blow striking true.

She hasn't heard me come in and her shoulders tremble just a little as she stares down at dishes smeared with food, shining with drops of water. Bubbles made of dish soap catch and splinter the overhead bulbs into a million tiny shards of light.

She's just so goddamn young.

'Was it Gloria going on about the children's bedtime routines?' I ask. The older woman hadn't bothered to hide her dig at the only non-mother in our little group, bringing up the topic of the kids anytime she could.

Trish startles and lifts her head. Her wide eyes, pink cheeks and the speed that she drops her hand give her away as she shakes her head. 'Not at all.'

'You'll get used to it,' I say, unable to prevent the weariness in my tone.

I don't expand and she doesn't query whether I mean the other wives, the parties or the shittiness of suburban life in general. Only with her husband, though, I'd say if she asked me. I know my Frank is different.

I hold out a cigarette. 'Want one?'

My breathy offer has the hint of rebellion about it. I know Ken, know how he feels about ladies smoking, but I sense Trish isn't quite as obedient as he'd like her to be. Not the man-stealing harlot the others claim either. They'd rather gossip than get to know her.

A tiny hint of a smile quirks those full red lips. 'No.' And then, with laughing eyes: 'Maybe later.'

She turns the tap, stopping the flow of water, then braces herself like a woman going to battle.

Three steps – I'm a little wobbly because Ken does import the best wine, the smug bastard – and I'm by her side. My hand on hers stops her like she's an animal, trapped. Powerless to fight back despite the crimson talons of her painted nails.

'Leave them,' I say.

She turns towards me, her dark-rimmed eyes a pool of indecision, of desperation. Her scent floral and heady like a tropical garden with a burst of summer-ripened fruit.

'He made me think I was interesting,' she whispers.

It's the answer to a question I'd jokingly asked her over coffee last week, after she told me how she and Ken met. We were alone, the others more interested in rumours than the truth, convinced she was a threat to their boring marriages. Two women flirting on the edge of properly connecting.

I hadn't meant to make her think she needed to justify being here and marrying him.

'Oh, honey,' I murmur, brushing a finger down a smooth, soft cheek damp with a single tear. 'You are.'

10

As Billie entered Restwell, the assisted living facility where her grandfather had resided the last few years, she held Lola close, the squirming weight making her wish she'd heaved the pram out.

After their visit to the hospital, they'd gone past the shops to pick up some groceries but had to leave empty-handed when Lola had a leaking nappy and began screaming. As Billie raced home for an emergency baby bath, she'd wondered again how Eve had managed so effortlessly with two. Mostly, Lola was a delight; it was just Billie who was struggling.

'Welcome to Restwell. How can I help you?' The smiling nurse at reception had to raise her voice to be heard over raucous sounds coming from a large airy room off to the left.

'Is there something special happening today?' Billie asked.

The nurse, '*Lisa*' according to the neatly pinned badge on her blue cardigan, smiled. 'It's a new drama improv program. They've taken to it with an enthusiasm usually reserved for bingo.'

Another burst of laughter came from the room.

'Looks like fun,' Billie said. 'But I'm here to see my grandfather, Frank. Frank Callaghan. He's in the secure wing.'

The woman showed no reaction to what surely must be their most infamous resident. 'Do you have the code?'

'No, I usually come with Mum. Do you need to see ID or anything?'

Lisa gave the licence Billie held out a quick look-over. 'You look just like your mum.' She bustled ahead. 'We've had a few folks from the media try to sneak in, pretending to be relatives. Not sure what they expect from him. Poor man deserves some peace.'

'Hope I don't upset him,' Billie said thinking of the test.

'He'll be glad of the company.' Lisa slowly punched in the code, allowing Billie to see it. 'Did you get that?'

Billie nodded.

'Good. Don't write it down. Our residents might not remember who they are some days but some are like Houdini with their escape efforts.'

'I won't. Thank you.'

With a cheery wave, Lisa returned to the desk and Billie entered the secure wing, making sure the door was locked behind her.

Then she headed to room twenty-two, where Frank Callaghan now spent most of his days. The carpet muffled her tread, not disturbing the quiet of the hallways, in stark contrast to the bustling activity of the rest of the facility. Pop's declining health had added to her mother's load over the last few years, the deterioration of his mind more painful when his body didn't follow suit. Her mum had tried caring for him but gave up on the idea when he'd gotten lost and turned up wandering a road near the conservation park.

Billie slowed as she approached Pop's closed door and with the swab kit feeling weighty in her bag, she pushed it open.

He sat in a green leather recliner by the window, his face turned to the sunshine. He didn't seem to notice she was there. The months where she'd been busy with Lola had changed him, the weight he'd lost made his skin hang off him and his grey hair turn fuzzy. A dusting of white hair decorated his jaw, and when he opened his mouth to mutter to himself it revealed pink gums. The missing teeth grinned cheerily on a small table next to the bed.

'Pop?'

He startled at the sound of her voice, but then his whole face brightened. 'Amanda, love, how are you? Let me put the kettle on.'

He moved to get up, but Billie quickly crossed to sit on the bed. 'I'm not Amanda.'

He frowned. 'Don't be silly.'

'No, it's Billie. I can ring for someone if you want a cuppa.'

His laugh was an echo of the rumble she remembered from when, as a child, she'd sat on his lap for him to read her stories. 'I know that, of course. How are you?' His gaze dropped to the child nestling into her side. 'And how is…'

'Lola,' she said. 'Her name is Lola. Remember, we brought her in to meet you?'

He nodded blankly. 'Of course, my first great-grandchild. How could I forget?'

She swallowed back the instinct to correct him by mentioning Max and Matilda.

'We took Plank to the beach last weekend,' she said hoping mention of his loyal mutt would spark some kind of reaction, but he didn't ask about the stray he'd taken in, nor even seem to have heard her despite man and dog being each other's shadows for years.

Plank, so named because Pop had found him dumped as a puppy on a worksite. White and black, and left like a couple of two-by-four pieces of wood. For those first two years the puppy hit Pop's life like an explosion of digging and chewing. The mix of a quick mind that took to training like he'd been born to behave, with a naughty streak that had Mum telling Pop he should surrender him for being too much hard work.

The day Pop could no longer pretend his brain wasn't troubling him was the day Plank was found at his side obedient and protective, keeping him from wandering onto a busy highway. He'd not chewed or dug since.

With Eve having her own dog, and Mum not an animal person, Pop had asked Billie to look after Plank when he'd been forced into respite care.

'He knows you, love,' Pop had said. 'Knows you're my best girl.'

And Pop had been right. She'd picked up Plank's stuff along with some other old things Pop had been meaning to throw away and tearfully loaded it into the car while Pop knelt, murmuring a goodbye in Plank's white, floppy ear that they all pretended wasn't final. From that day, the dog shadowed Billie when she was home, had accompanied her into work and more recently kept a safe distance from Lola's grabby hands then swooped in to clean up spilled food.

'It's a nice day,' Billie said, trying to keep her voice steady, pointing towards the window. It led out into a small courtyard garden, bursting with green shrubs and flowers.

She wasn't sure if he knew the time of year but didn't want to bring up the anniversary. With Mum refusing to be in the same room, Billie had been present when the detectives tried to interview him following up on the podcast revelations. His confusion and pain had her imagining kicking them out but instead she'd sat and tried to be supportive.

'Better sunshine than a grey old day,' he agreed.

'I'm sure the farmers could do with some rain,' she added, stretching her limits of weather conversation.

He nodded. 'It's a tough life on the land.' His face sagged. 'Tough in the suburbs, too.'

She tightened her grip on Lola who squeaked her disapproval.

This seemed to bring Pop back to the present. He smiled, showing his gums. 'Baby Billie looks just like you when you were little.'

Billie's throat ached but she didn't correct his mistake. 'She sure does.' Holding Lola with one arm she extricated the swab from her bag with the other. 'I need to put this in your mouth. Is that okay?'

'Whatever you need to do.'

Like an obedient child he opened his mouth wide, allowing her to get the sample. She'd not planned to explain why she needed it and seeing him only confirmed her decision.

Once she sealed it and returned everything to her bag, she could relax. She'd send it off before close of business. In the meantime, she'd do her best to brighten her grandfather's day. 'So,' she said cheerily, 'what did you have for lunch?'

A grin split his face. 'Roast. Beef with all the trimmings, just like your mother used to make.'

Billie didn't let herself think about whether he meant her grandmother, Carol, or her mum, Amanda. 'Sounds wonderful.'

11

Billie didn't mean to drift off but after collecting Mum from the hospital, she couldn't resist the chance to shut her eyes for a moment while Mum and Lola napped.

The feeling of someone standing over her had her fighting her way to consciousness, heart pounding. By the time she opened bleary eyes, there was nothing between her and the windows overlooking the conservation park.

'Sorry, did I wake you?'

Billie jerked towards the sound of Donna's voice.

She stood in the kitchen, hands full of shopping bags. 'I let myself in. Amanda said to arrive anytime.'

Billie blinked, trying to catch up. That's right, her mum had said Donna was cooking dinner for her first night home. Had Donna been closer? But why?

She shook off the sense of unease.

Getting to know Donna better would mean she could stop worrying about her mum getting hurt again.

'It's fine,' Billie said, getting to her feet. 'I should check on Mum and Lola anyway.'

'I took Amanda in a glass of water – she's doing great.'

Why did that feel like Billie had somehow failed?

'And,' Donna continued, 'Eve should be here soon with the kids. Tim has some boys' night, I believe.'

That much Billie did know as he was meeting Nathan in the city. 'I'll just be in with Lola if you need anything.'

Eve arrived when Lola was feeding, and delicious aromas had begun drifting in from the kitchen.

'I swear this place is haunted,' Eve said with a shiver. 'You wouldn't catch me staying here with a baby.' Then seeing Billie's face, she added, 'You probably don't believe in ghosts anyway, and you're the oldest.'

'I am simply responsible,' Billie argued. But inside she squirmed, knowing part of the reason she'd volunteered was because Donna had been about to.

As she finished up, Eve regaled her with a tale of how she'd coaxed her adorable dog Waffles into getting into the flour and the resulting picture had already practically gone viral.

It smelt even better in the kitchen, but the sight of a virtual stranger chopping spring onion behind her mother's kitchen bench jarred.

'That smells amazing,' Billie said with extra enthusiasm, like Donna might be able to read her unease.

'Amanda said at the hospital she was craving something with real flavour and my Thai beef salad fits the bill.'

'That's so kind of you.' Billie wondered if Mum had mentioned her dislike of spicy food in their sisterly bonding.

A few minutes later, when Donna set down the first bowl on the table, Mum actually clapped her hands. 'I can't wait to tuck in.'

Billie raised her eyebrows at Eve who smothered a laugh.

'This looks authentic,' Billie said. 'Have you lived in Asia?'

Donna placed the last bowl in front of Eve and sat. 'Only on holiday. I'm a cookbook enthusiast.'

'Carol, our mother, loved to experiment in the kitchen too,' Mum announced, like this was further proof of Donna's identity.

'Did she like to travel?' Donna asked.

Mum shook her head, a shadow crossing her expression. 'I'm not sure. She planned to, I think, but then… you know…' They shared a look, already communicating without speaking from just a few hours spent together on hospital visits.

As the thinly sliced beef in its tangy dressing melted in her mouth, Billie tried to think of other questions that might help fill out Donna's story. 'Where else have you lived?'

'Does Zach like spicy food?' Mum asked, cutting Billie off. 'That's her son,' she added for Billie and Eve's benefit, with a hint of showing off how well they already knew each other.

Donna smiled at Mum. 'He'll eat anything the way he's growing.'

'You should have brought him around for dinner,' Mum said.

Donna's hand tightened on her fork. 'This is all quite the change for him. I hope you understand that we'll need to take things slowly.'

'You've raised him alone?' Eve asked. 'Must have been tough.'

'His father passed away when he was a baby,' Donna explained. 'He's my world.'

'Did he get to meet your mother…' Billie cleared her throat. 'I mean, Janette Novak?'

Donna's eyes grew misty. 'They were close. It's been so hard for both of us to make sense of what I discovered.'

'You said you came because you needed to find out the truth of who you are?' Billie asked.

Donna nodded.

'But what do you want from all of this going forward?' Billie waved to indicate Mum and the house. She noticed Eve stop, spoon halfway to her mouth, and Mum hold her breath to focus on Donna's answer.

'I had a good life, didn't want for anything in terms of being loved by Janette, but now it's just me and my son and I believe in family. If, God forbid, something happened to me he'd be on his own.' She took a deep breath. 'I want to get to know where I've come from and give my son the family he would have had if I'd not been taken as a baby. In my line of work you can't forget that no one's invincible.'

There was something in her tone or maybe the openness of her gaze, but her vulnerability gave an intimacy to the conversation that stirred an immediate response in Billie. How quickly they'd moved deeper than the banal.

'Well, I can't wait to meet him,' Mum said before Billie could continue. 'How old is he? Does he look like you? What does he like? Is he at school? Is he—'

'Mum,' Eve interrupted. 'Maybe one at a time?'

Donna relaxed a little. 'Let me see, he has my colouring but his dad's body shape. He likes music and sport, but his focus is on his schoolwork. He's going to be a doctor.'

Mum made a noise of approval. 'How does he feel about starting a new school here?'

'We've moved around a lot, as I said. I like to travel, so he's used to it,' said Donna. 'But the science syllabus is different here. He wants to get into a special course for next year, but he has to qualify through an exam next week.'

'Science, did you say? Billie can help him; that's her specialty,' Mum said.

Billie felt them all look at her. 'It was. I haven't done high school science for a while.'

Eve muttered something about doing none at all while Mum waved away her disclaimer. 'Billie was going to be a doctor, too.'

'But she did something else?' Donna asked.

Billie's jaw clenched. Mum had always been a bit disappointed in her career choice. 'I studied business at uni,' she explained. A lifetime of being the responsible oldest and a logical thinker had come together when she'd spent a summer working for Pop. It was supposed to be short term but he'd been explaining a spreadsheet for a proposal he had to review when she'd pointed out two mistakes and made a suggestion that literally took his breath away. The workings of the business made sense to Billie, and at Pop's side she'd felt at home.

'Dad pushed her into the family business,' Mum added. 'After she'd won science awards at school it seemed a waste but what can you do?'

'As Billie said, she was at school a long time ago,' Donna said. 'I couldn't possibly ask it of her.'

Feeling a bit cornered and sorry for Donna trying to do her best for her son alone, Billie smiled. 'I don't mind. I did science tutoring through uni for spending money.'

'Let Billie help your son,' Mum insisted. 'You and Zach aren't alone anymore.'

Donna blinked rapidly. 'Your family is everything I'd hoped to find.'

'*Our* family,' Mum corrected. 'You belong now.'

A screeching cry from Lola who'd been sleeping broke the touching moment. Billie shovelled another mouthful of the tasty beef into her mouth, knowing it could well be cold by the time she was done.

'Excuse me,' she said.

Fortunately, Lola settled quickly and Billie returned to the table before the others finished their meal. They were talking about the drama of Donna's arrival and she was explaining how she'd had to steel herself to knock on the door.

'I have a question,' Billie said as she sat down. 'In your story you mentioned a man from Ridgefield giving you to Janette Novak. What was his name?'

Sudden tension flashed across Donna's features before disappearing so fast Billie wondered if she'd imagined it.

Donna hesitated. 'I was very young.'

Eve seemed to pick up on where Billie was going. 'What about a description?' she asked. 'You said he was older. Are we talking like mid-fifties or seventy-plus? And any other features?'

'Honestly,' Donna said, 'I don't even know how Janette knew him.' Her lower lip trembled. 'I'm sorry. I wish I had more answers.'

'But—' Billie began.

'I don't know,' Donna repeated. She wiped at her eyes, imploring Billie's mum with a tear-filled look. 'I'm sorry.'

Mum reached out and patted her hand. 'We'll work through this together and figure out exactly what happened.'

That faint disquiet in Billie's gut wouldn't go away. The less Donna shared, the more she craved answers. But Donna had the blanket. And that fact, as much as not wanting to stress Mum, kept Billie quiet.

'Anyone for a cuppa?' asked Eve into the tense silence.

Donna glanced at the time and stood. 'No thanks, I should probably get back to Zach.'

Billie studied the woman claiming to be her aunt. Did Donna really need to leave or was she making sure Billie couldn't ask any more questions?

Mum clasped Donna's hand and tugged her back into her seat. 'Before you go, I have something to ask you and I can't wait any longer.'

Something like dread solidified in Billie's stomach. What was Mum thinking?

Unable to sit still, Billie rose and cleared the dishes, putting herself on the other side of the kitchen bench from whatever Mum planned.

Mum's lips curved in a hopeful smile. 'Would you and Zach like to join us here for Christmas this year?'

Billie's smothered gasp was lost in Eve's instant, 'No.'

They all looked to Eve.

'I'm hosting Christmas. I've already planned the menu, got the back deck redone and brought in a special tree to decorate. It will be picture-perfect.'

'She means picture-perfect quite literally,' Mum explained. 'She's an influencer.'

None of them were paying Billie any attention. Right in front of her sat Donna's handbag, the top of it gaping open. Didn't they say a woman's life was contained in her handbag? What secrets were in Donna's?

Billie's hand hovered above it, but only for a moment. She shook herself from the impulse, sick that the thought had crossed her mind.

'I know all about Eve's brand,' Donna was saying. 'That Waffles is adorable. You're clearly a natural photographer.'

Eve practically purred. 'I work hard to keep my images fresh.'

Billie returned to her seat. It appeared Donna was quite the expert on Eve's social media. Could this be important? 'How long have you been following Eve online?' she asked.

'I flipped through her feed today during my lunch break after she mentioned it at the hospital last night,' Donna explained without missing a beat.

A time Billie hadn't been able to visit. She'd not realised they'd all been there together.

'And about Christmas,' Donna continued, 'I don't want anyone to change their plans for me.'

Mum folded her arms. 'I insist. Eve, dear, don't make things difficult. You can pick a couple of statement dishes and leave the traditional to me.'

'Have you forgotten your upcoming hospital procedure?' Billie interjected. 'Hosting Christmas is the last thing you need. It's more than food – there's the cleaning and the organising in preparation.'

'I need my family around me, in my home, for Christmas.' Mum's eyes shone with tears. 'Is that too much to ask?'

'Of course not,' Billie said, 'if it's what you really want. We'll all pitch in.'

Eve nodded her agreement.

Donna ran her finger under her eye in that way women did to try to stop their makeup running. 'In that case, if you're sure, I'd love to come, but it might be a bit much for Zach with all these new people at once.'

'I understand. Hopefully you can convince him.'

Mum and Donna shared watery, happy smiles.

Leaving them together, Mum sharing what she could remember of some Christmas traditions – pillow cases for Santa sacks and leaving out a beer and carrots – Billie made herself busy cleaning up. So busy that she almost missed Donna leaving, only looking up when the screen door closed.

The woman she'd thought so genuine and kind had shown a flash of something else at Billie's questions. A willingness to use her already-strong connection to Mum to keep Billie at a distance.

It only made Billie want to know more. She dropped the dishcloth and ran outside. 'Donna, wait.'

Donna turned, not trying to hide her surprise. 'Did you want something?'

'Your son,' Billie blurted. 'I can help him. If you'd like?'

Silence stretched between them. Billie couldn't help noticing that Donna wasn't exactly jumping to accept her garbled offer.

'Forget it,' Billie said. 'I'll let Mum know you don't need my help.'

Donna's lips pressed together, her mouth forming a hard line. It only lasted a moment, but Billie saw it.

Felt it.

But then Donna smiled. 'Yes, thank you. I didn't think you were interested.'

'Oh, I am interested,' Billie assured her.

Again, there was the briefest flicker of something. 'Great,' Donna said.

Just before bed, Billie sent Nathan a text: *'Interesting night here!'*

She waited, but there was no reply.

She switched off the light, rolled over, and tried to sleep knowing Lola could need attention any minute. But she couldn't stop thinking about Nathan.

Where was he?

EPISODE 04: CLOSE TO HOME

Music playing: 'Video Killed the Radio Star' – The Buggles

*The music fades to the voice of a **male reporter**:*
The inquest into the 1979 disappearance of Megan Callaghan opens this morning. It is expected that it will take weeks to question all the major persons of interest. Proceedings will begin this morning with Megan's father Frank Callaghan taking the stand.

Ruby:
I'm Ruby Costa. Welcome to Episode Four of 'The Callaghan Baby Podcast'. Along with my team, I've been investigating the forty-year-old cold case of missing baby Megan Callaghan.

You might be wondering how much can be achieved by an inquest twenty-five years after the event. Time passing was detrimental early in the case as people's memories blurred and physical evidence was lost. However, time can also be helpful as guilt weighs on a person's conscience.

When Frank Callaghan takes the stand at the 2005 inquest, the footage shows him as quite different to the man pictured in the photograph from that night at the party.

His thick sandy hair has turned a thinning grey and his skin now has the leathery look of someone who spent too much time in the sun before skin cancer was on anyone's radar.

This is a man who lost his daughter and, some would argue, his wife, on that fateful night and when he looks directly at the camera, the pain in his eyes is palpable.

Kate Emmett:
Mr Callaghan, I understand this might be difficult for you, but I am going to need you to answer the questions as fully as possible. It's you who discovered Megan missing, is it not? Please tell us what happened.

Frank:
It's just like in the police report. Larry and I went to check on the other children and then to our house. It was a bit of a hike up the hill and by the time we let ourselves in to the dark house my shirt was stuck to my back. Larry bumped into a chair trying to get a drink from the fridge. It was one of those moments that wasn't funny, but we were both trying hard not to laugh.

Ruby:
Frank is sitting there talking about laughter, but it's clear from his face that he's trying not to cry.

Frank:
The house appeared to be just as I'd left it earlier.

Amanda's room is the first along the hall. I peered inside the room, blinking to adjust to the darkness. Her bed was empty, and the sheet dishevelled. The blanket was on the ground but given the warm night, I thought nothing of it.

But then, I heard her. I stumbled in and found her hunched over in the corner, wild-eyed, keening. I fell to my knees. Grabbed her arms, but she didn't seem to know I was there. I shoved past Larry to get to Megan's room. On some level, I think I knew that only one thing could put Amanda in that state.

Ruby:

A hush falls on the room. They all know what's coming. They've all heard the story, but none of them, none of us, have heard it before from Frank himself.

It's important that we listen to what he says, knowing he's had an awful long time to prepare it.

Frank:

The door to the corner room was ajar, and despite having been wishing for a cold drink when we arrived, my hands were ice when I pushed against it. All of me was.

Ruby:

As Frank's voice trails off, his eyes are glazed. The raw agony in his face puts him back in that room. When he speaks again, his voice is wooden.

Frank:

The cot was empty and the only window in the room, smashed.

Megan was gone.

Ruby:
If people at the inquest came for the spectacle, expecting a dramatic breakdown from Frank Callaghan, then they would have left sorely disappointed. This man has lived with this haunting him for decades and you can tell he's practised at holding himself together.

Kate:
You said that you left Megan's bedroom door ajar so Amanda could better hear her cries. Does that mean you considered her to be in charge?

Frank:
No, no she wasn't. Fuck, Amanda was a baby herself. Sorry for the language, but Amanda was not at all responsible.

Kate:
What happened next?

Frank:
I called the police and when they arrived they took over. Carol tried to comfort Amanda and I gave my statement then helped with the search.

Kate:
You said there was a window broken in Megan's bedroom and cigarette butts left outside. Do you smoke, Mr Callaghan?

Frank:
I did then but not anymore. They weren't my brand as the

police confirmed. Anyway, I think I'd remember if I'd been out there smoking. I'd done gardening work that day and, they were definitely not in my yard that afternoon.

Kate:
You described the window as 'smashed' and I'm interested where the pieces of glass were found. Did you step on them?

Frank:
The glass was on the inside, smashed by whoever got in.

Kate:
Interesting. Had you heard of Dominic Snave before that night?

Mr Snave and the details of his previous crimes were widely referenced in the media leading up to the night Megan disappeared. Anyone could have copied the broken window and cigarette butts left at the scene in order to cast suspicion on him.

Frank:
Not me, because I hadn't heard of the guy. I had a new business and a new baby; I didn't have time to dally over the news.

Kate:
Witness evidence tells of you returning to walk the reservation on the nights following Megan's disappearance. And you were a builder with your own company, giving you access to tools?

Frank:
Yes, I was, but I'm not sure how this relates to Megan's disappearance.

Kate:
You had both the means and the opportunity to bury a body and you lived opposite a huge conservation park.

Frank, sounding indignant:
I was at dinner when Megan went missing.

Kate:
So, you all have said.

I understand this tragedy had a huge effect on your wife Carol. We'll talk more about her and what she was like after Megan went missing but I wanted to ask you, before the night of the 9th of December, were the two of you happy? Can you describe your relationship?

Ruby:
Frank's face softens. Some of the pain in his eyes seems to disappear and I dare anyone who sees him to doubt that he loved his wife.

Frank:
Our relationship? It was magic. Thinking about before, it's like it was a dream or something. I can hardly believe it. Life wasn't perfect, course it wasn't. We'd been through some heartaches trying to have another baby, but Carol was a trouper about the whole thing. I reckon it brought us closer as a couple. And when Megan came along, well

it was everything we'd ever wanted. We'd already planned family holidays for the four of us.

Some bloke at the pub said I had to be disappointed with another girl. I laughed in his face. Amanda was my princess and I couldn't be happier to have another one to spoil. I'd have done anything for my girls. All three. So yeah. I reckon we were happy.

Kate:
And afterwards?

Frank:
We all changed. How could we not? All that mattered was finding Megan.

My marriage took a back seat, sure. Did I miss what Carol and I shared? I'm man enough to say that I did, but I didn't resent her for changing priorities.

Mostly, I worked, for distraction and to give Carol and Amanda the best I could.

Kate:
Now, it's my understanding it was a warm night, the beginnings of a heatwave. You were all relaxed, there for a good time, and some nice cold drinks wouldn't go astray. Were you intoxicated?

Ruby:
Frank hesitates. His gaze flicks to the place in the room where I recognise a few of the others from the neighbourhood group sitting together. Although they were once such good friends, they now resemble students on a group project

forced to work together to save their grade. He coughs to clear his throat.

Frank:
I'd had a few drinks. We all had, I think. It wasn't like we were driving.

Kate:
No, nothing like that. You were only responsible for small children, one of whom – your newborn daughter – went missing and hasn't been seen in over twenty-five years.

Frank:
I know that. I bloody well know that and there's not a day that goes by when I don't think about what I could have done differently.

Ruby:
To find out what happened to Carol Callaghan, please join us again on 'The Callaghan Baby Podcast'. If anyone listening knows anything that could assist in making this podcast, please contact me on investigation@ thecallaghanfoundation.com. If you know something that could help the police, please contact them.

Thank you for listening.

12

Thursday December 12th

After spending half her night up with Lola, weary Billie spent the day trying to stop her mum overdoing things, in between searching the internet for anything to support Donna's story. The more she thought about it overnight, the more she feared Donna had acted so defensively because she had something to hide.

At least Nathan had finally gotten back to her, explaining his phone was broken.

Billie found nothing on Donna and she didn't have much more luck with Janette Novak. Her heart leapt when there was a small picture of young Donna with Janette at a fair from a local newspaper but, if anything, it only confirmed Donna's story with its Blue Mountains location.

Early afternoon, while Lola napped, she curled up next to Mum on her bed and they'd both read for a while. The easy peace of it taking Billie back to some of her favourite childhood memories of getting lost in *Black Beauty*, snuggled in Mum's bed at her side, while Mum devoured the latest thriller.

When Lola stirred, looking to feed, Billie realised Mum had drifted off to sleep and she crept from the bedroom, leaving her to rest.

Without Mum there to make conversation Billie found

being in that house, in the place where Megan had been taken, unsettling. Every gust of wind across the conservation park rattled the windows, bringing something ominous from the huge open space, trickling like an icy blanket over her heated skin until a call from Ruby Costa provided much-needed distraction.

Knowing Mum wouldn't want her to tell the podcast producer anything about Donna, she settled down with some trepidation to catch up with her oldest friend. They'd been inseparable once, being less than a year apart in age and thrown together because of Billie's mum's dogged insistence in keeping those involved in Megan's disappearance close. But they'd grown apart as they grew older.

Ruby's expertise as an investigative journalist, having won 'young women in media' awards and getting pieces into national papers, to potentially break open the case like others in the media that meant so much to all of them had convinced Amanda and the foundation to fund the podcast. Since Ruby was the granddaughter of the Marshes who'd attended the 'dinner party from hell', they knew she would handle the investigation with utmost care.

None of them had expected her to go after Pop, discovering that the group had dabbled in drugs and the timeline lies that put doubt on everything.

Billie promised to pass on to her mother Ruby's message regarding possible increased distribution of the podcast and then said what had been echoing through her head all day.

'Standing here, looking down at those houses in Wattlebury Court, part of me still can't believe they left the kids home alone,' said Billie. 'It's so different now, even from when we were kids, although Mum was pretty protective.'

Ruby murmured agreement. 'But you can feel it, being there? I know I did when I visited your mum.'

'Feel what?'

'A glimpse of how it was for them, with the houses facing each other, the close-knit community of what felt like friends all living nearby. Knowing all their neighbours by name and recognising people two blocks over at the supermarket. They all thought they'd found their own little slice of paradise at the edge of the world.' Ruby sighed. 'Times have changed, I guess. At least that's what Mum says, not that she talks about it much.'

Billie didn't reply.

'I'm sorry about Frank,' Ruby said guessing why Billie was quiet. 'I made a promise to get to the truth whether it was palatable or not.'

'I know.'

An awkward silence developed between them.

Billie wouldn't mention Donna but that didn't mean she couldn't ask other questions about the case. Over the morning she'd relistened to parts of the podcast, finding no matches with the story Donna had told them.

That would mean all the searching, all the years of looking and it was someone that no one had thought of at all. Impossible. Or the only possibility?

'What if the culprit is someone who didn't come up in the inquest or the podcast at all?' she asked.

'Why?' Ruby sounded suspicious. 'Have you found something?'

Billie pressed a hand to her flushed cheeks, thankful they weren't on FaceTime. 'No, just being here has got me thinking.'

Ruby chuckled. 'Don't overdo it.' She paused and then added, 'If ever there's anything you want to talk about, I'm here.'

'I know, thanks.' Billie disconnected before she could say anything else she'd regret.

With Lola still settled and Mum resting in her bedroom, Billie found herself standing in the small corner bedroom that had been Megan's, trying to picture it instead with lavender on the walls and a cot in the corner. It had been most recently decorated as a study. Painted in neutral light grey with a built-in wardrobe that hadn't been there back in the Seventies. Even the carpet had been replaced. She pressed her face to the window, staring out.

It was hard to believe a baby had been stolen through here.

Thanks to the curve of the hill and the street, she could see over the side fence and into the neighbours' yards. All the way to a glimpse of the very back corner of number five. To think if they'd not been having such a good time at the party someone might have been outside, looked up and seen something.

Unable to think of the what-ifs, Billie forced herself out of Megan's room to cook dinner.

The only hint Mum wasn't her normal self came after their meal. The baby books called this time of night the witching hour and from Mum's expression she'd be cursing Lola soon.

'Can't you settle her?'

Billie would have laughed if she wasn't so close to crying herself. 'I'll take her out for a walk.'

'Thanks, love.'

Billie strapping Lola against her chest was like hitting

pause on the remote, then tripping the volume to full. Mum winced and Billie hurried out the door.

'Shh now,' Billie murmured, hoping the vibrations of body-to-body contact might do what nothing else had.

Lola cried on.

But once they were outside, it was like the arching pink-tinged sky above swallowed the sound. Billie had worried about annoying the neighbours, but the houses each sat back on their expansive blocks. Built in the day of lush trees and solid walls.

She headed down and around to the front of the house, towards Wattlebury Court and the clumping of houses where the neighbourhood group had all built in the late Seventies. She'd listened to the podcast but only standing out here could Billie really get a feel of what Ruby had been talking about, seeing in her head the young couples building houses from empty blocks and then creating memories and milestones, and filling them with their own blossoming families to make them homes. That sense of safety indirectly leading to Megan's disappearance.

As they walked, Lola began to calm, blinking at the new sights around her, eyes widening at the swoop of a willy-wagtail from the low branch of a tree to dart about beneath a sprinkler striving to keep the grass from dying in the summer heat.

And the whole time, like it was a living thing, Billie felt the wide-open spaces of the conservation park overlooking the street with its trees and long grass and the sense that she could walk up there and be so completely alone that she could scream and no one would hear her. That park had watched on as those children were left home alone that night. Her mother and Megan. Her father and his siblings next door. And the studying teenager, Jennifer. All of them suffering so much for the choices of their parents.

Now Billie was here, her own baby nestled in this suburban community, her own baby vulnerable to whatever had happened to Megan?

Nearby, a door slammed, jolting Billie from her imaginings. The sound had come from number three where the Marshes had lived. It hadn't changed much, the red brick and white trimmings standing the test of taste and time. As she watched a teenage girl with long, dark hair stormed from the house, jumped into a small hatchback parked on the road and sped away.

Jennifer?

Billie shook herself from the silly thought but it didn't stop her seeing the street with images from the past overlying the neat quiet neighbourhood it had become.

Lola opened her little chubby fist and a small red and white bear she loved to carry fell to the footpath. Fearing more tears, Billie squatted to pick it up. A shiver raced along her exposed back. It would be so easy for someone watching from the conservation park to sneak between all these leafy trees and creep up...

She tamped down any further imaginings but couldn't help walking a little faster having retrieved the bear. She slowed to a stop outside number five, the only other house with one of the original residents still calling it home. Here in this low-slung Seventies home, Trish and Ken had thrown their dinner party.

She found herself at the door, feeling the ghosts of her

grandparents at her side, carefree and laughing as they'd arrived together all those years ago. She knocked.

The door opened. Trish, Billie's work colleague and friend, gasped. 'Oh, Billie it's you. You look just like...' Her voice trailed off, but it wasn't the first time Billie had been told she looked like Carol Callaghan. 'I hope this isn't about work,' she said breaking the moment.

The youngest of the dinner guests that night, Trish was a youthful sixty-five and well put together in her expensive activewear.

'I'm staying with Mum and I was going for a walk and thought I'd drop in.'

She didn't know herself if it was the podcast or maybe she was looking for work updates.

'I'd love a coffee,' Trish said. 'But I'm about to head out. I'm staying with a friend who had a fall for a few days.'

It was a stark reminder how old all those from the neighbourhood group were getting. 'I'm sorry. Is there anything I can do?'

'I'm good. But I appreciate you offering. Now, is there anything else?' It was then Billie noticed the overnight bag at Trish's feet. She really was right on her way out.

Billie studied the house in front of her, knowing it had been rendered and painted pale blue to cover the orange brick it had been built from, and the once-brown details changed to grey. In her head she could see each of the visiting couples arriving that fateful night with their apricot chicken and their trifle and their stroganoff.

'I wondered what you thought of the podcast.' With being on maternity leave she hadn't seen Trish properly since it all came out.

'I'm no journalist, but every story, depending on who's telling it, has a bias,' Trish said, after some thought. 'They can tell the truth but it's only the truth as far as they see it.'

'Did you know about the timeline being off? Did you know you'd confirmed a check that didn't happen?'

Trish looked at her feet. 'We were drinking. I'm not sure anyone knew properly to the minute. We didn't have reason to doubt Frank.'

Trish was making it sound like it was all on Pop. 'I thought you were all friends.'

'We were, like Ruby's your friend and that podcast is something she can rightly be proud of putting together. But it's the story she wanted to tell.'

'Are you saying she lied?'

Trish shrugged. 'I'm saying the truth depends who's telling it.'

Billie couldn't help thinking of how she herself hadn't lied but she was standing there not mentioning Donna. Guilt had her stepping back to let Trish past. 'I shouldn't keep you.'

Trish kissed first her cheek then Lola's. 'You're always welcome, you know that.'

Billie couldn't help the feeling as she waved farewell and then headed back to the house that there was something they were all missing.

13

Something had woken Billie.

She lay in the darkness with her eyes closed and listened for Lola's cries in the cot across the room, but there was only silence. And the relief of being allowed to succumb to the sweetness of sleep nearly made her groan aloud.

Except... she didn't.

Instead, she listened harder, eyes opening then closing again, limbs stirring to alertness. Why couldn't she sink back into oblivion? For once there was no one demanding her attention.

Wait.

No cries. And also, no regular baby breaths, no quiet snuffling in the crib.

An invisible fist squeezed her chest. She jerked up. Eyes wide open now. Straining to see in the darkness. Looking for the shape of Lola through the mesh sides of the cot.

Empty.

She stumbled from the bed on jelly knees. Regret beating in time with her hammering heart. What had she done bringing her baby here, to this house?

Pop's voice from the inquest recording rang through her mind like an accusation: '*The cot was empty and the only window in the room, smashed. Megan was gone.*'

Billie's gaze found the window. Intact. But the bedroom door was ajar.

'Mum?' The hoarse cry ripped from Billie's raw throat as she gripped the edges of the desperately empty travel cot. She'd put Lola there after feeding her only an hour ago, little eyes closed, rounded belly full of milk. There was an explanation. There had to be.

Because things like this didn't happen.

Except they did... and had done so in this very house.

'In here,' came the reply. The familiar voice answered straight away but it didn't come from the bedroom.

Billie followed the sound down the hallway and around to the living area. Her mum stood there in the darkness, in front of the huge windows, Lola held tenderly in her arms.

'My God,' Billie said. 'I thought...' She swallowed hard, unable to put into words the garbled terror that had filled her mind. She leaned against the wall drinking in the sight of her child safe and well.

Oblivious to the chest-hurting panic only slowly seeping from her eldest daughter, Mum stared out into the night, towards the dark empty reservation climbing beyond the houses across the road. A few streetlights in the court and a sliver of moon couldn't do much to penetrate the black.

'She was grizzling, upset, and I thought you could use the rest. These growth spurts are a hard time on the parents – I remember well enough. If I could take a little of that for you, I wanted to. And she seemed to calm with the view.'

Mum was right: Lola was now asleep again, content in her grandmother's arms, her little mouth open and drool on her chin.

'I'm sorry she woke you.'

'Oh, don't you worry. She didn't wake me. Too many memories and thoughts in this old head for me to ever rest easy.'

Billie, hands only trembling a little in the aftermath of her fright, took her sleeping daughter and managed to lay her in the cot without waking her. She lingered to breathe in her baby scent, rain air kisses over her and whisper, 'I love you, Lola-bug.'

In all the theorising about what happened she mustn't forget that a baby went missing that night.

When she went back out to the living area, her mum hadn't moved. Frozen and silent, she stared out into the night, her face inscrutable.

Billie hesitated, the words to berate her threatening to spill from her lips. Did Mum have any idea what she'd put Billie through by taking Lola?

Too tired for an argument, and aware of her mum's recent hospital visit, Billie instead asked something that had been playing in her head for the last few days. 'Is it just because she has the blanket? Is that why you're so sure?'

Mum didn't answer. Didn't even look Billie's way, or show she'd heard the question.

With a sigh, Billie filled a glass, drained it and rinsed it clean and still Mum remained in the same place. Her arms were folded over her chest and her thin nightgown couldn't hide how frail she'd become.

Billie moved to her side and looked out into the night, trying to see what Mum saw, trying to feel anything but creeped out by all that empty, dark space and the old red gum at the top.

Her mum wasn't much of a hugger and, to be fair, neither

was Billie. Maybe it was the darkness and the relief of a baby found, but before she knew it Billie wrapped her arms around her mother's stiff frame and held her. Held her, despite the fact that no arms lifted to hold her back.

And then, so slowly it was almost imperceptible, her mother's stance softened. Her head lowered, and brushed, almost leaned against Billie's shoulder. After a minute like that, Mum released a heartfelt sob.

Then she lifted her head and met Billie's gaze with shadowed eyes.

'You asked why I believe?' Her breath hitched. 'I don't have a choice. I was here, in this house, in a room just down the hall, right next door when she went missing. I was here. And from all reports I didn't sleep through whatever happened. This, all of it, is on me. I need this to be true. I need to believe.' Her voice dropped to a whisper. 'I need her to have been okay all this time, because I don't know if I can survive the alternative. Every day that passes I'm getting older. If I die—'

'Don't say that.'

'It happens to us all one day. Mortality aside, I don't know how long I can keep holding on to hope. And most of all, I need her to forgive me.'

THAT NIGHT

9.09 p.m. – Trish

Later, I find myself staring at Carol, replaying the moment in the kitchen. Part of me wishing I'd said more. Told her that I thought I would be something more one day than a rich man's trophy wife, how I'd been a quick study and smart at school until the male teachers couldn't lift their gaze from my chest.

Would she have understood if I'd shared my fears about where exactly Ken's money is coming from? Could I have risked that betrayal?

I hold her understanding, the sense of real human contact, close. Treasuring being seen. Fascinated by the fullness of her lower lip curved in genuine joy and the warm sparkle in her eyes. My heart is still skipping in my chest and I can hear my happy, breathy sigh as I suck in air.

It means I'm not listening properly to what the other two wives are saying.

Foolish mistake.

All the places I've worked, things I've seen – from dive bars to airlines in countries where women are less than chattel – none of it needed me to be on my guard as much as sharing a wine in a cloud of cheap perfume with these suburban mothers. I'd rather totter down a dark alley on high heels in

New York than let myself relax around a teacher and an office assistant four drinks into a dinner party.

I catch the last word – 'club' – and the gasp of scandal that follows. Like I don't understand what they're implying about where I've come from.

Their faces, shiny with sweat and flushed with alcohol, look at me with matching expressions, daring me to ask, practically begging for me to do it, so they can lie about not meaning anything like that, and then laugh some more.

Why don't you come out and call me a whore?

The words play in my head, tease on my tongue, but I don't say them. Don't point out the hypocrisy that falls so easily from their lips. We don't say things that aren't nice in this friendly neighbourhood group.

14

Friday December 13th

'Surprise!'

Billie didn't like surprises. Something her husband knew, which was the reason she didn't move from where she was sprawled under the air con.

'If there's a party in my living room, feel free to party without me.'

Nathan crouched next to the bed. 'I've made plans.'

'Unmake them,' Billie said sleepily. 'I barely got three hours' shut-eye last night and Lola's finally asleep.'

'This will be good, I promise.'

She opened one eye. 'You left me stranded at Mum's without messaging.'

'And I'm sorry I didn't realise getting my phone repaired would mess with my settings.' He pulled his phone out of his pocket. 'See, all fixed.'

She appreciated the proof, although she had no reason to doubt his word.

'*Not my type*' was her first thought on meeting him. Right alongside the thrill through her body at his smile. A thrill that became a kind of intoxication when she'd realised that the flashing dimples were aimed at her.

She'd been sure he was in the wrong place. His sun-streaked longish hair, lean tanned muscle and board shorts suggested he'd detoured past the lecture theatre for Advanced Mathematical Operations on his way to the beach. But when he walked across that courtyard and sat next to her on the stone bench, she didn't move away.

Turned out advanced maths was his elective in a finance degree as it was hers in her business degree, an attempt to placate her mother that she wasn't wasting her brains. He did extra math for fun because it made his brain hurt. He'd explained as much when she found herself having coffee afterwards and then skipping her final lecture for the day to go for a walk on the beach with him. She didn't understand how someone who loved numbers like she did could be so different to her, but she loved that he was. And before long she loved him with a reckless intensity that she'd never experienced in any other part of her life. It should have terrified her. But Nathan was all that and, somehow, safe.

'I might forgive you.' She closed her eyes. 'Once I've caught up on sleep.'

She opened her eyes at the sound of movement to see a glass of water poised over her head. She rolled out of the way before the first drop hit. 'What the—?'

He righted the glass. 'Now you're properly awake, I'll explain. Eve is waiting out in the living room to babysit.'

'You asked her?'

'She's excited, reckons she misses the baby stage.'

'Really?' Billie yawned as she dressed. 'Don't tell me it gets worse?'

'Hopefully not. Anyway, I've booked us a night away.' He named the best hotel in the city. 'Before you worry, we don't have to stay the whole night but for Lola's feeds there's all that pumped milk you've been saving.'

She couldn't deny it was thoughtful but dressing up felt like way too much effort. 'That's really nice but...' Her voice trailed off and she gestured to the shorts she'd pulled on with her singlet.

He laughed. 'That's perfect attire. I'm thinking room service and uninterrupted sleep, not fine dining.'

She kissed him hard, unapologetic when some of the water he was carrying spilt on his toes. 'I love it. You think of everything.'

'What were you two doing in there for so long?' drawled Eve when Billie trailed Nathan out into the living area a few minutes later, an overnight bag in her hand.

Billie shook her head. 'We were packing.'

Eve smirked. 'That's what you're calling it?'

'Are you sure this is okay?' Billie said, ignoring the teasing.

'We'll have fun,' Eve assured her, gesturing to where Max and Matilda were unrolling their little sleeping bags. 'I don't know what Nathan needs to make up for but I suggest you take advantage of it while you can.' She raised her eyebrows at her brother-in-law.

'Is it a crime to want to spend time with my wife?' Nathan countered.

Eve shook her head mock despairingly. 'Get out of here, you two, before I die of all the cuteness.'

Billie tried to think of everything Eve might need to know. 'Plank has one cup of his kibble, no more. Lola might want some of the pumpkin puree but she spits most of it out. There are a couple of marked bottles of breastmilk in the fridge and some in the freezer. You have to be careful thawing—'

'I know,' Eve interrupted. 'And where clothes and nappies are, and how to run a baby bath. I've got this. You relax. And if there's an emergency, I'll call.' Her smile gentled her brisk tone. 'I promise.'

'Thank you.' Billie tiptoed in to blow Lola a kiss, somehow managing not to disturb her, and then trailed Nathan out to the car.

A small tendril of guilt snaked through her at leaving Lola behind, but mostly she couldn't wait to have some time off and a chance to reconnect with her husband. She squeezed his thigh as he pulled out of their driveway. 'You're pretty great, you know that?'

'So are you.'

There was something extra nice about a hotel that was so fancy the staff didn't even blink when Billie and Nathan checked into one of the most expensive suites in singlets and shorts.

When they were finally alone Billie took in the stunning view through the floor-to-ceiling windows of the city skyline with the hills in the distance and then flopped onto the huge bed. 'This is even nicer than I imagined.'

'Drink?' Nathan lifted the bottle from the chiller and held it up for her perusal as drops of condensation ran down the side.

'Yes, please.' She turned up the air con and changed into one of the decadent robes.

He held out her filled glass and then when she took it, raised his. 'To you.' The care shining in his green eyes, the way his hair curled at the edges from the heat and the way his T-shirt pulled a little at the broad expanse of his shoulders – something she lately hadn't had time or energy to notice – had her body remembering she was more than just a mother.

'To us.' She clinked his glass and then lifted hers to take a small sip. The bubbles prickled on her tongue and liquified her muscles. Tension she'd thought permanent since having Lola slowly seeped away into the ether. She drained the glass.

Busy with careers and wrapped up in each other, a baby was a 'probably someday' thing until Billie decided to test after being unable to shake a stomach bug. It wasn't unwelcome but she'd wondered in her months of morning sickness whether the grind of broken sleep and nappies would bring unwanted reality into the fantasy of being with a man who still made her stomach flip.

But somehow Nathan the dad was even hotter than Nathan the husband had been.

He joined her on the bed in a matching robe and she couldn't resist grabbing the lapel and pulling his head down close. The champagne tasted even better on his lips.

They ordered a selection of food from room service and then sampled the complimentary chocolates while they waited for it to arrive. Billie sipped the bubbly and filled Nathan in on the last few days at her mum's place as he trailed his fingers along her bare calf in a lazy massage.

'Oh, and she volunteered me to tutor Donna's son.' She imitated her mum's tone: 'Billie can help him, that's her specialty.'

He made a face. 'Tell me you're not wasting your time with some snot-nosed high school kid.'

'I figured I could use it as an opportunity to get to know Donna, but she was reluctant. And although I've messaged the number Mum gave me twice, she's not answered. I'm really starting to think she has something to hide.' She stopped short of mentioning the changes in expression she wasn't sure she hadn't imagined. It had her holding back from believing this woman was Megan, had her unable to stop worrying about Mum.

'Call her.'

The alcohol fizzing through her veins made her reckless. 'Why not?' She shushed Nathan and pressed to connect a call to Donna's number. It rang, and Billie thought for sure she wasn't going to answer.

Then she did. 'Donna speaking.'

Billie jerked upright as Nathan's eyes widened. 'Hi, it's ah Billie. Just checking to see whether you got my messages about tutoring.'

There was a long silence. 'I did.'

Billie could hear her mum's voice in the background. Of course they were together. 'Shall I tell Mum you've changed your mind?'

'No. I really appreciate it. I'll send you the details including the syllabus.'

'Great.'

She disconnected and flopped back onto the bed, laughing as Nathan shook his head.

'Did I tell you Mum's invited her for Christmas?'

'I don't mind,' he said. He must have noticed her expression because he added, 'Unless you mind, which you clearly do. So now I definitely mind, and would you like another drink?'

After topping up her glass, he wrapped an arm around her.

'You spoil me,' she murmured against his chest.

'You deserve spoiling.'

She bit on her lip, reality creeping into the fantasy of the two of them separated from the world. 'This must have cost a fortune.'

He lifted her chin. 'How do you feel right now, right this very second?'

'Good? Great, even.'

He pulled her against him again. 'There, worth it.'

He'd always been thoughtful but not usually so extravagant. She couldn't help wondering why all this, why now. 'Must have been a big night with the boys,' she teased. 'Feeling guilty?'

'What? No. Was a bit of a fizzer really. Spent most of the night counselling Macca on his girlfriend problems. Tim bailed early and Stevo couldn't make it. But yeah, maybe listening to Macca whine made me appreciate just how good I've got it. Is that a bad thing?'

His oldest friend, who probably had a name other than Macca but everyone had forgotten it, was terribly unlucky in love despite being a good guy. And Stevo had a new partner and was probably too busy with him, Billie guessed.

When she didn't say anything, Nathan added, 'I wanted to make sure we didn't lose track of us.'

He'd said all the right things, but there was something... *off*. And she knew she wouldn't stop thinking about it until she knew what it was.

EPISODE 05: A MOTHER'S PAIN

Music playing: 'Bright Eyes' – Art Garfunkel

The music fades.

Ruby:
Thank you for joining us for Episode Five. I'm Ruby Costa and this is 'The Callaghan Baby Podcast'. Along with my team, I've been investigating the forty-year-old cold case of missing Megan Callaghan.

We turn our focus to Carol Callaghan, Megan's mother. She passed away more than twenty years ago. Before we begin, in this episode we talk about suicide, which may be triggering or upsetting for some people. If so, please call Lifeline on 131114 or talk to someone around you.

Carol Callaghan:
Please, if you know anything about Megan, or you saw anything unusual in the area of Wattlebury Court on the night of December 9th, no matter how small or insignificant you think it might be, please help me bring my baby home.

Ruby:

It's hard to watch and hear Carol's pleas to the media, knowing her entreaties would be ultimately unfulfilled.

Her husband Frank described their marriage as a happy one before Megan's disappearance and it isn't hard to believe when you examine photos of them together. Carol glows; her joy in life is a palpable thing. Her closeness to her husband evident in their body language – a hand held, a knee touching, a shared smile. We spoke with Barbara Jones, who was at the dinner party.

Barbara Jones:

Let me just say that I feel terrible about what happened to Megan, we all do, but you need to understand that times were different then. The world was a kinder place and things like that didn't happen in our area, ever. Or we'd never have left any of the children.

Ruby:

But they did happen. On your street. To your neighbour.

Barbara:

Yes, well, and it's awful. I said that. Besides, we lived right next door to the Williams house, and it wasn't like we're talking double stone. I heard Darren, my oldest, if he even got up to go to the toilet. It wasn't like they were really alone. And my youngest, Rachael, well she could scream, she could, and when she woke the whole street knew about it.

Look, I don't want to judge, but number eight is all the way on the corner, and I wouldn't have left my baby Rachael so far away at that age, but each to their own.

Frank and Carol were one of those couples, the ones they base romance novels on, that you don't quite believe exist outside a fantasy.

Ruby:
Could you explain this for our listeners?

There's the sound of someone tutting then a sigh.

Barbara:
One afternoon back before they had Megan, Frank popped around but it wasn't to see Larry. He wanted me to babysit Amanda overnight. It wasn't convenient having an extra for dinner but of course, being neighbourly, I agreed.

He took Carol away for the night as a surprise. It wasn't even their anniversary or anything.

She'd pop in to his worksite just to bring him a cold drink or some cookies, fresh from the oven. Then, once Megan was born, he didn't disappear to the pub to escape the kids but rather tried to get home more. He'd even change nappies.

Ruby:
You say that like it's award-winning behaviour.

Barbara:
Back then it almost was. Not sure my Larry changed a single nappy in his time. But it was more than that. You'd see it in their faces when the other one walked into a room, him often literally sweeping her off her feet to twirl her around. They'd brighten, come alive.

Ruby:
You don't sound entirely approving.

Barbara:
Romance is all well and good but it doesn't need to be slapped in people's faces. That's what some said anyway, I was their friend so it didn't bother me. They were happy and in love. Together they doted on their girls; they were a perfect family.

Ruby:
There are no family pictures of them together afterwards, not in the sense of happy snaps. There are only stills from news reports and photos for the media. In these, Carol and Frank could well be strangers given the distance between them, their lack of eye contact and the way they do not touch, their only connection the daughter they lost, and the daughter often photographed between them. In one picture, they stand rigid, eyes directed straight at the camera on either side of a lectern, which must be set up for a press conference. In another Amanda is between them. Another has them either side of a police spokesperson.

Medical records from the time show Carol visited multiple doctors seeking something to numb the pain. These days, I believe Carol's troubles would have been seen and recognised better by those around her, allowing her to get the support she needed.

We spoke about how Carol changed after Megan went missing, with Gloria Marsh. You'll remember her as the teacher from number three who was at the dinner party that night.

She is also my grandmother.

Gloria Marsh:
Of course, Carol changed. What mother wouldn't be heartbroken about what happened? Carol withdrew.

Ruby:
Are you saying, Gran, you gave up on your best friend?

Gloria:
I'm not sure I appreciate your tone. You don't understand how it was back then. We didn't have special hotlines people could ring. Christ, we didn't even have conversations about mental health. If you ask me, people these days are too quick to share everything with those around them. We had some decorum.

Carol knew I was there for her.

News presenter:
Carol Callaghan was found dead in her home this morning. The mother of Megan Callaghan, who sensationally disappeared nearly ten years ago, is believed to have died alone.

Ruby:
Mildred Winthorpe, the elderly neighbour who found Carol, was the same woman who was away the night Megan disappeared, the one known for complaining about the noise. She lived next door to the Callaghans.

Mildred has passed away; however, we have access

to her testimony from the 2005 inquest where she was interviewed by counsel Kate Emmett.

Mildred Winthorpe:
December was always a hard time of year for Carol with the anniversary of Megan going missing coming hot on the heels of Megan's birthday.

I liked to pop in, you know, and have a chat. Poor love, a cup of tea wouldn't bring her baby back, but she didn't have too many friends left after what happened.

Kate:
Can you tell us about the day you found her?

Mildred:
I'd done some baking. Date and walnut loaf with a drizzle of maple syrup. I thought Carol might eat a slice if she had company. She didn't eat enough if you ask me.

I remember I wrapped it in double alfoil to stay warm. Then I went next door, which means quite a hike for these old legs because that front door hadn't been used in I-don't-know-how-long. By the time I got to the back door I was a little breathless, one of the delights of getting older, although I was but a spring chicken then.

I knocked but there was no answer. The car was there and I'd not seen anyone leaving after Frank headed to work. I didn't know Amanda was away.

Kate:
So, you knocked and then waited for someone to come to the door?

Mildred:

Dear, we were neighbours and in Wattlebury Court that made us friends. I let myself in. Things are different now, but although times were changing it was still common to go on in. Honestly, I had a funny feeling. I called out, not wanting to alarm anyone unnecessarily, but the kitchen area was empty.

Kate:

And did you leave at that stage?

Mildred:

Obviously I didn't, or I wouldn't be sitting here taking up all these important people's time, would I?

There was something about that kitchen that put me in a right hurry. No dishes in the sink, no hum of the washing spinning the towels dry, not even the exhausted sighs of a person unable to leave their bed. I walked down that hallway and somehow, I knew. But I walked down that hallway anyway.

I believe that Carol knew exactly what she was doing, with Frank at work and Amanda away. They didn't need to be the ones to find her.

Ruby:

Carol died from a cocktail of prescribed drugs and we'll never know for certain if she intended not to wake up or she just wanted relief from the pain.

Kate Emmett asked Frank about this painful topic at the inquest.

Frank:

I don't know if she planned it. If I'd suspected I would have stayed by her side. Maybe it all got too much for her and, if so, who here could blame her?

All I could do was be there for her as best I could. And yeah, I guess that wasn't enough. Hell, some days it almost gets too much for me and I have work to keep me busy.

Kate:

I understand that you had dinner together the night before?

Frank:

We met in the city as I had a late meeting. After eating, we bumped into Larry and Barb, chatted for a few minutes about our children, particularly Amanda and Darren's budding romance, and went home for an early night.

Ruby:

If something changed for Carol at that time, I fear we'll never know.

To find out where the police turned next, please join us again next time on 'The Callaghan Baby Podcast'. If anyone listening knows anything that could assist in making this podcast, please contact me on investigation@ thecallaghanfoundation.com. If you know something that could help the police, please contact them.

Thank you for listening.

15

Number 14C was so blandly modern that Billie forgot what it looked like by the time she reached the front door.

Donna's message had been brief. Time, place, date and a link for Zach's exam syllabus.

Even as she rang the bell, Billie was second-guessing her decision to come. Although she'd prepared, high school felt like a lifetime ago. But she couldn't pass up the opportunity to find out more about Donna. Not when the DNA results still hadn't arrived.

A young man opened the door. 'Hi.'

'I'm Billie,' she said. 'And you must be Zach?' His narrow face, dark mop of hair and hazel eyes gave him away as Donna's son.

'Yeah.' He squinted at the shopping bag in her hand. 'You're not cooking, are you?'

Why did he sound so fearful? Oh, the apricot chicken debacle that Donna had stayed to clean up. 'Don't worry,' she said. 'This, my young friend, is science.'

Inwardly, she winced. *My young friend?* Ugh.

The click of shoes on tiles sounded and Donna appeared behind him. 'Billie, so glad you could come. This shouldn't take long, should it? I've been called in to a work shift and have to leave soon.'

And I don't want to leave you alone with my son.

She didn't say it but Billie couldn't miss the inference.

Zach smiled at his mum. 'I told you to go. I'll be fine.'

'Yes,' Billie agreed quickly. 'You can't rush this stuff.'

Donna looked between the two of them. 'I'll see where you're at when I finish getting ready.' She disappeared down the hall.

Zach held open the door and then offered to help Billie with her bags.

'Thanks,' she said, then checked the baby capsule where Lola was asleep.

'Are you coming?' Zach was already halfway down the hall.

'Yes.' She followed him.

Despite Donna saying they'd been here for months, the large canvas prints in the hallway were propped on a shelf rather than hanging on the wall. Billie tried to resist lingering to study each one. Most were of Zach alone, two with a smiling Donna and one with an older woman in a multi-coloured cardigan, who had to be Janette Novak. Zach was maybe five in the photo, and he had his arm slung around the woman's rounded waist. His eyes shone with adoration as he looked up at her. The woman's hair covered her face.

'My grandmother died,' Zach said.

Billie spun away from the picture. 'I'm sorry.'

He shrugged. 'She was sick.' His voice cracked a little. 'Anyway, I guess she wasn't really my grandmother.'

'Blood isn't the only way to be family,' Billie said quietly. Her heart went out to this gangly boy. Could Donna lie to a son she so obviously cared about? Because whatever doubts she had about Donna, she was sure this boy wasn't pretending.

Zach's frown betrayed his confusion as she pulled the experiment equipment from the shopping bag. The same experiment she remembered from year ten science with Ms Heathcote. She'd grabbed the necessary ingredients on the way, only realising how close Donna lived to the footy club where Tim worked when she'd literally bumped into him outside the supermarket. He'd been with a young physio from the football club and seemed to be embarrassed to see Billie, carting baby and shopping as she was, her hair escaping from her ponytail and with spit-up on her shoulder. He'd hesitated on making introductions and Billie had to ask for the poor young woman's name. He and Eve were always so well put together; maybe she'd cramped his style being a walking mess of new motherhood.

Soon, the digital scales and assorted chocolates were arrayed on the bench. A bench and surrounds, Billie noted, that was clean of any papers. No envelopes waiting attention, no calendars nor reminders of appointments to come. Simply tidy or had Donna guessed Billie's intentions to snoop? In fact, apart from the canvas pictures, the house appeared spotlessly clean and devoid of any personal hints about the people who lived there.

'Tell me what's going on,' Zach grunted. 'I don't get it.'

'Explain the difference between mass and weight, and I won't waste your time with the experiment,' Billie said, aware of Donna peering in the room as she passed, dressed in what appeared to be a hospital uniform. 'Although, you should know it does involve eating the main materials afterwards.'

She figured if he didn't know, he could pretend he wanted the treats.

He crossed his arms. 'Teach away.'

After a process reminder, he took over. It didn't take long to calculate the mass and weight of the treats on Earth compared to on Mars and explain why it wasn't equal. From there Billie went over other areas likely to be covered in his exam, the latter with Donna tapping her foot impatiently in the doorway.

'Is that all?' Donna asked. 'I'd rather you finished before I had to leave.'

Billie picked up the sheets she'd put together in the middle of the night after Lola had woken her and she couldn't sleep. 'There's all these examples, but if Zach doesn't need anything further...'

'Go, Mum,' Zach said without looking up. 'I'm not a baby. I'll lock the door after Billie leaves.'

Donna hesitated, then sighed. She crossed to Zach and brushed a quick kiss on his forehead while he squirmed. 'Don't get into mischief.'

He flushed. 'Yes, Mum.'

But Billie kind of thought the warning was meant for her, only relaxing when she heard Donna's car pull away.

They worked on the sample problems with Billie trying to steer the conversation to Donna. 'Does your mum get called in like that often?' she dared ask when he crossed to open a glass sliding door leading out into a tiny courtyard to let the air flow through.

'Yeah.' Seeing her looking at him battle the lock, he explained, 'This lock is dodgy as.'

She waited until he'd managed to get the door open. 'Does

she work a lot?' Every question sounded to Billie like an interrogation, but he didn't seem to notice.

'The hours at this new place are all over the place. Day, night, in between.'

'New place?' Billie hoped she didn't sound too interested. 'Since you moved here?'

He shook his head. 'Nah, she started a new job two weeks ago.'

Donna had implied she'd started at the children's hospital when they'd arrived in town. 'Where else did she work?'

He frowned. 'Does it matter?'

'Of course not.'

'Anyway, it won't be for long.'

'Why?' she asked.

'We move a lot,' he said simply. *Did this mean she wasn't planning to stay long?*

'But this program you're sitting the exam for, it's local?'

He shook his head. 'It's in the US. Although there's always the chance that even if I get in, it might fall over. Like the last one.'

'The last one?' Somehow it didn't come out as a squeak.

'Yeah, I should be in London right now. Mum says not to talk about it, like anyone's gonna judge. It's not my fault it didn't work out. At least it's warm here and I'm not away from Mum over the holidays.'

'Silver linings,' she agreed.

He wasn't even supposed to be here.

As Zach worked through more of the practice problems, Billie fed Lola discreetly on a couch across the room, her brain whirling with what she'd discovered. As she pulled a fresh nappy from the bag, a small Post-it was stuck to the front.

'*High school science is a cinch*,' it read in Nathan's distinctive scrawl.

She couldn't help smiling at the reassurance after her worry of forgetting every bit of science she'd ever learned.

Billie checked Lola was settled, and asked to use the bathroom.

'Sure, left at the end of the hall.'

This was her chance to see more of the house. Quietly opening the doors she passed didn't tell her much, showing neat plain bedrooms although the stacked boxes in the spare room added to the feeling of the home being a temporary one.

Although she didn't need to use the facility, she flushed and then went to wash her hands. The soap made her pause. Pears. She'd only ever seen that particular translucent amber in her mum's bathroom, something from her childhood. Mum claimed its few ingredients made it non-irritating.

A coincidence?

Opening the bathroom cabinet door felt a little like crossing a line she didn't let herself think too much about. Inside held only the expected assortment of bathroom spares but poking out from underneath a neatly folded hand towel was a small tube of antibacterial cream. And there in nondescript green font: 'for use in minor skin infections or after-tattoo care.'

A coincidence or had Donna gotten a birthmark tattoo?

When Billie returned to the living area, guilty sweat sticking tendrils of hair to her nape, she was sure Zach would guess she'd been playing detective but he was focused on the work in front of him.

When he finished the questions, she couldn't find any fault. 'I think you've got this.'

'Great.'

'Is your mum likely to be late?' Billie asked as she made sure she had everything. They'd already swapped numbers in case he had more questions.

Zach picked up a rattle. 'Not usually.'

'Was the other place she worked closer?'

He frowned. 'Why do you care?'

'No reason,' she said quickly, her voice sounding fake in her own ears. 'I remember loving time home alone at your age.'

'I don't mind it,' he said. 'I try to get dinner on if I can.'

Billie got the hint. 'I'll leave you to it, then.'

As she headed out to the car she couldn't stop thinking about how the place hardly looked lived in and about Zach's revelations. A change of jobs, his program being overseas and that tube of cream Donna might have used on a tattoo. Small details but they added to Billie's unease. Why would Donna have lied about her work? And why did she seem like she wasn't planning on sticking around?

THAT NIGHT

9.17 p.m. – Trish

All evening I feel the men's eyes on me, on curves and planes, on skin and the wispy fabric of my jumpsuit suggesting and hinting at my body beneath. Feel the hunger. Avarice. Not one of these happily married fathers bother to hide it.

They don't have to.

As I hand them beers, bottles wet with condensation. As I refill the salty, greasy bowl of nuts sitting between them in the middle of the coffee table. As I get a stinging slap on the arse and a 'good girl' from Ken.

It's been the same since puberty. The casual sweep head to toe as I walk past. The lingering assessment of my assets. The licking lips they probably believe is complimentary.

I could have me a bit of that.

Mostly they didn't touch. Not beyond a squeeze or fondle if I make the mistake of allowing one too close.

Nothing in it, love. Just being friendly.

And if a woman complained, well then she was cold. Frigid.

Obviously you wanted the attention, dressing like that.

The ring on my finger helps somewhat. Most of them respect another man's ownership of a woman, if nothing else.

But not all men.

I've been dancing around this one since the day I walked into that very first dinner party on Ken's arm.

Instinct told me he wouldn't be happy with looking for long.

16

Wednesday December 18th

'The house was strange, I tell you,' Billie said to Eve the next evening. 'It was like they didn't really live there at all and Zach said they'd likely move soon.'

Eve glanced through the glass doors to Billie's outside deck where the twins were playing with playdough – placed out there to keep it from Lola's curious fingers. Plank watched the children through the door, desperate to get out and play.

'She could simply be tidy.'

'And she could be Megan, but until we have DNA results her story isn't really adding up. She also had the same hand soap in her bathroom, the one Mum loves from when she was younger. Pears or whatever. That's creepy, isn't it?'

'Seriously?'

'What?'

'It's not like it's rare. Maybe she has skin sensitivities. Like Mum. Because they're sisters.' The latter was said deliberately, like Billie was a bit slow on the uptake. She shook her head. 'You sound like Mum.'

'How? She's convinced Donna is the real thing. She's inviting most of the family to lunch now, says she's going to explain Donna's a friend with nowhere else to be over the holidays. But the truth is she wants to show her off.'

'Donna this, Donna that,' Eve mocked. 'Obsession is obsession either way.'

A faint buzzing from Nathan's phone left on the bench prevented her having to think of a comeback. He must have forgotten it when he'd headed to the shops to get more for the barbecue after Eve dropped in.

'I should check that,' she said. She crossed over. Unknown number. She tapped in his access code, intending to pass on a message.

No access.

The side door leading to their carport opened.

Aware of Eve across the room, Billie pasted a smile on her face and held out the phone as Nathan entered. 'Forget something?'

Irritation flashed across his face. 'What are you doing?'

Embarrassed at his tone, she glanced pointedly at her sister. 'It rang and I thought it might be important...'

He exhaled. Smiled. And became again the Nathan she knew. 'Sorry, thanks, just thought I'd lost it. The kids like sausages, yeah?' he asked Eve.

'Love them,' said Eve.

'Have I forgotten anything else?' he asked Billie.

She shook her head, tensing as he kissed her cheek. He was probably just annoyed at having to come back, because he couldn't be hiding something.

'So,' Eve continued. 'About your obsession.'

'I'm worried about what this will do to Mum.'

'Only if she's not really Megan.' Eve's amusement had become annoyance. 'You haven't even asked about my big news.'

'I was getting to that,' Billie lied. 'Tell me everything.'

'I have all these new companies requesting me to be an ambassador for their brand.'

'All?' Billie didn't know a lot about what Eve did online but that sounded impressive. 'Why?'

'Some pictures from Mum's house have gained traction, probably because of the podcast popularity. That and rumours of a break in that case.'

'Rumours?' Billie did her best impression of a goldfish, trying to speak but no words coming out. Eventually she managed, 'You haven't mentioned Donna?'

'I'm not stupid.' The edge in Eve's voice was unmistakable. 'You don't know what it's like to have built a following largely because your husband once kicked a ball around. It's a fight for me to be recognised as an individual, not just a footballer's wife. And finally, I'm beginning to make my own name. You have your own career at the business. Is it so bad that I want something for me?'

As was her way, Eve managed to make a valid point when Billie had been sure she was completely in the wrong. Winning an argument with Eve was next to impossible.

And people thought Billie was the smart sister.

'In some ways we've orbited around the missing-baby thing our whole lives,' Eve said when Billie didn't respond. 'It's all Mum thinks about. I know she missed your uni graduation because of a lead.'

'Thanks. I was trying to forget about that.' Mum had been interstate and a flight cancellation meant she'd not made it back until after the ceremony. At the time she'd tried to focus on the fact Pop was there instead, but it had hurt given how close she and Mum were. 'Mum had good periods too. Remember the family holiday to the snow?' Sometimes Billie would play those memories in her head, trying to keep the normal un-Megan parts of her childhood from being lost.

Eve smiled grudgingly. 'I remember you slipping on the ice in the car park and getting a bump on your head.' She put on her imitation of ten-year-old Billie's voice. 'I will not leave the snow to go be checked at the hospital. I will live here forever.'

Billie grinned too. She'd been a stubborn kid.

'I wish I'd remembered that this morning when Mum was showing off to Donna about all your academic awards,' Eve said.

Something tightened in Billie's stomach. 'This morning?'

'They came by for coffee. Apparently Mum had been telling Donna about my renovations and they were in the area.'

It sounded perfectly reasonable but Billie knew the flare inside her was jealousy at them all getting together without her. She tried to push it down. 'And she was nice?'

'She was. Look, I won't give anything away about Donna.' Eve hesitated. 'As much as I can.'

Billie couldn't miss the qualifier. Eve was clever like that, always covered herself in case something went wrong. She swallowed her doubts. 'The brand stuff sounds great.'

Eve threw her arms around Billie. 'This is going to be fabulous; I promise.'

Billie extricated herself and sighed. 'Anyway, with any luck, the DNA test results come back before Christmas and the whole thing goes away.'

'By whole thing you mean Donna, right?' said Eve with a laugh. 'I don't think she's so bad. We were talking this morning about the latest trends and she suggested it was time to pick a new theme for my socials.'

'Huh?' Billie knew business operations, but she was lost.

'Changing the colour scheme and style to show my growth as a person. Don't look at me like that; I had to talk to the woman about something.'

Billie felt better but only a little. Eve got along with everyone, and she'd been overseas when Mum was at her worst. Part of her wanted to make her sister understand what they were dealing with if this all fell apart, and part of her still wanted to shelter Eve from the ugliness of the past.

A lifetime of being the big sister won. She cleared her throat. 'Just remember whose side you're on.'

Friday December 20th

Thankful Nathan had offered to park the car, probably to avoid more of Lola's crying, Billie made her way along the cardiac unit corridor to Mum's room after her procedure, carrying her now-content baby in her arms.

Mum wasn't alone in room 27. Eve, dressed in activewear, slouched in a chair by the door and Donna was perched in the one at Mum's side.

Billie crossed to kiss Mum's cheek. 'How are you?'

'I was only under six minutes,' Mum said with pride. 'It only took one shock to get everything back in order.'

'That's great.' She said a general hello to Donna and Eve.

'Tim picked me up from the gym,' Eve said. 'He's parking.'

'Nathan, too.'

'You shouldn't have come,' Mum said. 'I'll be able to go home in a couple of hours.'

'Do you need someone with you?' Billie asked.

'Donna's staying,' Mum announced. Her tone reminded

Billie of how she imagined those people who got to inform lottery winners would. She and Donna at her side wore matching grins, and again Billie could see a resemblance between them. Long hair, narrow faces, something around their eyes.

A sibling resemblance?

'What about Zach?' Billie asked. She glared at her sister. How had Eve not nipped this in the bud?

Eve looked a little guilty but only a little.

'He's pretty independent,' Donna said. 'He'll love having the house to himself.'

'I wanted him to come,' Mum added. Then, sensing Billie's hurt, she said, 'You've already rearranged your life once this month to look after me and I know how hard looking after a baby can be.'

'Well, I'm excited to be staying in my old room,' Donna continued, like she hadn't heard Mum at all. Then corrected herself: 'Megan's old room.'

Billie was the only one who seemed to notice Donna's obvious change in subject.

Mum's eyes brightened. 'It's different now of course. I just wish you could have seen it how it used to be.'

Donna patted her hand. 'I do, too.'

As Mum and Donna talked logistics of when Mum might be discharged, Billie put Lola on Eve's lap.

'Have a cuddle with Aunty Eve,' she said. Then lowered her voice. 'Did I miss anything else?'

'The DNA test results,' said Eve.

Billie just about choked. 'What?'

Eve chuckled. 'The look on your face…' She mimed eyes bugging and laughed again. 'It's nothing exciting. According to Mum, it's been delayed. She doesn't expect them until after the ball.'

The ball was the foundation's big New Year's Eve charity event held at the Convention Centre in the centre of Adelaide. With the use of the ballroom, the exquisite dinner and the auction items donated, they were able to raise a significant portion of their yearly budget.

'Next year?'

'It's only a few more days. And they call me melodramatic.' Eve shook her head. '*Next year.*'

Her sister could shake her head all she wanted. At this rate, Donna would have moved in permanently by the time they knew the truth.

Billie couldn't sit still. 'I'll see what's keeping the men.'

Eve nodded. 'I'll entertain this little smudgekin.' She made a face and Lola chortled.

Taking the rare opportunity of being alone, Billie quickly checked her work email but there was only sharing of good wishes for the festive season. At least from now they'd be shut down until the new year. Usually, they operated on a few important projects over the break but not this year with the drop in projects.

She headed towards the lift looking for Nathan and Tim. She spotted them at the end of the hallway, partially blocked from view by a Christmas tree.

They faced each other, chests all puffed up, like two strangers arguing in a pub.

'I said you should leave it,' Nathan growled.

She couldn't hear Tim's response, but his shoulders were stiff and hands clenched into fists. Was he threatening her husband?

Nathan shook his head. 'Like you can talk. Mind your business.'

'Or what?' sneered Tim.

Billie edged closer, keeping the tree between her and them. What the hell was going on?

Nathan stepped forward, but then he saw her and the annoyance on his face vanished. Tim turned and he, too, was smiling.

'Is everything okay?' she asked.

'Sure. Parking's a nightmare though.' He shook his head. 'People wanting to visit their loved ones in the festive season, who'd have thought?'

Tim shoved his hands in his pockets. 'It's pretty tense out there.'

She looked from one to the other. 'Is that why you two looked like you were going to have a punch-up?'

'You must have been imagining things,' said Nathan. He slung his arm over Tim's shoulder. 'Right, mate?'

Tim nodded. 'Yeah, bro. All good here.'

But Billie *had* seen them arguing. She was sure of it. As she turned to trail the two men back to Mum's room, her chest ached that Nathan would lie.

As the men entered, Donna left. Thanks to the shuffle and the small room, she and Billie were momentarily alone in the hallway.

'I'm surprised Zach isn't staying with you,' Billie said. 'Although he seems able to look after himself.'

Donna's ever-present smile from when Mum was around vanished. 'I don't know what you're implying.'

'Nothing,' Billie said quickly, but it seemed strange that as much as Donna had grown so close to Billie's mum so fast, they'd barely seen Zach. 'How was his test?' she asked to change the subject. 'I hope I helped.'

'Good. He said you did.'

'He mentioned it was for a program overseas, but you're not moving again so soon, are you?'

'He must have been confused with the details.' Donna's smile didn't reach her eyes. 'Anyway, can't chat. I have to prepare for my little stay.'

Billie watched her go while mentally replaying their conversation. There had been an undercurrent of something from the woman who seemed only too friendly to Mum and Eve, but what?

17

Sunday December 22nd

Eve waited, casual chic in white culottes and a luxe green top, on her front doorstep, hands on her hips, as Billie drove between the gates marking the entrance to her sister's driveway and then pulled to a stop. She hoped, as she always did, that her serviceable car wouldn't leave an oil stain on the light, pebbled surface.

'You're late,' Eve announced before Billie had the driver's door fully open.

'Sorry,' Billie said feeling the heat like a blanket on her skin. Was that smoke from the Hills bushfires adding to the haze? Or was it just her imagination from seeing so much devastation across the country on the news? The floral maxi-dress she'd thought cool and breezy at home stuck unpleasantly to her body. 'First Lola wanted to feed, then she needed changing again, then it took forever just to get her into her capsule...' She trailed off as she registered the lack of any other vehicles in front of the towering, white two-storey structure with its slate-grey detailing and warm wooden double door. 'Where's Mum?'

It had been a few days since Mum's procedure and Donna's stay at Wattlebury Court – a visit that had gone wonderfully by all reports.

'She's been held up apparently, wants us to start without her. That's okay, isn't it? The light is perfect out on the deck right now for pictures and the kids are desperate to begin.'

'It's fine,' Billie managed, fighting a stab of disappointment. Their annual gingerbread house making was one of her favourite family traditions and although Lola couldn't really participate and probably wouldn't remember, it was the first time she would share it with her and she wanted Mum there too.

'I'm sure she won't be long.'

Eve took the nappy bag so Billie could manage the baby capsule where Lola sat plump and smiling in a way that made Billie almost forget the grizzling of the last few hours, angelic in her white Christmas onesie with its red 'My First Christmas' across the tummy.

Along with the tasteful but festive lighting across the front of the house and the giant solar-lit presents on the lawn, a gorgeous small reindeer stood in the ficus pot by the door, delicate and already sparkling in the afternoon light.

'New decoration?' Billie asked.

Eve shrugged. 'It's from Donna. I gave her the number of my hairdresser and she brought it around as a thank you.'

Billie hoped her smile didn't slip. 'Lovely.'

She trailed Eve into the house, her shoes slapping against the cool, grey tiles where the faint hum of unseen ducted air conditioning maintained the temperature at perfectly cool. They passed the magazine-style spread of the formal lounge on their right, the natural tones highlighted by the skylights high overhead and the deep warmth of the thick rug in the middle of the room that Billie knew from movie nights with her sister was as comfortable as it was stylish.

They moved along the hallway, and around the stunning wood and glass staircase that led up to the second floor that boasted views of the bay, up where the children had their rooms and Eve had her own studio. Then, they continued into the huge back area where the open-plan kitchen and dining merged into the outdoor living by the tropical-styled pool and carols played through surround-sound speakers. A towering deep green Christmas tree that had to be at least twelve foot high and appeared too perfect to be real, despite the hint of pine in the air, overshadowed the usual gorgeous décor.

Matilda clapped her hands together at the sight of them, beyond cute in her white dress with a red bow where she was seated at the outdoor concrete-topped table next to Max in his red shorts and white T-shirt. Waffles the Insta famous caramel-coloured cavoodle lay on his dog bed, presiding over the scene with smiling eyes and a small wag of his tail.

Aware of how her beloved Plank accosted everyone who entered her home with knock-them-over enthusiasm, Billie could only sigh in admiration of how well Eve had her dog trained, as well as the fact that there were no hunks of gingerbread house missing from any of the sets arranged on the table, despite the twins being left unsupervised. She knew that Eve had personally baked every piece of the gingerbread houses they'd be assembling after her lengthy experimenting to find the recipe she'd deemed perfect for the occasion.

And Billie hadn't even managed to arrive on time.

At the table, Max and Matilda waited, jiggling a little with impatience and singing along with 'Santa Claus is Coming to Town', while Billie sat Lola in the highchair that Eve had set up down one end.

Eve let the moment build; her smile wide, love in her eyes as she studied her about-to-burst children.

Billie took a picture of Lola, who smiled gummily and seemed to bob a little to the music. She glanced to the hallway, hoping Mum would walk through it. What could possibly be so important that she was missing this?

'Now, we can start,' Eve announced a minute later with a dramatic swish of her hand.

'At last,' the twins cried in unison, reaching for the same bag of prepared icing. Laughter filled the air – somehow still cool from overhead fans despite being outdoors – as tiny hands played a brief tug-of-war, Matilda winning just as Eve was about to intercede.

Max grabbed the other bag on their side of the table and both children set to work. The smallest smear of chocolate on Max's lip when he frowned adorably in concentration, matching the one on Matilda's hands, suggested they'd explored some of the little white bowls filled with lollies for decorations even though they'd left no other trace.

Eve snapped pictures and another camera she had set up on a tripod filmed the event for her to put on her socials later, and in between she floated between Matilda and Max to help them hold gingerbread walls together or attach a roof.

Down the other end of the table, Billie hummed along to the music as she selected the walls of her and Lola's house and then taste-tested the icing that would glue the whole thing together. After placing the tiniest smudge on the end of her finger she put it in Lola's mouth, taking a picture to send to Nathan at the almost comical wide-eyed wonder from Lola at the sweet treat. His last-minute not being able to come hadn't bothered Billie, because it had always been her, Mum and Eve making houses together since she was little. Now, without Mum there, she wished he hadn't been caught up at work.

'That is not a Christmas face.' Eve showed her the picture she must have just taken to emphasise her point.

'I was just thinking,' Billie said without looking too close at the camera screen, knowing she'd been feeling less than joyous. She lowered her voice. 'Did Mum say how long she'd be?'

'She was vague.'

A knot of suspicion lodged like a pip in Billie's gut, growing larger the longer Eve avoided meeting her gaze. 'She's with Donna, isn't she?' Eve's lack of reply told Billie all she needed to know. 'Did she say why?'

'Something about the decorations for the ball.'

'But I always help her with that.' Billie heard the whine in her voice and tried to swallow past the lump in her throat. Had she come across as too busy now she had Lola or was she not needed anymore?

'She knew you wouldn't want to miss the gingerbread house making.'

Billie only just resisted pushing her wonky attempt off the table. 'She should be here with us and her grandchildren.'

Eve's expression reflected the pang in Billie's chest that their mum had chosen to miss this family tradition but her sister just shrugged. 'At least we're all together and she might make it before we're done.'

But she didn't sound hopeful.

EPISODE 06: VISITING THE SCENE

Music playing: 'Born To Be Alive' – Patrick Hernandez

The music fades.

Ruby:
Welcome to Episode Six of 'The Callaghan Baby
Podcast'. I'm Ruby Costa. Along with my team, I've been
investigating the forty-year-old cold case of missing Megan
Callaghan.

The Callaghans' house was built in 1973, only six years
before Megan's disappearance and at a similar time to the
neighbours'. It's located on the mouth of the cul-de-sac,
on the corner of Baden Avenue and Wattlebury Court.
Carol and Frank worked on the design with a local architect
and rented nearby until it was completed by Callaghan
Constructions with Frank himself picking up the tools when
he could. There was something about hammering a nail in the
forever home where they planned to raise their family that
solidified Frank's vision for Callaghan Constructions that to
this day is all about that dream home.

They moved in immediately with their daughter,
Amanda. Looking at the four bedrooms included in the

home, they planned a large family; however, it took many years for Megan to arrive.

I have several pictures of the street from the police reports. Although not the biggest or most expensive when it was built, the Callaghan house stands out, set apart by the western red cedar cladding. There's a classic timelessness about it. The building makes a stunning visual – perched on the side of the hill, wide balcony at the formal entrance, windows across the façade, overlooking a sloping lawn with small trees and shrubs. Pictures of the back of the house show a driveway off Baden Avenue, leading to a carport and another entrance, marked as the one more commonly used.

Pictures of the inside show typical Seventies décor. Lurid brown and tan patterned wallpaper cramping the main living spaces heavy with timber details accompanied by garish orange light fixings. The bedrooms are plainer, with cream walls and dark timber skirtings and beams, other than Megan's room that had been recently wallpapered for her arrival with a print of pretty lavender. In her room there's a wooden chest of drawers and a wooden cot, empty of course. The pictures show it bare of blankets and the mattress fitted with a white sheet. There's a teddy bear mobile, hanging on the edge of the cot.

There's the low rumble of an SUV. It comes to a halt. Quiet follows, broken by footsteps on concrete.

Ruby:
In my months of research for this investigation I've heard a lot about Ridgefield as well as details about Wattlebury

Court. I've looked at hundreds of photos, as well as floor plans and know it as my mother's childhood street.

But none of that has prepared me for today. Actually being here in this little cul-de-sac, on what used to be the edge of the city. Immediately, I notice the inclusive, friendly feel of the houses. Lush green trees provide shade from the blazing sun, trees that may have been mere saplings forty years ago. Across the road there's a trike, left on its side in the front yard, the signature of a child in a hurry.

It's hard to explain what it's like standing here in front of Megan Callaghan's house.

I expected to be creeped out, that there would be scarring from the tragedy that happened here, but if anything, it's the opposite. Homes closer to the centre of the city are like commuters packed into a train, all touching and breathing in each other's air but here... here is like friends seated spaciously around the table, all smiling into each other's eyes.

Before I can begin to study the familiar lines of Megan's home, my eye is drawn to something bigger, an expanse I couldn't really understand from the photos. The Tucker's Hill Conservation Park rises up behind Wattlebury Court like a tidal wave of dried grass. It's spotted with regenerated river red gums and grey box eucalypts. My research tells me many of these towering trees are new, adding to the native shrubs and wattle from which the street gets its name. I imagine the faint dip in the crest of the hill is in the direction of the long-abandoned bluestone quarry, but I can only guess. This stretch of land used to skirt the city and was claimed as a green buffer before more land was opened for development.

I'm sure the intentions regarding urban planning and recreation are well founded and admirable.

But standing here now, all I can think is that it's a bloody big space to hide a body.

There's the rap of someone knocking on a metal door, before the whine of it opening.

Ruby:

Amanda Callaghan now owns the family home where her little sister went missing. She says that she has a connection to the place and some deep instinctive part of her believes that one day Megan will come home.

She gives us the tour. Having seen crime scene photos, I recognise details that linger. Some of the dark timber skirting and the layout are the same although there has been remodelling by the intervening owners, like security blinds on the outsides of the bedroom windows, ugly things that Amanda tells us will be changed soon.

I comment that they kept the old light fitting in the hall, and she explains with sadness that only a few original features remain.

One change I notice is the large photograph that has pride of place in the living area. It's a photo I've seen before in the original case notes.

This isn't Megan alone, but instead she's with her mother and sister. A note in the original file mentioned that Frank handed it over with the simple descriptor: 'It's of my girls.'

Carol is gorgeous in the styled black and white image, with her long hair curled under, brown eyes perfectly lined, and lips open in a smile full of laughter. Amanda's hair is cut in a pretty bob and the dress is the old-fashioned, best-dress kind that could have been from any era, and she's staring down at her little sister who wears a simple white dress. Megan was nearly four months and my development knowledge isn't great but I would swear that baby is staring right back up at her big sister and her mouth is open in a huge grin.

I ask Amanda about it.

Amanda:

This photo? Dad always told the story of how they tried to get a picture with me looking at the camera but apparently when they got the proofs, I was looking at Megan in every single one. We didn't have long together but I adored her. I like to think we would have stayed close.

Ruby:

During my visit to Amanda's home, I was granted access to her collection of her mother's papers. We went through them together late into the evening and, well, I'll let her explain what we found.

Amanda:

I didn't expect to find anything when Ruby asked if I had any old papers of my mother's. I've gone through them and the police have combed them looking for clues, but fresh eyes are always welcome.

Ruby had my mother's old calendar. Ruby was glancing over the month of November when she gasped. There, indented on the page and only visible thanks to the angle of the lamp were three scrawled words: *They were here.*

My blood chilled. What did it mean?

Ruby:

We studied everything again, but didn't learn any more.

Please join us next time on 'The Callaghan Baby Podcast'. If anyone listening knows anything that could assist in making this podcast, please contact me on investigation@thecallaghanfoundation.com. If you know something that could help the police, please contact them on the relevant numbers.

Thank you for listening.

18

Tuesday December 24th

A children's choir singing carols greeted Billie when she entered the big sliding doors at Restwell in the afternoon on Christmas Eve. Red, green and silver tinsel hung across the ceiling and a huge tree awash with twinkling lights squatted in the corner.

Yesterday, when Mum had called to apologise for missing the gingerbread making, she'd announced that Pop was too unwell to come out for Christmas Day.

Not wanting him to be abandoned over the whole Christmas period, Billie volunteered to visit but time had gotten away from her.

She'd left Lola with Nathan, making him promise not to eat all the food she'd prepared.

'About that thing in the hospital with Tim...' she'd tried as she was grabbing her keys to leave.

'There was no thing.'

'And the calls?' There had been at least two from unknown numbers in the last few days.

He waved it away. 'They're not important.'

'Then tell me what's going on. I know you; something's not right.'

'For fuck's sake, it's just work stuff,' he'd said. 'Let it go already.'

Lola had started to cry at his raised voice, and Billie left before she could get sucked into dealing with any of it. She'd expected him to message to apologise the whole drive over, but she'd heard nothing. Merry Christmas to him too.

A different nurse was on the desk. 'Welcome to Restwell. Can I help you?' she asked.

'I know the code but thank you. And, ah, Merry Christmas.'

Billie quickly punched in the code, leaving the noise behind.

The tinsel and decorations that filled the foyer continued into the secure wing, but the festive spirit did not. Quiet filled the halls and most of the doors were closed.

The familiar figure of Lisa bustled down the hallway towards her. 'Good afternoon. This is my usual area,' she explained before Billie could ask. 'I was filling in out on the desk last time you were here.'

Just knowing this cheery woman worked with her grandfather lifted Billie's mood.

'You've worked with my grandfather for a while then?'

'Actually, I haven't. I've only had him under my care for the last few weeks. We had a few agency people in for a short stint but they like familiar faces.' She chuckled. 'Not that they always remember us. He misses your mother, asks about her daily.'

'I'll bring her in soon, unless you think he could come out tomorrow for a while?'

She asked the question on a whim. Her mum would have to deal with it. And, anyway, shouldn't Donna want to meet her father if she really believed she was Megan?

But Lisa was shaking her head. 'Your mum called

yesterday, and we had to tell her we didn't think it would be a good idea. He's likely to become upset. We'll look after him here.'

Billie didn't know what to make of that. Had her mother changed her mind?

Realising Lisa was looking at her strangely, she said, 'We appreciate everything you do.'

Lisa shrugged off the praise. 'I'd prefer he had some more meat on his bones. There's some dessert on his table and it would be great if you could encourage him to eat it.'

'I'll do my best.'

Billie pushed open the door and blinked to adjust to the dim light. The shades were drawn on the orange glow from the setting sun and her grandfather sat hunched in his chair.

'What are you doing sitting here in the dark?' She forced a bright tone into her voice even as her throat ached. Lisa was right: he did look thin.

He cowered into the chair. 'Who is it? Who's there?'

She crossed over and lifted the blind a little. 'It's Billie, your granddaughter. I've come to see you.'

'My granddaughter?'

'Yes, the oldest and the best if you ask me. Not that I'm biased.'

His features softened at her joke although he continued to regard her with suspicion. 'Your nurse told me you'd left some dessert uneaten,' she managed, voice almost steady. 'That's not like the Pop I know.'

'Pop?'

'You're my Pop and I'm your Billie.' This was the man who'd been there when she was growing up when her mum was too busy with Megan searches, who'd taken shifts at the hospital after her mum's breakdown, who'd taught her so much about running the business and then slowly stepped aside so she could largely take over the management side of things. She swallowed past a lump in her throat. 'You love dessert.'

'Don't want it.'

She picked up the small bowl of trifle and tried to keep her expression cheerful. Scooping some onto the spoon, she sniffed it. 'Smells pretty good to me. Are you sure you don't want some?'

His eyes didn't leave her face. 'Yuck. You eat it.'

Unable to help being reminded of her attempts to get Lola to try mashed peas, she popped the heaped spoon in her mouth. 'It really is good.'

He considered for a moment and then opened his mouth wide. With her help he devoured the whole bowl.

Her phone buzzed as she was putting the bowl on a small table by the door alongside a half-full cup of cold tea. The message was from Nathan.

'Sorry about before. Love you.'

'Love you,' she replied.

It wasn't an explanation, but at least it was some kind of truce.

Noticing Pop had dozed off, she crossed over, lowered the blind again and was about to leave when he startled upright, blinking at her in obvious confusion.

Were they going to have to go through who she was again?

But then his expression cleared, and his mouth curved into a happy smile. 'Oh, Carol love, there you are. I was wondering where you'd got to. I've missed you so.' His rheumy eyes filled with tears. 'Hopefully, we can go home soon.'

'Home?' she asked, heartsore that again he thought she was someone else, but at the same time curious what he might have to say to his wife.

'Don't sound so surprised. You know they don't keep second-time mums in for long. You're supposed to be an expert at this now.'

Her breath hitched. Could he be thinking...

'I'm glad we chose Megan in the end,' he continued, unaware of her racing thoughts. 'I don't think she's a Harriet after all. Amanda can't wait to bring her home and fuss over her. She's already such a good big sister.'

Billie nodded. 'She was always going to be.'

His smile spread wide showing all his false teeth.

No wonder Pop seemed so happy. He thought Megan was still a newborn, their much-tried-for second child only recently arrived safely at last, and his wife and child in hospital. In his mind none of the tragedy about to enfold them had happened yet.

Ignorance was bliss.

He clutched the edge of the blanket on his lap. 'Don't forget the special blanket,' he said trying to drag it free and hand it to her.

Special blanket?

Caught up thinking Megan was still a newborn, he could be talking about the one Donna had used as proof.

'Are you talking about Megan's blanket?' she asked in a carefully calm tone.

His eyes, usually so cloudy lately focused on her and again he was the man who'd helped her with her year twelve algebra and a few years later sat by her side in the office at Callaghan Constructions and explained the vision he held for the business, of making family homes that would last the test of time. They dabbled in other projects like businesses and a few developments but it was the creation of a forever home that was at their core.

'Pop, do you remember Megan's blanket?'

A hint of a smile curved his mouth. 'Blankets,' he corrected. 'Carol fell in love with this little set she found at a boutique. She insisted we didn't need the extravagance or the fancy embroidery, but I wanted to treat my girls. Her face when I gave them to her...'

Billie could feel the thrumming of her heart. 'There were two?'

A shadow crossed Pop's face and he looked down at his gnarled hands knotted together in his lap. 'I can't do anything to change the past.'

'What happened to the other blanket?' she asked. 'Where was it?'

But he wasn't answering, and it didn't matter how many different ways she tried to ask the same question, she couldn't get anything more out of him.

Somehow Donna had obtained the other blanket. The birthmark would be easy enough to fake and without the blanket, her story was about as substantial as fairy floss.

Billie dug her phone from her bag and went to ask her grandfather again, to catch his answer on camera this time, but he'd fallen asleep, and no amount of gentle nudging would wake him.

It didn't matter. Her mother would have to believe her. Donna's blanket didn't mean a thing.

A few hours later, Billie still hadn't been able to contact her mum.

'Eggnog liqueur?' Nathan asked.

Despite the desire to hurl it across the room, Billie dropped her phone so it fell face down on the couch. 'Do we even have that in Australia?'

He held out the bottle adorably hopeful. 'It was at the bottle shop. I make no claims to how it tastes.'

She tried to muster a smile. 'Why not? Tis the season.'

He was trying to make up for before but despite the traditional carols playing on the TV and Lola, adorable in the Christmas PJs that matched hers and Nathan's, she couldn't quite get into the spirit.

If Mum would answer then she could tell her what Pop had said and focus on Christmas Eve carols with her family. Or better yet Mum could walk through the door and explain why she'd cancelled another tradition at short notice.

'I'm sure she has a good reason,' Nathan said guessing her thoughts as he handed her a small glass.

'Am I that transparent?'

He grinned. 'It could be the ten million times you've mentioned the issue in the past hour.'

'I'll stop going on about it.'

'To Lola's first Christmas,' he said lifting his drink.

She touched hers to make a clink. 'Merry Christmas.'

As she sipped the not unpleasant concoction she tried to focus on the music and the twinkling lights of the tree. Even Plank – sprawled right beneath the air-con vent – had a red and green tinsel collar that she'd found in one of the boxes of Pop's things that still took up half the storage space in the garage.

A family Christmas.

Without half her family.

Eve hadn't answered her call either. Were they together with Donna? The creamy liquid she'd drunk curdled in her stomach at the thought.

19

Wednesday December 25th

By the time Billie and her family arrived at Wattlebury Court for Christmas lunch, she'd tried to call her mum so many times she knew exactly how many rings before it cut through to voicemail.

The only response had been a text message: *'Busy here, sorry love. If it's not about food for Christmas it can wait.'*

So much for Billie's plans to have Mum uninvite Donna to the festivities. Now, she'd need to get through the day knowing Donna was lying.

Unlike their mother, Eve *had* eventually answered her phone but had been sceptical as to whether Pop's admission meant anything.

Consequently, Billie had been distracted through Lola's very first Christmas morning, another thing to be annoyed with Donna about. Although she'd managed a smile for all the photos, and it wasn't like Lola would remember anything.

At least that's what Billie kept telling herself.

She'd burst into tears as she was about to get in the car and realised she'd nearly forgotten the Cointreau for the Golden Dream cocktail they always had, a drink that had apparently been a favourite of her grandmother Carol.

Nathan had caught her hand. 'Hey,' he'd said pulling her

against his chest. He wrapped his arms around her in the kind of bear hug that pushed the worries and even Lola's unsettled noises into the background. 'We'll get there soon enough and no one will mind if we're a few minutes late.'

It was what she needed to pull herself together.

The house on Wattlebury Court was already overflowing with people when they arrived. Mum had meant it when she'd promised to invite all the family. At least there was enough of a crowd that the 'friend with nowhere to go' excuse about Donna's presence wouldn't be questioned. Billie settled Lola with one of her dad's sisters and directed Nathan to unload the presents under the Christmas tree inside.

She kissed Mum's cheek and nodded to Donna, who was of course right by Mum's side.

'Is Zach here?' Billie asked. If Donna didn't plan on sticking around she might be deliberately making sure her son didn't get too involved with the family.

'It's so sad,' Mum said. 'He's come down with a tummy upset.'

A chill washed over Billie as Donna nodded confirmation.

'We've always celebrated on Christmas Eve so we've had our time together last night but I've promised him I won't be gone long and he has a phone to call me,' Donna explained. 'He didn't want me to miss my first Christmas with Amanda.'

'What terrible timing.'

Or convenient for Donna if she wanted to keep her son from the rest of the family as much as possible.

But Mum was talking again. 'Just to warn you, Donna and I have started a little project down the far end of the house so there's only one bathroom. Be considerate of others.'

'Together?' Billie looked between the two of them.

'Donna's had a fair bit of renovation experience and she's giving me the confidence to try things I never would have taken on by myself.'

So whatever this was had come from Donna, Billie guessed. Unable to help her curiosity, she peered down the hallway towards the tiny corner room that had once been Megan's before she headed back outside. A tarp taped across the opening prevented her seeing anything of what Mum and Donna had been doing for their little project other than a few tins of paint and wallpaper glue.

Outside, two huge tables had been set out on the deck that took up half the backyard, and the sizzling smell of roasting meat drifted from the barbecues. Nathan had come over before dawn to put the meat on like a kind of carnivorous Santa, so it would be cooked on time.

Tim and Nathan seemed to greet each other like usual. Maybe she'd misjudged what she'd seen in the hospital. Side by side the brothers-in-law went about the important business of carving the meat that would be kept warm while the guests ate the prawn cocktail starters. Anyone who didn't eat seafood could gorge themselves on the array of nibbles on the tables.

When Billie went to put some soft drinks in the outdoor fridge, her little sister physically blocked her path.

'There's no room,' Eve said. She waved at a sign stuck on the fridge door: '*FULL! KEEP OUT!*'

Billie kissed her cheek. 'Um, Merry Christmas?'

Eve grinned and gave her a quick hug. 'That too. I was up half the night putting the finishing touches on the dessert and I don't want it spoiled before the big reveal.'

'Which will be streamed live on your socials I'm guessing?'

'Got it in one. I'll make a social media queen out of you yet.'

'Who is she?' came a scratchy, weathered voice from behind Billie.

She turned and looked down into the shrewd eyes of Barbara Jones, her dad's mother. Granny B was a hard woman to evade but Billie had a ready excuse. 'Old friend of Mum's,' she said, already moving away. 'Better go and help with the prawns.'

She looked back to see Barbara looking at her. It was strange to imagine her as one of the eight at the notorious dinner party from hell when she was just Gran to Billie.

'Oh, Billie,' Donna said as she entered. 'Would you be a dear and serve these?' She pointed to the prawn cocktails.

She hesitated just long enough to assure herself she wasn't taking Donna's orders. Usually, it was Billie who helped Mum in the kitchen at Christmas. 'Sure.'

I know there's a second blanket, she tried to say with her narrowed eyes.

But Donna wasn't even looking.

Balancing the small crystal bowls Billie was struggling at the door when Mum stepped up beside her. 'Let me,' she said reaching out for the handle.

As Billie went to pass her, Mum stopped her with a hand on her shoulder. 'I'm sorry I missed the gingerbread and the carols. There was a clash and it couldn't be helped. I'll make it up to you and little Lola next year, I promise.'

Billie recognised the regret in her mum's voice and forced a nod. 'Next year,' she agreed.

Outside, the appearance of food had drawn people to

the table where they talked so loudly, they drowned out the Christmas carols.

Nathan caught her hand when she placed his dish in front of him. 'Thanks.' Then he pulled her down for the quickest of kisses. 'Better get close while I can.'

She made a gagging sound. 'Because there will be no kissing after you eat that.'

His playfulness lightened some of the dread that had been lurking in her belly since they'd arrived.

With Donna and Mum bringing the last of the entrées, Billie grabbed Lola's pureed sweet potato and trailed them outside. The day was heating up, but the large outdoor fan overhead kept the air moving and thankfully the flies weren't out in force.

Billie readied Lola for her lunch as Mum rose to her feet and tapped a glass to get everyone's attention. The conversations stopped, guests looked around and Christmas crackers were put on the table until everyone was looking her way.

She cleared her throat.

'I'm so grateful you could all be here today. It's been a big few weeks with the anniversaries, Christmas and the upcoming ball, which I'm thrilled to be able to announce is close to selling out. The foundation should exceed our fundraising goal for this year, allowing us to help more families than ever before.' Scattered applause followed the announcement. Mum waited for it to finish then continued, 'But what most of you don't know is this has been a more momentous time than I could have imagined.'

Billie tried to catch her eye, all too aware of Donna sitting at Mum's right hand. It couldn't be, could it? Is this what she'd intended all along by inviting everyone here?

Don't do this.

But Mum's shining gaze didn't look Billie's way. 'I have something to tell you all, something I'd begun to fear I'd never be able to say but I am so, so glad that I finally can.' She took a deep breath. 'Family and friends, I would like—' Her voice caught. 'I would like you to meet my sister.'

A collective gasp sucked the oxygen from the air around them. Billie's head swam as Donna took Mum's hand and stood at her side, smiling like they'd all gathered just for her.

Mum lifted Donna's hand aloft, a prize fighter exulting in victory. 'Everyone, this is Megan.'

'*How?*'

'*What?*'

'*It couldn't be, could it?*'

Mum picked up a piece of paper and spoke over the murmurs of wonder and excitement. 'The DNA results arrived last week, proving that this woman, who I introduced some of you to as Donna, is in fact related to me by blood. She is Megan Callaghan.'

Billie tried to make sense of what she was hearing. Proof? Mum had proof and she hadn't told them?

No wonder she'd relented and looked at getting Pop out of the home, no wonder she'd fudged and avoided conversations about the progress of the DNA results. Her mum had proof. Donna was Megan.

Donna was telling the truth.

Billie felt Nathan's hand on hers. She glanced his way. *You okay?* he mouthed.

She nodded. She'd been sure the science would back up her gut instinct, sure Donna was a fraud. And still, the niggle that something wasn't right wouldn't go away.

Mum raised her hands and the shocked conversations quietened. 'There's a lot to talk about and I know everyone will want to get to know the guest of honour, but I have a huge favour to ask.' Her gaze swept the table, taking in everyone seated around it. 'I need a week. A week of silence and confidentiality. I've trusted all of you to be here today, because you all have shared my pain these long years. However, I would like to make the official announcement at the charity ball.'

There were murmurs of agreement.

Looking around at all the happy faces, Billie squirmed. Why couldn't she be properly happy too?

But even as she thought it, even as she forced a smile onto her face, she knew why. The memory of Mum from those other times when she'd believed she'd found Megan. Even now, she didn't dare let herself trust Donna's intentions even if she was related. Maybe it was the strange house, the gaps in Donna's story, or the hints of animosity she seemed to reserve only for Billie.

Tim leaned across the table to Nathan. 'A week should give you time to get the big cheque ready, don't you think?'

Nathan had snuck a mouthful of prawn and this caught in his throat at the sudden onslaught of attention.

'What cheque?' he managed after a sip of water.

'From the money held in trust by the foundation, I guess,' Billie said, but she was wondering why Tim looked so amused. 'The reward. I guess she's found... herself.'

'That's not really how it was intended though, was it?' Nathan asked. 'It's more if someone else provided a lead. Like for the case where that missing student was found and they were able to distribute the reward. It's an ethical point.'

'It's not like it's your cash,' Tim said. 'Not the time to go all scrooge on us, bro.' He waved at the decorations. 'It's Christmas.'

Nathan grunted.

Billie patted his knee under the table. She appreciated his support on fearing Donna was only after the money, but he was taking it a bit far.

Before she could quell the line of conversation Mum called down the table to Nathan. 'Megan and I have talked about the reward and of course she has no intention of claiming it. We'd like to donate it on behalf of the family back to the foundation. I understand with the public holidays that the money might not clear by the ball but we can do a cheque and presentation?'

He nodded curtly. 'That shouldn't be a problem.'

Everyone else accepted his reply at face value, but Billie heard strain in his voice.

Conversation turned to how Donna had come to be there, and with her captive audience she told a shortened version of her story. A shadow man, a woman who couldn't have children and some newspaper cuttings in a safe box.

'Amazing,' Grandad Larry muttered when she finished. 'Somehow everyone was looking in the wrong place all this time.'

Granny B glared at her husband. 'It's a miracle.'

'A Christmas miracle,' Mum agreed, missing the undercurrents. She raised her glass in a toast. 'To family.'

'To family,' everyone echoed.

'We need a photo,' said Aunty Rach.

Mum's face glowed as she jumped to her feet. 'Great idea. Me and my girls.'

Donna beckoned to Billie. '*Refuse*,' said her expression. '*I dare you.*'

Billie couldn't miss the look or the gesture. She knew the picture would show three dark-haired women, with long faces and hazel eyes and then blonde Eve. Being part of the trend that made Donna blend into the family made her wish she'd dyed her hair red for Christmas. Billie rose, walked over and stood next to the woman everyone else believed was Megan Callaghan. She tried not to flinch as Donna's arm slid over her shoulder, pulling her in tight.

'Smile.'

THAT NIGHT

9.34 p.m. – Trish

We're laughing. All of us drawn together around the coffee table. The only light the orange lamp that Ken loves so much that I dare not tell him I picked it up cheap. Glasses are full of red or white wine, oh and don't forget fucking Gloria with the deep, dark brown of the fancy port I noticed she didn't offer any of to me.

Like I even want any.

I don't remember what the joke was or if I found it funny but everyone else seems to be finding it hilarious so I keep my smile in place, manage after another sip of wine to force a chuckle.

I meet her gaze, then. Carol's sitting just across from me, perched on the arm of Ken's beloved leather couch, her swing dress ridden up to reveal a long lean thigh. Her hand is touching her husband's leg. They are so ridiculously in love – it would be nauseating if it wasn't so sweet. And there's laughter in her brown eyes, and I think that maybe those eyes I could get lost in are laughing at me. That I'm so obviously faking this, and she sees it and she's amused, and suddenly it is actually funny.

Barb wipes tears from her eyes as Ken moves to the record player and selects something – that grin I know so well on his face. He's playing at something; this man loves nothing more than a game. As long as he wins.

Since the money started rolling in he thinks he's goddamn untouchable. Sometimes after they come around to do business – he tries to tell me it's a private dentist call – I lie awake imagining what we'd do if someone found out. Whether anyone would believe I didn't know.

They say love is blind, well, so is infatuation because I never thought for a second...

I push it out of my head in case one of our guests sees something on my face. Luckily my mam taught me to take care of myself and I'm already building a safety net.

The music starts. It's some old Sixties classic blaring from the huge speakers Ken was so damn proud of when he brought them home. He turns the knob and now it's so loud the baseline vibrates in my chest.

Ken is still on his feet and he does this little groove. A move that should look ridiculous with his belly wobbling and stumpy legs, but the man has so much confidence it's sexy.

He holds out a hand. 'Dance?'

But he's not asking me.

20

Christmas lunch was probably as delicious as every other year, but for Billie it might as well have been made from the paper she'd wrapped the presents in. All she could think about was the announcement of a DNA match. She'd been so sure Donna was hiding something.

The only interruption was when Eve did the big reveal of her dessert when she couldn't help but 'oooh' along with everyone else. Only Tim didn't seem impressed by the chocolate mint ice-cream combination, rolling his eyes out of his wife's sight.

'Since when did you know how to make cake like that?' Billie asked Eve later as they carried dishes in from the table and began loading the dishwasher.

'Actually, Donna gave me the link for this amazing site then she helped with some of the chocolate work. She was happy to be useful, said making all those birthday cakes for Zach was good for something.'

Billie tried to keep her smile in place. It seemed Donna was taking her place in her little sister's life as well as her mum's.

Eve reached out and touched Billie's earlobe and the diamond earrings Nathan had given her that morning. 'These are nice.'

'Aren't they though?'

'Expensive, too, I'm guessing.'

That's what Billie had said when she'd unwrapped them. She hadn't meant to sound ungrateful but with her on maternity leave at reduced pay she couldn't help wondering where the money was coming from.

'It's the thought that counts,' she said lightly. 'Anyway, on the subject of husbands, is everything okay with you and Tim?'

Eve's normally open features shuttered. 'It's fine.'

Billie blinked, trying to get her head around the bitterness in Eve's tone. She'd thought sister and brother-in-law had the perfect life, the perfect marriage. 'Are you guys going through a rough time?' Billie asked. 'Is that why he bailed early on the boys' night the other night?'

'Early?' Eve scoffed. 'He stumbled in around dawn.'

It had been a couple of weeks ago; maybe Billie had misunderstood what Nathan said.

The rest of lunch clean-up and the handing out of gifts passed in a blur. Billie had been tasked with getting Zach's gift but since he wasn't there she'd given the joke chemistry T-shirt to Donna to pass along.

Mum had copied the photo of her, her mother and baby Megan onto a canvas and Billie seemed to be the only one unmoved at Donna's tears.

She busied herself with cleaning up and packing away the paper and ribbon left on the floor around the tree as everyone else retreated outside. Billie was the practical one in the family. She never got caught up in flights of fancy. As a child Eve would dawdle in a park distracted by a butterfly, but Billie worried about running late.

And now here she was, still wondering about Donna despite her being confirmed as part of the family.

Crouched on her mother's living room floor, hands full of bright paper, with the sounds of the dwindling festivities trickling in from outside, she blinked back tears.

Why couldn't she just be happy?

Nathan's tanned arms slid around her waist from behind. 'Were you in here worrying?'

'How could you guess?'

He kissed the tip of her nose. 'Because that's what you do. Although I would have thought the science would have convinced you. Should I hold off on clearing the reward? Your mum is pretty keen to present the money at the ball.'

Her stomach tightened. The formal affair would be full of media attention and after that there would be no going back. 'Is there any way around it?'

His head tilted. 'You still don't believe?'

She closed her eyes. 'It's not the science, but her motives. I want to believe she means well, and at the beginning she seemed decent but when Mum's not around there are flashes of... I don't know, antagonism. And the house looks unlived in, and Zach said they weren't hanging around long. It doesn't add up. And why isn't he here?'

'Because he's sick?'

'Or because she wants to keep him at a distance. He wasn't supposed to be here with her and she lied about how long she's been in town and her work.'

He gave her a long look.

'Maybe I'm just imagining things because I'm tired and she is doing all the things with Mum I used to do.'

'You looked after your mum; that's not a bad thing.'

She raised her eyebrows. He'd told her often enough she wasn't responsible for making up for what her mum had lost.

'Even if she is Megan, what does she want with all of us, with Mum?'

'I can try and delay,' he offered.

'Thanks.' She sighed and held up a handful of wrapping paper in pieces to show Nathan. 'I reckon Max and Matilda shredded some of this when no one was looking.'

He chuckled and for just a moment all the unease between them vanished. He drew an imaginary line down the middle of the room and winked. 'Last one to finish has to change Lola's nappy.'

'Does she need a change?'

Nathan was already attacking his half of the room. 'You know she will soon enough.'

That was enough to move her into gear. She grabbed at paper and ribbons and labels and soon only had under the couch to go. She knelt to reach underneath.

'Nice view,' came Nathan's analysis from behind her.

She smirked and waggled her butt. 'If you're looking, you're not cleaning.'

She pulled out one last bit of paper that had been stuck to the underside of the couch. 'I'm done,' she announced.

'No.' Nathan pretended to collapse in horror. Then asked, 'What have you got there?'

She looked down at what she'd thought was wrapping paper. 'It's one of the newspaper cuttings about Megan's disappearance that Donna brought that first day and tipped out onto the table. One from Janette Novak's collection. It must have fallen.'

Dated early 1980 and reporting no new leads in the case, the cutting should have been on thin, flimsy paper of the age, probably turning brown.

Nathan peered over her shoulder. 'That is *not* from an old newspaper.'

'But does it mean anything?' She turned the white piece of paper over in her hands. 'Maybe Janette got a copy recently.'

'Or maybe, as you suspected, Donna's lying to everyone and she googled the case and made a print-out a month ago.'

Billie studied Nathan's face. 'You think she's suspicious, too?'

'I think you'll never rest easy until you know for sure. Until you've ticked off the things that are bothering you. What do you have so far, apart from feeling jealous?'

'Pop said there was more than one blanket. She lied about how long she's been here, the place looks like they could walk out the door at any second. And she said she worked at the children's hospital since she arrived in town, but Zach mentioned she had another workplace.'

He didn't look impressed. 'Why bother to lie about that?'

'I wondered the same thing. There has to be more to it. Maybe I could try to find out where she worked before?'

He nodded. 'It's a start. What's your plan?'

EPISODE 07: NEIGHBOURHOOD FRIENDS?

Music playing: 'Girls Talk' – Dave Edmunds

The music fades.

Ruby:
Welcome to 'The Callaghan Baby Podcast'. I'm Ruby Costa and this is Episode Seven. Along with my team, I've been investigating the forty-year-old cold case of missing Megan Callaghan.

Visiting the house and walking the neighbourhood changed the way I watched and listened to the inquest files. Particularly given Trish Williams still resides on Wattlebury Court. This is Kate Emmett speaking to Trish at the 2005 inquest.

Kate Emmett:
The dinner party was on a Sunday, but usually you gathered on a Saturday night. Is that correct, Mrs Williams?

Trish:
It's Taylor now, Trish Taylor. Since Ken died, I've returned to my maiden name.

We were married twenty years, not that it mattered in the end. When death looked him in the eye, he forgot about the years I stood at his side.

And yes.

Kate:

I understand there was some legal dispute over Ken's estate?

Trish:

He didn't want a bar of the kids from his first marriage when we were together, then the bastard left them everything when he died. I had to borrow to buy them out of the house. If I hadn't squirrelled some money away I'd have been homeless.

Kate:

You're saying Ken didn't like children. Is that why the dinner party was adults only? Was that Ken's idea?

Trish:

It certainly wasn't my idea. None of it was. Don't get me wrong, I enjoyed entertaining, but I didn't plan the evening. He'd bumped into a neighbour while he was doing the mowing and they'd gotten to talking. Ken would have been offering our place for that particular evening before the other guy had finished his sentence. We took turns every few weeks for the more formal parties but this one was last minute.

Kate:

I understand you were well known in the neighbourhood for putting on events.

Ruby:
Trish's smile is tight-lipped and when she eventually speaks there's bitterness.

Trish:
The alternative to having guests was spending time alone together in that huge house. And that wasn't enough for Ken. How would anyone know he'd gotten successful enough to have a trophy wife if he didn't put her on display?

Kate:
Is that how you felt then? Were you two unhappy?

Trish:
If you'd asked back then, I might have said so. He was only cruel if I did something he didn't like. He hated women wearing pants. Thought smoking was unladylike. Had to have his meals served on time. That sort of thing.

Kate:
In interviews in the aftermath of Megan Callaghan's disappearance, Ken is on record as saying you two were happily married. 'Besotted' is the word I think he used.

Trish:
Ken liked to say a lot of things.

Kate:
Was he lying?

Trish:

Not exactly. Look, that summer we were practically newlyweds. I was young and incredibly naïve. He was older and successful, and he'd promised to give me everything I'd ever wanted. I didn't have a lot growing up and he treated me like a princess at first, with presents of jewellery and dresses. Taking me out to shows and fancy dinners. He promised to devote his life to making me happy.

Kate:

You mentioned that Ken had children from his first marriage. Was keeping his distance from them part of his attempts to keep you happy?

Trish:

The opposite. I was twenty-five, not twelve. The estrangement was all on Ken. He wanted a lifestyle incompatible with 'rug rats' as he called them.

Kate:

Excuse me for approaching a delicate subject but is that why you had the abortions?

Ruby:

Watching the recordings it's clear how painful the topic is for Trish Taylor. Her face drains of colour, but then she collects herself and her eyes narrow.

Trish:

I discovered I was pregnant the first time in November 1979. I had my suspicions and the doctor confirmed it.

Having a baby wasn't in our plans but I was thrilled; maybe it was spending all our time with those family types in the neighbourhood.

Stupid, stupid me thought Ken's objection was to children in general. Not to mine.

Giddy with pregnancy hormones I told him after handing him a beer one night. He blinked, pulled out his wallet and gave me a number scrawled on a piece of paper. 'They'll help you get rid of it,' he said. Then he took a swig of his beer, turned on the TV and asked me what we were having for dinner. Bastard.

Kate:
You did as he told you? You got rid of the baby?

Trish:
Eventually. After I cried and tried all I could think of trying to change his mind. He told me if I had it, I'd be having it on my own. I'm not proud I caved to his demands and I've lived with regret ever since.

And yes, before you ask, it happened again a year later.

Kate:
How did you feel about Carol having a baby right around that time? It must have been hard seeing her with a newborn. And then you were expected to entertain her and the others?

Trish:
If you're trying to suggest I somehow snuck out of my house, that I might add was filled with people, and went

over there and did something to that baby out of some twisted jealousy then you're barking mad.

Some part of me still thought if I could just make Ken love me enough, he'd change his mind. I barely had a moment to myself that night, not even a bathroom break until eleven. Ask anyone.

Ruby:

Although the four couples at the dinner party that night appeared to be firm friends during the initial investigation, the further away we get from that night, the more cracks have begun to appear in their relationships. It makes you wonder, when hearing this change, what else they all are hiding.

This becomes clearer when I speak to Gloria Marsh about her new, young neighbour.

You two didn't get along?

Gloria Marsh:

There was always a veneer to her. Something superficial. We got along but only in the same way she pretended to get along with everyone. Like all of those young girls, she loved to throw herself at older men. You know they say she was an airline hostess? Well, I heard that she and Ken met when she was a hostess of a different kind. Working at one of those gentlemen's clubs.

Ruby:

She whispers the last part with all the excitement of someone sharing a scurrilous titbit of gossip.

We asked Trish about this rumour.

Trish:
Who told you?

Ruby:
Trish puts her hand up to stop any reply.

Trish:
Don't bother, it could have been any of them. Judgemental witches. All of them were, except Carol. You know, she's the only one who ever spoke about it with me directly. The others never had the nerve.

I remember she asked me straight out over a cup of coffee, asked how and when I met Ken. The *when* mattered too because Ken's ex had been spreading the rumour I was some sort of homewrecker. I told Carol how I'd worked part-time at a bar where the outfits showed some skin but the drinks were expensive. We had to look pretty and smile nicely, but the bouncers escorted us to our cars afterwards.

Ruby:
Trish pauses to suck down on a cigarette like the plane's going down and an oxygen mask has fallen from the ceiling.

Trish:
Ken had seen me at the club but he made his move when he saw me working on a flight Adelaide to Melbourne on one of my first shifts. I'd thought I was moving up in the

world, leaving the bar life behind. Just before landing he convinced me to give him my number. I didn't know he'd just left his wife.

Ruby:
It must have made it hard for you to fit in with those suburban housewives. You were more than a decade younger than them and without children of your own.

Trish:
They were Ken's friends and eventually, some of them, would become mine. None of the Callaghan family deserved what happened to them. It broke her... broke Carol.

Ruby:
Trish swallows hard, wipes a hint of a tear from her eye.

Trish:
But she couldn't be helped.

Ruby:
During the inquest, Kate Emmett examined each of the neighbourhood group's alibis rigorously. They were together all evening, apart from the checks on the children by the men. There were a couple of brief bathroom breaks from Gloria and Barb but neither long enough for the women to get over to number eight.

And Amanda Callaghan can confirm that Megan was alive at that check around ten p.m.

The police were stuck.

Please join us next time on 'The Callaghan Baby Podcast'. If anyone listening knows anything that could assist in making this podcast, please contact me on investigation@thecallaghanfoundation.com. If you know something that could help the police, please contact them.

Thank you for listening.

21

Friday December 27th

Sliding down in the front seat of her car so she could see the staff exit of the children's hospital without being seen, Billie waited. A quick glance confirmed Donna's blue hatchback remained in the far corner of the car park. Her shift should have finished a few minutes ago.

The hospital doors swished open.

Two women and a man exited, their happy chatter about work being over carrying across to where Billie watched, one window slightly open. None of them Donna.

This was not how she thought she'd be spending the day, two days after Christmas.

Lola whimpered and Billie reached back with one arm to rock the capsule. 'Hush now, Lola-bug,' she whispered. The movement did the trick and Lola quieted, until Billie stopped to look at the doors. She reached back to rock her again and pain shot through her shoulder. She flushed, thankful there was nobody around to witness her getting in a tangle.

'You're right,' she murmured. 'Mummy has no idea what she's doing.'

Movement from the hospital doors caught her eye. Her hand still on Lola, she squinted as the sun reflected off the glass. This woman was Donna. She'd know that stride anywhere. And that voice.

Donna was on the phone and a straining Billie caught a familiar name, 'Thanks, Eve.'

Billie remained frozen, heart thudding so loud she feared it would give her away as Donna waved cheerily goodbye to one of her co-workers and then got in her car and drove off, still talking to Eve.

Billie could breathe again but she couldn't help wondering what Donna was talking to her sister about now. It seemed Donna was getting close to everyone but Billie.

Although she longed to jump out of the car, race in there and get her task over, she waited for her cue. If she screwed up and Mum found out, she'd have made everything worse.

At last, the message arrived from Nathan. He was at Mum's where they'd guessed Donna would go after work. *'The eagle has landed.'*

He really was taking this detective stuff to heart. *'Hilarious,'* she replied.

Time to go in.

Getting Lola out of the car and putting her in the sling gave Billie an immediate task. Helped prevent her thinking too much, but too soon she was standing in reception and the young man was looking up from his screen and asking, 'How may I help you?'

'D-donna. Donna Novak,' she stammered.

He nodded and pressed something on the tablet in front of him. 'Sorry, there's no one of that name registered as a patient here.'

'She, ah, works here.'

His lips pursed. 'We're not in the habit of sharing information.'

'Could you just—'

'No.'

Her plan disintegrated before her eyes. 'Please, it's really important.'

He looked past her. 'Next?'

Unconsciously bouncing Lola, who'd picked up on her dismay and begun to grizzle, Billie stepped aside. Her shoulders slumped.

Head down and brain scrambling for a new plan, she headed outside only to collide with the ample chest of an older woman.

'Sorry,' Billie said.

The woman smiled, showing hot-pink lipstick on yellow-stained teeth. 'No worries, love.' She had a cloud around her of mint, tobacco and cheap perfume, so strong it made Billie's eyes water.

As Billie took in the nurse's uniform, she realised she was speaking to one of Donna's colleagues. 'Excuse me, do you know Donna Novak?'

The woman's smile widened. 'I certainly do, but I'm afraid you've just missed her.'

'How unfortunate.' Billie took half a step away then turned back as though struck with an idea. 'Maybe you can help me.'

The woman's thinly drawn eyebrows lifted.

The explanation Billie had prepared tumbled out. 'My son, Harry, was in here a few weeks ago and Donna was wonderful. I wanted to put her forward for a local hero award, but I need a few details to fill in the form.'

Holding her breath, she waited. Her efforts of wearing a

fake nose stud with extreme makeup and disguising Lola by putting her in a blue onesie didn't seem like enough for the woman not to report who she was to Donna. Any moment this woman would point and cry, '*Fake.*' But if Billie was right, Donna had worked somewhere else in Adelaide before here and had decided to keep that fact a secret. Finding out where it was might tell her the reason.

A grin split the woman's face. 'What a wonderful gesture. Follow me.'

The woman started walking and was already inside when it sunk in that she'd believed Billie's story.

She hurried to catch up, trailing the woman – who introduced herself as Maureen – to a staffroom, ignoring the glare of 'Mr Rules and Regulations' at the desk. There, she accepted a coffee that tasted like dirty water.

'What do you need?' Maureen asked.

'I have her name and the date but that's really all. Is there a specific name for the ward?'

'Was it north or south?'

Billie didn't have to fake her confusion. 'It was all so dramatic at the time I've completely lost my bearings.' She pointed vaguely. 'Maybe that way.'

Maureen nodded understandingly. 'Probably the Woodlands Ward. It's where most of the littlies end up after emergency.'

'Great.'

'Don't you need to write that down?'

Billie fumbled for the notepad and pen and scrawled down the information. 'And how long has Donna been working here?'

'A few weeks, although she's fit right in with the staff. I can introduce you to our boss if you like?'

More people to report her visit to Donna? No thanks.

'I'm sure you can give me everything I need,' she said. 'Do you know anything about her as a person?'

Maureen frowned. 'We're busy here while on shift. There's not much time to chat about life outside of work.'

It seemed Donna had been as cagey in her workplace as she'd been with Billie.

However, Maureen's face brightened when Billie asked, 'Do you know where Donna worked before?'

'*That* I do know,' she said. 'She mentioned she worked as an agency temp for Restwell.'

The name struck Billie like a slap.

Restwell.

The name of the aged care facility where Pop had been a resident these last few years. It couldn't be a coincidence. She managed to keep her excitement hidden for long enough to thank Maureen and escape the staffroom. 'Don't forget to keep it quiet,' Billie said in farewell. 'I want it to be a surprise.' Rather than messaging Nathan, she used some makeup wipes to clean her face and headed around to her mum's place.

'What are you doing here?' he demanded from up on the ladder.

She looked towards the house.

He shook his head. 'Don't worry about them. Your mum and Donna are knee-deep in old photo albums, being all secretive about their renovation project. Donna brought samples with her and they disappeared to discuss them in private. Oh, and Zach is apparently still unwell,' he added. Since she'd pointed it out, he'd noticed how Donna was keeping her son away from the rest of the family.

'Donna worked at Restwell,' Billie announced. When he

looked blank, she added, 'Pop is at Restwell. That can't be a coincidence.'

'So, she's what, stolen some of his DNA somehow? Is that why she was a match?'

It sounded even more unlikely coming from his mouth than it had in her head. 'I don't know. She could have gotten information from him, or about him, at the least, and she had the test kit overnight.'

'You should have gone there and asked around.'

She'd been tempted. 'I thought Mum and Donna might be heading around there. Doesn't she want to meet her dad?'

He frowned. 'Yeah, that's a bit odd.'

'What's odd?' The question came from the now-open door where her mother stood. 'Apart from you distracting my favourite worker?'

'I came to see you. Thought you and Donna might be going to see Pop and I didn't want to overwhelm him with too many visitors in one day.'

Mum folded her arms. 'The nurses said he wasn't well today and we've decided it could stress him too much. We have plenty to do here.'

'Nathan said something about your renovation. I know you hate those steel shutters but what else are you planning?'

Mum smiled. 'It's a surprise. For now it's for Donna and me to know. I'll visit Dad tomorrow while Donna's at work.'

'She's not going?' Billie grit her teeth, trying to stay calm. Mum wasn't usually so evasive; this delay must be coming from Donna. 'He deserves to know his daughter is alive. You need to tell him. Why are you worried about her going there?' Billie studied her mother's features and tried to imagine what was going through her mind. Probably not what Billie was thinking – that Donna didn't want to see Pop because she feared he'd figure out her story didn't match the truth or that someone at Restwell would recognise her. 'Do you think some nurse will guess who Donna is and give it away to the media?'

'That, too.'

'There's more than one reason?'

'Although I might not be happy with some of his choices that night, talking to Donna has helped me realise that I need to let go of the past so I can move on. She wants to meet him after I've made my peace with him.'

'How caring of her.'

Mum's arms folded. 'I don't like your tone, I thought you'd be pleased.'

Billie bit back a childish comeback. Mum usually listened to her but lately only Donna's opinion on anything mattered.

Since Donna's arrival the lifetime of it being her, Mum and Eve against the world had suddenly ended, and Billie didn't know whether she belonged at all.

She took a calming breath and tried for conciliatory instead. 'I'm glad you're going to see him. I think he's missed the company. He's been down and confused and the nurse said he's losing weight.'

Mum's face softened. 'You're a good girl going to visit him.'

Later that afternoon, Billie pressed the screen of her phone to call her sister and continued walking, pushing the pram while Plank loped obediently at her side. Hopefully, she'd be able to hear Eve over Lola's cries. Hopefully, Eve wouldn't be able to tell that Billie herself had broken down crying just minutes ago, dragging dog and baby outside lest she lose her mind completely.

'I'm baking for my socials,' Eve said when she answered. 'I don't have time to listen to you complain about Donna.'

'That's not why I rang,' she insisted, although it maybe had been. Eve was starting to show irritation any time Billie suggested Donna might be fake or that her intentions might be less than noble. She'd thought about telling Eve what she'd learned at the hospital but then she'd have to explain that she'd gone there in disguise. And her trip to visit Pop had yielded nothing thanks to him being asleep and no nurses able to answer her questions about whether Donna had worked there.

'Lola's fussy,' she said quickly as her sister gave a long-suffering sigh, a certain prelude to her hanging up.

'Get outside with her; put on some music. It will pass.'

Getting advice from Eve always felt a little like the world was upside down but Billie couldn't deny Eve had taken to motherhood like Billie had to algebra in eighth grade. 'I am outside, but it's not helping.' What she couldn't say was how much it made her long to be back in the office, where she had some control.

Eve laughed. 'Yep.'

'That's all you have to say?'

'Yep.'

'Twins are supposed to be harder than one, but you didn't have a crying baby all the time.'

There was the sound of the oven door opening before Eve replied. 'You're kidding, aren't you? They were bloody awful, bless them. Tim's mum was such a help, God rest her soul. I don't think we'd have survived that first year without her.'

Alice had died a year ago and Billie knew Eve had been

devastated. 'But you always had everything under control when I offered to help.'

'Because Alice practically lived with us until Max and Matilda were two.' Eve paused. 'And, not to be a bitch, but what were you going to do?'

As Plank stopped to sniff a clump of daisies struggling to grow in a crack in the pavement, Billie thought back to that time. Deep in the throes of building up the company with Pop, she wouldn't have recognised what a struggling mother looked like. 'I changed nappies when I was there and I babysat. Remember that time you guys went out for your anniversary?'

'You did and I appreciated it, but you really had no idea.'

'I guess I didn't.'

'Well,' Eve said, 'now you know. Hang in there and if you get desperate come here.'

'Thanks.'

Billie ended the call, her step a little lighter. At least, despite Donna, Billie still had a sister she could count on.

THAT NIGHT

9.37 p.m. – Barb

'*Dance?*'

Ken's single-word question snakes across the air between us, slithering, dripping with poison as he holds out a hand to me.

No.

The answer vibrates through me, begging for release. To be screamed so that it would shatter the glass of the fancy imported wine bottle he was just showing Larry.

My darling Larry who, bless him, is bobbing along with the music, each movement half a beat out of time. He catches my eye, gives an encouraging smile. 'Go on, love,' he whispers, slurring the words together, eyes out of focus. 'Don't be shy.'

Oh, Larry, if you only knew.

'Remember, we once danced to this back in the day?' Ken taunts, his gaze swinging from me to Larry, the threat hardly subtle. Wanting to remind everyone we have history.

I feel Trish's gaze and wonder, sweating anew, how much he's told her and more importantly whether she'll tell Larry. Given everything with the bank and the credit cards, he's already struggling. Like last week, buying some stupid new lawnmower to keep up with Ray's.

My fingers twist the top button of my blouse. The one chosen because Larry mentioned he liked the pattern in the catalogue. Spoiled by Gloria's not-so-innocent observation of having seen our ancient neighbour, Mildred, in one just like it when we arrived.

I stand. My skirt has ridden up. Stuck to the rounded flesh of my thighs in the heat. The sweat from the heat and the wine like glue on fabric, leaving nothing to the imagination. Each dimple revealed for eyes hungry for ammunition for weaponed tongues.

'Love to.' The lie falls easily from my lips and I wonder when the little girl who sat front pew in church learned the ways of the devil so well. I've had to since – in this case – the devil, who could ruin everything, lives just next door.

I stop, close enough to touch, and I don't fight when he pulls me against him.

Ken's hand when it takes mine is dry, and I know he feels the dampness on my palm. I see his eyes crinkle at the corners. Nothing he loves more than a game.

The heavy pulse of the music is excuse enough to hold me close. 'Remember how this feels?' he whispers so his hot breath tickles my ear.

The bare skin on my throat burns, but I don't give him the satisfaction of answering.

Larry is still smiling along with everyone else, but his eyes are bloodshot and uncertain. He's drained his glass of wine without his gaze leaving me and Ken, moving on the shag rug in perfect sync. He knows there's something happening here; he just doesn't know what.

Ken's smirking. He jerks his head at Trish. 'Dance with Larry.'

Of course, she does as she's told.

And when Larry, encouraged by Ken's hands on me, lets his hands wander across younger, firmer hips than mine, I laugh along.

We're all having such a good time.

22

Sunday December 29th

'What's with the huge box?' Billie asked as she entered the kitchen a couple of days after her call with Eve. She'd just been out walking the neighbourhood again, Plank in tow, to get Lola to nap.

Home from having ducked into his office to deal with some finance emergency despite the holidays, Nathan leaned against the kitchen bench, eyes glued to his phone screen, which was showing live cricket. 'Lola's Christmas present.'

She moved closer to read the side. 'Natural timber cubby house. Why do we have this?'

Nathan frowned but didn't look up. 'I wanted to get her something special for her first Christmas.'

'Didn't we give her the books, the ornament and the rocking horse? I distinctly remember because I wrapped them.'

'We did give her that stuff.'

'You didn't think to mention we also bought her what looks like an expensive play house when she can't even crawl?'

He folded his arms across his chest. 'Do you want to monitor my spending now? Tell me what I can and can't buy my daughter for Christmas?'

She went to speak but nothing came out. And while she was trying to come up with something, he was walking away.

'That's not what I meant,' she said to his back. 'Where are you going?'

Lola woke and began fussing, her little cheeks going red. A feeling Billie understood all too well.

'I was getting my bank statement,' he spat over his shoulder. 'Thought you might want to look through it, see if there's anything more you want to tell me off about.'

'Wow, that's mature.' She got Lola out of the pram and held her close, bouncing her up and down to try to calm her while feeling anything but calm herself.

Plank circled between them, head down at the tension between his people.

She thought Nathan was going to leave it like that, but he spun to face her and planted both feet. 'I don't like being treated as an idiot.'

'And I don't like you spending so much money without talking to me about it first.'

'I don't question what you spend.'

She sighed; she didn't want to argue but her being on maternity leave put pressure on everything.

'Maybe I should go back to work early?' Just saying it aloud brought a kind of lightness to her heart that she hadn't felt in ages. 'Not full time or anything, but it might help.'

He shook his head. 'We're fine, just let it go, will you?'

'But—'

'God, Billie, Lola's crying. Maybe you should worry more about that and less about what I'm doing.' He headed to the bedroom, slamming the door behind him. A moment later she heard the shower.

Billie stared at the spot he'd been, rocking Lola, long after he'd gone, long after Plank came and nosed her hand for a pat. But Nathan's words and the look of disgust on his face wouldn't fade. Her eyes stung and the world went blurry.

They were both tired thanks to Lola's night-time unrest but they'd never been so short with each other before.

Only Lola's hungry gumming of her knuckle got Billie moving.

Feeding and bathing Lola gave Billie an excuse to avoid Nathan, but the whole time she hoped he'd come and apologise.

He didn't. And she couldn't help but be aware of his movement through the house, shutting doors harder than needed, grumbling over everything.

Hating the tension between them, she put Lola down for her sleep and went out to him but without a clue of what to say.

Seated at the table, Nathan shoved a hand through his hair, scowling over the laptop screen. He was so intent on it that he didn't notice Billie enter the room.

She stopped behind him but the figures on the screen meant nothing to her. 'What's all this about?'

He slammed the laptop closed. 'Je-sus you scared me. Your mum is fixated on presenting the money to the foundation at the ball.' He covered his face with his hands, the heels of his palms pressing into his eye sockets. 'I don't think I can hold her off. You need to find out what's going on with this chick, if you're so sure she has bad intentions.'

'I'm trying.'

'Well, the foundation ball is in like two days, and your mum is expecting a cheque for a hundred grand to be given out. That's a fuckload of money we're talking about. That isn't to be thrown away you know.'

She dropped her gaze, noticing she had apple and carrot smeared on her elbow. 'I know.'

'What if you tell your mum you've done another DNA test and it came back negative?'

'You want me to lie?'

He jumped to his feet, pushing the chair away with a loud scrape. 'You already went into the woman's work and pretended to be someone else. Don't look at me like that. What about asking your grandfather? Can you try to get more out of him? That podcast stuff is damning.'

She froze. As far as she knew he'd not listened to the podcast. 'Have you been doing your own research?'

'A bit.'

'Since when?'

'Can we lose the twenty questions already? First the money, now this.' His raised voice turned him into a stranger and something cold trickled down her spine. It took a moment for her to register the feeling because she didn't associate it with Nathan. *Fear.* She noticed Plank had put his solid body between them and her heart ached that even he sensed it.

'Why does this matter so much to you?'

'Because it matters to you.'

It hit her then, like a blow, that he was lying. 'I call bullshit. There's something more going on. You're not yourself and that tone...' She swallowed hard, her hand finding the top of Plank's head. 'You're scaring me.'

He exhaled the shaky breath of a man trying to keep his temper. 'Look, you're really pushing it. I've just...' His gaze scanned her face, dropped to the dog, and whatever he'd been about to say died on his tongue. 'You wouldn't understand.'

She moved closer to him, reached out and touched his chest, felt the rough beat of his heart. 'Try me.'

His eyes closed, shutting her out.

Her chest cramped. He'd been acting more and more strangely but she'd been so caught up in Donna and her mother's drama – like always – and she'd ignored it. First Donna kept Mum busy through their Christmas traditions and then gotten close to Eve and now, without even trying, the woman was coming between her and Nathan. 'Please, Nathan, whatever it is, whatever is going on, we can work something out.'

He shook free of her touch and stepped back. 'I've got to get out of here.' He grabbed his phone and keys and headed for the door.

'Nathan,' she cried. 'Wait.'

But he was gone.

EPISODE 08: AN ANONYMOUS TIP

Music playing: 'Lay Your Love On Me' – Racey

The music fades.

Detective Paul Lennard:
We hold out hope for finding Megan Callaghan safe and unharmed. However, there are grave fears for the welfare of the missing baby.

Ruby:
Welcome to Episode Eight. I'm Ruby Costa and this is 'The Callaghan Baby Podcast'. Along with my team, I've been investigating the forty-year-old cold case of missing Megan Callaghan.

You just heard a grab from detective Paul Lennard from a news segment.

Back in the late Seventies, Paul Lennard was a relatively young man. The kind of police officer who believed that if you worked hard enough you could solve any case. Retired now, he's agreed to be interviewed for the podcast.

I walk into the café where we have agreed to meet and he's waiting. He stands to greet me.

Café sounds – the murmur of people. The clink of coffee cups on saucers, the muffled call of an order to the kitchen.

I've spent so long researching this podcast I felt I knew what to expect, but rather than the thin, young man with a full head of dark brown hair wearing a crisp uniform, he's in plain clothes. His hair is shorter at the back and sides and a steely grey. His gut strains at the buttons of his plaid shirt. But the ruddy cheeks are the same and his eyes still burn with a fire for justice. There's an intensity to his stare that makes even thinking about lying impossible. A stare he perhaps hadn't quite mastered back in 1979.

There's the scrape of a chair being pulled out, murmured greetings.

Thanks for speaking to me, Paul. I think it's fair to say that some cases stick with you, the disappearance of Megan Callaghan being one such case?

Detective Paul Lennard:

I will never stop wanting to know what happened that night. One of the most important parts of detective work is to allow the evidence to lead you to a conclusion, but this was the exact opposite of the initial handling of the Callaghan case. Once Dominic Snave was removed as a suspect, we were able to investigate without bias; however, there still came a time when we'd exhausted all leads.

Ruby:

It was then, on the 14th of February, Valentine's Day 1980, that Paul received an anonymous tip.

Paul:

I greeted the caller at two minutes past nine. She spoke fast, high-pitched and shaking. I guessed at once that she was trying to disguise her voice, but it didn't matter. There was a familiarity to it, and I knew I'd already spoken to her in some capacity.

She said, 'You should check out the teacher at the primary school. Nancy Blair. She knows more than she's telling. Her car was seen near the house on the day Megan went missing.'

I asked for more details but she hung up.

It was after hours on Valentine's Day and my girlfriend expected me home, but I'd lost track of time. That's how I was: the only relationship I could commit to was the one with my badge.

With no leads and hope dwindling, those in charge couldn't keep everyone working full-time on the case, but I couldn't give up.

I tried to let the Callaghans know we had a lead but could only contact Carol, something to do with Frank being at a school function.

Although there was no definite information, the woman on the phone was convinced. Sometimes you have to trust your instinct. We went around to speak to the young primary school teacher.

It was there I learned that sometimes instincts are plain wrong.

Nancy welcomed us into her home and allowed us to examine her car in which we found nothing of interest.

She was the epitome of a woman with nothing to hide.

Other than the car, her only connection was as Amanda Callaghan's teacher. Rather than be offended, she wanted to help.

We apologised for wasting Ms Blair's time.

Ruby:

By the 2005 inquest into Megan's disappearance the tip-off caller's identity had been discovered. Paul was correct in thinking it was someone closely tied to the case. But we'll reveal more about that later.

Sadly, Nancy Blair died two years ago after a short battle with cancer, so we were unable to speak to her for this investigation. As Ms Blair lived in England, she was interviewed for the 2005 inquest using video conferencing. The picture is a glitchy, rudimentary one compared to today's high-definition standards; however, it served its purpose.

Kate Emmett:

Thank you for joining us. I know it's very early in the morning for you there.

Nancy:

I don't mind – I'm happy to help.

Ruby:

Nancy leans forward, her face filling the screen.

Nancy:

Where is everyone? I thought I'd be able to see the proceedings. Can they see me?

Kate:

It's late here and the coroner and I are the only people here along with tech help. If required, your testimony will be screened in court for the relevant witness.

Ruby:

Nancy's frown deepens. She was a young and vibrant twenty-two years old back in 1979. She was Amanda Callaghan's teacher both that year and the following.

She's forty-eight in the video and still has the same long hair as she did back then but the brown has blonde highlights and new expertly cut layers allow it to frame her face. She's wearing a black fitted dress but the striking geometric-print knit cardigan over the top hints at the teacher Amanda Callaghan remembers so fondly.

Amanda:

It's no understatement to say that Ms Blair was the best teacher I could have had in that time. I'm pretty sure they don't hand out a manual when you leave teacher's college on how to deal with a student whose baby sister disappears.

When I couldn't, and later *wouldn't* talk, she gave me space and love and time. She understood.

I only went back to school because I had Ms Blair for a teacher. I'd had her the year before and she always decorated her classroom with a theme. When I walked into the class the first day after Megan went missing, it was through a barn door and into a stable. I don't think it's a coincidence she'd loaned me her copy of *Black Beauty.*

Ruby:
What is it about Nancy Blair that you remember most?

Amanda:
Mostly that she cared, but also how she dressed. Always bright colours, with block shapes and repeating patterns, whether it be scarves, jackets or even shoes. Most of the teachers were a variation on beige and she was a walking rainbow.

Ruby:
At the inquest, the lack of an audience for the video conference seems to bewilder Nancy. She's asked twice to speak by counsel Kate Emmett before she answers.

Nancy:
I taught at Ridgefield Primary School, a relatively new school literally up the road from Wattlebury Court. We heard about what happened quickly. I think it had filtered through to the staffroom by lunchtime. We were all shocked, but I worried about Amanda the most.

I visited the house and offered my help but there wasn't anything I could do. Carol was too upset to chat but Frank let me know how much he appreciated me stopping by. I made a point of requesting Amanda for my class the following year. I thought she'd benefit from some continuity.

Kate:
Did you get along well with the family?

Nancy:

I did. Amanda's parents were both supportive of her learning. Her father attended one of the children's drama evenings when Carol was in the hospital for Megan's birth. It was rare back then to have such an involved father.

And then, after everything happened, he stepped up for Amanda. It was he who was there for her parent–teacher interviews and her school events. He was a wonderful and dedicated father. If more of my students' parents were like him, it would be a better world.

Kate:

You were questioned by the police in February of 1980 after a tip-off from the public. Is that correct?

Nancy:

I cooperated as best I could. We all wanted answers about what happened to Megan. Amanda was my main concern, but my heart went out to that whole family.

Kate:

Why did you leave the area at the end of the 1980 school year? I understand Ridgefield Primary School were most sorry to lose you so abruptly.

Nancy:

I wouldn't call it abrupt. I'd been looking elsewhere for some time. That school was a great starting point for my career, but I'd always planned to move on.

Kate:
Do you know who made the tip-off to the police?

Nancy:
I figured it was a parent at the school who was upset by the extra time I spent with Amanda and her family. People will get offended by anything they can. I stand by the work I did with her out of hours and how she healed over that year. I would do it again in a heartbeat.

Kate:
What if I told you the call is understood to have been made by Carol Callaghan?

Ruby:
In the footage from the video conference you can see, despite its graininess, the moment Kate's revelation reaches the speakers where Nancy is sitting. Her eyes widen and she knocks over her glass of water.

There's a pause to clean up and by the time she answers she seems to have gotten her head around this revelation.

Nancy:
I can't understand why she would have thought I was involved. I always believed the Callaghans were grateful for my work with Amanda. Frank thanked me personally. Times were different then; we were part of the community and we all pitched in. In fact, they sent me a card when I left that I still treasure all these years later for its kind sentiment.

Kate:
Can you shed any light on why Carol might have thought you were involved with her daughter's disappearance?

Nancy:
Sorry, I have no idea.

Ruby:
It seemed police had reached another dead end.

Please join us next time on 'The Callaghan Baby Podcast'. If anyone listening knows anything that could assist in making this podcast, please contact me on investigation@thecallaghanfoundation.com. If you know something that could help the police, please contact them.

Thank you for listening.

23

Hours later, with Nathan still not home, Billie called Eve.

'Is something wrong?' Eve asked. 'It's not like you to call so late.'

Billie hadn't realised the time. Unwilling to mention her fight with Nathan, she resorted to the other topic of her relentless thoughts. 'I've listened to the podcast again and there's no such person as the Shadow Man that Donna talks about, who supposedly gave her to Janette Novak.' She had a thought. 'Unless it was actually Pop? But that doesn't make any sense.'

'This is about Donna.' Eve's annoyance was unmistakable.

'I've studied all the persons of interest in the case and not one of them fits. And there couldn't be someone completely new, not after all these years.'

Eve's exhalation sounded like it came through gritted teeth. 'There's a DNA test. Mum's happy. Why are you doing this?'

'She must have done something to it somehow; she had it overnight.'

'You were there. And you did Pop's sample.'

'Nothing is perfect. If there's a one-in-a-million chance of it being wrong then there is still that chance.'

'Can you hear yourself?' Eve asked. 'Maybe she's right

and you do have some sort of vendetta against her. I want to defend you given how hard it can be with a new baby but...'

Billie's stomach flipped. They'd been talking about her. She took a deep breath and tried to sound rational. 'I'm worried about her motives, what she wants from all this. Her story doesn't make sense. Mum is vulnerable to—'

'The science proves she's Megan,' Eve said cutting her off. 'Go to bed.'

Billie let Eve end the call but she couldn't do as she'd suggested.

There had to be an answer – Billie just needed to see it. In her head she heard an echo of Pop back when she started at the company. 'Once we know what we know, we're halfway to knowing what we don't.' Some twist on Confucius he'd heard as a lad on a building site. When she'd been none the wiser, he'd grinned and said, 'Make a list.'

So many of the statistics around the case lived in her head like she'd been born knowing them. Like that less than one per cent of missing children are kidnapped by strangers, with the majority, runaways, being impossible in this case. However, it meant whoever took Megan was most likely someone known.

Systematically, she went through people interviewed at the inquest and more recently for the podcast. With so many of the parties involved still in contact there were few possibilities. One by one she wrote down what she knew of each name from the neighbour Mildred to the high school friend Heather. Until she got to Nancy Blair. The young teacher who'd been interviewed by police but quickly discarded as a suspect, but who'd left the area afterwards. A woman about the age Janette Novak would have been.

She skipped through the relevant sections in the podcast, finding nothing until the description from the inquest of her wearing a 'striking geometric-print knit cardigan' and then Mum recounting her memory of Nancy loving 'bright colours, with block shapes and repeating patterns'.

The canvas in the hallway at Donna's home. The woman's face had been hidden but that gorgeous knit that little Zach had snuggled into was definitely bright. And patterned.

Lots of woman wear those styles.

Then there was Nancy being interviewed from her home in England, a place Donna had said that first day she'd lived for some time, and she still had the accent to prove it.

Although she was only investigated through a tip-off to the police and then quickly dismissed, she had left the area within a year of Megan's disappearance and she'd be about the right age.

Billie's pulse leapt with excitement. She brought up the picture of Donna and Janette Novak from the fair that she'd found that first day of searching. Janette's face was hidden by large sunglasses and a broad-brimmed hat and her hand was up to shield her face from the sun, but there again obvious despite the picture quality, that love for geometric print.

There were no online photos of Nancy Blair. There were notes that she'd attended the inquest via video link but the actual footage wasn't available.

However, Billie knew someone who would have it.

Ruby Costa had seen the recordings. Had she kept copies of the tapes? Would she share them with Billie, and did it matter when she had so little to match with? Only a remembered canvas print and a grainy newspaper picture, neither of which showed the woman's face.

Billie's eyes watered from too long staring at the screen and she stretched her arms over her head to ease the tightness in her shoulders. Then she reached down to pat Plank who'd curled up at her feet. The research had taken her mind off Nathan, but now she couldn't ignore his absence. Where was he?

A cry from the nursery broke Billie's train of thought. She waited a few seconds, hoping Lola would self-settle. She'd been fed and changed, had been rubbing her little eyes with exhaustion.

The volume increased, playing in stereo on the baby monitor.

Heaving herself upright Billie rubbed her own eyes, sticky with too many nights lacking sleep, and approached the little room they'd decorated so excitedly before Billie could have imagined just how hard a new baby could be.

She took a second on the threshold of the tiny nursery and exhaled hard. An article she'd read suggested babies could pick up on their carer's tension. If that was true, one touch from Billie right now and Lola would never settle again. Calmer, she crossed to the cot.

'Hush, now, Lola-love,' Billie said in her most soothing tone. 'Go back to sleep.'

Lola screwed up her features and let out a howl at a frequency that made Billie recoil. Her teeth ground together. Tears pricked her eyes.

Patting Lola she tried again. 'Shush, little baby. Sleepy time.'

Another wail and Billie picked her up. Too bad if the experts said not to – she couldn't stand the noise a second longer.

In her arms Lola began to quiet. Billie paced the nursery, humming low in her throat. Lola's eyes closed, her breathing grew deeper, more regular. Billie waited as long as she could, then slowly lowered her into the cot.

And the crying started again.

'Please,' she whispered, her voice breaking. 'Please sleep.' Billie could feel her own eyes stinging and blinked the tears away. She never imagined how many times she'd stand in the dark crying right along with her daughter.

Finally, Lola stayed asleep.

When Billie fell into bed it was nearly midnight. Alone, she lay in the dark, replaying everything Nathan and she had said, worrying about where he'd gone. The regular snuffling of Plank's heavy breathing from where he lay on guard near the bedroom door helped to soothe her racing thoughts.

Nathan crawled into bed long after midnight. 'Sorry for being a dick,' he said to her back.

She was still awake, but being awake and relieved he'd come home weren't the same as being ready to forgive. Holding herself stiff, she stared resolutely into the darkness.

He touched the hard line of her shoulder. 'I should have talked to you before I spent so much money. We've always discussed stuff like that. You were right.'

'Mark the calendar,' she said, allowing a hint of the smile on her face to creep into her tone.

'I am sorry.' He wriggled closer. 'I knew straight away I'd messed up but I felt really bad and that made me mad at myself. Which I took out on you. I got carried away.'

'Just talk to me next time.'

'I will, I promise. And I shouldn't have taken the stuff with your mum out on you. It's a lot of responsibility.'

She hadn't really thought of it like that. 'You can handle it though. Money is what you do; that's why the board voted for you to have the role.'

It didn't pay, but it was important, and he'd been honoured when Mum had endorsed him.

'Yeah,' he said. 'Thanks for giving me a chance to clear my head. Sorry it took so long.'

Her eyes were already closed and the warmth of his body against hers was the best kind of apology. He'd come home, and right then, that was enough.

24

Billie told Nathan her theory that Nancy Blair and Janette Novak could be the same person the next morning over breakfast.

He stopped, toast halfway to his mouth. 'Are you saying the teacher took her? But that would confirm Donna *was* Megan. Why would Janette Novak have concocted the Shadow Man story? Or if Donna knows, why lie?'

She'd wondered that, too, if she'd been doing all this only to prove Donna was Megan. At least then she'd know her mum was safe. Although Donna was a stranger who seemed to be taking Billie's place in the family.

'That's what I've been trying to work out. I think Ruby might be able to help, but I'd have to break my promise to Mum and tell her.'

'For your mum's good though. Doesn't the end justify the means?'

She was surprised at how easily that rolled off her husband's tongue. 'Maybe, but I didn't think she'd appreciate a call at dawn.' Billie yawned. Thanks to Lola, they'd already been up for hours.

'Don't wait. She's devoted months of her life to this podcast; she'll want to help.'

He had a point about Ruby's investment in the case, and she had offered help before. 'I'll message her.'

Ruby was up and she had plans to shop for a new dress for the foundation's ball that morning in the post-Christmas sales. They agreed to meet at a coffee shop in the city and Nathan volunteered to watch Lola.

By the time Billie walked into the small café Ruby was already there and had three bags with designer labels on the seat next to her.

Embracing her childhood playmate, Billie struggled to get her head around the slender young woman opposite being the same as the voice from the podcast. She looked more like a model with her olive skin, subtle makeup and short white summer dress.

'Tell me,' Ruby demanded before Billie had even sat. 'I knew there was something going on.'

'Can't a girl want to catch up with her old friend?'

'A catch-up?' Ruby scrunched her nose. 'Not when that girl's mother, who's usually on the phone daily about theories related to the podcast, has suddenly done her best impression of a ghost.'

Billie picked up a sugar packet and put it down. 'Christmas is a busy time.'

'It is. And I'll be seeing you at the ball, so what gives with the urgent meeting?'

'I didn't say it was urgent...' Billie stalled. In her head she'd been thinking about meeting the girl she'd played hide-and-seek with, and she'd forgotten this woman had grown into someone who'd won investigative journalism awards and who was almost as invested in this case as Amanda. If anything about Donna got out before the ball, Mum would never forgive her.

But the risk was worth it for the truth.

When the waiter had left with their order, everything came out of Billie's mouth in a rush. From Donna turning up, to Billie's doubts and the DNA test that seemed to be proof.

Ruby didn't interrupt once but her eyes widened. 'I can't believe Amanda didn't tell me.'

'I'm beginning to wonder why she hasn't.'

A deep frown line formed between Ruby's eyebrows. 'Megan alive… that might change everything. Why hasn't Amanda gone to the authorities?'

'She wants to make the announcement at the ball.'

'How does her story fit with what we found out about Frank?'

Ruby spoke about Billie's grandfather like he was a character in her story rather than a man who'd lived with the nightmare for forty years.

For the first time Billie really considered how biased Ruby might be. Whether she'd presented the facts to tell the story she wanted to tell, one that diverted attention from Jennifer Marsh.

But Billie kept the observation to herself – she needed Ruby's help. 'Donna has been vague on details. It's part of what makes me suspicious of her story,' she said instead.

The waiter delivered their drinks and Ruby drained her espresso in one go. 'Big night,' she admitted. 'Okay, so, what have you discovered that trumps a DNA test?'

'Not a lot,' Billie admitted. As Billie described the inconsistencies in Donna's story that had her concerned and then her investigative attempts so far, Ruby smothered laughter.

'As an investigative journalist, I'm guessing you make a damn fine businesswoman,' Ruby said when Billie was done.

'As a comedian, you're probably a pretty good journalist,' Billie retorted.

'Touché.'

Confider's remorse was already nagging at Billie's conscience. How far would Ruby go to control the narrative when any discovery of Megan being alive would reflect on her own work? 'This conversation is off the record, you understand?'

Amusement played on Ruby's lips. 'You know I'm neither a doctor nor a lawyer, don't you?'

'Promise.'

'I won't tell Amanda. Yet,' she added. 'But when this is done, however it turns out, I want this Donna's story in all of its messy detail for the podcast. Deal?'

'Deal.'

'Right. I assume you've listened to the podcast in full?'

'Yes, it was really good.'

'Thanks.' Ruby pulled out her glasses, put them on and leaned forward, suddenly businesslike. 'As far as your theory of Janette Novak being Nancy Blair, it isn't impossible. I can send you everything I have on Nancy Blair, but the files are all on my home computer. I'll check my other sources too.'

'I did an internet search.'

'And I bet there was somewhere between nothing and way too much information.' Ruby was sympathetic. 'I'll see what I can find on things like licences, credit cards and rental agreements in either of those names. I'll collate it and update you if, or when, I have something.'

'Sounds good.' With her business experience, Billie didn't usually feel like such a novice – unless you counted parenting – but she could only be impressed by Ruby's approach. And this was just a quick conversation; she was likely only seeing the barest hint of how she worked. Handing the load to someone capable felt a lot like relief, too.

Ruby's face lit up. 'Actually, something just came to me. There was something on Nancy Blair that didn't come up until after production for that episode was completed.'

'Something more?'

'Yes, it didn't seem to matter at the time but the school she was supposed to have transferred to contacted us. One of the office staff is quite a fan of the investigation and it turns out Nancy never took up the position.'

'She disappeared?'

'Yes. I did a cursory look, but it wasn't like Nancy vanished completely. She was at the inquest twenty-five years later.'

'She stayed on at Mum's school for the year after Megan disappeared.'

'While working full-time and living alone. I remember that much from the police report.'

Billie sighed.

Ruby shot her a sympathetic smile. 'The outcome of this might be nothing more than proving this Donna woman is everything she claims to be.'

'She's not.'

'That's my girl, keeping an open mind.'

Billie lingered for a moment before leaving.

Catching her eye, Ruby frowned. 'What are you thinking?'

'I'm afraid you're only helping me now because if Donna

actually is Megan then you might have to return all those awards and recognition they gave you for your hatchet job on Pop.'

'Hatchet job?'

Billie had listened to the podcast enough times to recognise Ruby's agenda. 'I know you wanted to protect your mum but you weren't there; you don't know what happened...' She swallowed hard.

Ruby looked away. 'I just want the truth.'

'Then that makes two of us.'

As she drove home a little while later, Billie didn't let Ruby's teasing bother her. She needed to make sure Donna wouldn't hurt Mum, sister or not.

Even if Donna was who she claimed it was becoming clear to Billie that she was intentionally forcing her to the outer. *Because she sensed Billie's scepticism or did she have a more sinister reason to keep the person who cared about Amanda Callaghan's welfare at a distance?*

By the time she'd driven the rest of the way home, fed Lola, and filled Nathan in on what had happened with Ruby, Billie already had three emails from her old friend, each with attachments including information on Nancy Blair.

The last email showed Ruby had kept to her word and begun her own search into the Nancy–Janette question.

Two items of interest. The first is that Janette Novak didn't seem to exist until she married Stefan in the early Eighties and that much at least fits with Donna's story. However, there's no clear evidence of what her maiden name might have been as we haven't yet been able to locate the wedding certificate.

The second is that Nancy did effectively disappear after she left Ridgefield. She was only contacted for the inquest via an old friend she had from teacher's college. Put simply, Nancy ceased to exist in terms of public record with the exception of the inquest, right when Janette Novak came onto the scene. It's hard to be certain but both of them also died of cancer at a similar time.

As she read the email again, aloud this time for Nathan's benefit, Billie couldn't hide her confusion. 'But even if Janette is Nancy, what does it mean? It seems impossible for Nancy to have taken Megan herself.'

'Are there pictures?' Nathan asked.

She'd opened the attachments, looking for a photo. There, that was it. She brought up the grainy picture of Janette Novak and the scanned class photo that included Nancy Blair and arranged them side by side on the screen.

The stir of Nathan's breath on her neck told her he'd moved to look over her shoulder.

She resized first one and then the other, zooming in on the women's faces. 'It's impossible to tell.'

'But not impossible that they're the same person.'

He returned to whatever he'd been doing on his laptop and she settled in to read over all the documents. She was nearly an hour in – wow police records were boring – when she spotted it. A detail that she'd forgotten from the podcast.

'It was Valentine's Day.'

Nathan looked up and frowned. 'What was?'

'The tip-off about Nancy. It was made on February the fourteenth, Valentine's Day.'

'You've lost me.'

She tried not to roll her eyes. This was what got men in trouble. 'An anonymous call was made to the police on that date only a couple of months after Megan went missing. The caller suggested that Nancy Blair should be investigated. The caller turned out to be my grandmother, Carol. As Carol searched for Megan she left everything else to Pop. Like teacher interviews, school events, pickups and sports days. All these things would have brought Frank into direct contact with the young and attractive Nancy Blair. Wait.'

With the ease of someone who'd listened to the podcast often, Billie quickly found Nancy's testimony from the inquest. 'She describes Pop as a wonderful man and you can practically hear the longing in her voice. Says more than once he thanked her personally when she went around to the house, which sounds like more than a wave at the school gate.'

Comprehension dawned on Nathan's face. 'You think Carol was jealous?'

'It would fit with her calling in the tip on Valentine's Day. Remember the detective couldn't contact Pop to tell him about the possible lead because he'd been at a school function? It was nine p.m. That's pretty late to have lingered at a primary school.'

She looked at the picture Ruby had sent again. It looked familiar somehow, and then it hit her. When she'd been going through all Pop's things looking for Plank's Christmas collar there had been some old school magazines.

Leaving Nathan frowning after her, she dashed out to the garage. Having looked through everything only days ago she found the stack quickly. And there, third from the top was the 1980 magazine, spiral-bound by thick yellow card on fading paper. Kneeling on the cement, she flicked through, aware of Nathan having followed her and now looking on.

And there it was, pictures of a parents and teachers 'get to know you' event from February. A much younger Pop standing with Nancy Blair, who was wearing that print she loved. They stood close, seemingly unaware of the camera. And when Billie used her phone to snap and enlarge the picture, Nancy's fingers were entwined intimately with Pop's.

Her stomach lurched like it was her own husband she'd found holding another woman's hand.

'That looks very friendly to me.' Billie brandished the phone at Nathan. 'This was early evening but he wasn't home at nine. Maybe Carol thought they had stayed on together. What if this call, on a day for romantics, was made because of pure womanly suspicion?'

'She'd caught them?'

'I don't know. Frank might have been careless, or Nancy deliberately let something slip to tell Carol she was taking her man. From the podcast it sounds like things could get pretty wild back in the day.'

'So, Carol drops Nancy in it with the police?'

'Precisely.'

'Then she leaves town. It fits but what does any of it mean for Donna?'

'I don't know. Yet. But I need to find out whether Nancy Blair was having an affair with Pop.'

25

'Oh, my, hasn't Lola grown? Can I have a cuddle?' asked Granny B.

'Of course,' Billie said.

Mostly, when she was with her grandmother, she saw the woman who'd been front row at every school event, but today, she couldn't shake the knowledge that to the rest of the world she was Barbara Jones, one of the neighbourhood group who'd left her children home alone the night Megan Callaghan disappeared.

'Granny B,' she began. 'Can I ask you something?'

'If it's about *that* night there's nothing much more to say, I'm afraid. Larry and I already told the inquest everything,' replied her grandmother without looking up.

'How did you know?'

Granny B flashed her a smile. 'You sound all nervous and that woman has appeared claiming to be your Aunt Megan. Had to be. Unless you and Nathan are having problems.' Her face fell. 'He did seem a bit distracted at Christmas.'

'We're good,' she said quickly. 'You said "claimed" about Donna. Do you think she's a fake?'

'It's not my place to decide, my darling.' She placed Lola down on the mat and faced Billie.

'But what about the DNA test?'

'I'm an old lady, what do I know about science? They're always so sure they're right until they're proved wrong. Does the rest of this interrogation require a cup of tea? Because I could sure use one.'

At home in her grandmother's kitchen, Billie added leaves to the ancient pot, boiled the water and then filled it to steep. Placing pot and cups on the small table, she settled on the couch next to her grandmother. She steeled herself. 'How were my other grandparents after Megan went missing?'

'Distraught, obviously.'

'I mean, how were they as a couple? In the podcast they said everything changed.'

Granny B poured them each a cup of tea. 'Something happening like that, well... They didn't blame each other but it was hard going. All Carol cared about was finding Megan, understandably. Anything of herself she had left over from that she gave to your mother. And Frank... I think he understood the change in Carol's priorities. He wanted to find Megan, too.'

'Was he lonely?'

Granny B sipped her tea. 'It's not hard to imagine he might have felt he also lost his wife that night.'

'Did it make him angry?'

'Not your grandfather. More sad and stoic. Worked harder, drank more, grieved in socially acceptable ways for men. The way he took over care for young Amanda showed he was about as forward-thinking as any man from that generation could be, but that didn't mean he was ready to sit and chat about his feelings.'

Billie tried to sound casual, aware of the photo of

Nancy and Pop from the school magazine on her phone. 'Looking after Mum must have taken him to her school a lot.'

Granny B nodded and her gaze sharpened. 'Aye, it did.'

'And that teacher, Nancy, she was pretty interested in Mum and the case, wasn't she? So interested that Carol tipped off the police to investigate her.'

'Aye. That's what they say. Carol had a lot going on back then. I'm not sure she was really thinking straight. The police never found any connection. If you're asking me if I think she took Megan then, no I don't think so.'

Billie placed her tea on the table and took a deep breath. 'I'm asking if Pop had an affair with her.'

Gran placed her cup on the table, her easy manner vanishing to be replaced by a wariness, as though Billie was an animal that could unexpectedly strike. 'That's a big question. Why do you think that?'

'A few reasons.' Her gran's closed demeanour had her faltering. What had been a theory at home, had become an accusation of someone she knew Granny B counted as a friend. 'At the inquest Nancy was gushing about how much time Pop spent at the school like she was a fangirl. How she personally thanked him, how he was such a wonderful man.' Billie couldn't help but have an imitation of Nancy Blair's simper in her tone. 'Then there was the tip-off on Valentine's Day that came out of nowhere, unless you think of it as a jealous woman's actions.'

Granny B didn't say anything.

'This is forty years ago. I'm not a little kid anymore.'

'You'll always be the little girl who sat on my knee – you know that.'

Everything in Billie wanted not to push. A lifetime of being her grandmother's good girl at war with the threat she felt from Donna to her mum, to her family.

Billie pulled out her phone, a bit fumbly in her haste, and pulled up the picture. 'This looks pretty friendly to me.'

Gran barely looked at it, but her lips pursed in that way she had when she didn't approve of something. 'You're not going to let this go?'

This was it: Billie could feel it. 'Please, when are you all going to realise that secrets fester? I only want the truth.'

Gran's hands tightened on the teacup, then she sighed, a sound of defeat. 'I guess you're old enough to hear the truth. Yes, there was a relationship. That young woman took advantage of his loneliness.'

'He was the one who was married.'

'Aye, he was. But Carol wasn't much of a partner in those days. It doesn't excuse him, of course it doesn't, but it's not our place to judge.'

Except that from her tone, Granny B was clearly judging Nancy. Billie's throat ached for both her grandparents. She couldn't hate her grandfather, but she could hurt for all of them. 'Did my grandmother know?'

Granny B shrugged. 'I'm thinking she suspected, thus the call. And I would imagine the whole thing was over in a matter of months.'

The revelation showed Pop's devotion to her as she was growing up in a new light. She and Eve had been the only girls in their school who were picked up several days a week by their grandfather and he'd always had unending patience with them. 'I couldn't have asked for a better grandfather.'

Granny B smiled. 'Don't let Larry hear you say that. Mind you, after all these years I'm quite aware that Grandad isn't a perfect specimen. Your little family, and – most importantly – your own growth and happiness should be your focus, not some long-ago dalliances.'

'I'm not mad at him,' Billie said. 'Although Mum probably would be.'

'Well, she and Frank were always so close. She's not always the most logical when it comes to all this.'

'I know,' Billie replied. 'Believe me, I know.'

'Well, I'm glad we had this little chat and I hope you're old enough to understand and not judge too harshly. Please, don't press me more on the subject. It's not something Larry and I like to talk about. Larry might have been with Frank that night, but he really did no more than hover in the hallway. Better to leave the past in the past.'

'Did you know the men were high that night?'

Granny B nodded, her mouth grim. 'You've probably heard this before but it was a different time. We were practically different people and it wasn't dangerous then like it is today, just a bit of fun. Some experimentation. He swore to me he'd never do it again.'

'And you forgave him?'

'I love him. Besides, none of us are saints and we all have our secrets. It was a long time ago.'

How Billie was sick of hearing what she was beginning to think was just an excuse for behaving badly. But in the slightly lifted chin and faraway look in Gran's eyes, she saw a glimpse of the woman who'd kept secrets for forty years and had no intentions of being guilted into revealing them now.

In that moment she wasn't Gran, she was Barbara Jones,

attendee at the dinner party from hell. Then she shrugged. 'Best you ask Frank anything else you want to know.'

'I'm not sure he's up to answering any questions.'

'Then perhaps that tells everyone whether or not they need to be asked.' Her grandmother shook her head. 'Leave it. Let the poor man end his days in peace.'

THAT NIGHT

9.59 p.m. – Trish

With my guests all occupied, with their drinks and a few with each other, I dare to take a moment out of sight ducking into the hallway. Breathing in and out, I lean against the wall. All the wine and the smoke and the pretending makes the whole night feel like a bad dream.

The wallpaper is rough against my back, even through the material of my jumpsuit. The print on the paper is hand-pressed and florid. Imported, because nothing local is good enough for Ken.

There, with the hall light seeming to spin above me, it strikes me I'm imported, too. It's how my husband likes things. Exotic, newer and better than those belonging to his friends.

Let's not forget unencumbered.

Not for him, needing to leave the party to make sure some tiny human is sleeping in their bed. That isn't part of the new life he's planned so carefully, so it's not part of mine.

Get rid of it.

Standing there, away from those people I'm never going to impress, eyes stinging, heart aching and aching and aching, I'm giggling at the prospect of Ken trading me in once I'm no longer new enough for his liking. More because it's inevitable, than because it's ridiculous, when I feel the man's bulk filling the hallway.

Someone's turned the music up. The languorous beat loud enough to cover all kinds of sins.

'Waiting for me,' Ray says, low enough that he knows it won't carry. It's not a question, and I know he probably believes that I have been. Because men like him do.

And I'm thinking of the wines that relaxed me leaving me introspective, and the food that was too rich and the smoke that's filled my senses and the confidence I stupidly felt that I could read each of these lame, suburban men. All the moments have compounded to put me here alone in a hallway with a man I should not have underestimated.

A dozen tiny mistakes.

The kind that women learn fast not to make if they want to survive in a man's world, and I regret them all.

He's bigger than me and stronger, and so boringly used to getting what he wants in a neighbourhood like this one. A community that gives men like him a title and a position of power.

My gaze flicks to the door, but retreat to the bedroom isn't an option and he's blocking escape back to the party.

Too late, he's got his hands against the wall either side of me. Boxing me in. 'I've seen the way you look at me. Gagging for a real man.'

'No.' But I might as well not have said it, because he doesn't care. What I want doesn't come into this.

I'm already back against the wall. There's nowhere for me to go.

26

Empty chairs and open spaces filled the main activity room when Billie made her way through reception at Restwell, Lola on her hip. One end of the tinsel that had fluttered cheerfully across the ceiling now dangled on the floor and the carers on duty at the desk were strangers. She couldn't begrudge the usual staff time off for the festive season, but their replacements' impersonal greetings had her feeling down before she entered the secure wing.

On the drive over she'd tried calling Mum but there'd been no answer, typical since Donna came on the scene. Hard to believe only a few weeks ago Billie had been so busy struggling with Lola she'd had to force herself to keep up their regular chats; now the too familiar sound of her mum's voicemail message had her chest aching. She didn't leave a message.

Like Pop had absorbed the anti-festive feel of the centre, he was in bed and barely awake. Unlike her last visit where he'd slept comfortably, each breath sounded like a battle.

'Pop? Are you awake?'

He blinked, like he was struggling to focus. 'Amanda? Is that you?'

'It's okay. You rest,' she said, not wanting to upset him.

He pulled himself up to sitting, wresting the pillow until

she stepped in to help make him comfortable. His rheumy eyes focused on her and a smile bloomed across his face. 'Amanda, my love. It's so good to see you.'

She sat on the armchair next to the bed, Lola propped on her knee.

He held out his hand, a little shaky, and Lola reached for his finger. His eyes lit up when she managed to get a grip on the end.

'How are you feeling?' Billie asked.

'Another day, eh? Could be worse.' His voice was scratchy and worn but where his mouth trembled and his hand remained unsteady, his eyes shone with a bright warmth.

'Shall I get you a drink?'

He took a sip through the straw she offered. 'Thanks, love. Should have given up the fags years ago. Your mum always told me I'd be one of those stinky old men with a hacking cough. I'll get around to it one of these days.'

As far as Billie knew, he hadn't smoked since she was a baby. 'The sooner the better,' she said.

'You're a bit kinder than your mum. She threatened to kick me out of bed if I didn't quit.' He faltered. 'I should have listened to her. God, I miss her. Every day. I'm so sorry. So bloody sorry.'

'I'm sure what Gra-Mum did wasn't your fault,' Billie said. She choked out the comfort even though everything she'd learned in the last twenty-four hours made her unsure if it was true.

Pop's eyes shut and a single tear seeped out of one of the corners. 'There was so much pain. We should never have gone to that blasted party.'

'It was a different time.'

'It was a mistake.'

Was he talking about simply going to the dinner, what Ruby had found out in the podcast, Nancy or something else? Billie kissed the top of Lola's head. 'I'm not a child anymore.'

'You'll always be my little girl.'

Billie had listened to the podcast so many times now in bits and pieces that she thought she could probably recite parts from memory. Now she knew about Pop and Nancy it had a different complexion.

'The night before Mum died, did you tell her? Did you talk about Nancy?' The question came out before she could stop it.

He frowned. 'How do you know about... Oh never mind. It's not something I'm proud of but I'd come clean to her years before. On our last night together, it was you we talked about. Our greatest gift.' There was something in the way he said it, something that told her he wasn't being entirely honest. 'Megan was gone. Everything I did was for you.'

'Are you sure it wasn't about Nancy?'

'I'm sure. She was my mistake and what I did hurt everyone, but not a word about her crossed my lips after the day I confessed to your mother. I'll be forever grateful for that second chance.'

'I'm glad you didn't go anywhere.'

His face softened. 'Me too. Now, tell me how you're handling your little one. Is that young Jones boy pulling his weight? Nice kid. Always thought he was a flighty thing though, wouldn't have bred with Larry's genes either, but who am I to judge?' He added the last with a grin showing his teeth almost falling out. He and Larry had been good mates and liked to tease each other.

'Darren's a good dad.'

'He'd want to be a good husband too, or he'll have me to answer to. You make sure you enjoy this time with Billie Mae. She'll be grown with babies of her own before you know it. Look out for her.'

'I will.'

His face shadowed. 'They can leave in an instant.'

'You mean Megan? She was taken.'

He cleared his throat. 'Of course. I just hope I get to live long enough to know little Billie. Take her for walks, read with her and spoil her.'

Billie nodded, the threat of tears making speaking difficult. 'I'm sure you'll do all of that. And I'm sure she'll love every moment.'

He drifted off to sleep soon after and she left.

With Lola balanced on one hip, she called Ruby before the centre doors closed behind her.

'What did he say?' Ruby asked.

'They definitely had an affair.'

There was a long silence and then a sigh. 'I can't believe I didn't see it earlier. I let myself be swayed by the detectives dismissing Nancy Blair as a suspect. The Valentine's call should have tipped me off.'

'The whole thing is a tangle of lies and hidden agendas,' Billie said.

'But I should have seen this. You'll be taking my awards next,' Ruby joked.

'It doesn't help with knowing whether Donna is telling the truth.'

'No but I have some people who owe me a few favours trying to get a photo of Janette Novak that shows her face.

Circumstantially, it makes sense that she's Nancy Blair but so far there's no proof. I'm thinking she would most likely have continued working in schools in some capacity. Unfortunately, most old school magazines aren't online.'

'If we assume that they are the same woman, what does it mean for Megan and Donna? Is all this going to prove she took Megan and somehow kept her for a year?'

Ruby's silence was answer enough.

As Billie drove the rest of the way home to prepare for a ball where Donna would be revealed to the world as Megan Callaghan, she feared she was only beginning to uncover the secrets from the 'dinner party from hell'.

EPISODE 09: THE CREEP

Music playing: 'I Don't Like Mondays' – The Boomtown Rats

The music fades.

Ruby:
Welcome to Episode Nine. I'm Ruby Costa and this is 'The Callaghan Baby Podcast'. Along with my team, I've been investigating the forty-year-old cold case of missing Megan Callaghan.

The information regarding Nancy Blair was not the only tip-off concerning the case. It came to light during the inquest that a woman near Wattlebury Court reported seeing something unusual around the time Megan went missing. The woman's history as a known busybody and her vagueness on the details meant it was dismissed.

No one returned her call until we contacted her for this podcast. This is the first time what she knows about that fateful night will be revealed.

Sharon McNamara was forty-three in 1979 and a homemaker with two grown children and too much time on her hands. Now, she's in a nursing home but when we went in to speak to her we discovered a woman whose memory of that time is crystal clear. She comes out to greet us in a wheelchair, her hair in a voluminous do atop her head, and she's wearing fresh peach lipstick.

Coincidentally, she resides in the same home as Frank Callaghan; however, his dementia places him in the secure wing of the care facility and she says the two haven't crossed paths.

We settle down in an open area of the home on two floral couches and I ask Sharon to tell me about the tip-off and her reputation.

Sharon:

I admit that my call regarding the early hours of the 10th of December wasn't my first to the local police station. We were pretty much on Christmas card terms by then as I rang them so often.

There's a rattle of a passing tea tray.

Would you like a tea? Coffee? No? It's no café, but it's not too bad. The tea girls here are just a delight. And the boys. Can't be old-fashioned, now, can we? And all of the nurses too. Some of the best in the world, I think.

Anyway, what was I saying?

Ruby:

You saw something in the conservation park?

Sharon:

That's right. My house back then looked out over the face of the hill and I could see all the way to the top. There was a figure with a shovel striding along the ridge through the long grasses. He looked out of place.

Ruby:
He? Are you sure it was a man? Was he alone? Was there a vehicle?

Sharon:
The figure didn't look small enough to be a woman, but the hooded jacket masked their features such that I can't be sure, particularly with the distance involved. It was not cold enough for the jacket. I think that's what made me remember. We'd all sweated through the warmest night in months. I didn't see anyone else, or a vehicle.

Ruby:
Unfortunately, Sharon couldn't tell us any more details about what she saw in the conservation park but her never being questioned is another example of the haphazard method of this investigation. She had more to say but we'll hear that in a later episode.

Back to the persons of interest. There was a creepy presence around Wattlebury Court at the time of Megan's disappearance. Desperate to make progress, police widened their search and called everyone involved back in for more questioning. This included young neighbour Jennifer Marsh who was sixteen in 1979.

The notes from her initial interview mention that she seemed scared, but put it down to the intimidating atmosphere of a police station. However, when Jennifer returned to be interviewed, the detective in charge believed her discomfort to be at odds with how she was treated. In short, they believed Jennifer was acting suspiciously because she had something to hide.

Jennifer refused to speak to us for this investigation; however, she did give us a statement.

'All I have to say on the subject has been said at the inquest. The case of missing Megan Callaghan is a tragedy, but it has nothing to do with me.'

Although we can't ask Jennifer any questions on the record, we do have access to her testimony from the inquest. The media described her as a neat, attractive middle-aged woman. And also, as a reluctant witness. In several places she is described as pale, almost fearful, eyes darting around the room.

The inquest testimony of Heather Thompson, her best friend from when Megan disappeared, sheds some light on Jennifer's behaviour, but we'll get to that a little later.

As mentioned earlier, Jennifer is the daughter of Gloria and Ray from number three, Wattlebury Court. Both her parents attended the dinner party that night, leaving Jennifer home. She'd previously babysat Amanda Callaghan and was known to be close to Carol, who was younger than her own mother. Rather than be jealous, Jennifer's mother Gloria encouraged the relationship.

Gloria Marsh:

Of course, I encouraged the friendship. Jennifer wasn't talking to me much and I remember being just so relieved she was talking to someone.

I've been a high school history teacher a long time and I know the trouble teenagers can find themselves in. I know that sixteen-year-old girls don't always feel comfortable talking to their parents. Carol shared anything she thought I needed to know.

Amanda Callaghan:
I loved spending time with Jennifer. She never made me feel like a baby. But she'd often just come around to talk to Mum. I thought she was Mum's friend as much as Mrs Marsh was.

Ruby:
Earlier in the podcast we heard details of the night Megan disappeared, but what about what was happening in the Callaghan household before the fateful party?

Megan Callaghan was a sibling nearly a decade in the making and Carol had several miscarriages between her two children. However, Carol was a relaxed mother. It was the Seventies and for the young and upcoming in the suburbs there were still good times to be had and these didn't stop with having kids. Jennifer could often be found helping with Amanda and Megan, changing nappies while Carol relaxed with a smoke or an afternoon wine.

But not everyone was glad about Jennifer's visits. And it was this person who became someone of interest in the case.

In a previous episode, we examined Carol Callaghan's mental health following Megan's disappearance. We heard from her neighbour who found her after she took her own life. In interviews Carol was described as becoming increasingly anxious even before Megan went missing.

What or who was Carol Callaghan afraid of?

It came up in the inquest that Carol was seen in a heated argument with a young man before Megan disappeared.

Mildred Winthorpe:
I saw him out the front of the house on the corner at around five p.m. on Sunday the 2nd of December. I remember very well because it was before I went away. I was just about to have my dinner, a casserole that always fed me three nights, when a commotion outside caught my attention.

I went to my little window in the second bedroom and peered out. From there I could see that end of the street without being seen myself. It wasn't that I was nosy, you know, but as an older woman living alone, I needed to be alert to my surroundings.

There was a young man, with terrible long hair and he was yelling at Carol. Towering over her, he was, and all red in the face. She didn't back down though, and she followed him all the way to his car, warning him to stay away.

He kicked their letterbox so hard as he passed it that he left a small dent, one I believe is still there to this day. He got in his car, slammed the door and then drove away with his tyres squealing rubber, as the young folk say.

Kate:
You said he drove away. Did he come back? Did Carol appear frightened?

Mildred:
I saw the car often enough, hard to miss it, orange and black with the loudest engine I've ever heard, but not

again that day. Carol appeared irritated as she headed back inside. There was a van though, a burgundy panel van that didn't belong to anyone in the street.

Ruby:
It was Mildred Winthorpe's mention of this van that police tried to connect to the one owned by Mr Snave. However, they found no evidence linking it to Megan.

Kate:
Had you seen the young man who argued with Carol before, Mrs Winthorpe?

Mildred:
Yes, and the car. It was always in the street coming and going at all hours. One day it blocked my driveway but mostly it was parked near number three.

Ruby:
It turns out the car's owner, Scott Allen, was there so often to see Jennifer Marsh, the teenager from number three Wattlebury Court. And it's he who we examine in the next episode of 'The Callaghan Baby Podcast'. If anyone listening knows anything that could assist in making this podcast, please contact me on investigation@ thecallaghanfoundation.com. If you know something that could help the police, please contact them.

Thank you for listening.

27

Tuesday December 31st

'Help.'

It wasn't the first time Billie had answered a call from her little sister that started as such and she doubted it would be the last. 'What's wrong?' Even as she spoke to Eve, her mind was going over the list of things she needed to do to be ready for the ball that night.

'It's everywhere,' Eve said, her voice breaking. 'God, Billie, I've really fucked things up this time.'

That got her attention. 'What?'

Eve just sobbed.

'Start at the beginning,' Billie said.

Eve took a few ragged breaths. 'I accidentally posted a picture with Donna and Mum on my socials. A website picked it up and the headline says she's Megan.'

Billie scrambled to think. The situation wasn't great but... 'It's New Year's Eve and people probably have other stuff going on.'

'That's what I hoped too, but all the big news sites have picked it up. They have it on the morning TV banners. It comes up right after the latest reports on the fires.'

Hand shaking, Billie turned on the TV. Sometimes she forgot how big the case was nationally. Missing kids get people's attention, and the podcast's success had added fuel to the conversations. 'Where's the picture from?'

The silence stretched so long she thought Eve had hung up and when she finally answered it was in a very small voice. 'Does it matter?'

It did to Billie, but only because she couldn't help wanting to know how much time the three of them were spending together. At least Eve had called her, not the woman who seemed to be displacing Billie from her family.

'I guess not. You need to talk to Mum.'

'She's going to be mad.'

'Probably. Better to get it over with.'

'Thanks for all your help. Oh wait, you gave me none. I don't know why I even called.' Eve hung up.

Holding her phone so tight it hurt her hand, Billie exhaled hard. She knew why Eve had called. And she didn't know what annoyed her more – that her sister expected her to intercede with Mum or that Eve wouldn't even come out and actually ask her to do it.

'What's wrong?' Nathan asked.

She explained Eve's latest disaster.

'She'll be fine,' he said. 'Leave it.'

'Leave what?'

'You were about to call your mum for her. Smooth things over.'

She glanced down at her phone, noticing she'd pulled Mum's number up without even realising. Perhaps the biggest surprise was that she hadn't yet called.

He gently prised the phone from her hand.

'She'll be fine,' he repeated. 'She doesn't need you to do this for her, even if she thinks she does.'

A timely cry from Lola gave her something to do along with the realisation Mum hadn't been answering her calls lately anyway. Not calling pressed on her but she resisted and by the time she'd changed Lola's nappy the urge had passed.

'See,' Nathan said, his gaze fixed on some sports results. 'That wasn't so hard.'

Across the room her phone flashed, ringing silently thanks to her general paranoia about waking Lola. On it was a picture of Mum holding Lola, from before Donna had turned up, the lines on her brow showing her stress. An unavoidable thought struck Billie – she's happier now.

Billie grabbed at the phone.

'Have you seen what your sister has done?' Mum asked before Billie could speak.

'Is this about Donna?'

'Of course it is. We need to present a united front. At least the foundation ball is tonight. None of us will make any comment today. The whole debacle might actually work in our favour; I've already had extra media asking to attend. Media is publicity, and that can only be a good thing.'

Billie didn't have the heart to point out that wasn't always true considering how business had slowed thanks to the podcast revealing Pop had been high and lying about checking a child who'd then gone missing.

Billie made the right noises while Mum complained before the call was cut short. 'I have to go, sorry love. Donna's here.'

With the aim of avoiding the media altogether, she and Nathan stayed around the house for the afternoon. He had the TV on something sport-related and would mutter or swear at the referees every few minutes while staring at a laptop screen full of figures. Lola was happy in her swing so Billie tried to read a bestseller that she'd been given by her in-laws for Christmas. The novel wasn't a match for her permanent sleep deficit so when Lola went into her cot, she drifted off in a luxurious nap.

She woke at Lola's demand to be fed then settled into the rocking chair in the nursery to express for the night ahead. She was nearly finished the uncomfortable process when she heard Nathan get up to answer someone knocking at the door.

Tell them to go away.

But he didn't get her psychic message. 'Billie,' he called. 'Are you done?'

'Coming.' With the precious milk in one hand and Lola on her hip, she hurried out to see who Nathan hadn't been able to turn away. 'Oh, hi.'

Mum didn't smile. 'Hello.'

Donna stood next to her and they hadn't made it past the small entryway. Billie noticed Plank was outside. Her mum had never been a fan but she kind of hoped he'd been put out because he'd been able to sense Donna wasn't a friend.

'Come in,' Billie said, shooting a questioning frown at her husband who shrugged and returned to his computer screen. Was he so annoyed about the reward cheque that Mum and Donna were donating back to the foundation that he'd forgotten his manners? With no proof Donna wasn't Megan any hope of avoiding that outcome was gone. 'Would you like a tea or coffee?'

'A glass of water would be nice,' Donna said.

Right at the same time as Mum said, 'We're not staying long. The media are camped out at Wattlebury Court. I'm surprised they're not here, too.'

'We haven't forgotten, no talking to the media.'

'I need to make sure you're on board for tonight.'

Billie swallowed guilt. 'I can't wait.' She placed Lola back in the swing before moving around the bench to get Donna's glass of water. After handing over the glass, she leaned back against the bench. 'Is that all?'

'Eve said something about DNA tests not being one hundred per cent accurate. I want to know where she got that from.'

Hoping the heat rising in her throat wasn't making the outside red to match Billie scoffed. 'An internet search?'

At another pointed look from Donna, Mum continued, 'I don't think so. Do you?' Before Billie could reply, she continued, 'Did you go to Donna's work?'

Billie's stomach dropped to her feet. 'Why would I—'

'That's what I want to know.' Mum had her arms crossed. 'It's important that everyone is on the same page before tonight.'

'Everyone has your best interests at heart.'

Mum shook her head. 'Maybe some people prefer me unhappy. Maybe they're afraid I won't need them anymore.'

'I'm sure that's not it at all.' Billie met Mum's gaze although she knew part of her distrust of Donna was the way the newcomer had stepped so easily into the role of Mum's support person and become instant friends with Eve.

Some of Mum's gruffness disappeared. 'You might be ri—'

'Oops!'

Billie turned towards Donna as the glass she'd been holding fell from her fingers, striking the rug at her feet and sending water in every direction.

'I'm so sorry,' Donna said sweetly. 'At least the glass didn't break.'

'It could be worse,' Mum agreed.

Billie couldn't miss the perfect timing to stop any softening from Mum, but knew pointing it out would only make things worse. 'I'll get a towel.'

She took her time, trying to think of how she could explain the hospital visit if Mum pushed, how to smooth things over and make sure she didn't end up shut out completely. She was beginning to think that's exactly what Donna wanted, but why? Could it be more than just wanting to be first in her new sister's affections?

'What do I have to do?'

Billie didn't need to look to know who was standing in the laundry doorway behind her. It could only be Donna. Despite the others being just down the hall, her pulse spiked like an animal cornered. Hopefully, Donna couldn't sense it. 'I don't know what you mean.'

'I have the blanket, the birthmark and a DNA test that prove I'm Megan Callaghan. What more do you want?'

'Nothing.'

'It's only the two of us here now. No need to pretend. What I don't understand is, why are you so against me? The whole family have welcomed me home, but not you.'

Billie faced Donna, towel held against her chest, and raised her eyebrows. 'Welcome.'

'I have tried. Tried so hard to make ground with you but still you're there testing everything I say, trying to trick me and your poor mother. Now you've stooped to harassing me in my workplace. What have I done to deserve any of this?' The tone was pleading but her expression glinted with pure malice.

Billie stared her down. 'I don't know what you're talking about.'

'No.' Donna's lip curled but her tone was wounded. 'You don't know what *you're* talking about, and I'm the one suffering. Me and your mother. What lengths will you go to next?'

Confusion made Billie hesitate. Everything coming out of Donna's mouth sounded so sincere but her face... Her face was saying something else entirely.

'I want us to be close,' Donna continued. Her voice hitched, as emotion apparently overwhelmed her. 'Please, Billie, won't you give me a chance?'

Billie realised then, right as Donna's mouth curved into a smirk that there was a shadow behind her. They weren't alone after all. Her mother must have trailed Donna, and had probably heard every word. No wonder the tone didn't match the expression. She'd been performing for her audience.

Billie struggled to recall if she'd said anything that might upset Mum.

Too late, Mum stepped into view, her expression cold. 'I thought you were on my side, Billie, but it seems Donna... it seems Megan was right about your bad treatment of her.'

'I haven't treated her badly,' Billie insisted. While she'd been busy looking into Donna's story, Donna had been turning Mum against her. 'What am I supposed to have done?'

But Mum wasn't listening. 'If you can't support us in this then I'd prefer you didn't come tonight.'

Billie's chest cramped. 'What?'

'You heard what I said. I only want those who want to be part of my family going forward to be there tonight. What you do is up to you.'

Mum spun on her heel and strode away.

Donna flashed Billie a triumphant smile and followed.

A moment later the front door slammed shut and then Nathan appeared. 'They walked out with your mum in tears and that woman smiling like she'd won bloody lotto. What the hell just happened in here?'

Billie's eyes stung as she realised she'd been played. 'Mum just chose her fake sister over me.'

28

Billie couldn't miss the ball, but her fears that she wouldn't be able to look her mum in the eye and declare she believed Donna was Megan proved unnecessary. Standing there that night in the middle of the stunning ballroom, Mum walked past her as though she didn't exist.

Mum touched Ruby's arm. 'Excuse me, Ruby, could I speak to you in private for a moment?'

Ruby smiled. 'Of course.'

Without another glance at the group, Mum strode off towards the small stage where Ruby would soon be opening the gala event.

Ruby was a professional and had promised not to tell, but Billie couldn't help bracing for all her secrets and lies to blow up in her face. By coming when Mum had insisted only those who supported her with Donna should attend, she'd made a promise of sorts, one she wasn't sure she could keep.

Fairy lights glittered overhead and lavender centrepieces on each table were reminiscent of the foundation's logo taken from the wallpaper that had decorated Megan's nursery. Billie tried not to think how usually she'd have been the one to be with Mum when she had her meeting with the events people to plan the decorations and how she'd taken Donna with her instead.

'Relax, Ruby's got this,' Nathan said as he handed her a glass of bubbles.

Her gaze on the two women – Ruby was doing a good impression of being stunned by whatever it was that Mum was saying – Billie took a seat at Nathan's side. She sipped, only able to enjoy the sparkling wine when Mum and Ruby had moved apart.

'Careful, it will go straight to your head.'

At Nathan's warning she glanced down at her empty glass. 'I hope they bring out the food soon.'

'Not until after the big announcement,' Eve said, joining them at the table. Tim trailed behind her and the two of them made a stunning couple. Eve's silver dress with its plunging neckline was an eye-catching contrast to the navy velvet of Tim's dinner jacket.

Billie tugged at her own black dress, so tame in comparison, but her only option thanks to the stubborn baby kilos clinging to her frame. Mum not talking to her didn't help the feeling of being completely out of place.

As though she'd telegraphed her sudden insecurities Nathan leaned over and whispered, 'Have I mentioned how hot you look tonight?'

She mustered a smile. 'Not in the last five minutes.'

'Rookie mistake,' he declared. 'I'll do better.'

Listening to him she could almost forget his pacing while she got ready, ranting about the cheque and Donna's treatment of her and how that woman was a menace.

'What's your part tonight?' she asked, half hoping Mum would need to come over to talk to him and sort it out, while dreading another cold shoulder.

Nathan patted his jacket pocket, the one with the cheque.

'She'll announce it and then I'll toddle up there and hand over the fake money like a good little boy.'

She winced at his tone, but no one was listening. On one side Eve and Tim were having what appeared to be a low-voiced argument and, on the other, Aunty Vicki and her partner, Kim, were holding the rest of the family's attention with a hilarious story about their son Ralph getting stuck in his dinosaur suit.

Donna had yet to make an appearance. Billie guessed Mum must be keeping her big surprise hidden in one of the smaller rooms behind the stage. Probably where some of the raffle and silent auction items had been stored. Like other family events, there was no sign of Zach.

The music faded to silence, there was a tap on the microphone and the crowd hushed. While Billie had been lost in thought, the place had filled up. Each table now with guests seated or standing nearby, each person having paid a high price as a donation to be there.

Ruby, gorgeous in a dress that matched her name, had stepped up onto the stage.

'Ladies and gentlemen, honoured guests, friends and family, my name is Ruby Costa and it is my great pleasure to welcome you here this evening on behalf of The Megan Callaghan Foundation and the Callaghan family.'

She paused to allow the smattering of applause that followed her announcement to finish and then she gave the Acknowledgement of Country before continuing.

'Many of you will have already seen the headlines before coming out tonight and...' Ruby smiled towards the media throng '... others of you are here as a direct result. In previous years I've used the opening of the evening to share the history

of the foundation and then invited someone the foundation
has helped up here to tell their story. It's important to connect
with the human side of all the foundation does in its search
for missing loved ones.'

More applause.

'Tonight, it is my deepest joy to invite Amanda Callaghan
to the stage.' Ruby held out her hand towards Mum.

Mum climbed the few steps slowly, soaking in the moment.
Twice, she glanced back to where Donna must be standing in
the wings. Mum wore a gown Billie had never seen before.
A long black dress, embroidered with tiny lavender flowers.
Billie knew with a lurch of her gut her mum had this hanging
in her cupboard, possibly for years, waiting for this night to
wear it.

Mum's eyes glistened with emotion, but when she spoke
her voice was steady. 'Thank you, Ruby. And thank you for
your brilliant work on The Callaghan Baby Podcast. The
award-winning production has broken all kinds of records
and it is a credit to you and your team. Without your hard
work I don't think I'd be standing here tonight with such
incredible news to share.'

Expectation built as Ruby left the stage.

Around the room were those long-time supporters of the
foundation who'd come to this event for as long as Billie
could remember. And at a table of their own were those still
left of the neighbourhood group. Wariness lay over their
faces like a photographic filter, distorting their features. From
Grandad in the same black suit he always wore and Granny
B in a lovely matching navy skirt and top. Alongside Trish
Taylor, still able to pull off a tasteful plum-coloured, fitted
gown, with Gloria Marsh in a jacket and skirt that almost

perfectly matched her steel-grey, bouffed bun and Ray Marsh in his trademark brown jacket. Even Jennifer had come.

Trish caught Billie's eye and lifted her hand in greeting. Billie probably should have sought her work colleague out but she'd been too focused on the impending announcement.

'A few weeks ago, a woman knocked on my door,' Mum began. 'She'd heard the podcast, and she believed she might be able to help me find my missing sister. Understanding I had experienced disappointment before, this special person allowed me to take the necessary steps to ascertain the truth of her claim before going public. Tonight, I have the joyful honour to tell you that due process has confirmed her story.'

Mum visibly set herself, battling the waver of emotion in her voice. 'Please allow me to introduce you to my sister, Megan Callaghan.'

Donna stepped from the wings of the stage like a pageant queen, wearing black in a similar cut to Mum and with a lavender brooch pinned to her chest. She looked from Mum to the guests, eyes shining.

She smiled. 'I am so happy to be here at last. At my sister's side. Where I belong.'

Her arm slipped around Mum's waist and the tears Mum had battled now ran freely down her face. They posed as cameras flashed and the guests rose as one in a standing ovation.

At the table with the neighbourhood group there were tears and embraces. Exclamations she could make out even at this distance.

'*At last!*'

But it was Granny B and Grandad who caught her eye. Her reaction was mild compared to the others, to be expected since she'd been there at Christmas. But his – she could only describe Larry Jones's reaction to the announcement as forced. And his eyes, his eyes were fixed on Donna, and Billie would have sworn she saw something like hatred in them. Then he was being embraced by Gloria and whatever she thought she'd seen was gone.

Billie stood with the others, her smile brittle.

When the applause eased, Mum spoke again. 'The podcast that helped Megan find her way home was only able to happen thanks to funding from this foundation. Funding available thanks to nights like this and the generous donations of people here tonight and in the past.' Mum leaned forward. 'One of the biggest roadblocks people who are missing face... is being forgotten. Not by their loved ones, but by those in authority, the media and therefore the public. It's been so important to keep Megan's name alive.'

The applause grew to deafening.

'Tonight, we have succeeded.' Her gaze swept the room. 'Thanks in no small part to every one of you.'

Billie couldn't miss the emotion in the crowd. Every person in this room was emotionally and financially invested in the woman at Mum's side – the great success of bringing Megan Callaghan home. Now if Donna somehow wasn't Megan, more people than Mum would be devastated.

Mum cleared her throat to gain a little quiet. This time she looked to the media. 'There will be an opportunity for photos with Megan, but afterwards we'll be spending the rest of the evening with our guests. I hope you can understand and respect our privacy. But first, we have one last formality.'

She beckoned Nathan to the stage with an imperious flick of her wrist.

Those watching him walk across the small distance would have seen a fit, handsome man, in a well-made suit, but Billie noticed the stiff set of his shoulders and the pulse throbbing in his jaw.

When he stood at her side, Mum spoke again. 'Part of the foundation's work has been in being able to offer a reward for any information leading to finding Megan Callaghan. It is incredibly difficult to have the government authorise rewards for information resolving missing-people cases. To be able to do so privately through the fundraising of the foundation not just for Megan but other cases, has been one of our great achievements.'

Mum stepped away from the microphone, her arm still entwined with Donna's and allowed Nathan to step forward.

He pulled the piece of paper from his pocket and cleared his throat. 'Good evening.' His voice cracked and he tried again. 'Good evening, everyone. My name is Nathan Peters and I am the finance officer for The Megan Callaghan Foundation. It is my role to present the reward cheque that Donna and Amanda are choosing to donate back to the foundation to help other families with missing loved ones.'

He held it out to Donna, who took it with a pose for the cameras.

Nathan didn't waste any time bolting off the stage. 'It's done now,' he said when he returned to the table. Then he drained his glass of beer.

On stage, Mum had one last thing to say. 'At its heart, our foundation believes it is imperative that those who are out of sight are never out of mind. Thank you.'

THAT NIGHT

Ray's finger is damp and sweaty when it makes a slow, stomach-churning trail along my jaw. He's leaning closer now, and my brain is still scrambling with how to get out of this and not make a scene. Because Ken didn't need to drill into me that not making a scene was right up there with not telling anyone about the nights he can't get it up or where the money is coming from.

'Gloria won't like this.' I hate the weakness in my voice as I say it, hate that I'm using her name like I give a shit about that woman who looks down on me.

'She'll blame you,' he murmurs, his meaty breath warm on my face. 'She always does.'

He's right.

My hand swings to slap his face, scene be damned, but he catches my wrist before I make contact, then he grabs the other. Holds them easily in one hand above my head so I'm pinned painfully in place. I'm exposed.

His knee is hard, pushing between my legs and his eyes are just a little unfocused and I'm still trying to get out of this without causing a fuss, because I've been programmed that way my whole goddamned life.

I should have scraped my nails across his face when I had

276

the chance, grabbed his balls and twisted until he screamed in pain, but I couldn't risk making Ken mad. A mate touching his wife, versus that wife embarrassing his friend?

Whatever is happening in this hallway is not all in good fun.

My breath is loud in my ears, matching the thudding of my pulse. What do I know about this man with his sagging jowls and grey-spattered sideburns? Not much beyond the wife who doesn't approve of me and the daughter he doesn't know.

But I have heard rumours...

'Don't you usually like them younger?' I taunt. 'Only the pretty ones get sent in to see the principal.'

He laughs.

My attempt to shock, based on whispers I've heard in the neighbourhood, doesn't make him angry or ashamed. And I see it, then, in the lift of his chin and the curl of his lip. It's not that he doesn't care that people know, he's proud.

A hand comes out of the darkness, lands heavily on my aggressor's shoulder pulling him away. 'Another red, mate?'

And just like that, my wrists are free and the two men are walking down the hallway like nothing happened.

As I collapse against the wall, legs trembling, my flight response still trying to register my escape, I catch the eye of my saviour.

Frank, back from checking his adorable girls are safe at home shrugs as if to say, what can you do?

I'm grateful. He's done enough.

29

Billie stopped just before where the hallway she'd been walking through backstage turned a corner. She could hear people talking up ahead and hoped they'd move on before she had to make conversation about how wonderful it was that Megan was home.

'Your investigation was seriously impressive.' The low masculine voice was slurred. 'Nearly as impressive as that neckline.'

'Thank you, but if you'll excuse me, I should probably get back to the ball.'

'Why? I've been watching you and I know you're here alone tonight. Stay with me, babe. I'm sure no one will miss us.'

Listening to the exchange, nausea climbed in Billie's throat.

She recognised that voice, knew it almost as well as she did her own husband's. It was Tim speaking, and he was speaking to Ruby, if she wasn't mistaken.

Tim and Ruby.

Ruby and Tim.

The two of them talking alone in the back reaches of the huge function centre where they were hosting the ball, only hours since the excruciating rounds of family photos for the media celebrating Donna's return as Megan.

The woman spoke again. 'Sorry, I really do need to leave.'

As a female, Billie recognised the tone. Still trying to be polite, but also trying to be assertive to a man who you feared wouldn't take no for an answer.

Tim was one of the good guys, wasn't he? She'd known him for years, watched him cry at the birth of his children. She'd noticed some tension between him and Eve lately but hadn't thought anything of it. And to be doing this here, and with a woman who was practically part of the family.

'Please let me go.'

A woman who clearly wasn't interested.

Sudden rage filled Billie. How could he?

How *dare* he?

She strode forward, but when she rounded the corner, the narrow corridor was empty.

Lack of sleep, a couple of drinks and shock combined to make her head spin. She had to find Eve.

She heard a voice behind her.

'Wait,' Tim called.

She didn't.

Out in the main ballroom the noise from the jazz band hurt her head. She registered Nathan where she'd left him at the table, Ruby looking relieved to be away from the situation in the hallway and Eve doing the rounds. Keeping a smile in place in case there were media watching, Billie crossed to where her sister stood, engaging an elderly woman who Billie recognised as one of their biggest donors, a woman whose husband had disappeared on their honeymoon sixty-three years ago.

'Excuse me,' she said. 'Do you mind if I borrow my sister for a moment?'

'Go ahead, dear,' she said. 'I know what these things are like. It is a wonderful night indeed. My Frederick will be found next – I just know it.'

'What's wrong?' asked Eve once the woman had moved on. 'You look bloody awful.'

Deciding to tell Eve what she'd heard was one thing, telling her another.

But then her sister looked over Billie's shoulder. Whatever she saw drained the colour from her face. 'Oh,' she said. 'I see. Please tell me it wasn't you.'

'What?' Billie asked.

'Tell me he wasn't so drunk that he actually hit on my big sister.'

The sick feeling in Billie's stomach climbed into her throat. Eve was not surprised. 'Not me,' she said. 'I heard him with Ruby.'

'God, she's practically family.' Eve suddenly stepped past Billie, her eyes narrow. 'Seriously, you couldn't keep it in your pants here?'

Billie turned to see Tim standing behind them.

He swayed on his feet. 'She's lying.'

Eve shook her head. 'She's not.'

'You're going to take her word over mine?'

'You don't even know what she said. And yes, I am,' Eve said simply. 'Billie wouldn't make this up, and look at her. She's shocked by the whole thing.' Eve's laugh was bitter. 'Congratulations, you've managed to turn the opinion of one of the few people left who didn't know the kind of man you are.'

'What were you even doing, spying on me?' Tim sneered.

Billie blinked at the sudden attack, still trying to make

sense of Eve's resignation, the implication that Billie was the last one to know. 'I was going to check the auction items, not that it's any of your business.'

'And my relationship isn't any of yours,' he replied, voice rising. 'Didn't stop you running out here to tattle. Seriously, you're as uptight as everyone says.'

As everyone says...

She shrugged. 'If having my little sister's back is uptight, then that works for me.'

He stepped right up into her space, all six-foot-four, former professional athlete in a cloud of red-wine fumes. 'If you know what's good for you, you'll keep out of it.'

Billie's heart thudded hard against her ribs. 'You're embarrassing yourself, Tim. It's time to leave.'

'Please, Tim,' Eve added. 'She's right: go home, don't make this worse.'

'Don't you bitches tell me what to do.'

Nathan suddenly appeared in front of Tim. 'I think you should get out of here.'

Tim laughed. 'Well, well, well, what do we have here? If it isn't Mr Perfect Husband.'

'Mate,' Nathan said, 'it's a big night for the family, don't make any more of a scene.'

'It is a big night,' Tim agreed. 'For you, too. I mean you had the important role of handing over the money. Standing up there like the performing monkey you are. Saying the right things, doing the right things, but little do they know.'

Nathan's jaw tightened. 'Watch it.'

'Or what? What are you going to do?'

Billie heard someone ask if they should get security, but she didn't hear Eve's answer. The commotion had drawn a crowd. She'd started something and there was no way she could stop it now.

Nathan put up one hand. 'Leave it, mate. Please.'

'I'm not your mate,' Tim snarled. 'And I'm not the only one who should be in the shit tonight. What do they say? Misery loves company. Want to join me?' He shook off Nathan's hand and whirled away. He strode straight for the stage and the microphone, tapping the top so hard a screech echoed over the sound system. 'Ladies and gentlemen and any other PC terms I can't be fucked with right now,' Tim began.

The crowd turned as one. Surprise on most of their faces, some clearly thinking it was time for the countdown to midnight although that was still a few minutes away.

'I feel you all should know something about the precious foundation's finance officer.' Tim leaned forward covering the microphone and asking Nathan, 'Is that your title, bro? I guess it doesn't matter, won't be for long.'

Nathan tried to grab the mic, but Tim held it out of reach. 'Whatever you call him. The guy in charge of all the money. That money that so many of you have donated over the years. Well, our friend Nathan has a little problem. And his little problem got him involved with some rather persuasive people and if I was you, Aunty Megan, or whatever your name is, I wouldn't be in too much hurry to cash that cheque because it's sure as fuck going to bounce.'

Nathan's head dropped into his hands.

Billie's knees went to water. *God, it was true.*

EPISODE 10: DANGEROUS PRESENCE

Music playing: 'Fire' – The Pointer Sisters

The music fades.

Welcome to Episode Ten. I'm Ruby Costa and this is 'The Callaghan Baby Podcast'. Along with my team, I've been investigating the forty-year-old cold case of missing Megan Callaghan.

Last episode we were introduced to Jennifer Marsh's boyfriend, Scott Allen. You may recall Jennifer was the teenager from number three, left home alone to study the night Megan went missing.

Jennifer's friend from that time, Heather, was interviewed by counsel Kate Emmett at the 2005 inquest.

Kate:
How would you describe Jennifer and Scott's relationship?

Heather Thompson:
Intense. She'd be all deliriously happy one moment and then they'd fight, and she'd be miserable. Jennifer changed

283

when she was with him. She pushed her friends away and even skipped school.

Kate:
You say you were friends with Jennifer, yet there are suggestions you'd grown apart by late 1979 and are no longer in contact.

Heather:
She was always busy with that wanker, sorry, with Scott. He didn't like her to be unavailable. We were still close, then.

Ruby:
Heather pauses for a long time, her lips pressed together.

Heather:
I don't think Jennifer is close to anyone from those days anymore. She and her family left Ridgefield and never looked back. It was sad because we not only lost a friend but one of my favourite teachers. We all liked Principal Marsh.

Ruby:
Scott Allen was twenty-one in 1979 although he liked to let everyone believe he was nineteen, making for fewer complications dating younger girls. He had a mullet of boyish curls, and was tall and powerfully built. His blue eyes have been described as both dreamy and chilling. He liked people to be afraid when he entered the room but it's hard to know how many of the stories about him were true.

At the inquest, Kate Emmett questioned Heather about Scott and Jennifer's movements on the afternoon of the 9th of December.

Heather:
Jennifer came to my house that afternoon and she seemed upset. She claimed it was about the math test but I didn't believe her. It had to be Scott. I didn't like him much and I didn't try to hide it, you know? She got mad with me when I said she should dump him.

I knew the second my mum let her into my room that there was something wrong. When I pressed her, she admitted that she was worried about what Scott might do. There had been this big argument when he found her at Carol's place. Carol had lied saying Jennifer wasn't there, but he found her. Carol told him to leave Jennifer alone.

Scott was the kind of guy who didn't like people standing up to him. Jennifer said they'd fought and she feared he'd get revenge on Carol. He said he'd teach the old bag a lesson about interfering with his stuff. I remember I felt kind of sick then cos I realised he meant Jennifer. She was his stuff.

Kate:
Did Jennifer give any more details?

Heather:
No. But she was wearing a long-sleeved top and was kind of favouring her wrist. You need to understand it was like a million degrees that day. I asked if he'd hurt her, but she wouldn't give me a straight answer.

Ruby:

Heather goes on to talk about the threats she received on social media leading up to the inquest. An anonymous user told her to keep her mouth shut and showed pictures of her house and her kids' school. When asked who she thought was responsible she didn't hesitate, pointing to the back row where a man had been seated for much of the proceedings.

Heather:

It was him. He can deny it all he wants, but I know Scott Allen didn't want me talking today.

Ruby:

Let's hear from Jennifer herself at the inquest.

Kate:

Your best friend at the time, Heather Thompson, says that Scott came looking for you on December 9th at the Callaghan family home. She says you hid in the baby's room while Carol lied for you, telling him you weren't there. We understand he forced his way inside.

Jennifer hesitates, then finally speaks in a small voice:

Yes. She tried to keep him from entering but she wasn't strong enough. He pushed her, she fell and it was lucky she wasn't hurt. Out of respect for her and the children, I left with him.

Kate:

And what happened next? Heather told us you were injured and fearful for Carol.

Jennifer:

We drove around for a while and then he dropped me near Heather's house. I was fine, and I'm sure Scott was only talking crap with what he said about Carol.

Kate:

It's clear Megan, who went missing that night, was Carol's biggest point of weakness. I ask you, Jennifer, whether you believe Scott Allen was involved with taking that child?

Ruby:

A tear slides down Jennifer's cheek.

Jennifer:

Honestly, I don't know.

Ruby:

Knowing what we now know about Carol's altercation with Scott, it is possible that the note found on her calendar – 'They were here' – and the person who made her seem afraid was him. However, Scott Allen didn't become a person of interest for police until more than a year after Megan went missing.

A woman speaks:

Tonight, we air a special investigation around the case of missing baby Megan Callaghan. What really happened that night at the dinner party from hell?

Ruby:

The airing of a TV special around the first anniversary

of Megan's disappearance could have passed as nothing more than a painful blip for those left behind, except seeing Jennifer Marsh on the television jogged apprentice plumber Eddie Snyder's memory. He was interviewed at the inquest in 2005. In the footage, he's a young-looking forty, solid with muscle, and dimples appear when he flashes a nervous smile.

Just a warning, what you're about to hear from Eddie, well, it's pretty disturbing.

Eddie:
I was just a punk kid back then, but I was working on a building site in Bremner Park where Scott hung out. We were on smoko and I remember his face turning real ugly when someone asked about his girl. He kicked a crate and said some older chick was trying to interfere. He said that people reckoned that having a baby made them think they could lecture people, when all it did was make a good target.

Kate:
You believe he was talking about Jennifer and Carol?

Eddie:
Well, yeah. Jennifer was his girl and Carol had the baby... He also boasted he knew more than the police about the Callaghan case.

The other thing was, he made these jokes about putting bodies in the foundations. And not just in passing but with detail that suggested he'd thought about the logistics. One day I was levelling this tiny little square for a toilet when he smirked that it would be perfect to hide a baby. I thought I was going to be sick.

Ruby:

There were searches at a number of properties where Eddie Snyder had worked as a labourer in 1979, but these searches didn't find anything.

Kate Emmett recalled Jennifer Marsh's parents after all the evidence of their daughter's relationship. Although Ray didn't have a lot to say, Gloria became quite defensive.

Gloria:

I didn't like it, but she was nearly an adult and what could we do? Any attempt we made to discourage her from seeing him only made him more interesting to her.

Heavens, we moved all the way across town to try to break them up. She didn't have a car and we hoped it would be out of sight, out of mind for him.

Ruby:

At last Scott Allen was called to the stand. When his name is spoken, he approaches with swagger. And once he sits, it doesn't take long before any hope of getting answers disappears.

Kate:

I understand that you are choosing not to speak, as is your right?

Ruby:

One side of Scott's mouth lifts in a smirk.

Scott:
Yep.

Ruby:
If you're wondering why Scott Allen wasn't compelled to answer questions, it was decided that doing so might contaminate future evidence if he was able to be charged. After twenty-two long days of questioning and more than a dozen witnesses, the inquest closed.

Evening news introduction plays, **Male news presenter** *speaks:*
The inquest into the disappearance of Megan Callaghan wrapped up today with the coroner handing down his findings after a long deliberation. The coroner has found given the signs of forced entry and there being no sign of a body along with the testimony of those involved that Megan Callaghan was most likely taken that night. Likely she died on, or close to that night.

There are suspicions that a number of people know more than they're telling. We hope that whatever threats, fears or circumstances are keeping these people from talking one day changes, and they share that information. Her family, led by her surviving sister, Amanda, have put together a foundation to continue the search for answers. They continue to hope Megan will walk in through their front door one day, safe and well.

Ruby:
The Callaghan family were ultimately left without answers. This could have been the end of this story.

But it wasn't.

Tune in to the next episode of 'The Callaghan Baby Podcast' to find out more. If anyone listening knows anything that could assist in making this podcast, please contact me on investigation@thecallaghanfoundation.com. If you know something that could help the police, please contact them.

Thank you for listening.

30

A rushing in Billie's ears drowned out the noise of a hundred conversations breaking out around her at once. An arm came over her shoulder, led her away, almost before the words had finished ringing out across the ballroom.

The arm belonged to Eve. 'It's going to be okay,' she murmured as they weaved through a crowd stunned enough to part to let them through.

'This can't be happening.'

'It is.'

Eve pushed at a door and they'd reached the privacy of the small backstage area. Billie straightened then and stared into her sister's eyes, looking for something to make sense of what she'd heard. 'Did Tim say Nathan took all that money?'

Eve nodded.

'Could he be lying?'

'He could be, but Nathan's reaction...' She pulled out a tissue from somewhere and handed it over. 'I don't think he was. Not about that anyway. He's a cheating pig but that much I already knew.'

It was too much to take in. Her brain veered from what

Nathan had done, settling on Eve's problem. 'How long has this Tim stuff been going on?'

'He was a famous footballer. Overseas it kind of came with the territory. He'd be away on trips and have girls throwing themselves at him. He promised that when we had the twins he'd do better.'

'But?'

She shrugged. 'It didn't last long. Like that time when you were staying at Mum's and he'd bailed on Nathan but didn't come home. I guess I've tried to forgive each time he's promised it won't happen again, turn a blind eye if I could. I don't want to be a single mum; it's bloody hard.'

'Why didn't you tell me?'

Eve stared at Billie for a long moment and then shook her head. 'Seriously? You have to ask? Failure isn't an option around you. If it's not perfect, don't bother. Not everyone can live like that.' She wrapped her arms across her body. 'Not everyone wants to.'

'You haven't spent your life trying to make up for what Mum lost.' Billie's voice shook. 'Someone had to, and as always the responsibility falls to me.'

'Only because you demand it.'

Billie spluttered. 'Me? Demanding?'

'Yes. You think you're the only one Mum's obsession has affected? With missing Megan and Billie the clever one, how much of her attention do you think has been left for me? Being pat on the head for looking pretty isn't the great compliment you seem to think it is.'

Guilt sat heavily in Billie's chest. 'It's not a competition for Mum's affection.'

'Then why do you always have to win?'

The question, so quietly spoken, cut right through Billie. She couldn't look at her sister. She'd thought she was the only one who ever felt like she wasn't good enough.

Maybe that had made her competitive in herself, but she'd never thought Eve was feeling that way too.

'It's not winning, but I've just always been so scared to lose,' she admitted, the words coming from a place of shame deep inside.

The fragile balance they'd all existed in, dancing around Mum's fixation with finding Megan, had shattered tonight and she didn't know if she had it in her to put the pieces back together.

Billie's head dropped into her hands.

She felt a touch on her shoulder.

Eve, reaching out to her. Eve closing the gap between them emotionally and physically. Doing with touch what neither of them could manage with words.

She blinked back the sting of tears, her gaze swinging between Eve's perfectly manicured fingernails and her understanding eyes. 'Making this right between us should be my job,' Billie said.

'No,' said Eve. 'It's not. You've always been the smart, sensible sister. I guess I didn't tell you about Tim because I didn't want you to know I'd gone and messed up another part of my life.'

Speech failed Billie. Crying freely now, she pulled her sister to her in a fierce hug.

After a moment Eve squirmed free, dabbing at her perfectly lined eyes. 'Stop it. You'll make me cry too and I'll mess up my makeup.'

Billie sniffed. 'Because that's a priority right now.'

'Yep. About that, should I mention you now bear a striking resemblance to a racoon?'

'By all means. Hopefully those media people still left in the ballroom got a good picture and I can see for myself.'

Eve winced. 'It's late, maybe they've all gone home.'

She couldn't worry about who had seen what. 'I'm going to have to stop hiding and talk to Nathan. And Mum.' But Billie didn't move. 'She is not going to be happy.'

'Better to get it over with.'

Billie didn't miss Eve's smile. 'Thanks for that, yes. I remember doling out such clichéd advice myself only this morning.' Eve's media drama seemed a lifetime ago.

'You did,' Eve said. 'And you say I never listen.'

'Then listen to this.' Billie held her sister by her shoulders. 'I'm not saying you're a perfect wife but Tim's the one who messed up here. You should have told me.'

'Maybe.' Eve's eyebrows arched. 'Then again you can't talk, everything's been great with Nathan, has it? He's managed to steal from the foundation and given no signs that have you worried. Because if there's one thing my big sister likes to do, it's worry.'

'Point taken. We're as hopeless as each other.'

'I don't know,' Eve said. 'At least I knew what was coming from my husband.'

She had a point. Part of Billie wanted to defend herself, wanted to 'win', as Eve had so helpfully pointed out. But she bit back the urge and not only because it wouldn't have been true. For all she'd worried about Nathan she never imagined this.

Wanting to be a better person was a start, wasn't it?

Billie dabbed at her eyes. 'Right, as a great woman once said, better get this over with. I need to know exactly what Nathan's done. So many lies…'

'Men!' Eve declared.

'Men,' Billie agreed.

But she'd only got as far as the small corridor when Mum bustled in from the ballroom. Alone. 'Megan's gone,' she said as though that's all that mattered. 'This whole thing has been a slap in the face for her.'

'What about Nathan?' Billie asked.

'He'd want to have left. To have done such a thing after he was put in a position of trust on my personal recommendation.'

'He must have had a good reason.' Billie's defence of him was automatic.

Mum's lips pursed. 'He blamed some sort of debts, but that's no excuse. He's off the board, obviously, and we'll be speaking to the police in due course.'

'The police?' Billie echoed dumbly.

'Of course, they'll be involved. What did you think? That we'd sweep the whole thing under the rug? This is a lot of money. Money donated in some cases by those who don't have much to spare and he's gone and taken it from them. Taken it from Megan.'

'Donna.'

Mum crossed her arms. 'Did you know anything about this?'

'What?' Billie sputtered.

'Answer the question. You haven't tried to hide your antagonism towards Megan. She warned me about you but I was too foolish to listen. I need to know how much you were involved.'

She stared at her mother for a long time, unable to form a coherent sentence. She wanted to blame Donna for such an accusation, for coming between them, but right now this was all on the woman standing in front of her.

With nothing left to say Billie slowly turned and walked away.

31

Billie arrived home, paid the babysitter and checked on Lola before sitting on her front steps to wait for her husband, cup of tea in hand. She breathed in the chamomile aroma, hoping for the relaxing properties to have an effect, but couldn't bring herself to sip.

Rather, she stared down the street, watching for his familiar shape to appear in the splashes of light filtering through the tree branches. They'd forecast a shower, but it had yet to appear. Even though it was only an hour or so after midnight, the street was quiet, and there was no sign that a new year had just dawned. Nothing to show it was different to any other evening. Except she was sitting outside in a ballgown in the dark, and her life had just exploded.

The first drop of rain landed in her cup, sending tiny ripples across the surface. The next on her arm, the big fat droplet running over her wrist like a tear. Then the sky cracked and the heavens opened.

And she waited.

So much of the last few weeks now made sense. She could only imagine the pressure he must have been under to do what he'd done.

All. Those. Lies.

He stepped into view in a pool of light on the other side of their low front fence. Gone was his usual confident stance, replaced by sagging shoulders and a bent head. Without his dinner jacket, his shirt had soaked through and his hair was slick against his brow.

He stopped and lifted his head.

Their gazes met and locked. Something flashed in his eyes as the sky rumbled overhead. He looked different.

Her whole body tensed as she swore for a moment he was going to run, keep on going away from her and their family and the consequences of his mistakes. But then he pushed at the gate and approached like a man headed for the gallows.

'What have you done?' She'd meant to give him time, but the question ripped from her throat before he reached the foot of the stairs. She wanted to scream at him, wanted to slap him, but she kept her hands on the teacup, revolted by her own wild thoughts.

He was shaking his head. 'I'm sorry. So bloody sorry. I fucked up.'

'Not good enough.' She'd ached for him but now the rage simmering inside her wiped out everything else.

'You don't understand.'

'Then explain it to me. Step-by-fucking-step until I do.'

He pushed at his hair, but it flopped back on his forehead. 'It started with the footy. There was that game back around Easter, the huge upset when the Doggies got up. I had fifty bucks on it and the payout...' He whistled. 'After that I had a couple of good wins and started betting a bit more. And then some losses. Then another win but I'd lost a fair bit.'

'You were gambling?'

His Adam's apple worked in his throat. 'Saying it aloud sounds so stupid. It's on the app and it's like it's not even real money. All the guys do it. I had it under control.'

She thought back to how she'd seen him on his phone more and more and how animated he'd be about sports she didn't realise he even followed. Was this better than an affair? Was there a scale of shitty secrets your partner could keep?

And then she realised what was different about him. He wasn't holding his phone, wasn't checking some score or following some live update.

'But you didn't have it under control.'

He jerked a hand across his red eyes. 'No.'

'How do we get from messing around with an app to tonight?'

'The feeling when I'd win would put me on top of the world. I'd be high for hours. Until I lost. I had a few good wins and this guy put me onto a website with a little more grunt.' He must have seen the confusion in her face. 'Bigger spends, bigger odds.'

'Bigger losses,' she filled in.

His head bowed. 'That's how it turned out. Not straight away, not at first. They have these incentives, these can't-lose options, that made me feel fucking invincible. And then I owed them.' He swallowed again. 'Owed them more than I had. There were threats.'

The odd calls and secret messages suddenly made sense. And the clash with Tim at the hospital.

'Tim knew?'

'A little.' He hesitated. 'I borrowed some cash off him when I needed to make a payment.'

'We owe him? We owe them?' This was only getting worse.

Now she might owe her baby sister money – her baby sister who she'd always tried to set an example for.

'Only a couple of grand.'

Her eyes closed. Only… She opened them. 'And all that foundation money was just sitting there, earmarked for information on someone who'd never return.'

He nodded. 'I thought I could borrow it and get it back into the account before anyone was the wiser.'

'How were you going to get that much money back?' She could read the answer on his face. 'Let me guess: more gambling.'

'I didn't plan for her to show up, did I?'

'It doesn't matter. You took the money. You didn't borrow it; you stole it.'

He slumped again. 'I know.'

'And the gifts, the extravagance?'

'I had these wins and I felt so bad about everything. I just wanted to be happy again.'

Her lip curled. 'You lied to me. You stole from the foundation, and that is something you'll have to deal with through the police, but you betrayed me and our marriage. I trusted you. That's why you were so helpful with my investigation. You were covering your own arse.'

'I was,' he admitted. 'But I supported you too. I still don't trust that woman.'

'I'm not sure your judgement counts right now.' The lukewarm tea that had been a comfort might as well have turned to cement, too heavy for her to hold a second longer. She placed the cup on the step beside her and clasped her hands together, pressing them to her lips. 'God, Nathan, all those people, that money. It was never yours.'

She could see in the lines in his face, and the curve of his shoulders that he knew all this.

'I'm really sorry,' he whispered.

She jumped up, knocking the cup and spraying tea across the veranda. 'You've broken something. Shattered the trust underpinning our marriage, and I don't have a clue where we go from here. Right now, I can't stand to look at you.'

Mouth trembling, he nodded. 'I don't blame you. Can I grab some things, say goodbye to Lola?'

Had she meant for him to leave? She didn't know, but she didn't move to stop him when he walked past her into their home and then a little while later came back out, with an old sports bag slung over one shoulder.

She didn't say a word. But she couldn't help watching his every movement, eyes stinging, as he got into his car, started the engine, reversed onto the street and drove away.

If this was what she'd wanted, why did it feel so damn awful?

THAT NIGHT

10.22 p.m. – Gloria

It's not like I wouldn't have given her some port. I understand this is a potluck dinner party and we all need to contribute. Unlike her I've been coming to these for years.

All she had to do was ask.

But she didn't. Likely thinks she's too good for it. The same way she does everything else in the street. Does she think we haven't seen the deliveries coming thick and fast to the house since she moved in?

Even now, three glasses of wine in, cheeks pink, she can't bring herself to look any of us in the eye. Us women anyway.

'Can I get you a drink?' she asks.

Her eyes are wide, a light blue like the sky in spring, rich with promise and the skin around them smooth as the day she was put on this earth. Which was about five minutes ago compared to the rest of us. Mary mother of God, she could pass for one of my Jennifer's friends.

It registers through the haze and the liquor flush in my veins that the question is to me.

We both look at the crystal I'm holding. Ostentatious and heavy, the cuts in the base are tiny prisms catching rainbow light. Empty, but for a single crimson drop.

It's a dig. Plain as day. Delivered perfectly beneath the

conversation swirling along with smoke and melodies around the room.

This, *I want to cry at Carol, who always defends her.* This, *is what I mean.*

'I can serve myself.' It's my bottle after all. I do not need this child-playing-host's permission.

Her mouth curves. 'Of course.' She waves towards the table with an elegant flick of a wrist sparkling with a delicate gold bracelet. 'Be my guest.'

My teeth clench. 'Only because I have to be.' I hold her blue-eyed gaze, the shadow above it a perfect match.

She doesn't flinch. Shows no reaction. It's all I can do not to scream it in her smooth, unlined face.

Only because I have to be.

But now she's not even looking my way. Not much of a hostess if you ask me. I'd have made sure my guest wasn't stuck with an empty glass parched from the heat. Instead, she's talking to Carol. Their heads bent together, voices lowered, like schoolgirls sharing secrets. My stomach knots. I've seen enough mean girls in the classroom.

Talking about me.

My hand, damp from it being way too goddamned hot in here, tightens on the crystal. Bitches both.

I stand. There's a slurp as I peel from the leather couch. Imported of course. I bet that's her influence. What's wrong with a nice floral material that matches the drapes?

I've left a wet patch in the shape of wide thighs and a rounded behind where I was sitting. Heat suffuses my throat, but a glance at the others shows no one is looking my way.

Barb and Larry are canoodling on the leather, her probably whispering they should get one for themselves. Originality is not exactly Barb's forte and they're always trying to keep up with the neighbours. Ken is reaching for a vinyl off a shelf filled with records. Frank, as always, only has eyes for Carol. It's enough to make a person sick.

And my Ray... The knot in my stomach twists. Unsurprisingly, he's watching our hostess. Practically has his tongue hanging out. Does he think I didn't see him follow her earlier?

Hardly his fault the way she's advertising herself. Does she think that I haven't faced this before in the last twenty years? It takes commitment to keep a marriage going in this day and age and I will not let some hussy derail the twenty years of work I've put in.

Ray is only a man and it isn't his fault that women throw themselves at him.

It's up to me to make sure he remembers that we made a vow before God and it is not something to be so easily thrown away.

So much for the sisterhood.

32

Something nudged Billie's arm.

'Nathan?' she murmured. Then consciousness slammed into her, and with it all she'd tried to forget. He'd gone. Nathan had fucked it all up and then left her to pick up the pieces.

She blinked and made out the stocky shape of Plank, whimpering by the bed. 'What is it, boy?'

But Plank just nosed her hand until she rubbed behind his ears, and the whole time he kept making that same sound softly in the back of his throat. Made uneasy by his distress, she forced herself to her feet to let him out and then checked on Lola. But even when the door was wide open Plank stayed so close, she felt his wet doggy breath against her bare calves. And for a change when Billie peered into the nursery Lola slept soundly.

She locked up and stumbled back to bed. There, the exhaustion dragged her back into oblivion, her hand on Plank's soft, warm head.

Billie's phone was ringing.

She fumbled in the dark. It was still the middle of the night. 'Eve? What's wrong?'

'It's Pop.'

Billie staggered out of bed, squeezing her eyes tight for a moment to stop the threatening tears. 'I'm coming.'

There was a long pause. 'It's too late. He's... he's gone.'

She fell back onto the bed, meeting Plank's mournful brown eyes. Could that have been why he'd woken her? Did he know his master had gone?

'But I just saw him. He wasn't great, but I didn't think...' Her throat was too tight; she couldn't go on.

'He was old, Billie. The doctor said it was his time.'

Tears spilled from aching eyes, tears when she'd thought she couldn't cry another drop. 'How's Mum?'

'She called me after the care facility called her. She's gone down there but said there was no point us running all over town in the middle of the night. Yeah, anyway, I figured you'd want to know – you were always his favourite.'

She had been. Pop had adored – just thinking past tense brought a fresh wave of tears – both girls but Billie had spent more time with him through the family business and it was Billie he was closest to.

And it struck her then. 'Mum called you?' she asked, leaving the unspoken, *and not me*?

Another silence. 'She was pretty upset.'

'But not upset enough not to make sure I know she's pissed with me.'

'Anyway, she said she'll be going through the arrangements at her place tomorrow around mid-morning.'

'Arrangements' meant funeral and estate plans and Billie's name was on some of the paperwork. After Mum had been uncontactable following some lead on Megan when Pop had had a fall the year before, they'd decided it was better to have more than one person able to execute his wishes in case of emergency. They didn't imagine that when such a time came Mum wouldn't be talking to Billie.

'Will Donna be there?'

'I guess. But Mum didn't say *not* to mention it to you.'

'Oh goody.'

'Don't growl at the messenger. I'll miss him too.'

'Sorry,' Billie said. 'I know you will. How's things there?'

'I have the whole house to myself. Tim hasn't dared show his face and the twins are sleeping over at his sister's place. All the better for receiving late-night calls, really. After you left I tried to apologise to Ruby but she wouldn't hear a word. She said I'd done nothing wrong.'

'You haven't.'

She grunted. 'What about you, have you spoken to Nathan?'

Billie twisted around so she was propped against the pillows. It felt strange to be chatting to Eve like so many other calls they'd shared over the years except this one was happening at four in the morning, they'd both lost their husbands and their grandfather had just died.

'We spoke,' she said. 'Out in the freaking rain, while tea spilt everywhere.'

'And?'

'I don't know what to do. I'm not sure it was something he could control in the end.'

There was a pause while Eve considered. 'You mean not like Tim?'

'I don't want to make this a shitty husband competition.'

'Don't.' Eve snorted. 'Because I'd win.'

Billie couldn't argue with that. It came down to whether she thought she'd be able to forgive Nathan. From what Pop said, her grandmother had forgiven his straying with Nancy and Billie wouldn't judge that, but she knew herself. She'd never forgive Nathan cheating. But this... if he truly had a problem, recognised that and if he got help, maybe one day she could.

'I'm sorry that Tim's done this to you and Max and Matilda,' Billie said.

Eve took a shaky breath. 'I'm mostly mad that I'll have to deal with it now. I liked pretending everything was fine and I'd have preferred it not to make headlines.'

'Ouch, I haven't looked.'

'Don't. Anyway, the publicity should be great for my socials.'

'That's good,' Billie said, and meant it. 'Maybe Nathan will get the help he needs, and you'll become a household name.'

Eve laughed. 'Who'd have thought my logical sister could put such a spin on the debacle. Oh, Billie, I hate the circumstances, but it's so good to talk to you.'

They'd gotten so busy dealing with their own lives and the ever-present shadow of the search for Megan, they'd not connected like this in so long. And as the rain came down outside and her body ached with the pain of Pop's passing and Nathan's betrayal, Billie didn't hesitate in replying, 'It's good to talk to you, too.'

'You still suspect Donna?' Eve asked.

Billie had nothing but two blankets, some holes in Donna's story and her antagonism to prove the woman wasn't everything she claimed.

'I suspect her intentions,' Billie said eventually. 'She's turned Mum against me and there's this current of antagonism when she's sure no one will know. Maybe it started out as wanting to prove her wrong but mostly I just want to know what she really wants. As far as her being Megan? I don't know,' she admitted.

'That's a first from you,' Eve teased.

The late night and raw emotions combined to make her more honest than she would normally be, less afraid of letting the world see the truth. The pretending she thought she needed to do, so what... people would think she was perfect?

'I've been struggling,' she whispered to Eve. 'Even before all this. With Lola, with wanting to be at work and thinking I should be at home every second. Of trying to work out who I am now I'm her mum.'

'Oh, Billie, we're all struggling. That's what this is all about. All struggling and all kicking butt at the same time. It's pretty incredible really.'

For now, she had an ally in her sister. She'd face up to the fallout of the night's events in the morning.

EPISODE 11: A CHANGE OF HEART

Music playing: 'My Life' – Billy Joel

The music fades.

Welcome to Episode Eleven. I'm Ruby Costa and this is 'The Callaghan Baby Podcast'. Along with my team, I've been investigating the forty-year-old cold case of missing Megan Callaghan.

Sometimes in life bad things happen to good people, but sometimes, someone like Scott Allen find themselves barely middle-aged and with only weeks to live. We'd contacted him in the preliminary phases of putting the podcast together, but he'd never replied.

Then, out of nowhere, he did, asking to meet.

Although never convicted of anything relating to the Callaghan case, Scott Allen remains a strong person of interest for those in charge of the investigation. This is a man who openly talked about where to dispose of a body, bragged about having inside information and who had a well-documented history of violence. Not only that but he threatened Carol Callaghan and was seen at Wattlebury Court on the day Megan went missing.

After hearing of the possible break in the case, Paul Lennard requested to accompany us on the visit.

There are the sounds of a hospital. Air conditioning. Medical conversations.

We enter through double glass sliding doors and I'm immediately struck by the drab walls. This is a place where those without families come to see out their final days. We're directed to 'poor Scott's' room.

The first thing I notice about Scott Allen is that he's smaller in real life. His illness has wasted his body, leaving hollowed eye sockets and pinched features. He holds out his hand to shake in greeting but neither Paul nor I accept. There will be no fake civility here.

Scott:
I don't have the time or energy left in this world to play games. You might not believe this but I'm a changed man. Ask me whatever you want, and I'll do my best to answer.

Ruby:
Did you kidnap Megan Callaghan?

Scott:
No.

Ruby:
In your determination to keep your hold over Jennifer Marsh and put Carol Callaghan in her place, did you lie in wait, watching the house until Frank had made that last check on his children? Did you break a window to that baby's room, when you knew the adults were at a

dinner party and take the child in order to teach Carol a lesson?

Scott:
I did not.

Look, I'll save you the time. I hit women I dated; I cheated on them. I was the worst kind of bastard, and if there's an afterlife I'll pay for what I've done, but none of it has anything to do with that kid.

Ruby:
You admit you've hurt these women but think you get to decide they're not part of the story. Jennifer Marsh was sixteen when she was abused at your hands. *Sixteen*. You seduced her with your charm, and you hurt her. This was what you taught her love looked like, how love felt, but you have the nerve to sit there and tell me that it is not relevant?

Scott:
I am sorry for that; I am. But I stand by what I said. Your mother is not important to the case. I know who you are. Christ, you look just like her – I'm not stupid. But I think your connection to this is making you blind. This isn't some dying bedside confession if that's what you're hoping.

There's a long silence, only punctuated by the sound of a woman trying to control her ragged breathing. Then it stops and there's only the whirr of recording and a mechanical clunk.

Ruby:

Then why call us here? Did you want to screw around with us one more time before you died? Because so far all I'm getting from you is what you didn't do.

Scott:

You're right, but this is harder than I thought it would be. I'm struggling with my life being summarised by my mistakes with women, and whether I took that baby.

Ruby:

Then make it mean something more. Tell me something.

Instinctively, I know that Scott is on the edge of revealing something that could smash this whole case wide open. My heart is racing, and tiny beads of sweat are forming on Paul's forehead. This is the moment where the answers might finally be within reach. We're recording and in those seconds my brain is dredging up everything I know about criminal law. Could a confession here be used in court? Should I stop him from speaking in case it compromises the case?

And that's when he says it...

Scott:

When I was first dating Jennifer, I had to do the right thing, get in good with the parents. Good girls are a challenge for a guy like me; they take a bit of charming to win over and that was never going to happen without Ray and Gloria's permission. I played the game, turned up at their house in my best shirt, used my manners, the full show.

But the bitch hadn't warned me there'd be a cast of fucking thousands there. It was one of their parties, wasn't it?

I got stuck standing there with some of the blokes cooking the barbecue. They began talking up what tough guys they were in their youth. One of them asked whether I could get them a little something.

Here I was trying to come across as clean-cut and they were asking me to get them drugs. What could I do? I wanted to date Jennifer, so I hooked them up. They had the dinner party that night because they scored that day.

Ruby:
Are you saying that the adults on Wattlebury Court were all on drugs?

Scott:
That's exactly what I'm saying. Now I don't know what it means for the case, but those guys speaking on the stand never once mentioned their little party habit.

There's the clunk of a door closing and two people releasing their breath in an astonished sigh.

Ruby:
Paul and I have waited to speak about what we've heard until we're out of the treatment facility.

Paul:
It's gut-punching. In all my years of investigating this case,

we never even heard a whisper of this kind of thing, but I believe him. He has nothing to lose.

Ruby:

In the days following our meeting with Scott, we go to the police who promise to look into the new information but cast doubt on Scott Allen as a witness.

However, what we do know is every single statement from the people at the party that night must now be called into question. And most importantly, if they could hide this for so long then what else are they hiding?

Amanda:

This revelation has forced me to see everything in a new light. These adults were responsible for a four-month-old baby when they put short-term personal pleasure ahead of her safety.

Ruby:

How does Frank being on drugs that night change things?

Amanda:

I believed his version of what happened that night for nearly forty years. I had no reason to suspect he might not have been thinking straight, that he might have worried as much about sobering up as calling the police, that he may not have been acting rationally.

And now I can't ask him.

Ruby:

Please join us next time on 'The Callaghan Baby Podcast'.

If anyone listening knows anything that could assist in making this podcast, please contact me on investigation@thecallaghanfoundation.com. If you know something that could help the police, please contact them.

Thank you for listening.

33

A few hours later Billie stood outside her mother's house, adjusted Lola's weight to free her hand and went to knock. Usually, she'd have let herself in but after last night she felt like a stranger. From the cars arrayed in the driveway, Eve and Donna were already there.

She'd planned to come early to speak to Mum alone, but everything had taken three times longer than she thought it would. She'd had two messages from Nathan. The first a simple, *'I love you and I'm sorry,'* and the second sending his sympathies about Pop, neither of which she'd been able to reply to.

Before her hand could connect with the surface, a figure appeared on the other side of the wire screen. 'Oh, Billie, it's you,' Donna said. 'Come in out of the rain.'

Donna held the door wide so Billie could enter and smiled as though neither last night nor the afternoon at Billie's house had happened. In black and red floral activewear, Donna's outfit could have come from Mum's wardrobe.

Mum and Eve were at the table and her sister jumped up and hurried to give Billie a hug. The human touch threatened Billie's self-control and by the time they pulled away, they were both teary.

Her mum hadn't looked up from the paperwork spread out on the table. 'Mum?' Billie's throat ached. 'I'm so sorry he's gone.'

For a moment Billie thought she'd be ignored again, but then her mum got to her feet and they met in a brief embrace.

Mum wiped at her red-rimmed eyes. 'Thank you for coming. I'd like to put all the nastiness behind us and move forward together as a family.'

'Me too,' Donna echoed. 'Family is the most important thing.'

Mum nodded. 'You're so right. I'm so glad you understand.'

Unwilling to fracture the fragile truce and aware of Donna already taking the chair at Mum's side, Billie swallowed her confusion at the about-face. Considering she wasn't talking to Nathan; she could hardly expect Mum to just get over what he'd done. Now was about her beloved Pop and his last wishes.

And as to why Donna was playing nice, Billie could only assume it was for Mum's benefit. Her limbs fizzed with the tension of pretending she hadn't seen the malevolence from the other woman. Mum would need proof her intentions weren't good and Billie would only get one chance to plead her case.

As they went through the paperwork, Donna's sniffling in that way that said, *Look at me everyone, I'm grieving*, had Billie having to clench her jaw to stop from yelling: *You didn't know him.*

Didn't know him and hadn't tried to. Whether she'd been there at the home otherwise was a different question. It was too much of a coincidence that she'd worked at Restwell. One that even now churned in Billie's gut along with everything else that didn't quite add up. How far would Donna have gone to quiet him?

The horrifying thought made her miss the first part of the discussion on where to hold the service.

Mum was nodding at something Donna had said. 'Obviously, he couldn't have known what would happen when he suggested he'd like to have it at the chapel.'

'I'm just saying it could be a tight squeeze with the numbers likely to attend.' She gave Mum a wobbly smile. 'You know him best; after all I didn't really get the chance.'

Billie's new efforts at diplomacy could only be pushed so far. 'You can't be thinking of moving it. That's where he wanted to have it. It's where he and Carol got married.'

Mum wavered. 'We need to make sure there's enough room.'

Billie didn't have to ask what had changed. 'You mean for the gawkers?' She tried for a calmer tone. 'The chapel will fit the family and his friends, and he made his wishes quite clear.'

Donna tutted. 'As your mum said he couldn't have known what would happen. Are you suggesting she doesn't know what her father would want?'

But none of this is coming from Mum.

Somehow Billie didn't say it aloud, but she shared a pointed glance with Eve. Surely, at least her sister could see what Donna was doing?

Mum made a note on one of the papers. 'Now, he loved Nat King Cole, and I think the duet of "Unforgettable" would be lovely. On so many levels.' She smiled at Donna. 'We never forgot you.'

Billie couldn't argue the choice. She'd never forget him playing it on his old record player one rainy afternoon when she'd mentioned the approach of her first high school dance. There in the kitchen of his tiny unit, he'd tried his best to teach her to waltz.

She snuggled into Lola as the memory of his rough, calloused hand gently holding hers threatened to bring her to tears once again.

It was that kind of morning. Mundane details and cups of coffee and then the sudden attack of a memory that would nearly bring her undone. And then it was over.

'I guess that's it, then.' Mum sighed and straightened the piles of papers. She shook her head. 'I just can't believe he's gone.'

'Sometimes it's better for them to be at peace if their mind is failing them,' Donna said comfortingly.

Billie's eyes narrowed. How did Donna know about his mental state?

Mum rubbed at her eyes. 'I'm just so damn tired. Lately, I get to bed, and all of it plays over and over in my mind and I can't sleep.'

Donna murmured sympathetically. 'I can probably get you something to help with relaxing. Something a little stronger than you can get over the counter. Has to be some advantage to having a nurse for a sister.'

Mum sighed. 'I might have to take you up on that. There's so much to do and I'm struggling. At least now I have you.'

Billie clenched her jaw to keep in her instinctive response: *What are the rest of us, chopped liver?* Rather, she caught Donna's gaze and held it.

'*I see you,*' Billie said with her eyes. '*And I'm not going to stop until Mum sees you too.*'

She cleared her throat. 'What about Pop's things?'

Mum frowned. 'Donna and I are meeting with someone from a magazine who wants to do a story on us later today, and we have the funeral director tomorrow. Besides, there's not much there.'

'Magazine?' Billie asked. 'You hate that stuff.'

'We talked about it and we've agreed that in this hard time it's important that we manage the story, and that means select interviews. People are interested in Megan coming home.'

Donna's expression told Billie all she needed to know about where that plan had come from. 'We can talk to them about the ceremony,' Donna added like she'd just remembered.

'What ceremony?' Billie asked. She felt Eve's gaze on her, pitying almost, and she guessed the answer before Mum confirmed it.

'For the award. You understand it makes sense for Donna to be the one at my side considering she was my inspiration.'

Billie would have sworn a smirk twisted Donna's lips, but of course it was too fast for anyone else to notice. She swallowed back an argument and said instead, 'Let me go to the home for you, then. I want to help.'

'Good idea,' Eve said.

A rush of gratitude flooded Billie at her sister's support.

'It would be good to get it sorted out,' Mum said.

'Although, we could probably fit it in together later,' Donna was quick to point out.

Mum considered. 'You need to check in on poor Zach,' Mum said. Then to Billie: 'It must be so sad for him to be struck with this virus over the holidays.'

'There will be plenty of time to get to know him,' Billie said, thinking of how he'd let slip they wouldn't be around long.

Billie didn't dare move, watching as Mum stared into space, mentally going through all she had to do. Long seconds passed, until finally she nodded. 'Thank you, Billie. That would be a big help.'

Donna opened her mouth but then seemed to think better of whatever she'd been going to say and nodded too.

It felt petty to be thinking in such a way, but as she stood to gather her things, Billie couldn't help but feel she'd had a minor victory. With Mum and Donna getting coffee in the kitchen, Billie was about to begin her goodbyes when Eve, just back from the bathroom, caught her eye. So softly she might as well have mouthed it, Eve whispered, 'Go to the end of the hall. Pretend you need the bathroom.'

Maybe it was the grief or lack of sleep, but Billie did not follow what her sister meant in the slightest. Still, she obeyed, knowing Eve would be at her until she did what she wanted.

The tarp she'd noticed after Christmas was hanging open so she could see down to the corner bedroom with its door partially open. The light grey that had been on the walls was gone.

And after noticing the colour, she'd seen enough from photos of the past to guess the rest. Still, she had to see it for herself. She approached with slow steps and her chest cramped.

'Oh, Mum, what have you done?'

She pushed at the door and it swung open. The stench of adhesive didn't take her breath, but the four walls of lavender-print wallpaper did. She reached out to touch it but recoiled short of contact.

How had Mum found the exact replica of wallpaper that had been on these walls more than forty years earlier? Why would she want to recreate this room?

Although Billie had grown up with her mother's obsession, she couldn't be sure if details from the white polished drawers and the small cupboard next to the window were a match to the original, but in the corner, she couldn't miss...

The cot.

The old-style wooden cot was identical to that which had been the last place her mother's baby sister, Megan Callaghan, had been seen.

She pulled Lola tight against her until she squirmed to get free.

Back out in the living area, Eve met her gaze with a silent, *WTF?*

Billie could only shake her head.

'You have to speak to her,' Eve muttered.

'And say what?'

'What are you two nattering about?' Donna asked.

Billie hesitated. Knowing Eve would be annoyed, she put on a fake smile and headed for the door. 'Just saying our goodbyes.'

This would have to wait. For now, she needed to be allowed to pack up her grandfather's things the way he'd want her to.

At Restwell, most of the Christmas decorations were down already but the staff remained friendly when she stopped at the reception desk to gift some flowers and chocolates she'd picked up. Then she made her way to his room, pushing a gurgling Lola in her pram.

At the door, she froze. It was empty as she'd known it would be. But without him in it, the four walls closed in and his favourite green leather chair sat tattered and worn. Her eyes stung.

Lola's hungry cry forced her into action. She settled in the scuffed chair, her grandfather's old cologne enveloping her in a woodsy hug. As Lola fed, she allowed the memories to come. By the time Lola finished, Billie was ready to face the task ahead.

With Lola asleep in the pram, Billie made short work of going through her grandfather's things. A small part of her had hoped for some clue left behind, but there were only the belongings of a man who'd come here to end his days.

All the furniture except the recliner came with the room and she messaged Mum, asking what she wanted done with the one thing she couldn't load into the car.

Mum's reply came quickly: *'I'll organise for it to be delivered here.'*

There went her hopes of keeping it for herself. Not that it would fit in their small house... Suddenly it hit her. Nathan would need to pay back the money. They could lose their house.

Her head bowed.

'Sorry for your loss,' came a voice from the doorway.

Billie wiped her eyes, pulled herself together and turned to face the kind nurse, Lisa, who she'd met before. 'Thank you. I'll miss him very much. We all will.'

'I saw the headlines. It's a pity he passed without knowing his Megan had been found.'

'Yes,' she agreed. But she thought he'd known more than he'd ever said.

'Thanks for the flowers and chocolates,' Lisa said. 'But caring for the residents is our job.'

'Our family appreciate it all the same.'

Lisa nodded. 'Take however long you need. And if there's anything I can do, please ask.'

Then she was gone again.

Billie forced herself to her feet and picked up the last photo frame. In all she'd filled one box. His clothes fit in in garbage bags, one for charity and another to be binned. A life didn't take much to pack up.

But she didn't leave.

He was gone but she still had so many questions. Why had Donna been so reluctant to meet Pop? Would seeing him have blown her story out the water? And if so could she have done the unthinkable to prevent it happening?

Heart thundering and stomach sick she called for the nurse.

A moment later Lisa looked in. 'Did you need something?'

'Pop mentioned one of the agency workers but not by name. The family would like to extend our gratitude to her, too.' Billie hated how smoothly the lies came. What had she become?

Lisa's face brightened. 'Funny you should ask. There was one. Notes suggest she spent some time with your grandfather. I can get you her name and see if we have any contact details.'

Billie tried to keep her voice steady. The fear of Donna silencing Pop would not go away. 'Was she here yesterday?'

Lisa frowned. 'I had the night off. I'll just see what I can find out.'

'I'd appreciate it.'

If Donna had worked here, she would have had ample opportunity to question him, discovering details about the blanket and the birthmark. Working nights, she'd have avoided visits from the family and would have had access to his DNA.

Lisa returned a minute later, in her hand a piece of paper with a phone number and a name. 'Here you go.'

For the first time in hours, Billie's spirits lifted.

34

Billie left Restwell with her grandfather's last few possessions and a piece of paper with Donna's phone number. More puzzle pieces, but still the picture refused to fall into place. Had Donna been there to help Pop to the other side to protect her story?

At the car, she dialled Ruby's number.

'You've saved me a phone call,' Ruby said when she picked up. Excitement thrummed in her voice. 'We've found the marriage certificate through Stefan Novak. It confirms Janette Novak and Nancy Blair are the same person.'

Billie nearly dropped her phone. 'Are you sure?'

'My source is sending me paper copies, but from the scanned images it's pretty clear that Janette must have been a middle name that she took to using, and then with the marriage changing her last name she became Janette Novak. I'm sure.'

'Donna is Megan.' The words she never thought she'd say rang loud in the cabin of her small car.

'It certainly looks that way.'

Billie sank into her seat, deflated. 'That information puts a different light on what I was about to tell you.' She explained about her proof of Donna working at Pop's facility but didn't mention her fear of how far Donna had gone that seemed silly now. 'She was probably trying to get the lay of the land before coming forward. Maybe she was uncertain of her reception.'

'With good reason,' Ruby said gently.

'Me,' Billie admitted. She closed her eyes, replaying everything she'd said and done since Donna turned up at Wattlebury Court, stomach sick. She'd been worried about Donna's intentions, when maybe it should have been the other way around. 'The woman must hate me.'

'You were only looking out for Amanda.'

The consoling words didn't make Billie feel any better. 'Thanks for your help. I'd better go apologise and hope she'll forgive me.'

'Good luck,' Ruby said. 'And I'm sorry to hear about Frank.'

'Appreciated.' Her throat tightened again, and she blinked back tears. The headlines would paint him as Frank Callaghan, father of the returned Megan, but to her he was Pop and she'd miss him as such for the rest of her life.

They discussed the tentative plans for the funeral arrangements, with Ruby assuring Billie that the whole family would come and pay their respects.

'Maybe Donna was able to spend time with him before he passed,' Ruby said.

'It would have been such a relief for him,' Billie said. 'Although whether he was lucid enough to understand is something I'll never know.' She tried to picture them together, Pop smiling as Donna gave him the peace he'd craved for so long. 'I can't exactly ask Donna about it.'

'I won't tell her about your role in finding the new information but after the dust has settled, I'll share the evidence I've found with her and Amanda. Do you think she'd do an interview, give the podcast a proper ending?'

'I can't claim to know her that well, but I think they'd be interested.'

After ending the call, Billie headed back to her mum's house. She tried to call Eve on the way to share the latest developments, but her sister wasn't answering. She tried again when she reached Wattlebury Court but mostly as a delaying tactic.

With no answer, she steeled herself to go inside.

Holding Lola in one arm, she opened the unlocked door. 'It's me,' she called ahead, not wanting to interrupt anything. 'It's Billie.'

They were together at the table, heads bent close together, looking at some papers but both rose to their feet as Billie walked in.

Mum frowned. 'I didn't need Dad's things straight away.'

Billie had almost forgotten the load in the back of her car. 'That's not why I came,' she said. Her heart thudded hard against her chest. Maybe she shouldn't have come; maybe it would have been better to leave things as they were, and hope time healed the rift she'd caused.

'Then why?' Mum asked.

Donna said nothing but folded her arms and studied Billie with a narrow gaze.

With both of them staring at her, and the new knowledge from her conversation with Ruby, it was impossible to miss the likeness between them. It made sense; they were sisters after all.

And this made Donna the most important person in her mother's world. Billie had to clear the air.

She took a deep breath. 'I wanted to apologise.'

She had the small satisfaction of seeing surprise on both their faces. Mum was the first to speak. 'I'm confused.'

Billie wished she'd thought more about what to say on her way there. 'Going through Pop's things made me realise just how short life is. I didn't want to go forward with any bad feeling.' She looked Donna... Megan in the eye. 'I'm sorry for doubting and I hope you can forgive me. I'm not sure Mum has had time to tell you, but she's taken being let down by fakes badly before and I wanted to protect her. That's all.'

Whatever Donna saw in Billie's face must have convinced her it wasn't a ploy. 'I'm glad Amanda had someone looking out for her. I look forward to getting to know you properly.'

Billie couldn't trust herself to speak. She nodded.

Mum's smile was wide. 'That's wonderful, darling. I'm glad you've finally seen sense. You can be the first to congratulate your aunt.'

Billie couldn't help the wariness in her reply. 'On what?'

Mum shared a look with Donna. 'Your grandfather didn't have a lot to give, but apart from a few personal bequests to you girls there's enough left in his estate for me to purchase a small unit. It's all I need.'

'What about the house?' Billie asked. 'You've put so much work into it.' She remembered the disturbing renovation project and realised she would have to ignore it for now.

'I'm giving it to Megan. She missed her childhood here and this is the least I can do, considering the unpleasantness with the reward.'

Heat bloomed in Billie's cheeks, but she couldn't argue. 'If you think it's for the best.' She turned to Donna. 'Congratulations.'

Donna reached out and squeezed Billie's hand, the touch oddly dry. 'Thank you, it's been a long time coming but finally I'm home.' She took her sister's hand in her other so the three of them were linked. 'Finally, I'm where I belong.'

By the time Billie let herself in her empty house, she could barely muster the energy to smile at Plank's warm doggy welcome.

'Your dad's supposed to be here,' she muttered to Lola as she prepared her some pureed carrot, the smiley face Post-it from Nathan she found stuck to the crisper almost bringing her to tears. She held the little sign of his love, wishing she could go back to before she knew what he'd done. 'He's supposed to be my shoulder to lean on.'

Lola's gargled response didn't make Nathan appear but her happy gargle watching Plank lick up a fallen splodge of carrot helped. As did talking to Eve on speaker while she bathed Lola and readied her for bed. Eve didn't question Billie's change of heart regarding Donna and she was grateful not to have to explain.

When the doorbell rang around eight, Billie's heart leapt. Nathan, she thought. But when she opened the door with Plank at her side, his tail wagging, it wasn't Nathan standing there wanting to hold her tight and make everything better.

It was her grandfather, Larry Jones.

EPISODE 12: BACK TO THE NEIGHBOURHOOD

Music playing: 'Too Much Heaven' – The Bee Gees

The music fades.

Welcome to Episode Twelve. I'm Ruby Costa and this is 'The Callaghan Baby Podcast'. Along with my team, I've been investigating the forty-year-old cold case of missing Megan Callaghan. I spoke to Sharon McNamara, the elderly neighbour from the next street over.

Sharon McNamara:
I tell you; they know what happened to that baby. Everyone who was at the dinner party that night knows something.

Ruby:
There's been an investigation and an inquest and they have been repeatedly questioned by police. Are you suggesting they're lying?

After I ask this question, there's a pause before Sharon answers but not because she's uncertain. Rather she's shaking with the anger of someone who's waited far too long to see justice.

Sharon:

Are they lying? Yes. Every damn one of them left alive.

They should have been under more scrutiny.

In a close-knit neighbourhood like ours I couldn't help seeing them afterwards, going about their business. And sure, Carol was obviously devastated, but the rest of them just kept on. It didn't sit right somehow.

Ruby:

Maybe they were doing the best they could.

Sharon:

I don't expect you to understand, but they were close to each other. Not like friends. More that they had some kind of unnatural connection between them. It was there in the way they stood and spoke and acted. There in the families intermarrying, others in business together. All entwined. As though between them all they had something to hide.

Ruby:

If you were so sure they were up to no good, why didn't you go to the police again?

Sharon:

I would have. I almost did. But things back then were different. Who was I to question what the police were doing? I thought they knew best and I'd already been rebuffed.

Ruby:

This is something we found repeated through this whole

investigation, the faith of so many involved in a police force who were at best understaffed and struggling.

Over the months making this podcast there was one person of interest who proved surprisingly reluctant to open up. My mother.

Previously, I've referred to the damage done to Jennifer Marsh by the persistent public perception that her boyfriend at the time, Scott Allen, was involved in the disappearance of Megan Callaghan. She's been stalked and harassed by amateur sleuths sure she can help them solve the case.

I visit her in our family home, a long way from Wattlebury Court.

Jennifer Marsh, thank you for speaking to us today. Please, tell us your story.

Jennifer:

I don't think I appreciated just how young I was back then until I looked back from the other side of fifty. Like most teenagers, I felt grown up but I was just a child. A child who made the mistake of falling for a charmer – an adult who should have known better – and I've been punished for this ever since.

It's a long time ago, but when I close my eyes I can see that page of calculus notes like it's right here in front of me. I had a desk, an old wooden thing handed down from someone, but I preferred studying on my bed. I'd spread my textbook and revision questions out in front of me but I couldn't concentrate for the heat. The fan was on and I'd opened the window looking for a breeze... And also, because sometimes Scott came by late after everyone else was asleep. Yeah, I'm not proud of sneaking around but I was sixteen and infatuated. We'd fought that day so I didn't really think he would, but it meant I could hear the music from the Williams place and the occasional cry of laughter.

Thanks to where my bedroom was – towards the front but on the side of the house – I could also hear anyone approaching the front door so I could make sure I looked extra busy if Dad came by to check I was studying. He was principal at the school and he'd heard through the grapevine about my last math result and had read me the riot act. But he hadn't told Mum.

He came by sometime before nine. I don't remember looking at the time but I remember the 'I can't keep covering for you' lecture Dad gave me.

Ruby:
The adults at the dinner party are on record saying that check was at eight-thirty p.m. Specifically.

Jennifer:
I remember I got a lemonade ice-block from the fridge only a few minutes later and Mum's old grandfather clock struck nine.

Ruby:
And what about the final check? Any late-night snacks to confirm Frank's visit at ten p.m.?

After my questions, there's a long silence while Jennifer turns a blue and silver ring on her thumb around and around.

Jennifer:
He didn't visit.

Ruby:
All along you've agreed that he must have come by but you couldn't be sure. This now sounds definitive.

Why the change?

Jennifer:
I thought if I ignored all this, pretended it had nothing to do with me, it would go away but it hasn't.

They were all so sure of the timelines and I was only sixteen. But I didn't fall asleep. I didn't get caught up in my work. I listened and I watched out for a boyfriend who never showed.

And I'm sure Frank Callaghan did not enter my house that night.

Ruby:
Of course, Frank might have believed the teenager didn't need the check in the same way as the younger children. This revelation, this certainty of Jennifer's, might mean nothing for the timeline of the night a four-month-old child went missing.

We asked Amanda about that touching memory of the very last time she saw Megan.

Given Jennifer's revelation that Frank didn't enter number three Wattlebury Court at ten p.m. as he stated to police, and then again at the inquest, can you confirm that he came to check on you at that time?

Did you have a clock in yours or Megan's bedroom?

Amanda:

I'd wanted my very own clock radio but didn't have one, and I don't remember seeing the time. I just always believed that memory had to have been then.

Ruby:

But you can't be sure?

Amanda:

No.

Ruby:

An increased window where Megan could have gone missing, combined with Scott Allen's revelation at least some of them were high, places doubt on what exactly happened and the convenient alibis that prevented them from ever being properly investigated.

For me, that meant the prospect of returning to the beginning and requestioning everyone involved to try to ascertain concrete details of that now questionable timeline.

In fact, I'd made preliminary contact with both Heather Thompson and Eddie Snyder to try to get the bigger picture, when an anonymous source sent me a new piece of evidence.

The sound of a doorbell ringing and a man's voice: 'Delivery for Ruby Costa.'

Despite the envelope being no bigger than an A4 piece of paper, light and thin, there is something about the innocuously printed address and small but striking 'URGENT' in the lower left corner that has my heart clamouring in my chest.

In it are two photographs, similar to that which became so well-known showing the dinner party from hell. But it is clear from the clean table and neat dress of one that it is early in the night, and from the flushed cheeks, glazed eyes and food remains that the other is later.

In the background is a digital clock and in both photographs it reads 4.22 p.m.

Combined with none of them wearing watches, it is quite possible they had no idea what time it was at all.

In the nursing home where Frank Callaghan resides, Sharon McNamara places her teacup down with a rattle towards the end of our interview.

Sharon McNamara:
He was involved.

Ruby:
Three words hang in the air. Echo through space and time, spreading out like the ripples of a wave washing over everyone who has ever been involved in this case.

When you say 'he' who are you referring to?

Sharon:
Frank. Frank Callaghan.

I believe it was him in that conservation park with a shovel. He knows what happened.

Ruby:
For our final word, we look to Amanda, she who has worked so tirelessly to find her missing sister over so many years.

Amanda Callaghan, I ask you this simple question: Do you believe that Megan is still alive?

Amanda:
Yes.

Ruby:
And do you have a message for her, if she's out there listening to this podcast?

Amanda:
I love you, little sister, and I will never give up on you. Wherever you are, if you can hear me, please, please come home.

Ruby:
This is the end, but it is not over. I have known this family my whole life. I have seen the pain they live with every day. All those who were there that night carry this tragedy with them.

I believe that the truth will be found. I hope this podcast has contributed to that goal. Real breakthroughs have been made and there has been pressure applied to those in charge to do better. The response from the public has been overwhelming and I ask again that if you know anything please come forward. We will find out what happened to Megan Callaghan. I believe this with all my heart.

This was the final episode of 'The Callaghan Baby Podcast'.

Thank you for listening.

35

Billie looked for Granny B to appear on the path, but Grandad was alone. She didn't realise he even knew where she lived. 'Is everything okay? Is it Granny B?'

Red flushed his cheeks and there was a cloud of whisky coming from him. 'She's fine, but I had to come.'

She stepped back to let him pass. 'Can I get you anything?'

As he shook his head, she noticed his puffy eyes and how the small motion made him sway on his feet. 'I heard about Frank,' he said. At the sound of Pop's name, Plank lifted his head in question. The sight of it seemed to hurt Larry because he quickly looked back to Billie. 'And that your mother is giving her the house. Is it true?'

Suddenly, she remembered his face at the foundation ball, the disgust she'd thought she'd seen as Donna was presented to the world. And then it hit her: Frank Callaghan wasn't alone when he found Megan missing.

Larry had been there at his side. Gruff Larry who'd been a silent bystander through her childhood, who never had much to say, always letting his wife do his talking for him. Even in the inquest he'd barely featured.

'She feels it's the least she can do after everything her sister has missed.'

Grandad sat heavily on the couch, his head in his hands. 'She can't.'

Billie perched next to him, her brain racing. 'Why?'

When Grandad lifted his head, tears leaked from his bloodshot eyes. 'Damn Frank for going and leaving this with me. Damn him.' His voice choked. 'My best bloody friend in the world, you know? I'd do anything for him.'

'I don't understand.'

He shook his head, covering his face again, sobs rocking his shoulders. Plank seemed to appear at Grandad's side, his warm body right there for Grandad to pat him, which he did. The gnarled fingers finding the soft white fur of Plank's head.

Part of Billie wanted to dismiss all this as grief. She could call Granny B, get him collected, and never know what had driven him to come to her doorstep. But that was only a small part. Like everyone else in her family the burning question of what happened that night back in 1979 affected every facet of Billie's life and she could no more turn Grandad away now than she could stop breathing.

'What are you trying to say, Grandad? What has he left with you? Do you know something about Donna? Do you know what happened to Megan?'

He didn't answer for the longest time, but the sobs stopped and he sucked in gasps, getting himself back under control.

'Grandad?' she whispered.

He stood. 'No, I shouldn't have come. This was a mistake. Listen, don't mention to your grandmother I was here.'

He moved to take a step past her, but she caught his wrist. Held it. 'No.'

'What do you mean?'

Tightening her grip, she rose so she could hold his gaze.

'You came here to tell me something and you're going to sit back down on this couch and finish what you started. This is a burden you've been carrying for far too long and I promise that you can trust me to shoulder with you. Tell me, Grandad.'

'I'm sorry. I'm so damn sorry.' He buckled at the knees and she helped him onto the couch again.

She sat at his side and placed a hand on his shoulder. 'What are you sorry for?'

He lifted his head and his gaze searched her face. 'You might have Callaghan blood but you were born a Jones. You're my granddaughter. And the smartest of the lot of us.'

'You can tell me.'

Slowly, he nodded. 'That's why I came. Because I think maybe, with your brains and with the Jones strength of character. Maybe I can.' His hand shook as he dragged it over his face. 'You have to understand, I wanted to tell, all these years, it burned in me. But I made a promise.' He shook his head. 'Made a promise and broke a promise and I have to live with that.'

His words slurred a little but that wasn't why Billie was confused. 'Start at the beginning,' she said. 'You're not making any sense.'

'Once I tell you, I can't take it back.'

'I can handle it.'

His rough and weathered hand gripped hers. 'I think you can.' His throat worked. 'You know about the party and that we went to check on the kids. And I guess you know about the drugs?'

She nodded, afraid if she said anything he'd stop talking.

'We weren't really thinking straight when we found her.

343

Maybe if we had been we would have done things differently. I've thought about it enough.'

'You found Megan?'

He shook his head. 'No and yes.' He hesitated. 'We found Amanda. She had the baby with her. It was that SIDS thing, likely, that terrible thing where no one really understands it. A bloody tragedy. And when she woke up... I've never seen anything like it.'

'Megan died in Mum's bed.' Saying it aloud didn't help, only the lifeline of Grandad's grip kept Billie upright.

He was quick to argue. 'A baby dead, with a ten-year-old. It was SIDS. There was no sign of harm or trauma on her body and your mother was so gentle and caring with that baby. And we were high as bloody kites, weren't we? We panicked. Amanda was so out of it and Frank was terrified what would happen to her, to us if the police discovered what had happened. He wrapped up the baby, hid the body in the ceiling, then we made it look like that guy on the news.'

Billie suddenly remembered her mum from the podcast, *I can hear a sound I'm sure is her crying*. She would have gone in there and tried her best to comfort her, taken the baby back to bed with her. 'But if it was SIDS?'

'We weren't thinking. And Frank's pain – I can't tell you how he was hurting. I promised Frank I'd go along with whatever. Figured he knew best for his family. I can't explain what it was like that night, but he was desperate to protect the child he had left. He would have done anything. He must have buried the baby under the guise of searching over the next few days; we didn't discuss the details.'

'What did you tell Gran?'

He ducked his head, avoiding her gaze. 'I didn't grow up in

a nice place like this, or the house at Ridgefield. I'd changed my name and had relatives I'd pretty much cut out of my life. I told her the baby was missing and we didn't want the police investigating us. Also back then, my career, well it wasn't what I made it out to be. We were up to our necks in debt.'

'The others?'

He shrugged. 'Everyone has secrets; no one wants their lives examined too closely.'

Billie tried to comprehend what he'd told her. 'There's been so many resources, so much time put into this case and all along you knew what happened and didn't say anything. How could you?'

He winced. 'I know.' He pulled his hand away and stood, pacing the small room with a heavy tread, nearly tripping over Plank who'd returned to his dog bed to watch it all unfold with sad eyes. 'Over the years I almost told a bunch of times, but then I saw what the searching and the not knowing was doing to Carol and I couldn't keep quiet anymore. She was my friend too and I couldn't bear to see her in pain anymore. I told her the truth; I told her Megan was never coming home.' His voice cracked. 'And I have to live with that.'

Billie's heart hurt remembering the detail from the inquest that they'd bumped into Larry the night before Carol died. 'She took her life the next day.'

Grandad nodded. 'I live with that. I told Carol and she couldn't take it. Frank knew I'd done it. Knew the whole thing was my fault. Things were never the same between us. I'd broken my promise and killed the love of his life.'

'You can't be blamed for what Carol did.'

'Can't I?' He shook his head. 'It didn't take much to see that Amanda was her mother's daughter. And her obsession with searching for Megan… What would the truth do to her? I didn't want another Callaghan death on my hands.'

'But you've told me.'

'Because you're *my* granddaughter, you've got Jones blood, and you said you could handle it. And because someone needs to stop this woman. But I'm not going to the police. I can't. It's too late for all of that.'

Billie had no cause to doubt her grandfather. Part of her understood why he'd kept his silence and why he'd never tell Amanda what had happened to her sister, but it was a heavy burden to carry.

She wasn't bound by Larry's promise to Pop, and she had a responsibility to take care of her mother. That responsibility that had filled so much of her life. But who was she to make a judgement on an accident forty years in the past? If something happened to Eve, she'd do anything to make it right.

She couldn't let Donna go on pretending to be Megan. She must know the truth and she'd manipulated Mum into giving her the house. What else would she take?

'Tell Mum,' Billie begged, knowing she wouldn't be believed if she tried to do so herself.

Grandad's chin lifted, a stubborn look she knew well. 'We both know what that will do to her. There has to be another way. You have to find it.'

As she saw him out, the weight of it all nearly made Billie's knees buckle. But her brain was working overtime. Grandad's confession raised the biggest question of all.

If Donna wasn't Megan, who the hell was she?

THAT NIGHT

10.57 p.m. – Trish

Across at the alcohol-laden shelf he thinks of as his bar, Ken is mixing a cocktail, showing off with extra flourishes for Carol's benefit. He's poured vodka on ice and topped it with orange juice.

'What's that?' she asks. 'A screwdriver?'

He smirks, reaches to the back and pulls out a new bottle. He breaks the seal and waves the bottle at her. 'A splash of this, too.'

She leans close enough to read the label of what I know is the sloe gin. 'So, it's a…?'

His smirk turns lascivious. 'A slow screw.'

Ken might be drunk and high, but when he gives her the drink, his hand is steady and he doesn't spill a drop. 'You'll like it.' He takes the opportunity of her husband gone to check their children, to let the touch on her arm linger. 'Trust me.'

It's not the way he talks about Frank's wife that tells me she's what he wants me to be, rather it's that mostly, he doesn't.

But his gaze follows her when she moves around a room. He shows off just a little more for Frank.

I don't blame him.

The two have this joy between them that I'd envy if I wasn't happy enough just to bask in its glow.

Ken, however, doesn't like any light that's not on him.

She lifts the glass to her lips. They're pink and shining, and curved like she's about to laugh at a private joke only you and she understand. The liquid inside glows deep orange like a sunset and when it tilts towards her mouth it's like the whole world tips with it.

I hold my breath.

Smoke and wine and the candle someone lit mix in my lungs so I'm heady as she swallows. Every one of us watches. Her neck arching back, and the muscles there moving beneath smooth, pale skin.

She lowers the glass and I think there's still music playing but it's disappeared into the background as we wait for her to speak.

'Nice.'

Her eyes are dancing with amusement and there's a drop of burnt orange on her lip.

Ken's mouth works and for a moment no sound comes out. Is he angry? He stands. Awkward. Supplicating. Right in her space but not intimidating so much as desperate. 'A thank you for the host?' he begs.

She considers for a heartbeat and I know – I know – she wants to refuse but she must see something in the clench of his fist or the sweat beading on his brow.

Even women like her must play along.

She leans close and kisses him. Playful, friendly. All in good fun.

Her gaze meets mine and those eyes are still amused as she walks across our lounge room, hips swaying to a rhythm that makes my heart thrum in my ears.

She doesn't touch me but she's so close I breathe her in, that hint of vanilla I caught earlier in the kitchen. Her breath is orange-juice sweet and just a little sour as she leans closer still. She doesn't blink and I can't because I know where this is going and I know it's just part of a good time but it's more.

Right then, it's everything.

Then her lips are on mine. Heat spreads through me from the lightest of contact. A brush of skin on skin, with a softness that melts all the barriers I've worked so hard to build on my heart and my body and I don't dare move in case I reach for her.

'Thank you,' she murmurs.

She steps away, and I smile so somehow I don't cry.

It's all part of the fun.

36

Thursday January 2nd

Unable to sleep properly after Grandad's confession, Billie got up early the next morning and went through all her evidence again. She listened to parts of the podcast and stared at the copy of the wedding certificate that Ruby had sent through. She had to be missing something.

And if Grandad wasn't going to talk, she needed evidence before this stranger swindled Mum out of everything she had, let alone the emotional damage.

After loading Lola into the car before she could change her mind, Billie headed for Donna's house. If she was at home, Billie would pretend she wanted to further make amends, and if she wasn't, Zach had said himself that side door leading to the small courtyard often didn't lock properly.

Minutes later, she sat in her car outside an apparently deserted Number 14C, but she didn't turn off the engine. Sweat slicked her skin despite the air conditioning blowing cool air. What was she thinking? She'd never broken into anywhere in her life.

But if the door was open it wouldn't really be breaking in. Would it?

As she got out, Lola started to cry. Although grey clouds filled the sky, the air was thick and warm.

Never ever leave a baby in a car. Even for a few minutes.

She unstrapped Lola from the car seat and held her against her chest, shushing her softly until she relaxed. As she walked quickly towards the small house she murmured, 'Mummy is actually doing this. Zach will probably be home and the whole thing will go to crap but we're doing this. We're walking down the path, pretending like we have some reason to be here.'

She knocked on the door. Then knocked again harder.

'It looks empty,' she said to her tiny accomplice. Lola smiled happily, probably soothed by the rhythmic hammering of Billie's heart.

Riding the wave of shock and grief she didn't let her doubts kick in, striding around the side of the small house. A simple reach and flick of the latch let them through the small side gate and they were nearly at the door. It really was a tiny box of a house.

'It will probably be locked,' she murmured to Lola.

At the glass door she paused next to a bedraggled-looking fern and peered inside. No sign of anyone home. The woman had to have some identifying papers somewhere. Crossing her fingers on one hand, she used the other to try the handle.

It didn't budge.

The rush of blood pumping in her ears drowned out any neighbourhood sounds as a familiar figure approached from inside. Zach. Of course he was home. He'd hardly be anywhere else with Donna keeping him away from the family as much as possible.

He opened the door, his head tilted in question.

'You don't look sick,' she blurted. And then, the thud of a car door nearby turned her bones to liquid. Donna was home.

Billie waited, heart trying to beat out of her chest. Maybe this was why she'd come; she needed to confront Donna now she knew the truth and needed to see what that meant for her intentions. Would she try to pretend, or would she show her true colours?

A hand appeared at the top of the gate. The latch flicked and it swung open.

Donna stood there, eyes wide. 'You? What the hell do you think you're doing?'

'I wanted to speak to you.'

Donna's arms folded. She must have heard in Billie's tone she no longer believed she was Megan. 'You said everything you needed to this morning. In front of your mother.'

'But now I know the truth. I know you're not Megan. And I believe you know it too. That's why you never intended to stay long, why you didn't plan for your son to be here, the reason you want to keep me as far away as possible, the only one willing to question the fairy tale.' She could feel Zach watching on behind her.

'We've heard it all before,' Donna snarled. 'Billie with her overactive imagination, her relentless harassment, her jealousy making her see things that aren't there.'

'But, Mum,' Zach said. 'She's right about—'

'Enough,' Donna snapped. Although she cut off Zach her icy glare remained fixed on Billie. 'I won't let your wild rantings come between me and my son. Please leave before I call the police.'

Zach made a distressed sound.

It brought Billie to her senses. She'd find no more proof

here and she didn't want this young man caught up in the crossfire of pushing Donna too far.

She walked past Donna, heading for her car and what suddenly felt like safety compared to the frisson across her skin when she had to pass Donna. As she buckled Lola in with fumbling hands, she half expected to feel Donna's hand on her shoulder. The idea of Donna physically attacking her was ridiculous but her body felt otherwise. With Lola in, she hurried around to the driver's side. As she opened the car door, she dared a look back before sliding inside.

Zach must have gone inside but Donna remained, her gaze fixed on Billie in a way that made the fine hairs on the back of her neck prickle to attention.

'I know you're not Megan.' Billie didn't plan to say it but once she started, she couldn't stop. She'd heard the pain in her grandad's voice, knew his story of that night to be the truth.

'The evidence was in Pop's things,' she lied, unwilling to reveal her true source. 'You weren't careful enough.'

Donna had looked angry before but, at Billie's taunt, her face changed. It smoothed like a child flattening the features of a plasticine person. Anger became intent. And intent was much, much worse.

Billie pulled into the driveway, her heart yet to settle from the confrontation with Donna. What had possessed her to goad the other woman?

She took a deep breath, tried to relax and then she saw

him. Nathan, sitting on the front steps with Plank beside him. Wearing shorts, a soaked T-shirt and an air of contrition, Nathan waited for her to turn off the car and get Lola out. As she approached, he remained on the step but held out his arms. As much as she wanted to be the one to run into them, she handed Lola over instead.

'I'm sorry about Pop,' he said. 'I came by yesterday, but you weren't here.'

'I was at Mum's and then at Restwell, packing his things.' She took in his damp T-shirt and the water on the driveway. 'What happened? Were you watering?'

Nathan hesitated, then sighed and jerked his head towards the side of the garage. 'I was trying to clean that.'

Confused, Billie went around and there she saw it. In a neat grey paint still visible despite Nathan's efforts. 'LEAVE IT ALONE.'

Three words screamed at her in a slow-bubbling violence despite being faded, thanks to their size and the fact they'd been painted here on her home, in her space.

Tears pricked her eyes. 'Who could have done this?' She tried to think back to when she left earlier. Had it been there then? She'd had her hands full with Lola and struggling to keep her eyes open enough to focus on the road, let alone anything else. The thought of whoever it was out here while she slept just the other side of the wall had her stomach churning.

Staring at the faint words, she pictured Donna's hand, then some stranger's. Tried to remember if Plank had been restless through the night.

Nathan shifted from foot to foot. 'I'm sorry.'

'It's not your...' Her voice trailed off. She'd guessed it was her pushing for answers, but she didn't know who he owed money to; maybe it wasn't directed at her at all.

'I'll get the stuff to clean it properly, but maybe you should listen.'

She dragged her gaze from the message. 'Maybe,' she said, but she didn't think it could be that simple. Now she knew Donna wasn't Megan she had to wonder what her motivations were. She had to know the truth.

'How's your mum?'

'Devastated. Pissed at you.'

'No less than I deserve.'

'You know that the police will have to be involved. She wouldn't keep it inhouse even if she could.'

'I know.' He hesitated. 'I've been pretending nothing's wrong, but I can't hide from it any longer. I'll pay what I owe and take the punishment coming, as long as I can spare you and Lola as much as possible.'

He turned his attention to Lola, taking the time to kiss her nose and examine every finger and toe as though it had been a week rather than a day away.

Billie used his distraction to study him in turn, noting the faint lines of worry on his brow, dark rings around his eyes and the stubble on his jaw. 'I don't know you anymore and I really hate that.'

'I don't know how to fix this.'

She swallowed hard. 'Maybe we can't.'

He turned to her then. 'I'll do whatever it takes so you can trust me again. I'll get help; I know I have an addiction. I've already arranged to speak to a counsellor. God, just saying that feels like a relief. It sucked that you found out that way, but I'm glad you know.'

'Me too, I guess.' The truth was better than all she'd been imagining.

'I'm staying at Macca's place, on his couch.' He mentioned his oldest friend, the one who usually had the women problems. 'Anyway, I'm there if you two girls need me.'

Maybe he expected her to beg him to come home, but she just nodded.

'I love you, Billie,' he said. 'I've messed up, I know I have, but you and Lola are the most important parts of my world. I'm going to do whatever I can to rebuild what I've broken.'

'It's going to take time.'

'Then I'll make time. I'm not asking for promises that you'll forgive me but I'm begging you to let me show you we can have a future together.'

'I'm mad at you. But I'm not saying no.' She couldn't offer him more right then.

'That's a start.'

He helped out with Lola and then left, promising to come back for Lola's bedtime routine.

Eve had called but Billie couldn't begin to know how to tell her sister what she knew about Donna, not until she had some plan of what to do about it.

Her grandad's explanation about that night echoed in her head: 'No one wants their lives examined too closely.'

She needed to go back to where it all began.

37

Lola in her arms, the physical reminder of just how small Megan Callaghan had been that night when her parents had come to this very house leaving her behind, Billie walked the path to the front door of number five Wattlebury Court and knocked hard on the door.

Like the night of that tragic dinner party, Billie knew that when the door opened Trish would not be alone. She recognised one car parked in front and could guess the owner of the other.

'Billie?' Trish said as the door opened. 'I wasn't expecting you.'

The sound of whispers came from beyond the woman Billie had thought she knew so well, the familiar voices of her gran, Barbara Jones and of course, schoolmarmish despite years of retirement, Gloria Marsh.

'Casual catch-up is it?' Billie asked. 'Or have you heard that Mum's giving her the house and you're asking the questions you should have asked forty years ago?'

Trish sighed. 'You're coming in whether I like it or not?'

Billie hesitated. 'It's time to stop the lies. But I'm not going to push you over if that's what you're asking.'

Trish stepped backwards. 'You won't get the answers you need here, but you might as well ask the questions.'

Billie led her work colleague inside, into a cloud of old-lady scent thick with powdery perfumes of rose and lavender. She didn't argue when Gran took Lola from her, before returning to where she'd been sitting at the table while Trish took the spot at her side away from Gloria.

While Billie remained on her feet, the three surviving women from the 'dinner party from hell' looked at her from a table, more modern than the one in all the pictures, but in the same room as they'd partied that night. Although it had tea and coffee cups on it today instead of wineglasses, and eyes were glazed with old age not with other substances.

'I don't know what you think we have to tell you,' Gloria muttered, disapproval in her turned-up nose and crossed arms. 'There's no crime in getting together for a chat.'

'No crime in that,' Billie agreed as she tried to get her thoughts in order. 'But there is in what Donna's doing. It's fraud at best and we don't know her full intentions. She is not Megan. You have to tell Mum what really happened that night.'

Gloria tutted. 'We don't know.'

Billie studied the three faces before her. Gran prim and proper and born to be someone's grandmother, her opposite alongside in the so much younger, and still stylish, Trish who Billie thought of as a friend, and the stranger among them Gloria, who she'd known as Ruby's grandmother. Gloria's forever stern demeanour making Billie grateful for her own grandmother.

Could they really not know?

She thought about the famous photo and those sent

anonymously in to Ruby, adding to the doubts around the timeline. It had to have come from one of these three.

'You lied,' she said. 'About checking the children and about being high and you kept proof of that lie in the photographs taken that night.'

None of them flinched. All of their faces coated with a thick layer of makeup filling age lines that weren't there forty years ago, they could have been wearing masks.

'Someone must have seen something,' Billie insisted. She thought back to the podcast, what they'd said to the police and to the inquest and then she remembered the view from Megan's bedroom window, right into this very backyard.

She turned to Trish.

'You smoked. Still do when you think no one's watching. Ken hated it, thought it wasn't suitable for a lady – you said that much in the podcast. And you took a bathroom break around eleven and that must have been when it all happened. Did you see something?'

Trish didn't answer.

Billie swallowed back a scream of frustration that would only scare Lola and let these women dismiss her as a child. 'You saw something and you had the photos?'

As she spoke she realised who she was talking to. A woman who'd somehow become a partner in the family construction firm after her marriage broke down. Billie's breath rushed out as realisation hit.

'You blackmailed Pop to join the company but you didn't go to the police with what you knew. Were you having an affair with him, too?'

The snort of laughter burst out from deep within Trish. 'Hell no.'

'Explain.'

Trish stared at her hands, her nails perfectly manicured as they always were, even if she had to go out on a construction site. Today's colour a gorgeous light blue. 'You've got it wrong. I helped the business at a time where Frank was struggling. Put money into it that I'd kept aside. I didn't have any photos.'

'How did you have money? You said at the inquest he cut you out of the estate.'

'I never trusted Ken,' Trish admitted. 'No one ever stopped to ask how a dentist made so much money. An average one at that. But I saw the men coming by with briefcases of cash after hours. I don't know what the scheme was but you can be sure as hell I made sure I kept aside enough for myself.'

It clicked for Billie. 'No wonder Ken didn't want the police looking at him too closely.'

Trish's sigh was like a weight being lifted. 'None of us were thinking straight, and having one story and sticking to it was the only option. None of us wanted the police poking their noses into our affairs.'

'We were broke,' Gran blurted. She was holding Lola in front of her and making an exaggerated smiley face to make her great-granddaughter giggle, not even meeting Billie's gaze. 'In debt, trying desperately to keep up with our fancy neighbours. We were trying to put Larry's family connections behind us. We wanted a fresh start.'

'So that makes lying okay?' Billie retorted.

Gran lifted her head, eyes flashing. 'Don't complain when you don't like the truth. Anyway, I didn't take any photos that night, couldn't afford to.'

That left…

Along with the others, Billie turned to Gloria Marsh.

Under the almost white of her thick foundation there were two slashes of colour on her cheeks as her lips pursed. 'I simply wanted to help Ruby's podcast.'

'Bullshit.'

Billie swung to face Trish at the snarled exclamation.

Trish shook her head, glaring across at Gloria who glared right back. It was like they'd been shadow-boxing for forty years but someone had torn off the gloves and they were toe-to-toe bareknuckle, all pretence of politeness gone.

'You just can't help yourself, can you? With the lying and protecting him.' Facing Billie again, Trish's jaw worked. 'One might wonder why Ray Marsh, respected principal, didn't tell Scott Allen where to go when he was abusing his only child?'

Billie hadn't really thought about it. She'd heard Gloria's explanation that her daughter was too grown up to be locked up and kept from Scott but there was no such interview with Ray.

'Why?' Billie asked. 'Was he connected to the drugs too?' That might be why Ruby hadn't asked the questions of her own grandfather. The realisation of the gap made her feel uneasy, like she'd been tricked as a listener.

Trish shook her head. 'Sure, he gave it a try; we all did. It was the Seventies. But drugs weren't what Ray Marsh was hiding. There was more.'

'She doesn't know what she's talking about,' Gloria screeched.

But Billie kept her gaze locked on Trish. 'Tell me.'

Trish hesitated so long that Billie feared she was going to

be foiled again by the ties that kept those who'd attended that dinner party from speaking out, keeping each other's secrets all this time.

'Please,' Billie said. 'Whatever you're all hiding, it's festering, seeping like something rotten through the generations. I can handle it. I need to know it all and then maybe I can end this before that imposter takes everything'

Trish nodded slowly, and then with a final glance at Gloria she said it: 'He had a particular reputation at the school. Everyone knew about it. Scott knew about it. No one talked about it.'

As she spoke, Billie remembered the odd comment from Heather Thompson, Jennifer's friend: 'We all liked Principal Marsh.'

Trish was still talking. 'It was okay back then for teachers to keep their students back alone in a classroom. Okay for them to drop a favourite home after dark. A community thing. Okay for a private tutoring session on the weekend.'

Gloria pushed back from the table, leaping to her feet. 'I don't need to hear any more of these lies.' She picked up a teacup and it looked for a moment like she would hurl it at Trish.

'Sit,' Gran snapped. 'We all know it, and we know you sent in the pictures because Ruby was going to go back and speak to young Heather Thompson and you thought she might hear about Ray.'

Gloria's mouth opened and closed but then she lowered the teacup and sat. Her head bowed. 'We just didn't want them asking questions.'

Trish's eyes beseeched Billie, asking her to understand. 'You know the women who were at that dinner party. We're your grandparents, your family friends, and in one special case your colleague and godparent.' She managed a weak smile at her reference to herself. 'But all of us are old in your eyes. We weren't always worrying about blood-thinning medication and crook backs.'

'O-kay.'

'We were young and wild and our bodies… they were for fun and sex and we used and abused them. Particularly the women. It was different then. We had to use whatever we had at our disposal for power, to keep safe.'

She must have seen something in Billie's expression because she gave a low sultry laugh and for a moment Billie could almost see it.

'All of us,' Trish said. 'Even your grandmother. And I'm not only talking about Carol.'

Gran flushed, but didn't argue.

'Everyone had their own reasons for backing Frank and not asking too many questions about what really happened in that house,' Trish continued. 'No one was thinking straight. We never thought our white lies would snowball the way they did.' She hesitated. 'We trusted our husbands, because, to be honest we didn't have a lot of choice.'

It was beginning to make sense. In Billie's mind a new picture was forming, replacing the original photo of those at the dinner party published so many times in connection to the case.

The surface congeniality of the happy group seemed to have changed before Billie's eyes. The smiles now appeared faked on some of the faces. Desperate on others. The tension between them like the smoke swirling from the ashtrays and weaving between the couples. A front they'd maintained all those years. All for their own reasons.

At last she had their truth.

Somehow in all of it was the answer to who Donna really was.

THAT NIGHT

11.01 p.m. – Trish

I manage to sit until the conversation starts up again then I'm on my feet. Carol's gaze is on me, concern and kindness. She didn't mean anything by it.

I just need to get out of here.

A moment to myself.

'Bathroom,' I lie to Ken so he won't follow.

I'm outside in the warm night air in the farthest reaches of my garden, lighting up at fucking last, when I hear the slam of a door. Larry's voice, raised but not enough for me to make out what he's saying.

Then, a single woman's cry that brings me to my knees.

38

Eve and her twins arrived at Billie's place at the same time as Nathan returned with the takeaway. 'Sorry,' Eve said looking from Billie to Nathan. 'I didn't mean to interrupt anything.'

'You didn't,' Billie said quickly. He'd come for Lola's bedtime routine and she couldn't resist his offer of dinner from her favourite Italian place. *Just dinner*, she'd warned him.

'And I've bought enough to feed a small army,' Nathan added holding up the bags.

'In that case,' Eve said, 'I'll stay. Mostly to make sure you're doing right by my sister.' The tone was light but the look she gave Nathan was anything but nice.

'Fair enough. I've got a lot of making up to do.' Nathan was quite serious. 'To everyone.'

They shared a look and then Eve nodded, apparently convinced by whatever she'd seen. 'Max and Matilda have already eaten but they might try a bit. They're impossible tonight.'

'Impossible,' Matilda agreed with a grin.

Standing there in his truck pyjamas Max nodded proudly. 'Adsolutely.'

Nathan convinced the twins to help him serve up, and

Eve collapsed dramatically onto the couch next to Billie. 'Is Nathan why you've been missing in action?'

'No, Donna.'

Eve shook her head. 'Truce broken then?'

'I'm sure she's not Megan.' Billie didn't know how to explain why she was so convinced without breaking Grandad's confidence. The realisation that Megan was dead and never coming home was still sinking in. The responsibility of that knowledge weighed on her. She dropped her gaze.

Eve knew her too well. 'Spill. What do you know?'

Over creamy carbonara and spicy amatriciana Billie told her sister and Nathan about Ruby's revelation confirming that Nancy and Janette were the same person and about Pop's affair. 'She couldn't have taken Megan and kept her hidden for a year,' she finished lamely. 'She was at school with Mum every day.'

'But Donna passed the DNA test,' said Eve. 'Are you saying it's all a coincidence?'

Billie liked logic; the most likely answer was most likely true.

'I'm sure she's not Megan, but the chances of the test being wrong are so low as to be negligible. And I can't work out how she could have fudged it without me noticing one of the seals being broken. It's a paternity test not an identity one; it doesn't prove she's Megan. It does prove, however that she's Pop's daughter.'

'Pop's daughter, but not Megan?' Eve echoed.

Billie's spoon slipped from her fingers bouncing onto the floor as realisation hit. 'That's it. It's obvious.'

Nathan picked up the spoon. 'What's obvious? Spit it out.'

'What if Jannette loved Donna like a mother because she *was* Donna's mother?' Billie tried to connect everything

REBECCA HEATH

she knew for sure. 'We know that Nancy and Pop had an affair and then she left town and left a school she by all accounts adored. Then, she didn't take up her new position. She couldn't teach because she was busy having her baby, having Donna. Donna could easily be a year younger than she says – it's not like we've seen a birth certificate.'

'Didn't Donna say Janette couldn't have children?' Nathan argued.

'She would,' Eve said. 'If she needed to for her story.'

'What about the birthmark?' Nathan asked.

Billie shook her head. 'Easy to fake and there was aftercare ointment in her bathroom cabinet.' She made herself busy collecting her spoon. 'I just happened to see it when I was there.'

'The blanket then?' Eve countered.

'Pop said to me the other day that they had two.'

Eve didn't appear convinced. 'I don't know.'

But Billie couldn't sit still. She jumped up. 'It fits with everything. I knew it; I knew she wasn't Megan.' It also fit with the secret Larry Jones had shared about what really happened to Megan.

She faced the others, wondering how they couldn't understand. 'Even the DNA testing. Of course it came back positive. She's Pop's daughter, but not Carol's.'

Their faces showed their thoughts. Nathan's slow comprehension so easy to read she wondered how she hadn't guessed about his gambling problems.

Eve, however, was still unsure. 'But why?'

'She's part of the family she probably always felt had been denied her, and Mum's sister,' Billie suggested. 'Mum's signing over the house.'

368

'And lots of people like attention,' Eve mused. 'All the fame and press that is going to come from this. She'll have talk show offers, magazine spreads, the works. No wonder she encouraged Mum to do those interviews.' She shrugged. 'But how can we prove any of it?'

Billie grinned. 'Another DNA test, but match to Mum. I'm no DNA expert but I reckon full and half-siblings will give different results.'

'You're right.' Eve had already done a quick search on her phone while Billie was talking. 'Full is like fifty per cent match and half twenty-five per cent.'

'Why did Nancy leave town?' asked Nathan.

'Rejection,' Billie guessed. 'Pop broke up with her and she was pregnant. She must have wanted to leave the past and her association with the famous Callaghan Baby behind her for good.'

'Maybe Donna thinks she is Megan.' This was from Eve who'd gotten along with Donna from the start. 'She could be a victim, too.'

Billie considered. 'No. There's been something off from the start. She never intended to stay here for long. If she was Megan, I'd have welcomed her with open arms,' said Billie.

Eve scoffed. 'Would you?'

'I want to find the truth as much as anyone.' Billie couldn't shake the image of Donna staring after her as she drove away from her house. 'I told her I knew,' she whispered. 'I lied because I had to say something.'

'So what?' Nathan said. 'You do now. Well, if any of this is true.'

The more she'd seen from Donna the more Billie worried

about her intentions. Even if she had been Megan, the way she'd splintered the family, the malevolence she'd only let Billie see, like she knew Billie couldn't do anything about it.

If Donna truly was family, then that made this personal. And that changed everything.

'What if,' Billie said slowly, the tangle of possibilities knotting into a hard lump in her belly, 'she's not getting so close to Mum because she loves her and wants to be her sister? What if it's the opposite?'

Eve held her gaze while she considered. 'Then Mum's in danger. We have to warn her.' She grabbed her phone, and pressed to call Mum's number.

It went to voicemail.

'Please,' Eve said. 'If you get this, Mum, call me back. It's urgent.'

Billie tried too but, again, there was no answer.

'It's after nine and it's been one hell of a day,' Billie said trying to remain rational. 'Maybe she's gone to bed early.'

'Probably,' Eve agreed.

Nathan had grabbed her a fresh spoon and when the others ate so did Billie. But she might as well have been eating glue.

Max and Matilda had fallen asleep in front of the TV with Plank curled up between them. The three matching low snores the only break in the quiet. They finished eating, Billie and Eve both leaving limp strands of fettuccine in their bowls.

Nathan stood. 'I should probably get going.'

Billie hated the thought of him leaving but didn't want to ask him to stay. 'I'll walk you out.'

'And I'll clear the plates,' Eve said, quickly making herself scarce as Billie trailed Nathan out the door, Plank watching their progress but not moving from his spot with the children.

Nathan paused at the car, making no move to open the door. 'Give Lola a kiss for me.'

She wrapped her arms around her waist to keep herself from reaching for him. He needed to make changes before she could let him fully return to her life or her bed. Asking him to stay now would be forgiving him before he'd done anything to earn it. 'I will.'

'Your mum is fine; you don't need to worry there. Donna might be hiding some things but she's been in your mum's life for weeks now and done no harm.'

'I know.'

'I love you.'

She nodded, her aching throat preventing her answering even if she knew what she'd say.

He waited a heartbeat and then sighed. 'Night, Billie.'

'Night.'

She didn't watch him leave, instead heading back in to Eve who'd cleared the table and stacked the leftovers in the fridge.

Billie checked her phone, but there was no reply from her mum. Was Donna really the kind of person they should fear? Could she harm someone who'd let her so warmly into her life and been willing to give her everything?

'Mum's probably okay,' Eve said, guessing her thoughts.

All the way along she'd been sceptical about Billie's doubts, wanting to believe as much as their mum, and she'd immediately got along with Donna, but now the worry Billie felt was all over her sister's face.

Without Nathan there Billie could think more clearly. As Eve put the dishwasher on, Billie fired off a message summarising her latest theories to Ruby.

'*We think Nancy left town because she was pregnant with Pop's child, and Donna is impersonating Megan for revenge.*'

Ruby replied with an attachment only minutes later. '*That makes sense. I wouldn't have realised it was her if you hadn't raised the possibility of her being pregnant.*'

Attached was a picture of a woman who could be Nancy Blair and she was obviously expecting. The date on the grainy shot put it a few months after Nancy left town. Proof at last.

Moments later Ruby called. 'I know it's late but I had to tell you this in person.'

'What?' Billie put it to speaker so her sister could hear.

Ruby hesitated. 'I was following up on Donna's work history at various care facilities and hospitals. There was a hush-up at one of her places of employment around her having a temper. The redacted report described her as "unstable".'

'Unstable? What does that even mean?'

Billie couldn't miss the fear vibrating through her own body reflected there in Eve's wide eyes and blood-drained cheeks.

'I followed the trail to find out,' Ruby replied. 'In this case, it refers to an assault charge that was handled out of the courts. God, Billie, I'm sorry. Maybe if I hadn't been so focused on your grandfather I would have looked into Nancy more and might have found this all sooner.'

'Thanks to you we'll hopefully be able to warn Mum in time.' Billie ended the call and met Eve's gaze. 'I think I should go to Mum's place.'

Eve chewed on her thumbnail. 'I could go. Or we could call the police?'

'And say what? All I know is I'm not going to sleep until I know for sure.' Billie grabbed her keys and headed for the door. 'Look after the kids; I'll be back in half an hour. Oh, and keep trying Mum.'

It didn't take long to get to Ridgefield. Billie stopped the car on the side road and killed the lights. The street was dark and quiet, the reservation across Wattlebury Court ink-black. No light or movement came from Mum's house. Hers was the only car in the driveway. Nothing signalled Donna's presence but when Billie rang her mum's number it again went straight to messages.

Before she could get out of the car, her phone buzzed in her hand.

'You're there aren't you?' Nathan asked as soon as she answered.

'Maybe.'

He sighed. 'I would have come with you.'

'I know.' Like Eve, he'd not been convinced that Donna could pose a threat, but they hadn't seen the woman's face that afternoon.

'I'm guessing you won't wait for me to get there before going in?'

'You can stay on the phone,' she offered. 'It's deserted. You and Eve are right: I'll knock on the door, get Mum out of bed and probably get told off.'

But I'll know she's safe.

She didn't talk to Nathan as she got out the car, careful not to make too much noise closing her door. Few lights shone from windows in nearby houses. Nothing moved in response to her presence. These days people minded their business. As she headed towards number eight on the corner, the red timber almost black, she thought she saw movement on the reserve. She spun to scan the grass and trees but all remained still.

Her husband's regular breathing kept her company as she made her way down the sloping driveway, along the side of Mum's car towards the side door.

Something rustled in the shadows of the backyard. Donna?

Billie peered into the darkness but couldn't see a damn thing. The thudding of her heart and comforting rhythm of Nathan's breath drowned any other sound. Then, a scrape of shoe on concrete alerted her to company a moment before the voice spoke.

39

'Why am I not surprised?' came the growled question in the darkness.

Billie must have made a sound because she could hear Nathan's voice in miniature coming from the phone. 'What's wrong?' But she couldn't answer him.

Her hand went to her chest as Donna stepped forward from the shadows. Without hanging up, she slipped the device into her pocket. 'I've come to see Mum.'

Donna shook her head. 'Oh, honey, I don't think that's a good idea.'

'I'll let Mum decide.' Billie moved towards her, but Donna widened her stance to block the narrow gap between car on one side, and the western red cedar cladding of the house on the other.

'You think you're so clever,' she snarled. 'You should have heard my boy: Billie this, Billie that. Enough to make me ill.'

'I don't think I'm that smart.'

Donna's face brightened. 'You're not.'

'If I were smart, I would have come here hours ago.'

Donna bared her teeth in a smile. 'Yes. And now you're too late.'

Her stomach lurched. *Please let Nathan be hearing all this,*

please let him be on his way. Let him have called the police.
This woman was unstable at best. At worst... She wouldn't
know that if she couldn't get to the house.

'Am I too late? You're still here.' As she spoke, Billie let her
voice rise, hoping to alert Mum, hoping she could be alerted.
Donna's *'too late'* could be talking about gaining Mum's
confidence and signing over the house or it could mean she'd
harmed her half-sister. How far would Donna go?

Billie tried to judge the distances and angles. Could she get
around the car and beat Donna to the house?

Donna noticed the direction of Billie's gaze. 'You could
try,' she said. Then she lifted her hand so the needle on the
end of the syringe in it glinted in the faint light. 'With what's
in this, you'd want to be sure I won't catch you.'

Billie's feet stuck to the ground and fear snaked up her
spine. Despite all her suspicions, the sight of the weapon so
casually brandished chilled her blood. A nurse with expertise
and access to who-knew-what drug concoctions.

'Poor Amanda has been so tired,' Donna said. 'Lucky I
could give her something to help her sleep. You were there
when I offered, remember?'

Billie could only nod. She could picture her mum's grateful
expression that Donna was a nurse and could get her
something strong to sleep.

Donna shook her head. 'Your mother held out her arm
for me. She was so trusting that my only concern was her
wellbeing.'

'What have you done?' Billie lurched closer, pulling up
short of the needle.

'And there's all those renovation things she has lying around
from our little project,' Donna continued. 'Solvents and paint

thinners and the like. So dangerous to keep so much of it inside, but Amanda couldn't have known that she'd fall so heavily asleep with a candle going. Oh, to watch her recreate that room, it was sickening. The whole thing is an accident waiting to happen.'

'I know the truth. You're Nancy Blair's daughter and you came here for revenge.'

'But your mother will never know any of it. The last thing she said as sleep sucked her into its web was how tremendously happy she was that I'd come home.' Donna's face hardened. 'But she meant Megan. It's always her with Amanda.'

Something like recognition spiked inside Billie. 'Believe me, I know.'

Donna's eyes narrowed, assessing. 'I guess you would understand. Her obsession with finding that child taking over everything, no one ever able to fill that gap of a baby missing forty years ago.'

Billie edged closer, feeling a night breeze on her back, fresh like it had blown straight off the conservation park. 'Is that what you wanted, to be the one to fill the gap?'

Donna's laugh held derision. 'To be Megan Callaghan? No. Like everyone else with a brain I'm pretty sure she's dead. Such a waste. My sister should have been out there looking for me.'

The whole time she spoke, Donna didn't try to keep her voice down nor look back to the house. Clearly, she didn't think anyone was coming from inside. Whatever sleeping concoction she'd given Mum must have her knocked out.

Billie sensed she was running out of time, but what was Donna's plan? If she gave Mum an overdose it would point to her and she'd risk losing her son, something Billie was sure she didn't want.

'Mum didn't look for you because she didn't know you existed. None of us did,' she said, trying to work out what Donna had planned. 'You can't blame her for your parents' mistake.'

'That's where you're wrong again, Little Miss Know-it-all. There's enough blame to go around.'

'Have you always known?' Billie asked, stepping closer still.

'That I'm not Megan?' A bitter laugh. 'Of course. My mother didn't tell me about Frank until her last years. Only then did I see the pain *your* family caused her. Frank chose Amanda and his dead baby over me.'

'And you decided to try to get revenge?'

'Try? I think you'll find I've succeeded.' Donna's eyes flashed pure rage. 'A little research, and that podcast was a goldmine of information. A fake birthmark and my mother's most beloved possession: that stupid blanket. And a house that I don't even want but will resell quite well even if it's somewhat damaged. No one will blame me if I can't live here after what is going to happen tonight.'

'You'll lose Zach.'

Donna laughed. 'Not when no one can prove I've done anything wrong. As far as he's concerned this will be a strange blip, soon forgotten.'

That's when Billie caught the faintest whiff of smoke.

Fire. No wonder Donna had mentioned the paints and solvents and the candle she'd left with a sleeping Amanda. She'd planned it all to look like an accident so she could get revenge and then pretend to be devastated. Now she was stalling, she needed to give whatever she'd lit time to catch and burn so Billie couldn't stop it.

Billie moved then, fast and straight at Donna. As the older woman jerked back in surprise, Billie helped momentum with a two-handed shove in her chest.

'You little bitch,' Donna cried, stumbling back against the car.

Billie was almost past her when... Ouch. Something pricked her skin. Instinctively she flung her arm up and away, her nails grazing Donna's cheek.

'I'll get you for that.'

The syringe flew through the air, rolling into the darkness under Mum's car. Donna dropped to her knees, scrambling after it, choosing recovering her evidence because even if Billie managed to get to Mum she'd have no proof this fire wasn't an accident.

Billie grabbed at the phone in her pocket, pressing the speaker. 'Nathan?'

'I heard everything; the police are on their way.' His voice carried to where Donna crouched.

Her head turned. Their gazes locked. With one last glare at Billie, Donna pushed up onto her feet and took off up the driveway.

Billie headed in the opposite direction, towards the house. As she reached the door, an engine roared to life out on the street. Donna would get away, but Billie couldn't waste time chasing her because she tasted the thick tang of smoke on her tongue.

Slamming her fist against the screen door, she called, 'Mum?'

Nothing.

No movement, no sound, nothing at all came from inside the dark house consistent with Mum being not simply asleep. Smoke filled her lungs with every breath. She touched the door. It was cool, but not cold – the weather? Flames unseen on the other side?

The eerie quiet of it pricked at her senses. Even if Mum couldn't hear the warning or smell the smoke, the alarm should be screeching.

The door didn't budge. Locked. Suddenly instead of the one or two she might as well have had a hundred keys on her keyring. Finally, the lock clicked and she pushed at the door, listening for the crackle of flames, feeling her mouth coat with smoke. Nothing broke the quiet.

Didn't fires make a sound?

The kitchen appeared normal. A pile of papers stacked neatly on the table. A small vase of freshly picked lavender the centrepiece.

But more smoke now. The air blurred with it. No flames, no but a faint hint of something else in the air. Burning solvent?

'Mum!' she screamed, but there was no response.

Shouldn't the police have come by now? Had she told Nathan to call the fire brigade?

When she went to ask him, she realised she must have dropped her phone outside. He'd be worried, but she had to find Mum. She followed the smell and the smoke towards the door leading to the hallway. This she touched just in time, recoiling from the heat. And now she could hear the crackle and hiss coming from the other side.

Opening that door would give the whole thing a rush of oxygen fuel, likely to feed the fire, or worse see Billie enveloped in flames.

Think.

She ran outside and around to Mum's bedroom window. The solid outdoor security blind installed by the last owners might as well have been concrete. She banged on it anyway. 'Mum!'

But she couldn't see in, let alone know if Mum had heard. Besides, Donna had a syringe. Her mum was probably unconscious. Hopefully, only unconscious.

Then it came to her.

Megan's room.

Like the rest of the room, the small window had been renovated to be just like it was forty years earlier. Plain, ordinary glass.

On shaking legs, she ran around the side of the house.

40

There, at the end of the path along the fence Billie spotted the small window into the room that had been Megan's. Thanks to the podcast, part of her searched the ground but there were none of the cigarette butts that had so long ago diverted the investigation into Megan Callaghan's disappearance.

Hopefully, she could get in this way and be inside the house on the other side of the flames she'd heard in the hallway, on the side where her mum lay asleep and vulnerable.

The room inside the window showed no hint of flames, the glass cool to the touch. She banged against it. 'Mum?'

No response.

She searched the surrounds, loosening a hand-sized paver from the uneven path. It came free. She swung as hard as she could, lifting her other arm to cover her face and turning away.

It shattered, glass spraying around her in a tinkle of sharp edges. The jolt through her arm made her cry out. They never showed that it hurt in the movies.

Smoke came out on wisps of stronger scent and a blurring and stinging of her eyes.

Thankful she'd slipped into her Converse rather than sandals, she kicked out as much of the pane as possible.

Then she climbed up and in, looking and listening for the fire deeper in the house. Hoping all the time to hear sirens in the distance.

She used the top of the cot to balance and jump down into the room. On the ground, she glanced back at the window, broken and gaping, lit by faint light from outside and with the black wall of the fence beyond. And beneath it, with stray flecks of glass glinting in the cot. Empty.

Pop's words from the inquest rang in her head:

The cot was empty and the only window in the room, smashed. Megan was gone. She was gone.

Billie shook her head to clear it. She knew Megan was long dead, but unlike the tragedy of the past, tonight could have a happy ending.

Every step forward she longed for someone else to come in and take over. Someone more capable, more competent, someone who knew what they were doing. But there was only her.

She could see the stretch of hallway. There at last, almost welcome, the first sight of orange flames through thick murky grey darkness. Now she could see the enemy. Donna must have lit it in the laundry next to the bathroom and from the smell she'd made some sort of cocktail from Mum's home renovation supplies. A renovation Donna had encouraged for the secret special project for bonding with Mum.

She must have been planning this all along, leading Mum to purchase the supplies and then when Mum commented on her exhaustion, pushed her to ask for the help with sleeping that would allow it all to come together. Mum dead in a terrible event that would seem like an accident, with Donna left the grieving sister.

Billie's heart raced, but knowing she had some space and time was calming, better than the towering inferno she'd imagined.

She coughed.

The fumes coated her mouth with every breath, and her breath came in shallow gasps to compensate. The room spun and she made herself stop and recalibrate, lifting her T-shirt to cover her mouth and nose, before moving forward into the hallway. If only she'd stopped to wet them when she'd passed the hose. Too late for if-onlys now.

Crouching low to the floor she headed for Mum's bedroom, away from the source of smoke.

Bang!

She flattened herself to the floor, but when the ceiling above didn't fall in, she pushed on. She had to keep moving.

The air cleared when she entered Mum's room, allowing her to see the motionless outline of her mum under a light sheet. She fell to her knees beside the bed. 'Mum?'

She didn't expect movement and didn't get any, but there was a pulse, she was alive. Donna must have been sure the fire would reach here and given Mum enough sedative to keep her from escaping before it did. There would be no evidence Donna was to blame for any of this.

Hand on Mum's shoulder, Billie shook hard. 'Mum, wake up. You have to wake up.'

No response. And worse, Billie could hardly move her.

She crawled back to the door, peering out towards Megan's room. Flames there now definitely. Another bang and the light fitting down the far end of the hallway crashed to the floor. With every breath the smell of solvent grew stronger. Donna must have spread it through this end of the house.

Then, the wallpaper caught. Sheets of flame skidded across the walls, eating through the cheap paper.

Billie gasped, choking on the billowing smoke.

No way back.

Working quickly using everything she knew about fire safety, she shut the bedroom door, rolling up one of Mum's long dressing gowns from the back of the door and using it to block the gap at the floor.

Then, she examined the window. The glass opened easily but the shutters wouldn't budge. She cleared the exit as much as she could.

Then she heard it. The sweetest wail she'd ever heard. Fire engines were coming.

Tears pricked her eyes, adding to the sting from the smoke.

But they weren't out of here yet. Again, she doubled over, coughing. Each breath hurt but she returned her attention to Mum. Hooking a hand under each arm, she dragged her off the bed and along the floor, edging backward on her knees, right over to the window and the small hints of fresh air coming through the gaps in the shutters.

'Help,' she shouted, hoping for a crowd gathering outside. 'We're in here.'

If Nathan had come, he'd know where Mum's room was, might know where to find them. But had he come?

Each breath hurt, like she was breathing in cotton wool. Terrible, throat-burning cotton wool. The sirens were closer; the faint sound of an engine filtered in from outside. People talking, shouting, giving orders.

She pressed her mouth to the gap too small to even see through. 'Help!'

She pushed Mum's hair back off her forehead. 'They're

coming,' she managed. Hoping she was telling the truth, hoping Mum could hear it through whatever Donna had given her to knock her out. 'Hold on.'

Then she pushed herself up and placed her lips to the gap again. 'Help, someone, please.'

Over the fire and smoke feeling like it was plugging her ears she heard water hitting the house. But not close.

'In here.' But her voice was loud only in her head, the whisper pitiful through the material covering her face. Had it always been so weak? Had she shouted at all?

'Help.'

Her knees sank beneath her despite her hand gripping the window ledge. She thought of her daughter, home and sleeping, and suddenly she didn't care about all the million ways she failed as a parent, she just wanted to see her face again.

The light got further away. Was she falling?

Help.

She wasn't stupid, knew as she lost sight of the window completely that she hadn't made a sound but as darkness closed in, she cried it again anyway in her head.

Help.

41

It could only have been seconds between her last cry and the whine of the metal window covering being torn away that brought consciousness crashing back to Billie.

Coughing and gasping for air, she tried her best to aid the suited-up firefighters who helped her and Mum free of the smoke-filled bedroom. But her head spun and her legs didn't work properly.

'Thank you.' It barely came out of her raw throat, but she couldn't stop trying to say it. 'Thank you.'

And then Nathan was there, his face red from tears and fear, and she knew in that moment that they would be okay. She wanted to tell him as much, but couldn't manage the words past coughing up blobs of disgusting grey mucus.

As soon as she could breathe better again. Billie shrugged off the kind hands of the ambulance officers and, leaning heavily on Nathan's arm, she stumbled on wobbly legs to where they'd placed Mum on a stretcher. Her eyes were open now but didn't have their usual sharpness. She looked straight at Billie but didn't show any signs of recognition.

'Mum, you're okay. There was a fire, but you're okay.'

'I'm sorry,' Mum said.

It came out so quiet and slurred Billie almost missed it.

She leaned down close to Mum, fighting nausea and the people trying to do their job as they moved her towards the waiting ambulance. 'You don't need to be sorry; this isn't your fault.'

'She needed me.'

And then Billie had to shuffle backwards to avoid a crunch.

She stared after her mum as they loaded her in. She couldn't know about Donna yet. What had she been sorry about? And were those tears in her eyes?

The ambulance officer she'd escaped earlier was there in front of her again. 'You need to see a doctor.'

She shrugged off their concern. 'I'm okay.' But the cough that followed made a lie of her claim.

The woman smiled, kind but firm. 'We probably won't keep you long. And you'll be able to be with your mum. Your hubby can follow in his car.'

Billie looked to Nathan. 'Will you?'

He pressed a kiss to her forehead. 'Let anyone try to stop me.'

Billie didn't get to go home that night. The tests for the effects of smoke inhalation took forever in the busy hospital and then more tests when she remembered the sting in her arm from the syringe.

The tests came back clear but by then it was almost morning.

She tried to snatch a few hours of sleep, and Nathan spent the long hours in a chair next to the hospital bed when he wasn't going to get updates on her mum for her.

Eve and the twins stayed the night at her house to care for Lola and Plank who Eve said started getting restless as soon as Billie left, like he'd known she was in danger.

Nathan had reported that Mum would be okay. But he couldn't completely assuage Billie's worry, because there would still be fallout to come from this mess.

Mum would wake up and have to lose her sister again, along with having to face how someone she'd trusted had used her and tried to hurt her. As well as come to terms with who Donna really was and what that meant about her father's betrayal with her teacher. It would be a lot to take in and Billie worried for Mum's mental state.

But strangely, she didn't feel responsible.

Billie had never been the type for 'I told you so,' and she wasn't happy to have been right about Donna. In that long night in the hospital when she lay awake staring at the ceiling in the darkness, with only Nathan's snores and the distant hum of the hospital activities to distract her, she returned again and again in her mind to those moments with Mum when she'd woken briefly before being placed in the ambulance.

Because Billie's gut said that in the shock and trauma of the night, Amanda Callaghan found herself back in the past. Specifically, December 9th 1979.

And she'd felt to blame for the tragedy that had taken her baby sister.

And lying there, as the first rays of the morning sun brightened the bare hospital room and lit up the drool on the edge of her husband's mouth Billie understood that she could never solve the mystery for a mother who couldn't bear to know.

And it brought tears to her eyes.

She cried, curled up in the glow of the rising sun with the taste and scent of smoke still filling her senses. As Nathan woke and moved to offer the comfort of his arms without demanding she put this feeling into words, hot tears filled her stinging eyes and ran down her cheeks. Tears for baby Megan dead from SIDS and for her mother who'd felt to blame. Tears for all the relationships warped and twisted by that summer night in 1979. But most of all for her beloved pop. A man who'd carried the painful secret of Megan's death with him. Taking the burden on himself to protect his daughter who was still alive, the one he'd loved more than anything in the world.

Friday January 3rd

Spending the night in the hospital meant that Billie was there at Mum's bedside when she woke. Nathan had left a little while earlier to shower and take over looking after the kids.

Mum blinked a few times, confusion creasing her features. 'Where am I?'

Billie took her hand. 'There was a fire at Wattlebury Court but you're okay.' Her voice was mostly back to normal but each painful breath reminded her how close they'd come to not getting out of the house the night before.

The creases in Mum's face became crevasses. 'What about the house? And Megan was there. Is she okay?'

And suddenly, despite having doubted all along, Billie couldn't bring herself to take Mum's sister from her again.

Mum jerked her hand free. 'Tell me.'

There was a knock and Eve poked her head around. 'Good, you're both here. Is there room for me?'

Billie moved to let her sister past so she could kiss Mum's cheek, then enveloped Eve in a hug. She'd visited briefly the night before, but the night's events had made Billie grateful for every chance to show her family how much she loved them.

'What happened?' Mum asked again.

Eve took over the explanation. 'There was a fire at the house. They can't rule out an electrical fault, but the likely ignition was from a candle. Did you have one burning?'

Mum shook her head. 'Megan gave me one for Christmas but I don't think I...'

Billie took a breath, coughed a little and then spat out the bad news. 'Donna was there. She told me she set it.' She exhaled hard. 'I caught her coming from the house. Donna drugged you and then lit the fire, planning for you to be caught in what would appear to be a terrible accident.'

Mum was already shaking her head. 'That's impossible. She didn't drug me; I asked her to give me something to help me sleep.'

'Mum,' Eve said. 'The doctors have confirmed you were given more than necessary.'

'People make honest mistakes,' Mum snapped.

Billie's stomach sank. 'She threatened me and tried to stop me getting to you to help. If I hadn't then you wouldn't have gotten out.' But even as she said it, she knew that the tox screen hadn't found anything and the police hadn't found a syringe. 'And she's admitted she's not Megan.'

Mum's mouth trembled. 'Billie, this time you've gone too far.'

Eve took Mum's hand in hers. 'It's all true.'

At least this Billie could prove. While Mum's expression remained stony, Billie explained as best she could how she'd worked out about Nancy Blair and Pop and who Donna really was. 'The police are fast-tracking a new DNA test to prove it.'

Mum's mouth worked; she turned her head away from Billie. 'I'll wait to talk to her myself. You've had it in for Megan since the day she arrived home.'

Billie swallowed the painful lump in her throat. She understood how much Mum wanted to believe, but couldn't be a part of the delusion, not knowing everything she knew.

She stood.

Eve looked from one to the other. 'Mum, Billie is telling the truth. You're being awful.'

Mum stayed with her back to Billie.

Eve tried one more time. 'She saved your life.'

Mum lifted her head then, her eyes filled with pain and sadness and managed a soft but sincere, 'Thank you, love.'

As Billie hugged her sister goodbye and walked from that hospital room, she didn't feel mad, or even surprised that her mum would cling to the hope of Megan for as long as she could. Instead, the feeling coursing through her felt a lot like freedom.

Mum would have to accept it eventually. And she'd probably even apologise, but Billie didn't need to wait until then to get on with her life. They'd shared too much to keep a distance for long but Billie needed to learn from this and put her own relationships above a terrible night that happened before she was even born.

Pop had chosen to protect his daughter right at the start and Billie knew he'd want to continue to do so.

Nathan would be back soon to pick her up and there would be interviews and more statements to police. It was too soon to know what or whether Donna would be charged. All

Billie had was her report of being threatened with a syringe and circumstance to say that Donna had meant any ill will, and she figured she'd probably have a cover story by the time the police spoke to her. They'd probably never know if she'd done something to Pop.

Then there was the small matter of figuring out how they were going to repay Nathan's debts.

'Excuse me, are you Amanda Callaghan's daughter?'

Billie lifted her head at the question from a young orderly, pausing from his task of relocating an empty bed. 'I am.'

His hand went to his chest. 'My sister has been missing for three years and the foundation—' He broke off, his mouth working, then continued. 'It's helped my family so much. Would you pass on our gratitude?'

Billie's eyes stung at the obvious emotion on his face. 'I will. Good luck.'

'Thanks.'

Watching him walk away she thought of the aunt who she now knew had died tragically that night of the dinner party, but thanks to her big sister Megan Callaghan had left a legacy that meant so much to so many.

She and her mum would work things out, and in the meantime Billie had plenty of other things to worry about. As she heard Lola's familiar squeal and spotted Nathan at the end of the corridor, she realised she had plenty to enjoy as well.

42

One month later

Before Billie could get out of her car, her phone rang. 'Tell me you're not stranded somewhere,' she said upon answering.

Eve chuckled. Not because it was impossible – she'd always call Billie in times of crisis – but because lately her calls were mostly good news. 'They officially offered me the job.'

'Brilliant,' said Billie as she climbed out of the car. 'They came through on the work-from-home stuff then?'

'They didn't take too much persuasion.'

Eve had connected with a local specialist homewares company through her social media and convinced them she could lift their profile as long as they allowed her to work from home around the twins' pre-school schedules.

'Single mother and career girl – I'm impressed,' said Billie, meaning it. Everything that had happened with Donna and the separation from Tim had shown her just how strong her little sister was, as well as brought the two of them closer than ever.

Slowly, their mum was returning to the fold, too, after having to realise the truth about Donna's identity. She'd asked Billie to be at her side when she accepted the award for her work with the foundation and Billie had never been prouder.

'Helps I have you to look up to,' Eve replied.

'We can look up to each other,' Billie countered. 'I'm just home so I should go. Talk to you later. Love you.'

'Love you, too.'

As Billie clicked the button to lock her car and shifted her bag onto her shoulder her mouth watered at the unmistakable smell of garlic bread coming from the tiny rental they'd moved to when it became clear the only way to settle Nathan's debts was to sell their house.

Advantages – the two-bedroom, one-bathroom cottage was close to work at her beloved Callaghan Constructions where Billie had returned four days a week. And well within their budget despite Nathan's reduced wages after being let go from his role in finance as a result of his misappropriation of funds. Luckily, he'd avoided jail time and was now working for his mate Macca in his landscaping business.

Disadvantages – it wasn't really home. Not yet. Their old place overflowed with memories. From their early days as newlyweds to pregnancy and bringing Lola home.

Billie shrugged off the gloomy thoughts and opened the door, the last of them chased away by the sight that greeted her. Nathan lay on the floor on his back, holding a happily squealing Lola above his head, both of them so joyful her heart hurt.

Discarded on the table across the room was Nathan's phone, a flip model he'd found with no app or other smart functions to help avoid temptation. Along with his weekly counselling sessions it meant he'd managed to make real progress on his addiction.

He spotted her in the doorway and grinned. Still smiling,

he lowered Lola onto her playmat, stood and crossed to kiss her hello.

She kissed him back. The very best thing about being back at work was how happy she was to come home. 'Missed you,' she said against his mouth.

'And us you,' he replied. 'Made your favourite for dinner.'

She sniffed the air appreciatively. 'Thank you.' She allowed her bag to slide to the ground and looked over at Lola. 'Any updates on Operation Mobile?'

Nathan chuckled. 'No, but not for want of trying.'

Lola had been able to get up on her hands and knees for a few days, but crawling had so far eluded her. As though understanding the topic of their conversation Lola had rolled onto her stomach and was up again. In her sights, the '*You are incredible*' Post-it from Nathan that had tumbled from Billie's bag to land just a few feet away. Lola rocked back and forward, a determined crinkle on her forehead.

And then, as Billie and Nathan watched on, she did it, managing to halve the distance to her goal in a few jerky movements.

'She crawled,' Billie cried, happy tears stinging her eyes.

Nathan did a kind of jig, his eyes shining too. 'At last.'

He picked Lola up and they both smothered her in kisses.

Then Billie smelt the smoke. 'The lasagne!'

Nathan bundled Lola into Billie's arms and raced around to pull the charred dish from the oven. 'Oh crud.'

'It's all right,' Billie said, returning Lola to her playmat. 'You can't keep me from pasta. We'll scrape off the top.' Her phone buzzed, and she glanced at it but didn't pick it up, continuing around the small bench to help him save their dinner.

'Do you need to get that?'

She shook her head. Mum's message, *I think I have a new lead on Megan,* could wait.

Billie had more important things to do.

EPISODE 01: THE OTHER CALLAGHAN

Music playing: 'Like a Prayer' – Madonna

The music fades and a woman speaks:
It's December 1989. Donna Novak is nine and lives with her beloved mother Janette in a small community in the Blue Mountains. She's interested in the same kind of things as any other girl her age. Her netball team, her library books and her chances of getting a Cabbage Patch doll for Christmas. She's oblivious to the ways of adults until her mother, getting her a glass of milk, drops the glass and stands stunned in the shards at the sound of a news bulletin.

Male reporter:
Carol Callaghan was found dead in her home this morning. The mother of Megan Callaghan who sensationally disappeared from her cot nearly ten years ago.

Ruby:
That was the first day Donna remembers hearing about the Callaghan family. She didn't understand then why they were so important or how they would shape her own life.

I'm Ruby Costa and welcome to 'The Other Callaghan'.

This extended bonus feature covers the sensational story of Donna Novak's arrival into the Callaghan family. It includes exclusive interviews with Donna herself and at last explains what happened earlier this year on the night her family home burned to the ground.

Acknowledgements

I'd like to acknowledge the Kaurna people and the Kaurna Country on which *The Dinner Party* was written.

Although writing a book takes hours alone at a keyboard, getting it to the hands of readers needs a dedicated team. So much thanks to anyone not explicitly mentioned below who has helped in this book's journey.

A huge thank you to my editor, Martina Arzu, for her boundless belief in me that I could make this book into something special. And also, to the wonderful team at Head of Zeus Publishing. Thanks to Helena Newton for the copyedits. Thanks also to the Australian Bloomsbury team for your continuing support. I'm so lucky to work with two great publishers.

Special thanks to Hattie Grünewald for her brilliant support and the way she makes everything seem possible. Thanks too, to all the team at The Blair Partnership for always being in my corner.

Much thanks to Andria, Megan, Kerryn Mayne and Malcom S for your help answering my questions on policing matters. All mistakes are my own and your advice is much appreciated.

Lots of people helped with my research for this book.

Thanks to Barbara Denton for the chat about careers in the Seventies and Shirley Sampson who told me about heart arrythmia without questioning why I wanted to know. Thanks to all the readers at the Rachael Johns Bookclub Retreat who were also helpful with character naming. Particularly Phil whose suggestion was picked from the box.

This book started with a 'what if', drawn from my hazy memories of the dinner parties of the 'Ridgefield Avenue mob' back when I was a child. My dinner party is entirely fictional, of course, but I must thank this wonderful group of neighbours who became friends. Jan and Tony, Anne and Ron, Mandy and John, Liz and Alec and Pauline and Bob. My particular thanks and love to Auntie Anne Jantzen for all her help.

Writing friends make showing up at the keyboard so much easier. I've felt so warmly welcomed into the crime and thriller community and I'm so lucky to be a part of it. Thanks to the Monday Murder group who heard about this so long ago. My Writers Camp friends help to keep me sane in this rollercoaster business. Lisa Ireland and Emily Madden you are so appreciated. Thanks for reading an early draft and everything since Amanda Knight. And of course, to Rachael Johns who is there through it all, wise and entertaining and sometimes the only thing keeping me at the computer!

Thanks so much to all the friends who listen to plot problems and when I talk about characters like they're real people. Caroline and Rowan, Alison, Amy and Julie, your support means so much.

Harriet (the very best dog) and more recently Karma (is a cat) were great company in the long hours of writing and editing. Plank, however, takes so much from Barcley who came to Mum as a rescue, dumped for being too energetic, and quietly and stoically saw Mum through her final months, always by her side. Dogs are just the best.

I couldn't do this without family. Thank you to Dick, Shirley and Lyn and remembering Dad. To Wendy, who listened way back when this was just a dream. Thanks to Chloe and Mitch for answering young people questions for me any time of the day or night. To Fiona and Kirsty – you girls are simply the best and I adore you. Growing up with you helped inspire parts of this story. To Mum – you were with me in spirit every day while writing this one. I miss you.

Such huge and heartfelt thanks to all the readers, booksellers, bloggers, podcasters and reviewers who supported the release of *The Summer Party* and made it more than I could ever have dreamed. Thank you.

Finally, to Dave, Amelie, James and Claire, thank you for everything! I love you more than you could imagine and I couldn't do any of this without you. Nor would I want to.

About the Author

REBECCA HEATH studied science at university, worked in hospitality and teaching, but she always carved out time to write. She lives in Adelaide, Australia, halfway between the city and the sea with her husband, three children and a much-loved border collie. Her debut adult novel, *The Summer Party*, was released in 2023. This is her second adult novel.